Praise for *The Bo*…

‘I loved this book – tightly plotted, edge-of-seat gripping’

Sophie Hannah

‘I raced through it – edgy, tense and wry with great foreshadowing’

Harriet Tyce

‘I just finished reading *The Book Club* and I for one am terrified of the woman next door!’

Louise Candlish

‘A dark, twisty, claustrophobic read. I love those locked room novels (albeit locked village in this case!). A thrilling psychological debut’

Jo Spain

‘Smart, sassy, *The Book Club* is *Midsomer Murders* meets *Desperate Housewives*. Immensely entertaining, the growing sense of menace – of ‘where have I seen you before?’ – grips and chills in equal measures’

Cath Weeks

‘Intricately plotted, this gripping thriller is written with great style’

Lisa Ballantyne

‘Intuitive and addictive’

Alison Bruce

‘An irresistible slow descent into darkness, with twist upon twist upon twist’

Catriona McPherson

‘A fabulous, page-turning read! Beautifully written and I loved the humour’

Caroline England

C. J. Cooper grew up in a small village in south Wales before moving to London as a student. She graduated with a degree in Ancient History and Egyptology and spent seven months as a development worker in Nepal. On her return to Britain she joined the civil service, where she worked for 17 years on topics ranging from housing support to flooding. She hung up her bowler hat when she discovered that she much preferred writing about psychotic killers to ministerial speeches. She lives in London with her husband and two cats.

Follow C. J. Cooper on Twitter @CJCooper_author.

THE BOOK CLUB

C. J. COOPER

CONSTABLE

CONSTABLE

First published in Great Britain in 2019 by Constable
This paperback edition published in 2020 by Constable

1 3 5 7 9 10 8 6 4 2

All characters and events in this publication, other than those clearly in the public domain, are fictitious and any resemblance to real persons, living or dead, is purely coincidental.

A CIP catalogue record for this book is available from the British Library.

ISBN 978-1-47212-967-3

Typeset in Minion by SX Composing DTP, Rayleigh, Essex
Printed and bound in Great Britain by Clays Ltd, Elcograf S.p.A

Papers used by Constable are from well-managed forests
and other responsible sources.

Constable
An imprint of
Little, Brown Book Group
Carmelite House
50 Victoria Embankment
London EC4Y 0DZ

An Hachette UK Company
www.hachette.co.uk

www.littlebrown.co.uk

For Mark, for everything

Now

There's that noise again. It's a shrill, beeping sort of sound. Sometimes it's so quiet I forget about it. Sometimes I can't hear it at all. And then all of a sudden it's back, and I know it was there all the time, hiding just beneath the other sounds: the voices and the footsteps, the scrape of a chair against the floor.

It's strange, it's familiar somehow. I think I should know what it is, but when I try to reach for it, the memory slips away. I tried asking them, the voices. I asked if they could hear it too, but they didn't reply. That should have annoyed me – I could feel the edges of the anger against my brain – but when I tried to focus on the feeling it dissolved like smoke. I forgot my question, too.

What was it? Oh yes, that noise.

It's high pitched; like I said, shrill. Like a whistle, almost. But no, not like that. Not continuous, more a series of sounds. Like a tap dripping, or a heart beating. Only not like that either. It's almost musical, like a piano. No, a synthesiser. That's right, electric. Just the one note, again and again.

It's getting louder now.

It's so bright in here. It must be those big windows at the front.

They're concentrating the glare of the sun. I try to turn my head away, but the light is still there, so I screw up my eyes instead.

That noise, that note: can't someone make it stop?

I want to move but I feel so tired, like I've been here too long and melted into place. Everything is heavy. Maybe I'm ill. Maybe I'm having a heart attack, or a stroke or something. Perhaps this is what it feels like.

The noise is still there, not growing in volume now, but persistent, clear. And there's something else – something low and uneven and jagged-sounding. It rises and falls. There's a pressure on my eyelid, but that can't be right, because my eyes are open.

That can't be right.

The low sound is still there. It has a pattern, I can hear it now. *Hmm*-hmm, *hmm*-hmm.

The light is too strong, but I can't shut my eyes, not with this thing on my eyelid.

And now the sound is getting clearer, almost like words.

It's a voice, a woman's voice. I try to look around, but my head is so heavy and something's still pressing against my eye. The noises have gone: no more hum of conversation, no clatter of chair legs. Just that high electric beat and the sounds that are almost words.

Hmm-hmm, *hmm*-hmm.

And then I know what they are.

'Lucy.'

I'm not afraid any more. I open my eyes.

Before

Chapter 1

It was so hot the grass had turned to straw right there in the ground the day I opened my door to the woman who'd try to kill me.

Of course I didn't know that was what she was there for then. I just wished I'd cleaned my teeth after I'd got back from Tom's, because when I opened my mouth to say hello and welcome her to the village, I could tell from her half-raised eyebrow and the way her lips turned down at the corners that she could smell the alcohol on my breath. I wondered later if that was when she got the idea about the wine bottle, but I suppose there's no way of telling.

I'd returned from The Gables an hour or so before. The visit hadn't been a success, though I had only myself to blame for that. I'd gone to ask Tom's advice, but I hadn't managed to get to the point. That's what happens when you don't want to tell people the truth: you spend so much time testing possible reactions in your head, filtering out anything that might take the conversation in a direction you don't want it to go, that all of a sudden you find you've been there for twenty minutes and the other person is halfway into a story about Cynthia in the post office and her attitude to undelivered mail, and it's too late to do anything but nod along and pretend you were just dropping by for a chat. *Time's up, ding ding!*

So I'd sat there, hmm-ing in the right places, and every so often passing a surreptitious dog treat under the table to Ferdy, Tom's cairn terrier; and just as I was thinking I should leave and let him get back to work (Tom, that is, not Ferdy), there was a scrunch of gravel and a ripple of laughter at the open door, and Maggie and Rebecca were bustling in.

I took in their Lycra leggings and rolled-up mats and told myself I didn't mind that they hadn't invited me to yoga or Pilates, or however they'd been spending their morning. They'd both lived in the village for years, after all. I couldn't expect to be included in all their routines right away.

As if she'd read my mind, Maggie installed herself on the bench next to me and gave my arm a reassuring squeeze. 'Wonderful that you're here, Lucy! Saves us another visit. You'll *definitely* want to hear this too.'

On the other side of the table Rebecca sat upright, eyes sparkling. 'We've got news. We have a new arrival.'

For a moment I was confused, my eyes flicking down automatically to where the table would hide any sign of a pregnancy bump; but Tom caught my eye and laughed. 'You mean someone's moved into number 1?'

'Got it in one!' Maggie thumped the table, the large rings she wore cracking against the wood.

'Well, not quite,' Rebecca corrected her. 'According to Cynthia, the postman said he's been delivering mail there.'

Maggie was nodding vigorously, her glossy black bob swinging perfectly back into place. I'd considered asking for the number of her hairdresser before now, but suspected he or she was out of my price range.

'So whoever's taken it must be moving in soon,' she said, swivelling to face me. 'I bet you'll be pleased to have someone next door, Lucy.'

I started to reply, but Rebecca cut across me. 'Cynthia didn't have any details, apparently.' She pursed her lips. 'I just hope whoever it is will make the effort to fit in.'

I half listened as they speculated. Truth be told, I wasn't much interested in a new neighbour; years of living in London had bred what I considered a healthy lack of interest in the people the other side of a party wall. But clearly Tom, Maggie and Rebecca felt differently. Had it been the same, I wondered, when I'd moved into number 2? Had they sat around discussing whether I was going to 'fit in', whether I had anything more in common with them than membership of the village's select under-40 demographic? And when they'd met me, had I passed the test?

I stopped myself. I was here, wasn't I? They wouldn't be talking like this if I hadn't.

Tom had gone to a cupboard and returned with a dusty bottle with something dark inside. 'We should toast the incomer,' he said. 'Anyone for a tipple?'

Maggie grinned. 'Is that . . .?'

He nodded. 'Oh yes. Aunt Lydia's sloe gin. Once drunk, never forgotten.'

Rebecca tutted. 'Really, Tom. It's eleven in the morning! Besides, I have things to do.' She got to her feet and smoothed back a strand of blonde hair. 'There's a cake sale at Ellie's nursery tomorrow, so I'll be in the kitchen all day.' She gave a martyred sigh. 'My honey and oat cookies are in demand.'

I caught Tom rolling his eyes and suppressed a smile. Next to me Maggie was reaching for her yoga mat. 'I'll come with you, Becs. Much as I love you all, I need to get back to the grindstone.'

She pulled me into a brief hug. 'But you should stay, Lucy. That sloe gin is quite the experience!'

For a moment I considered leaving with the two of them, checking some job adverts, brushing up my CV . . . But then Tom was sloshing purple liquid into a glass and pushing it across the table, and I put it to my lips and told myself the day was still young. It went down like gasoline, streaking fire down the back of my throat, and Tom confessed afterwards that he sometimes used it for cleaning his paintbrushes; but it was surprisingly drinkable after the initial shock, and I was two glasses down and swaying gently by the time I made my way back to the cottage.

It wasn't long after that that the lorry turned up. I'd been on the laptop, battling with Willowcombe's erratic broadband signal, when I heard the rumble of its engine. I paused, head cocked like a meerkat. I love the village, but there's no denying it does something to you, living in a place like this. The sound of traffic, the slam of a door, noises that in London I would barely have registered, are significant here, echoing against the silence of the Fosters' holiday home on one side and number 1 on the other, the fields stretching up beyond the hill behind. Sometimes I like to hear them, the reminders of other lives; but I didn't like the sound of that engine.

I heard it chug and hiss the way big vehicles do when they come to a stop, and braced myself for what would come next. Satnavs don't work well in Willowcombe, and once or twice before lorry drivers had called at the cottage to ask for directions. There I'd be, standing in the doorway explaining that I'd only just moved in, while a white guy of a certain age and taste in T-shirts huffed and puffed like it was my fault he couldn't read a map. Perhaps this time I'd pretend to be out.

I heard a door slam, then voices; but there was no creak of the gate. I ventured into the living room and poked my head around the corner of the curtain, registering even as I did so that it had taken me only three months to turn into the archetypal village snoop. The lorry had stopped outside number 1. I peered closer, squinting at the lettering on the side: *Abaddon Removals, Pimlico.* So the new neighbours were ex-Londoners too. Maybe we'd have something in common: we could reminisce over functioning mobile phones and the existence of public transport. Still, I wasn't sure how it would go down in the village. I could just picture Cynthia in the post office muttering about an invasion of townies, how they'd all be making unreasonable demands about courier services and asking Willowcombe Supplies to replace jacket potatoes with quinoa.

I watched for a while, but the men were leaning against the lorry chatting and hadn't even opened up the back. They must be waiting for the new tenants to arrive with the keys. I wondered if I should go over there when they turned up, introduce myself. That was what Rebecca would have done; she'd arrived on my doorstep the day I'd moved in, complete with a homemade sponge cake in a wicker basket. I thought I'd moved to Stepford.

I twisted my head in the other direction, half expecting to see her outside now, pretending to water her plants or take out rubbish while she kept her own lookout for a glimpse of the newcomer – *incomer*, that's what they call us here. But there was no sign of movement outside number 4, and her car was gone. Maybe she'd interrupted her baking for some child-related errand, taking Oscar to football or Ellie to ballet.

The lorry drivers were smoking now, obviously not expecting to be called to action any time soon. I let the curtain fall back into place, trying not to ask myself whether this was really what my life had come to: spying on the new neighbours in the hope of having some gossip to relay to the others, sitting in the pub with Tom, Rebecca and Maggie, recounting the colour of next door's sofa or whether they preferred brass bedsteads to wooden ones. If Richard could see me now, he'd congratulate himself on a lucky escape.

He's probably doing that anyway. And why do you even care?

I told myself to get a life and went to the living room to watch *Loose Women*. And yes, as it happens, I do appreciate the irony in that.

She got me on the back foot from the beginning, but I suppose that was my own fault too.

I'd heard them moving about outside, the rattle as the back of the lorry was opened up. I thought if the new tenants had arrived I could offer them a cup of tea while the removal men did their stuff. I liked the idea of welcoming someone else to the village.

I didn't want them to think I was nosy. My plan was to take a casual look out of the window, get the lie of the land. I picked up a book (*Pride and Prejudice*, in case they had exceptionally keen eyesight; I wanted to make the right impression) and took the three steps from one side of the living room window to the other. But it was no good; I'd been too intent on looking absorbed in the book to see anything more than a blur of figures and furniture. I counted to five in my head and tried again, this time pausing at the window, holding the book at chin height, the slightest of turns . . .

'Jesus!'

I was looking directly into a pair of grey eyes. The book slipped from my fingers and fell to the floor, pages fluttering. I bent and snatched it up, feeling the blood rush to my face. Blushing is a great look when you've got red hair: *Welcome to the neighbourhood, you've moved next door to a giant beetroot.*

The woman outside the window was staring at me. She was about my age, I guessed, late twenties or perhaps a little older, with small, even features and light brown hair cut so that it brushed her shoulders. For a second we stood looking at each other through the glass, and I had a momentary sense of something cold and absent; but then she gave a short laugh and mouthed, 'Sorry.' She was one of those people who looked much nicer when they smiled.

I hurried to the door.

'Hi, hi! You must be my new neighbour! It's lovely to meet you!'

'Yes, you too.' She almost looked as if she meant it. 'Sorry about . . .'

'Oh no, my fault. I mean, I was just, er, having a lazy morning with a book.'

I'd leaned forward as I said it with suitable levels of enthusiasm, hoping to distract her from my root vegetable appearance; but as soon as the words left my mouth I realised my mistake. She pulled back and grimaced as the noxious fumes of Tom's sloe gin washed over her. Oh, this was getting better and better. Not just any beetroot, but an alcoholic beetroot – as M&S definitely would not say, ever.

But the woman on the doorstep had steeled herself for introductions. She gave me another little smile, pretending she hadn't noticed. 'No need to be embarrassed. I don't blame you for wanting to see who's moving in next door.'

I peered over her shoulder, searching for a neighbourly response, then realised it looked like I was trying to check out her furniture. She moved slightly to one side, blocking my view. 'I'm Alice Darley.'

A formal introduction: we'd got off on the wrong foot. I effused away, hoping to repair the damage. 'Hi, Alice! Good to meet you! I was going to come over and introduce myself once you were settled.' Her raised eyebrow suggested she didn't believe a word of it, but I rattled on. 'I didn't want to get in the way when you were moving in. It hasn't been that long since I got here myself, actually! I remember what it was like. Just chaotic!'

'Yes, it certainly is.' A pause. She looked like she was waiting for something.

'Oh God, I'm sorry! I'm Lucy. Lucy Shaw.' I reached out to shake her hand, the response automatic from too many client meetings. I had a momentary impression of her stiffening, a subtle tension in her shoulders; but then she held out her own hand and clasped mine with sudden warmth.

'Lucy. So lovely to meet you.'

I stepped aside for her to come in. 'If you've got time for a cuppa?' And now I sounded like a cockney builder. *Owzabout a cuppa Rosie, love?* Alice followed me into the kitchen and settled herself at the small table while I bustled around making fresh coffee, hoping she wouldn't think it was a hangover cure.

She looked about the room as we attempted small talk, taking in the decor (still the pale yellow it had been when I moved in; the lease prohibited redecorating); asking me where I'd got the old-fashioned kitchen scales I'd bought when I was still imagining myself swanning around all Kirstie Allsopp, wearing a gingham apron and making jam; tipping up her mug when she thought I wasn't looking to see if it had 'Tesco' stamped on the bottom (it did, damn it). Her movements were contained, careful, grey eyes scanning the room, missing nothing. And despite being in the middle of moving house, everything about her was neat and fresh: the crisp white T-shirt, the flat silver pumps, not a strand of light brown hair out of place.

'So, what made you decide to move to Willowcombe?'

She fixed me with a steady gaze. 'Oh, you know, I just felt I needed a break from London. There were some . . . relationship issues.'

Join the club. 'I'm sorry. I didn't mean to pry.'

'No, really, it's fine. Or it will be in time.' Her fingers were suddenly restless, pulling at the sleeves of her cardigan. 'How about you? You said you hadn't been here long yourself.'

'I was made redundant.' Practice kept my tone light. 'Thought I'd take the chance for a change of scene – get some perspective on things. Everyone kept saying it was a great opportunity for that.'

'And were they right?'

'I'm not sure yet. I hope so.' Her scrutiny was a shade too close for comfort; time to change the subject. 'I saw this place advertised in the *Standard*. I suppose they were looking out for the second-home market. I don't know why I came, really – I've never lived anywhere like this. But the photo was so pretty. And of course, it's great to have some outside space. Though I'm not very green-fingered, I'm afraid. As I'm sure you'll have noticed.'

Now I admit I was fishing for a compliment there, because I *had* made an effort with the garden. I might not have known the names of any of the plants, but I'd tried to keep them neat, pulling out the obvious weeds and tying up the climbers when they were getting straggly. I'd gone to a garden centre just outside Tewkesbury and returned triumphant with terracotta pots, compost and red geraniums, a combination of which now sat on the strip of gravel that ran in front of the cottage. The colours didn't really go with the spires of blue and pink flowers that rose from the borders, but they were bright and cheerful and I loved them.

Clearly my efforts hadn't impressed Alice, who was nodding patiently.

'Well, you don't get a lot of chance to practise until you have a garden yourself. I could give you a hand if you like – my gran was a great gardener. I picked up quite a lot from her over the years.'

I tried not to bristle. 'No, really, I wouldn't want to put you to any trouble . . .'

'No trouble at all. It would be my pleasure.'

'But you'll have your own to do . . .' I could hear the whiff of desperation in my voice.

Alice put down her mug, adjusting it so that the handle was precisely parallel to the edge of the table. 'That's the problem with having most of your garden at the front, isn't it? Anyone not keeping on top of it brings down the appearance of the whole street.' She smiled sweetly. 'Don't worry, Lucy. I'll have plenty of time for both of us.'

She looked up at the clock on the wall. 'Goodness, is that the time? I've been enjoying our chat so much I completely lost track!' She rose to her feet. 'I'd better get back and see how they're getting on. Thanks for the coffee. I'll return the favour soon.'

And with that she was gone, a hint of fabric softener lingering in the air behind her.

I worried away at that conversation for the rest of the day. I told myself it was stupid, but I couldn't help it. Maybe even then I knew on some subconscious level that Alice was someone who deserved to be worried about. Or perhaps I was just paranoid about her comments on my horticultural shortcomings, anxious that it was what the others in the village were thinking too. I told myself it didn't matter what Alice thought; that she was new to Willowcombe and didn't know how things were done, didn't understand it was all cottage roses and jumbled hollyhocks here, not clipped topiary in stainless-steel planters. She'd probably offered to help with the garden as a way of getting to know me. I wouldn't mention it again and it would soon be forgotten.

But what had Alice thought of me? It didn't take a lot of guessing: a nosy cow, stinking of gin at two in the afternoon while she tried to snoop on her neighbour's belongings. And had she noticed my evasiveness when she'd asked me why I'd moved to Willowcombe? Had she spotted the way I'd been unable to meet her eyes as I trotted out my half-truths?

For I hadn't, of course, told her the real reason I'd left what friends I still had in London to move to this little cottage in the middle of nowhere. The redundancy had been merely a symptom of the disease, the rot in the apple, the cancer in my bones that had been my time – I refused any longer to dignify it by calling it a 'relationship' – with Richard. An affair with a married man, my boss no less; I wasn't about to confide that to some woman I'd just met.

Of course, I know now there was no need.

Alice already knew.

Chapter 2

Maggie rocks back onto her heels, trying to take the pressure off the balls of her feet. She should have worn flats, but she hadn't expected to be here long. 'Just half an hour while the first rush is on.' That was what Rebecca had said, and like a fool she'd let herself be talked into it. And the toy stall, of all things: couldn't Becs at least have got them on tea and cakes? She checks her watch. With any luck, Tom will be here soon. He's promised to put in an appearance and he's bound to be up for sloping off to the pub for an early lunch.

'How much is this?' A grubby-fingered boy with golden ringlets is holding up a toy car.

'Er – ten pence.' She hasn't got a clue, but it's only small.

The boy holds out a palmful of change. 'Have I got enough?'

Maggie smiles in spite of herself. Kids are cute sometimes, there's no denying it. She bends down and selects one of the coins. 'Here. This is a ten-pence piece. Do you see that number ten there on the bottom?'

He looks uncertain. Maybe he's too young to have learnt his numbers.

'Yes, you've got enough.' She straightens up. 'I'll take this coin, and the car's yours.'

He grins at her and runs off to show his loot to a statuesque brunette in designer jeans. So he's Claudia's little boy – Maggie knew he looked familiar. No doubt she'll be tripping over that car the next time she's there for a consultation on the design scheme for the new studio. For someone wanting 'modern industrial', Claudia seems remarkably impervious to the bits of primary-coloured plastic scattered throughout her home. That's what having children does to you, Maggie supposes; she's glad she's never had to find out.

'Has the Paw Patrol car gone then? I thought it wouldn't last long.' Rebecca leans past her to drop some coins in the cash box.

'Poor Patrol?'

'That blue car that was at the front. The one with the dogs in the window.' Rebecca is smiling brightly, but Maggie can see the suspicion beginning to dawn.

'Oh yes, that one.'

'Oscar used to love Paw Patrol. He's too old for it now, of course.'

'Hmm . . .' Maybe she should have checked the price.

'You did check the price, didn't you, Maggie?'

'Of course I did!' She'll take a look later and make up the difference. Rebecca will have everything inventoried down to the last wax crayon. You'd never guess this was a church bring-and-buy, not the Harrods sale. And where the hell is Tom?

She scans the crowd. She knows most of the people here – has even, as with Claudia, done work for one or two of them, though most of her commissions come from outside the village. Willowcombe has its share of incomers looking to remodel their quaint Cotswold cottages as far as the planners will allow, but the majority of villagers are still Combers born and bred, as likely to hire an interior designer as to take up base jumping or vote Labour.

There, though, is a face she doesn't know: a woman on the edge of the crowd near the tea stand, small and slim with light brown hair in a neat shoulder-length bob. She's talking to Cynthia Sullivan from the post office – or rather, Cynthia is talking at her. The woman is only half listening, Maggie can see that from here, looking over Cynthia's shoulder as though searching for someone. Maybe she's hoping to be rescued.

A flash of red hair over by the door distracts her attention. At last – hope for her own escape. She waves madly. 'Lucy! Over here!'

Lucy weaves through the crowd, flushed in the heat, hair escaping from a straggly ponytail. She arrives slightly out of breath, clutching a pile of books to her chest as Maggie pulls her into a one-armed hug. 'Hey, both. Who knew the church jumble sale was such a crowd-pleaser? There's a proper scrum at the bookstall.'

'Oh yes, we always do well.' Rebecca has the air of the seasoned organiser. She nods at the books in Lucy's arms. 'Pleased to see you contributing to the church funds. If you find a first edition in there, mind, we'll expect an appropriate donation.'

Maggie laughs. 'I'm impressed you managed to find anything that wasn't a Mills & Boon. So what have you got planned for the rest of the morning?' *Because if the answer is anything less than root canal surgery, you're about to take over from me . . .*

'Well, I was supposed to be meeting Tom for lunch . . .'

Maggie surveys the room again. 'Yes, he told me he'd be here too.' And there's still no sign of him. Typical. Still, if he hasn't arrived for Lucy's lunch date . . .

Her train of thought is halted by the sight of the woman with the light brown hair. She's stopped pretending to listen to Cynthia and is staring at them. Maggie blinks and looks again. If she didn't know she'd never set eyes on her before, she'd think she'd done something to upset her: the expression on the woman's face is pure dislike.

She nudges Rebecca and lowers her voice. 'Don't look now, but do either of you know the woman with Cynthia? Over there, by the tea stand.'

Lucy swings around, craning her neck. So much for subtlety.

'Tourist, maybe.' Rebecca is dismissive, but Lucy has raised her hand in acknowledgement. Maggie sees the woman wave back, a friendly smile lighting up her face and making her almost pretty. She must have been imagining things.

'That's our new neighbour, Alice something. You were right about number 1. She's just moved in.'

'Lucy, you should have said!' Lucy is about to protest, but Maggie rolls her eyes at her and shakes her head. There's no point trying to argue when Rebecca is about to go into hostess mode. 'So they're in? I saw the car, of course . . .' She turns to Lucy with a questioning look. 'Silver Renault, yes? Fairly new? But I just assumed . . . She'll think I'm so rude for not going round. Call her over, for goodness' sake!'

But Alice has already detached herself from Cynthia, and a moment later she's joined the group.

'Hi, Alice. Lovely to see you.' Lucy's tone doesn't quite match the sentiment, Maggie thinks. Surely they can't have fallen out already?

'I'm Rebecca.' Rebecca almost pushes Lucy to the side as she stretches out a perfectly manicured hand. 'I live at number 4, just a few doors along from you. And this is Maggie.'

Alice's handshake is surprisingly firm, and Maggie winces as the edge of her ring is pressed into her finger; but Alice is still smiling and doesn't seem to notice.

'So how are you settling in?'

'Good, thanks. I've almost finished unpacking.'

'Goodness, that was quick!' Rebecca shoots Lucy a look of reproach. 'So it's just you, then?'

'Just me.' Is there a tightness to her jaw as she says it? Perhaps it's man trouble. Maggie glances at Alice's hands, but there's no sign of a ring and no mark where one might recently have been. Maybe it was the terseness of the reply, but a pause has formed and it's on the verge of becoming uncomfortable. Maggie racks her brains for something to say, but it's Lucy who comes to the rescue.

'I don't know how you managed to sort everything out so quickly.' She smiles at Alice. 'I know it took me weeks. It was the books that were the problem – I took loads to the charity shop but still ended up moving six boxes—'

Rebecca interrupts her. 'You should get an e-reader.'

'Becs, no!' Maggie and Lucy are almost in harmony.

'It's just not the same . . .'

'The feel of the pages . . .'

'The smell of the paper . . .'

Rebecca looks put out. 'Well, I love mine. And when you have children, you don't have the luxury of being sentimental about your stuff. Believe me, you need every bit of storage you can lay your hands on.'

'Excuse me!' A voice pipes up from hip level. 'How much are the Top Trumps?'

Rebecca turns to their latest customer and Maggie sighs. 'I'd better get back to the excitement, I suppose. Unless either of you ladies fancies taking over?'

'Sorry, Maggie. Since Tom's stood me up, I've got a hot date with Agatha Christie.' Lucy nods at the copy of *Sparkling Cyanide* topping her pile of books. 'Besides, I need to check for those first editions.'

Maggie is about to try to convince Alice what a great opportunity it will be to get to know the villagers, but something in her expression tells her it's not worth bothering.

Sure enough, Alice says, 'I'm afraid I've got things to do this afternoon. But it's been lovely to meet you all . . .' The rest of the sentence trails away, and for a moment she looks lost. Maggie feels sorry for her; it must be hard, coming alone to a new place, especially if there's some kind of relationship break-up behind the move. She reaches out and places a hand on Alice's arm.

'Why don't we all meet up tonight?' She turns to ask Rebecca if she's free, but she's deep in negotiation with a small girl. 'I'll check with Becs. And I'll get hold of Tom, too. The Red Cow, seven o'clock? We can get something to eat and welcome you to the village properly.'

'I'd love to.' Alice shrugs and Maggie's hand falls away. Then she smiles and Maggie thinks again how much it suits her. 'I feel I'm already amongst friends.'

* * *

The phone is ringing as Tom opens the kitchen door and receives Ferdy's rapturous welcome. He bends to scratch the terrier's head, then strides into the hallway to snatch the handset from its cradle.

'No rest for the wicked,' he mutters, then, 'Hello?'

Maggie. Oh Christ, he'd forgotten all about that bloody bring-and-buy. And he'd been supposed to be meeting Lucy for lunch too, though he knows she won't mind. She doesn't get upset about that kind of thing; it's one of the reasons they get on so well.

Maggie hasn't paused for breath – something about going to the pub to meet some incomer.

'So I said tonight, but Rebecca's doing an overnighter for a conference – women with start-up businesses or something. Can you do Tuesday instead?'

Tom mentally checks his diary, but Tuesdays are usually quiet. 'Should be fine . . .'

'I've heard that before, Thomas. So what happened to you earlier? I was relying on you to rescue me from the ankle-biters.'

'The what?'

'Becs had me on the bloody toy stall.'

He laughs. 'Your idea of heaven. Rebecca knows you so well.'

'Hmm.'

There's a catch in Maggie's voice and all at once he remembers: it's July, nearly the anniversary. Christ, of all the times to be surrounded by kids.

His voice when he speaks again is soft. 'Are you OK?'

'Yes, fine, you know me.' The forced jollity doesn't fool him and she knows it. She sighs. 'It's not the children . . .'

'I know.'

'I was fine until I got home. I walked through the door and it just hit me . . .' A pause. 'I don't know why I still get like this.'

'Is David there?' He knows he won't be; Maggie wouldn't be having this conversation if there were any chance of her husband overhearing.

'He's in London. They're such slave-drivers at that surgery; the weekends are the only time he gets for his research.' She sounds like she's apologising for him, and Tom murmurs something non-committal. 'Anyway, I'll be OK. I've booked myself in at Armitage Hall for a couple of days.'

The spa; it's where she always goes. 'You know I'll be here if . . .'

'I know. Thanks, Tom. I don't know what I'd do without you.' She laughs, but he knows she means it. 'So I'll see you on Tuesday, then.'

After Maggie's hung up, he heads for the studio; the day is still fine, and if he leaves now, he can get in a couple of hours' painting the irises by the river before the light fades. They're a rich shade of indigo and the prints will sell well – Tom knows his buyers appreciate a bit of colour to go with their cushion covers and cashmere throws.

His thoughts drift back to Maggie. He wonders if being relieved she's been distracted from asking him about his no-show makes him a bad friend. He meant what he said, though: he'll be there if she needs him. Experience suggests she will. She can't carry a secret, that's Maggie's problem. She has an urge to openness.

Tom's only glad he doesn't suffer the same affliction.

* * *

Three doors down, the woman who calls herself Alice Darley sits at the brand-new dining table covered with a fresh white cloth. In its centre stands a crystal vase filled with roses and sweet peas, the only object brought with her from her grandmother's flat. On the wall in front of her, the one that divides 1 Mellingford Cottages from number 2, a print of a field dotted with red flowers hangs in a gilt frame. The writing underneath it reads: *Poppy Field near Giverny, Claude Monet.*

There's something about the scene that's wrong, a discordant note. Perhaps it's only that the woman has just moved in and the room hasn't yet taken on her personality. Perhaps it's that there's no personality for it to take.

She sits upright, her shoulders tense, only her neck bowed as she looks at something on the table in front of her. A notepad. It's open at what appears to be a list, until you look more closely and see that the words seem to bear no relation to each other. It reads:

Her
Rebecca (4 MC)
Maggie
Tom (??)
books (Christie)
e-reader
Pub, (?) Cow

She is sitting very still, her eyes fixed on the page. Her lips move but make no sound as she reads what she has written. Slowly her left hand moves towards the notepad. A pen is clutched between her fingers and it scratches as it moves across the paper, round and round, circling the first four lines, bringing the words together inside a blue boundary: *Her, Rebecca, Maggie, Tom*. The pen moves quicker, the blue circle growing fat as the lines multiply. Round and round it goes, and then suddenly it stops. Her hand moves up the notepad and now the pen is moving left to right, short lines, the nib pressed hard into the surface of the paper.

There's a salty taste in her mouth. She puts down the pen, and when she touches her fingers to her lips, they come away red. She rises and leaves the room through a door at the back, the one that leads to the kitchen.

The notepad sits there, its edges aligned precisely with those of the table. The list looks messy now, the circles like a bird's nest around the first four entries. One of the words has been underlined again and again, and if you ran your finger beneath it you'd feel the sharp indentation where the surface has been almost worn away.

Her.

Chapter 3

The book club was her idea, of course. Alice's. She was subtle about it, though; I don't know if the others would even remember how it happened. They might say it was a group decision, something we'd all been talking about. But it wasn't.

I wondered once whether she'd had it planned from the beginning, but now I think she just intended it as a way to get to know people. A way to get inside their heads. It's brilliant, when you think about it. Get people to talk about characters, motivations. See how they respond, what strikes a chord, what gets under their skin. She couldn't have known then how else she'd use it in the end, not when she'd only just arrived in the village.

Even Alice has limits. She's not superhuman.

She's not.

It was the day after the bring-and-buy and I'd been searching online for information on setting up a business. After chickening out of asking Tom's advice, I had to do something: my dwindling redundancy pot wasn't going to last for ever – no matter how much extra cash had gone into it courtesy of Richard's desperate desire to get me out of Waites – and I was determined not to just exchange one tedious office job for another. I wanted to do something I could be proud of, something I could talk to my parents about without their eyes glazing over. That's the problem with having a family like mine: it's hard to measure up.

For once, Willowcombe's broadband was behaving itself, and I'd bookmarked a stack of articles on everything from business planning to tax. In an impressive display of self-control, I'd barely glanced at Waites's Twitter feed. Richard had told me once he abstained from social media, and I'd been surprised when I checked to find he'd apparently been telling the truth; but as finance director he featured now and again in one of Waites's tweets, unexpectedly dry for a PR firm, announcing quarterly outturn or profit forecasts. I'd watched the page load, my palms sticky, but there'd been no mention of him, and no photos.

After a couple of hours of what I told myself was research, I got up to stretch my legs. The day was hot, and even in the kitchen, in the shade of the hill behind the cottages, a sheen of sweat coated my skin. I poured myself a glass of apple juice and opened the back door to get some air.

The slope of the hill behind cut off the space for gardens to the rear of the four houses that made up the terrace of Mellingford Cottages. At number 4, Rebecca benefited from the bit of extra land that ran around the edge of the house, but for the rest of us there was room for only a small yard. Mine was given over entirely to a patio with a table, a couple of chairs and a few flowerpots. I took a seat and rested my head against the cool stone of the cottage, breathing in the sweet fragrance of jasmine.

'Hello, Lucy.'

I jumped, splashing apple juice onto my leg. Alice was studying me from across the fence, a smile hovering at the edge of her lips.

She held up a pair of secateurs. 'I was just cutting back some of the overgrowth. Technically, I think I'm supposed to throw it back onto your side, but I'm guessing you'd rather I just got rid of it for you?'

I opened my mouth to reply, but she hurried on.

'All this jasmine is strangling my honeysuckle, you see. Lovely as it is, it has to go. You know what they say about the definition of a weed?'

'No, I don't think . . .'

'A weed is any plant that's somewhere you don't want it. Any plant that's getting in your way.' She stared at me in a way I didn't like. 'You just have to rip it right out.'

I nodded, and tried to wipe my leg with the hem of my skirt.

'I meant to say how nice it was of you to introduce me to your friends the other day.'

'I don't think you could have avoided Maggie and Rebecca if you'd wanted to.'

She smiled then. 'I expect they wanted to check out the newcomer.'

'Well, you know what it's like in a small village . . .'

'No, not really.' She was looking down now, china-white fingers unwinding a tendril of jasmine from a honeysuckle stem. 'Actually, Lucy, that's something I wanted to ask your advice about.'

'Oh?' I stopped dabbing at my leg.

'You've been here a while now, haven't you?'

'Well, yes, I suppose so. I mean, I still feel like the new girl, but I guess I'm not quite so new any more.'

'How long since you moved in?'

'Three months. That probably counts for about thirty seconds in Willowcombe time.'

'That's exactly what I think!' She was holding a stem of

jasmine, stretching out the little kinks where it had bound itself to another stalk. 'I know everyone says it takes ages to get to know people in a place like this – but you've made friends here, haven't you?'

'Well, yes . . .'

'I mean, you and Maggie and Rebecca all seem very friendly.'

'Yes, they've been great.'

'And your other friend – the one we're seeing at the pub. Tom, isn't it?'

Yes, Tom. I wondered belatedly what had kept him from meeting me for lunch. Probably he'd decided it was safer to stay away from the bring-and-buy than risk Rebecca roping him into a stint on one of the stalls.

Alice was waiting for an answer.

'Yes, that's right. Another of our neighbours – well, close enough anyway. You pass his driveway on the way to the high street.'

'Oh! The big house?' I nodded. Let her think Tom had money if she wanted to; she didn't need to know he'd inherited it from his aunt Lydia, she of the paint-stripper gin. 'Are you and he . . .?'

She must have got the wrong idea about our lunch date. I couldn't help laughing. 'God, no! I'm not sure I'm his type.'

I watched the penny drop. 'Oh, so he's . . .?'

'Gay, yes.'

'Do you all hang around together then?'

I felt like a kid again, standing in the playground while another little girl pulled up her socks and asked to be my friend. It *was* hard being new to the village; surely I knew that better than anyone. 'Well, yes,' I said. 'But it's not like we're some exclusive club or anything – you'd be very welcome to join us any time. I mean, it's not like we actually do very much.'

'Don't you?'

She sounded mildly shocked and I saw how we must appear: a bunch of twenty- and thirty-somethings, cooped up in a village where the average age was well past bus-pass eligibility, meeting up for bridge and sharing stories about our geraniums. I hurried to dispel the image.

'I mean, we do *do* things, obviously.' I groped for examples. 'We meet for coffee quite a lot and, er, we go to the pub . . .' Jesus, was this the best I could do? 'And Tom cooks for us all now and again.'

'Oh, well that sounds nice.' Alice's tone suggested it actually sounded duller than a wet weekend in Bognor. She opened the secateurs around a stem of jasmine and the jaws came together with a snap. The tendril hung from her fingers for a moment before she dropped it out of sight behind the fence. 'I wouldn't want to intrude or anything. It's just that sometimes I don't make as much effort as I should to meet people. And somewhere like this . . .'

She trailed off and I found myself nodding. 'Yes, I know what you mean. It can be too easy to shut yourself away.'

'Can't it, though? Sometimes I just get my nose stuck in a book and that's it – the whole day's gone by and I realise I haven't spoken to a soul!' She beamed at me.

'Me too. I'm supposed to be doing something useful, but if I've started a good book . . .'

'What kind of stuff do you read? Other than Jane Austen, of course.'

For a moment I thought she was assuming sisterly membership of the Jane Fan Club, but then I remembered the incident with *Pride and Prejudice* and found myself blushing again. Why did she do that, just as I was beginning to relax with her?

'All kinds of things, actually.' I was determined not to apologise again. 'The classics, of course.' God, could I sound more pompous?

'Oh, of course! They're classics for a reason.'

'But plenty of modern stuff too. Literary fiction, crime, thrillers. As long as it's well written, I'm not fussy about genre.'

'I couldn't agree more.' Alice had selected another strand of greenery. 'Though I draw the line at sci-fi.'

'Oh, I don't know – I've enjoyed a bit of Asimov in my time. And Wells, of course, Burroughs . . .'

'Goodness, I see I've run into quite the fan!'

The clipping was speeding up. Lift, hold, snip, drop. There must be more of the jasmine on Alice's side of the fence than I'd imagined. I could hear the blades sweeping softly over one another, each little swish punctuated by a snap at the end.

'Oh, but Lucy!' Swish, snap. 'I've had an idea.'

'Really?' I forced enthusiasm into my voice.

'Why don't we start a book club?'

'A book club?' What was wrong with me? I sounded like I'd had a lobotomy. *Books, you say? What be these things of which you speak?*

Alice was looking at me patiently, the secateurs on hold. 'Yes, Lucy. Do the others like reading?'

'I'm not sure . . .'

'Oh, but you talk about books, I know you do. Rebecca was talking about her e-reader just the other day.'

'Yes, that's true.'

'And you and Maggie were saying you both preferred physical books.'

'Yes, we were.' Why was I so reluctant? A book club was a brilliant idea.

Alice brandished the secateurs. 'What about Tom?'

'Well, I know he reads . . .'

'There we are then!' Swish, snap.

'But I'm not sure he likes the same kind of thing I do. Or that Maggie or Rebecca do, for that matter.'

'Excellent!' Alice was unwinding another green stem.

'Excellent?'

'Well of course! That's the whole point of a book club, isn't it? So you read things you wouldn't pick out for yourself.' She freed another tendril and held it out. A few tiny white flowers trembled at the end. 'Will you talk to the others, then? I wouldn't want them to think I was . . . well, you know, pushy or something.'

The secateurs were poised over the fragile little stalk. I told myself to get a grip.

'Yes, of course I will. It's a great idea, Alice. I don't know why we haven't done it before.'

She smiled at me again and squeezed the handle of the secateurs.

Snap.

I'll be honest: by the time I left Alice that day, I knew I didn't like her. It wasn't anything I could have put my finger on; just the certainty that if I'd had any choice in the matter, I wouldn't have wanted her living next door. Now I might call it instinct.

Back then, though, I tried to ignore it. I knew my antipathy was at least in part because I saw Willowcombe as *my* place, my sanctuary. I'd moved there wanting to leave behind my old life, to meet new people, swap the daily toil of the office for something creative in beautiful surroundings; and now here was Alice moving into a cottage just like mine, another refugee from London, another woman fleeing 'relationship issues'. She brought with her an echo of things I wanted to forget. Worse, she seemed to see me as a shortcut to establishing herself in the village. I didn't like the idea of her muscling in on my friends, telling me how to look after my garden, instituting a bloody book club when *I* was the one who loved reading.

I knew they were feelings that did me no credit.

Later that day, sitting across from Tom in The Gables' lofty-ceilinged kitchen, I tried to talk to him about it. I'd gone there to fill him in on the book club idea, and he'd been lecturing me that literature didn't stop at the year 1900 and he wasn't going to participate if we were going to 'lie around on couches swooning over Mr Darcy'.

Ferdy had settled himself on the quarry tiles at my feet and I reached down to scratch behind his ears. 'No one's arguing with that, Tom. In fact, Alice said that was the point of it – to read things you wouldn't normally.'

'Good. Then that means we take it in turns to pick the books.'

I nodded vaguely, trying to work out why the idea made me so uncomfortable.

'She's the one we're meeting at the pub, isn't she? This architect of Willowcombe's new social scene?' Tom inspected me over the rim of his coffee cup. 'I see.'

There was a note of satisfaction in his tone. I said, 'See what?'

'You don't like her, do you?'

'No, no, it's not that . . .'

'I agree, it's a little presumptuous, instituting a new social gathering when she's only been here five minutes. But I didn't think you were the type to mind that kind of thing?'

'I'm not. I mean, I don't.'

'So what's wrong with her?'

I sighed. 'I've been asking myself the same thing.'

I looked down at the table, the pine scrubbed nearly white from decades of use. The table in my parents' kitchen had come from B&Q. It was nice enough, but I couldn't see Nat or me transferring its beech veneer to our own homes when the time came.

I struggled to find the right words. 'It's just . . . She's just . . . Oh I don't know. This is going to sound ridiculous.'

'Fabulous. I like ridiculous explanations the best.'

'She's just a bit *creepy.*'

Tom raised an eyebrow. 'Creepy how?'

'I don't know. I can't put my finger on it. It's like – she's friendly and nice enough and everything, but she's just . . . cold.'

'Are you going to say she's dead behind the eyes?'

'There's no point talking to you if you're just going to laugh at me.'

'Sorry, Lucy.' But he *was* laughing – the corners of his mouth were twitching. 'Look, I'm sure she's just shy. People can come off a bit chilly when they're nervous. Not everyone can have the happy knack of blending easily with any society, whether high or low.'

I recognised the words. It was a quote from the BBC adaptation of *Pride and Prejudice*, the hapless vicar, Mr Collins, addressing Elizabeth Bennet.

'You're misquoting Austen. That's a capital offence.'

'Just practising for the book club.'

Not long after that, a phone rang out from somewhere in the depths of the house and Tom jumped immediately to his feet. I tried not to mind that he sometimes let it ring for ages when I called; perhaps he was expecting to hear from someone important.

Traipsing back down the gravel driveway, I told myself he was right: Alice was just nervous and I was too willing to think ill of people. It was probably a legacy of my time with Richard.

Which of course brings me to my second reason for not trusting my instincts.

I wish I had a more romantic story. It's where everything starts, after all. It feels like it should have been a grand passion, something irresistible, a once-in-a-lifetime yin meets yang that would have made whatever came afterwards worth it. Even a disaster, an ending filled with blazing rows and recriminations, would have been better. Instead, it was just *ordinary*.

I'm not going to try to blame it all on Richard. He was a flirt, yes, but it wasn't as if he hid the fact he was married – with two kids; we may as well get that on the table. I suppose in a strange way it made everything easier; I thought his having a wife and family meant that nothing would ever happen. I thought it was safe to look, to enjoy the casual touches and the lingering glances, the feeling of possibility when he was around.

We had sex for the first time on my desk – a terrible cliché, and I'll warn you now it wasn't the last. It was a few months after he'd joined Waites, and over the previous weeks our flirting had intensified to fever pitch. I don't need to go into details. Suffice it to say it was late, we were alone in the office and 'one thing led to another' – that's what people say, isn't it? He made the first move, but I escalated things; by which I mean he was the one who kissed me, and I was the one who reached for his belt buckle.

It lasted a little over four months and I'm ashamed to say that at one point I persuaded myself I was in love. It was a defence mechanism, I suppose; believe it or not, I take marriage seriously. My parents have been married for thirty-three years, and while they've both had their admirers – even in the world of classical music there are fans who get too enthusiastic – as far as I know they've always been faithful. I admire that. I respect it. And yet somehow there was Richard; smooth, charming Richard with his blue eyes and his strong hands and his penchant for risky sex, and for a while I didn't care that someone else had got there first.

In the early days, the fear of being found out added to the thrill. The clandestine visits to the hotel near the station, the military planning to get Richard in and out of the flat when Liz wasn't around (having a flatmate who worked at the same office added an extra dimension of difficulty to proceedings, as you can imagine), even the pay-as-you-go mobile phones he'd insisting on buying, as if MI5 had a special department devoted to catching out adulterous spouses – all of it brought a frisson of excitement that was entirely new to me. It was like a drug.

Over time, though, it began to lose its potency. I remember the jolt the time I saw Richard turn away from me in bed and stretch out to pick up his trousers from the floor, the shock that was almost physical as I realised I knew exactly how he'd swivel his hips as he got to his feet, how he'd reach for his shorts and give them a little shake before putting them back on, left foot first, then right. It felt too soon to know those things; it felt like failure.

I think Richard felt it too, that the spark was fading. I believe now that's why he did what he did that day. I'm sure it's why I went along with it.

Neither of us ever guessed where it would lead. That sounds like I'm trying to justify myself, doesn't it? That's not it. I just want to say: yes, we knew what we were doing was wrong, but we couldn't see it then, the chain of cause and effect.

We didn't understand what it would do to other people. And we didn't know the price we'd have to pay.

Chapter 4

The Red Cow is the fifth pub Alice has ever visited.

The first, the Three Feathers, was her grandfather's local. He'd taken her there now and then when he said her nan wanted to get them out from under her feet. Alice had liked those times, sitting in the booth in the corner, a glass of lemonade in front of her. Every so often someone would come over to talk to Grandad and he'd introduce her solemnly, as if she were a grown-up: 'This is my granddaughter, Emily Alice,' and when they'd gone, he'd go back to squinting at his paper and Alice would return to her book.

She'd discovered reading by then, the relief of escaping into a world where she wasn't picked on for her old-fashioned coat, or because her nan wore a pinafore when she collected her from school. She didn't blame her nan, not really; she didn't know any better. It was her parents who were responsible, her mother who had lied to her and left her. Sometimes, when she was reading, she forgot all that – but the time always came to turn the final page, and then she'd look up and find everything was just the same.

The second pub had come a lot later, but she'd been there only once and didn't remember the name. She'd gone with some girls from the shoe shop where she'd got a Saturday job. They hadn't really wanted to invite her, she knew; she'd overheard them conferring in urgent whispers in the little space behind the curtain that divided the shop from the storeroom. She couldn't hear most of what they'd said, but she'd caught the words 'weird' and 'creepy' and knew with a sinking heart that they were talking about her. But they were well-mannered girls, and they'd asked her to join them anyway – probably they'd thought she'd say no – and she pretended that they hadn't been talking about her after all, and smiled and went with them, and ordered a lemonade, and tried to join in as they talked about their boss and her husband and their son, Liam, who occasionally helped in the shop and who they thought was fit, and a bit of a flirt even though he had a girlfriend. She'd thought it had gone OK, but then the next week she'd waited and hoped, but they hadn't asked her again; and she thought perhaps they weren't going and they'd ask her another time. But she knew really that wasn't it.

The other two pubs had both been near the office, places where people went after work and sometimes even at lunchtime. It hadn't taken long after she'd started working in the admin team to be invited on one of the regular jaunts; they never seemed to be planned and no one appeared to know or care who came along. It was usually one of the PAs who'd get people moving. There'd be a big sigh, and a slap of a cardboard file on a desk, and then Lissa or Jenny or whoever it was that day would announce they'd had enough, and they didn't know about anyone else, but they were off to the Manx for a bevvy. Alice had never supposed they were talking to her, hadn't supposed she was invited at all; but then one day Lissa was pulling on her coat as she walked past Alice's desk, and she paused and said, 'Are you coming then?' and so Alice did.

She hadn't known where they were going at first; she'd never heard of the Manx and it turned out that it was called the Black Cat really. After a few weeks, when she'd been out with them a few times and no one seemed to mind, she'd plucked up the courage to ask Lissa why they called it that. She'd said, 'It's 'cos of the sign outside – the cat's got no tail, like one of them Manx cats.' And then one of the other women, Alice didn't know her name, leaned across and said, 'And it's 'cos most of the men in here are manks and all!' and they started laughing so hard that people turned around and stared at them and Alice laughed too even though she didn't know why it was funny, and thought: *I'm here, in a pub, with a group of people who look like they're having fun.*

It had been the fourth pub where she'd met the boy. By then Lissa had persuaded her to add vodka to her lemonade, and she couldn't remember how it had happened and whether he'd come over to her or she'd spoken to him (though surely she wouldn't have plucked up the courage to do that, vodka or not). But however it had happened, they'd spoken to one another, if only a few words over the thud and clash and twang of the band that had been Lissa's or Jenny's or someone else's reason for getting them all to ditch the Manx for the evening. And when that bit was over, he'd leaned into her and abruptly (a little rudely, Alice thought) put his tongue in her mouth and, seeming unsure what to do with it, rolled it around hers, first in one direction and then in the other, reminding Alice of watching her grandad's socks going round and round in the washing machine.

And then they'd gone back to his flat and taken off their clothes and made what her nan would have called the Beast With Two Backs – if her nan had ever talked to her about such things, which she hadn't. And Alice hadn't enjoyed it but she hadn't minded it; and she didn't mind either when he'd said afterwards that he didn't want her to think he was a tosser or anything, but he had to be up early in the morning and his flatmates got pissy about people staying over, and did she have money for a cab 'cos he'd thought he had some but the barmaid must have only given him change for a tenner instead of a twenty; and so she'd got dressed and caught the night bus and walked down two shiny black streets to her grandparents' front door, and let herself in as quiet as a mouse, and was just about to close her bedroom door behind her when her nan stuck her head around her own door and said wasn't it late to be coming back, but in a way that Alice knew meant she was happy really because she thought Alice was doing normal things that normal girls did, and Alice said yes, she was sorry, and her nan smiled and said, 'Well, just don't wake up your grandad.'

The Red Cow isn't like any of those other pubs. Alice had known it wouldn't be, but still, the beams, and the slate floor, and the big fireplace with its basket of dried flowers, which surely, when winter comes, will hold a roaring log fire, are a reminder. She doesn't belong here.

For a moment, she feels the old nervousness tighten her throat. She looks down at her clothes: the dove-grey cashmere sweater, the tailored capri pants, the silver ballet pumps in the softest of soft leather. Her outfits now are carefully assembled, the product of hours of research, leafing through magazines with names like *Country Living* and *Homes & Garden* and even, as her preparations became more focused, *Cotswold Life*. She straightens the hem of her sweater and thinks: *I don't belong here. But they don't know that.*

***

'Seven o'clock for Ellie. Oscar can have another half an hour, but that's it. Sam. *Sam?*'

'Yes, I've got it. Seven and seven-thirty.' Sam grins and gives Rebecca a mock salute. There's a time when it would have made her laugh, but the hapless male routine has long since worn thin. He sees her expression and tries again. 'I've got it, love, honestly. You go and enjoy yourself.'

He's been on his best behaviour for the last couple of days, trying to get on her good side after the incident with the Coco Pops. She'd lost her temper then, and who could blame her? She'd wanted to enjoy coming home after a night away, to remember how much there was to be thankful for in family life; but the moment she'd stepped through the front door, he'd started: thank God she was back, the kids had been little brats all weekend, could she put the kettle on, what was for tea?

She'd dumped her bag on the floor of the hallway and said, 'Perhaps if you took the time to discipline them now and again, they wouldn't be so bad.' And then she'd walked into the kitchen and things had gone from bad to worse.

Piles of washing-up overtopped the sink, and on the kitchen counter pools of varying size and colour documented the children's beverages of choice. And then her gaze had fallen on the table.

A bowl of brown milk sat on one side, a sticky spoon protruding from the top. Takeaway flyers, unopened post, Sunday supplements and a box of sugar-laden cereal jostled for the remaining space. The box lay on its side, but it was empty, its contents strewn across the table and the floor below.

She'd turned to him, white-faced, scared that if she opened her mouth she didn't know where it would end. He said, 'Sorry it's a bit of a mess. Oscar wanted to pour them himself.' He glanced at her nervously. 'I was about to clean it up, but Ellie was crying that she'd lost Trixie. You know what she's like about that bloody rabbit . . .'

She cut him off, pushing past him wordlessly and collecting her bag from the hallway. For a second she entertained the fantasy of opening the front door, leaving the three of them to wallow in their squalor; instead, she stomped upstairs to the bedroom, slamming the door behind her so hard it shook on its hinges.

She moved about the room robotically, unpacking the contents of her bag then turning to Sam's clothes, still lying on the floor where they'd fallen: boxers, T-shirt, an old pair of jeans. She placed them in the laundry basket, burying the clothes she'd worn that weekend. How long, she asked herself, would it have taken him to get around to moving them? Would she have had to stay away for a week? A fortnight? A month? Would they have just multiplied on the floor until she came home to restore order?

This would be how it went if someone dug through the laundry basket: a thin layer of his-and-hers clothing at the bottom, the few things she wasn't able to get into the last wash before leaving; then a thicker layer of her own clothes, neatly separated into colours and whites as she'd emptied out the laundry bags from her suitcase; then Sam's detritus, gathered up and deposited there on her return – the jeans with one leg inside out, the balled up socks, the boxers and the T-shirts and the favourite 'sleeping shorts', stale-smelling and jumbled together. Someone could sift through those layers and determine how long she'd been away. They could tell how many times Sam had been to the pub, and how many times he'd made himself beans on toast instead of defrosting the meals she'd cooked and frozen for him. They could count the grass stains from the garden kickabouts with the kids, and the beer stains from the evenings in front of the telly when they'd gone to bed. Maybe they could guess what she'd been doing too.

All those secrets that could be unearthed. The archaeology of a marriage.

That was two days ago, and Sam has been making an effort since, bringing her the odd cup of tea and putting his dirty clothes on top of the laundry basket, even if they haven't made it inside.

He's probably got a night out planned with his mates, and doesn't want her kicking up a fuss. It won't last, but she knows she should make the most of it while it does.

Now she says, 'I won't be late back.'

He shrugs in a way intended to demonstrate that it doesn't matter. 'It's under control, love, honestly. Don't do anything I wouldn't do.'

She closes the door behind her, thinking: *He hasn't got a clue.*

* * *

He'd known he'd be cutting it fine, but Quinn is a regular and Tom can't, won't, disappoint a regular. Besides, he'd told himself it would be a challenge: by how much could he speed things up and still get the job done, and – more interestingly – how adroitly could he move from the imperative-laden vocabulary of his time with Quinn to a genteel discussion about the mechanics of a book club with four Willowcombe ladies who lunched?

He still feels a frisson of pleasure in these moments of arrival back in the midst of village life, fresh from an appointment with Quinn or Seb or any of the other owners of the initials that appear discreetly alongside the dates in his Moleskine organiser (Tom is a great believer in the security of the low-tech approach). He still gets a kick out of standing in the village store discussing the late blooming of the daffodils, or listening to Cynthia in the post office lament the continuing failure of the council to tackle the speed of traffic, thinking: *If only they knew . . .*

Quinn hadn't noticed the difference; had seemed, if anything, even more appreciative of the urgency of Tom's manner, and after they'd finished, he'd gone through his usual routine in just the way he always did, his thumb jabbing at his phone as he checked the next date for what he referred to as their 'meetings'. (Tom knew, because he'd asked – one couldn't be too careful – that those meetings were recorded in Quinn's electronic diary as 'Conversational French – Philippe'.) Tom didn't hurry these formalities: experience had taught him their importance. It was all too easy in his line of work to find a client who'd been an enthusiastic participant one moment consumed by second thoughts, uncertainties, even downright self-loathing after his departure. That wasn't good for business; more importantly, it wasn't good for his clients. So he made a point of putting things on a businesslike footing at the end of appointments, consulting diaries, checking arrangements; subtle reinforcements to the subliminal message: *This is OK. This is normal. This is a service like any other.*

By the time he'd got back to the Daimler, he'd known he was going to be late. Now he winds down the window, slides a cassette into the ancient tape deck, and pulls out of the driveway. A last glance in the rear-view mirror confirms that Quinn is already on his mobile.

No rest for the wicked.

* * *

Maggie drains her glass of Merlot – something decent to start the evening with, and after all, isn't David always talking about how good for you it is? – and scans the bar for Tom. The conversation so far has been stilted. She's been doing her best to keep it ticking over, but Rebecca is distracted and Lucy is out of sorts, and Alice . . . well, Alice is trying, but after all, she's new to the area and doesn't know anyone very well. She'll fit in in time, no doubt – Maggie hasn't yet found the person she can't talk to about something – but for the moment, it is, not to put too fine a point on it, awkward.

'He's late.' Rebecca has seen Maggie looking. 'Typical Tom.'

'Yes, that's our boy.' Maggie gropes for a topic. Perhaps she should have tried harder to get David to join them – at least

Rebecca could have asked him about his research. She always seems interested, though heaven knows why; Maggie knows for a fact that Rebecca didn't even pass GCSE biology.

'Perhaps he's been held up at work?'

'Ha! There speaks a woman who's never met Tom!' Maggie glances at the door again.

'What does he do? For a living, I mean?'

Maggie smiles to herself at Alice's old-fashioned formulation.

'Tom's an artist. A botanical artist – you know, flowers and grasses and things.' There's an unmistakable note of envy in Lucy's voice. 'He's really good. You should get him to show you some of his work.'

'This must be a wonderful place for a painter.'

'Oh yes, there are loads of creative types in Willowcombe.' Maggie picks up the thread with relief. 'You can't turn around without tripping over one of us!'

'I can see that.' Alice casts a smile around the table. 'Painters and interior designers – and Rebecca, you have your baby clothes business, don't you? I always think that kind of thing needs its own type of creativity.' Rebecca looks pleased. 'And what about you, Lucy? I'm sure you have your own hidden talents?'

Maggie darts Alice a glance. Was the barb deliberate? But Alice is all smiles; she hasn't realised how it sounded. Besides, she seems to like Lucy – she made a beeline for the seat next to hers when she arrived, and listens attentively whenever she speaks, tucking her hair behind her ears as though to hear her better. That hair is a little mousy, Maggie thinks, not unlike her own in its natural state – at least, as far as she can remember.

'... especially with parents like yours!'

She really shouldn't let her mind wander like this – Alice has said something and is looking around the table, evidently expecting an answer. No one else looks ready to supply one;

perhaps they haven't been paying attention either. But Lucy looks embarrassed, sheepish, like she's arrived at a party in a little black dress when everyone else is wearing jeans. Alice was saying something about parents. The silence is stretching on – oh God, is no one going to answer her? Maggie will just have to make something up. Or there's always that story about her own parents coming to visit and asking for quinoa at the village shop . . .

'Oh, there's Tom!' Lucy sounds every bit as relieved as Maggie feels.

'About time.' Rebecca peers at her watch, a frown puckering the skin between her eyebrows. 'I wonder what his excuse is this time.'

Chapter 5

Thank God people started to relax when Tom turned up, or I don't think I could have stood it. I'd have had to make an excuse to leave, something involving a splitting headache (the favoured approach in Willowcombe, as I'd learn in time) or suddenly remembering that I'd left my hair straighteners plugged in. That last, of course, is a mistake I'd never make; but no one but Alice would have known that.

I'd got to the pub after Maggie and Rebecca, and was sitting facing the door – it's what I always do these days, I have to see the exits – so I was the first to spot Alice arrive. She was looking around as she came in, seeking us out, and when I caught her eye and waved, she froze for a second. It was odd, and odd too that that no one else noticed; but I didn't imagine it. She paused mid step inside the doorway, turned her head as I waved, and stared at me – just stared. It can only have lasted for a second, and then she smiled and waved back as if nothing had happened at all.

She went to the bar for a drink, and when she returned, she sat on the bench next to me, asking about the people in the village, who was who and what they were like. Out of all of us, she was making the best attempt at conversation – and yet it hadn't seemed strained before she'd arrived. Perhaps it was just that everyone was still getting to know her, trying to make a good impression. Maybe that was what it was like for Maggie and Rebecca and Tom when I first joined their group; maybe they felt they had to make an effort, though honestly, I can't see it, especially not from Rebecca.

And then Alice was asking about everyone's jobs. I suppose that's just what people do when they're getting to know you, the shorthand they use to classify you. And Maggie has such an interesting job, and even Rebecca, with her baby clothes – she's a businesswoman, after all, an entrepreneur. And then there's Tom with his painting. What did I have to say after all that? 'I used to work in marketing but I hated it and then I had to leave anyway because I had sex with my boss.' I'd have sounded like Bridget Jones.

So I tried to keep the conversation focused on everyone else. Usually that's a sure-fire winner because almost everyone likes talking about themselves, especially when there's a passing chance that the person they're talking to is actually interested. This time, though, it didn't seem to work: Alice wouldn't let it lie. She kept asking about my 'hidden talents' (*rude*), and saying how inspirational creative people must find it to live somewhere so beautiful; and I was wondering whether to tell her that she might think better of that when she'd seen the Willowcombe Players' infamous murder mystery *All's Dead That Ends Dead*, when she said it. She tipped her head to one side and looked at me from under her lashes and said, 'You must enjoy expressing your creative side, Lucy, especially with parents like yours.'

I don't think anyone else was listening. Not that it's a secret who my parents are, but I hadn't told anyone in the village. I knew how it would go, somewhere like this: people making excuses to come round so they could tell me my mother played the cello like no one else, or that the Berlin Philharmonic had never had such gravitas as when conducted by my father; and when did they plan to visit, and would I perhaps like to bring them over for supper, nothing too formal, just to meet one or two friends who enjoyed discussing 'the arts'? And then there'd be the questions: what instrument did I play, was I going to follow in their footsteps? And I'd shake my head, seeing their surprise as I admitted I didn't have a musical bone in my body, pretending I didn't mind.

No, that I could do without.

So I hadn't said anything, and I liked it – just being Lucy Shaw, not anyone's daughter, just me. So how did Alice know?

She'd expected to surprise me, that much was obvious. She was watching for my reaction and I suppose she must have seen she'd got one. I didn't say anything, though, and that was stupid. I should have asked her what she meant, made her explain how she knew about my parents. I expect she had her cover story ready, but I didn't even make her use it.

At the time, it crossed my mind that she was some kind of Annie Wilkes character, you know – 'I'm your number one fan!' Or Mum or Dad's number one fan, anyway. They'd had them over the years, turning up at the same supermarkets, stopping Mum in the freezer aisle and asking about her favourite composers while I stood on one leg and then the other and started tugging at the edge of her cardi until she said that she'd love to carry on talking but the peas had started to defrost. Or some woman with pearl earrings would come up to Dad in the car park and tell him how much she admired his work, touching his arm and gazing up at him while Mum rolled her eyes and said he'd have to go back in because Nat had lost his Batman figure somewhere in the bakery section.

But Alice didn't seem like a fan – she didn't strike me as the type to get excited like that, not about anything. Her words took me by surprise, and as I was trying to decide what to say, the door opened and Tom came in and that was it – the moment was gone.

Things got easier after that, thank God. Tom made his apologies and told some ridiculous story about his car getting stuck behind a flock of sheep on the way back from shopping, and overheating. I suppose it was plausible enough with that old banger he drives, but everyone knew all the same that it was a lie. Tom lies all the time – he doesn't even try to disguise it. It should be annoying, but there's actually something sweet about it, as though he's making things up because the truth is too boring for words and he's sure you'd prefer to hear something more entertaining. Perhaps everyone should lie like that. Perhaps I should give it a go – after all, it's got more charm than my usual approach, the sin of omission; which isn't even technically lying when you come to think of it. Funny that it can feel so deceitful, while being on the receiving end of Tom's fibs instead feels oddly flattering. Perhaps that's what a public-school education does for you.

He disappeared to the bar soon after arriving; I could hear him flirting with the barman. But then he was back, plonking two bottles of wine and a clutch of glasses on the table. Alice introduced herself, leaning across the table to shake his hand in a way I thought was strange but no one else seemed to; perhaps that's what people do in places like this. At first she had his attention – I saw him watching her as he asked about the book club and what he called 'the rules', no doubt looking for signs of the oddness I'd told him about. But Alice gave nothing away. She replied politely, smiled sweetly, said nothing original: the idea for the book club had come up as she and I were talking, she wasn't sure who'd first suggested it; she liked reading, but we'd all been discussing books – Maggie had far more sophisticated tastes than hers, and I read so widely ('Even sci-fi!'); she thought e-readers were terribly convenient – perhaps Rebecca could recommend the best model?

Her every answer was an evasion, an attempt to deflect the focus of the conversation to someone else. But if Tom noticed, he didn't seem to mind; and Maggie and Rebecca followed up their cues to keep the discussion flowing, chipping in ideas for what we should read first.

'We could have themes! Thrillers and whodunnits one month, then feminist literature or – what do you call it? Magical realism! Magical realism the next.' Maggie had knocked back her second glass of wine and her volume had climbed a notch.

Rebecca's lips tightened at the mention of feminist literature. She said, 'Couldn't we have more of a mixture? Perhaps the classics? Loads of them are free on the e-reader, you know – out of copyright.'

Maggie shrugged. 'Fine with me. I like my men in breeches.'

I waited for Tom to argue, but he was eyeing up the barman.

'Lucy? What do you think?' Alice had turned to me and I thought there was something nervous in her expression. Her fingers pulled at the wrists of her cardigan.

Tom remained oblivious and I decided he'd have to fight his own battle on this one. Besides, it was too warm to argue – the air in the pub was getting thicker. Perhaps it was all the bodies around the table. I ran my finger around the neck of my T-shirt; the skin there was hot and sticky.

'Yes, sounds good to me.'

'Well then. That's settled.' Alice looked as if her lottery numbers had come up, and I found myself warming towards her; she was trying so hard to fit in.

The wine was making me drowsy, and talking became more and more of an effort as the evening drew on. Now and again

I felt Alice's sidelong glance on me as she asked a question or commented on something on which she evidently thought I should have a view. I wondered vaguely what she wanted from me, but I was too hot and tired to care.

Gradually I became aware of Tom and Rebecca bickering, their voices taking on the edge of people pretending their argument was trivial while becoming ever more annoyed. It was something about where the book club should meet – I didn't have to listen carefully to guess that each would be staking their claim to host it first. Then Maggie was interjecting, her blurry voice cutting through the clipped tones, saying she'd do it instead as long as no one cared that she'd only feed us shop-bought canapés.

The wine glass had grown heavy in my hand. Maggie was still talking, but her voice now was a distant murmur. She was saying something about going away, a trip to a spa; but then her words ran into each other and I couldn't understand them any more. I put down the glass and tried to stand, but my legs felt as though they belonged to someone else, someone older and weaker and infinitely more disposed towards staying where they were.

Tom was looking at me, his lips moving, and there was a pressure, a hand on my arm, pale skin, slim white fingers. Then I was on my feet, an arm around my waist. My head was spinning and I thought I would fall, but the arm kept me upright, surprisingly strong, a bite of fingernails in my side. There was a face next to mine, pale grey eyes, warm breath in my ear. I caught the words 'down' and 'home' and felt myself nodding.

Shapes slid past me – chairs, I think, a coat stand. Then a car, its seat scratchy against my legs, the smell of pine coating my throat.

A door slammed. Green and flashes of sunlight, then cool air again. Alice's hair against my cheek as she leaned across me, undoing my seat belt. I tried to get up, and hit my head, hard. For a moment the world wobbled and I thought I would be sick; but

Alice was pulling at my arms, and somehow between us I was on my feet. Gate, path, door – my door. But it was too late, my stomach was churning. I doubled over. There was red, something red, then blackness closing around the edges. My stomach heaved again and I vomited over the geraniums.

The front door was open now; I could see into the hallway, the big knot at the end of the rope handrail that ran beside the stairs. Alice must have found my keys. Somewhere beyond the nausea, embarrassment stirred to life. I tried to lift my head, to force my useless, flabby tongue to form an apology. But an acrid taste rose in my throat and I was sick again.

Alice's hand was on my arm, pulling me forward. I tried to shake her off, sure that any motion would make me vomit. But she was strong and I found my feet moving, just managing to summon the strength to lift them over the doorstep.

I had to get to the bathroom; but the cottage had only one, and that was up the steep, narrow stairs. Climbing them seemed impossible. The hand on my arm had gone – had Alice left, or was she in another room? Perhaps she'd gone to the kitchen to get me water. I longed for water. My mouth was parched and sour.

I stood there for a moment, watching the floorboards tip and slide. There was a scuff mark on one of them. I tried to focus on it, but the floor tipped again and I fell forward, my hands and knees hitting the edge of the stairs.

I tried again to speak, and this time I heard a small, cracked voice say, 'Alice.' It sounded like it was coming from a long way away. There was no reply. She must have left. Perhaps she thought I was drunk and would be better left alone to sober up.

The bathroom.

I raised my left hand and felt my fingernails scratch the wall. My arm felt like lead. It fell to my side and I breathed in deeply, once, twice. Pause. Try again.

I summoned all my strength, and this time my fingertips brushed something coarse. The handrail. I tried to curl my fingers around it, but it was too high, too far away. My arm fell to my side once more.

I heard a sound, a sob, and realised it had come from me. My heart was hammering in my chest, and for the first time, fear sliced through my clouded mind: something was very wrong.

I had to get upstairs.

I stretched my arm forwards this time, reaching for the stairs above me. The wood was warm and smooth against my palm. My fingers found an edge and gripped it. I took a breath to steel myself and pulled. My body slid upwards, my useless legs following. Another breath, the other arm, an edge; grip, heave, rest. Again.

Sweat ran down my forehead and stung my eyes.

Somehow, eventually, I was lying face down on the landing, the thud of my heartbeat in my ears. I wondered whether I should try to get to my bedroom, to reach the phone there and call for help. An ambulance; yes, I needed an ambulance. But there was water in the bathroom, cool water I could splash on my face and drink from the tap. And who knew how long it would take an ambulance to reach me here, in my pretty little cottage, in the pretty little village, down all those pretty, winding country roads.

I reached out again and saw my hand white against the floorboards as I pulled myself towards the bathroom. There was something black at the edge of my vision. My heart was thundering now, shuddering in my chest as if it would burst from my ribcage. The blackness was creeping closer. I knew I had to keep moving, I had to keep going or it would close in on me, and that – it came to me with a sudden, piercing clarity – would be very, very bad.

Ahead of me I could see the bathroom door ajar. I closed my eyes against the tiredness in my bones and reached ahead once more.

My fingers struck something and I opened my eyes. A pair of feet in silver ballet pumps barred my way.

And then the darkness closed in.

I awoke surrounded by softness. My lids, still heavy, restricted my view to a strip of greyish gold, a mist through which various darker shapes loomed. My throat was hot and dry. I blinked once, twice, and the shapes began to resolve themselves into objects: a wardrobe; a doorway; a chest of drawers; a chair. With a rush of relief I realised I was in my own bed.

There was a glass of water on the bedside table and I reached for it, my arm shaking. The water was tepid, but I drained every drop. I put down the glass and shuffled to a seated position. My shoulders and abdominals ached in protest and a memory surfaced: I had dragged myself up the stairs. Could that be right? Had I really been in such a state? But I remembered it: stretching out each arm in turn, the drumming in my chest, dragging my legs behind me.

What had happened to me?

I had to go to the bathroom. The urgent need carried the echo of a memory. That was where I'd been trying to get to when I pulled myself up the stairs. I swung my legs out from beneath the duvet and got to my feet gingerly; but they held my weight. I set off at a gentle hobble across the room.

The door to the landing was closed and I paused there, my hand resting on the old-fashioned latch. My muscles ached and I was tired, but that was all: no sweating, no streaking pain through my skull.

It was then that I noticed what I was wearing.

The T-shirt and skirt I'd worn to the pub were gone, in their place an old, baggy nightshirt I hadn't seen for years. With a start, I realised I wasn't wearing underwear.

Alice. She'd been there; she must have put me to bed. It was she who'd left me the glass of water, who'd drawn the curtains. I should have been grateful, but a knot of unease was forming in my stomach. Where had she been while I was dragging myself painfully, inch by inch, up the stairs? Why hadn't she helped me?

I tried to remember what had happened after I'd reached the landing. Had I made it to the bathroom? Maybe – my cheeks flamed to think of it – I'd had some kind of accident. Perhaps that was why she'd had to remove my underwear. *Dear God*, I prayed, *please, please not that.*

But it was all a blank. Perhaps that was for the best. If I'd had to remember something like that, I'd never be able to face her again.

I began to lift the latch and then stopped: perhaps Alice was still there.

I had a sudden fervent longing to be back in my parents' house, Mum bringing me soup and cold drinks and insisting she was going to call the doctor. I didn't want Alice there. More than that, I realised with a jolt, there was something about her that frightened me. The coldness, the patronising offers of help that seemed to conceal a real dislike, the way she watched me when she thought I wasn't looking. A vivid picture flashed across my brain: Alice holding a stem of jasmine, her eyes on me as she sliced through the fresh moist sap.

I shivered.

I lifted the latch quietly and padded onto the landing. There was a stillness to the house that told me I was alone, but I had to be sure. I said, 'Alice?' It was too quiet for anyone to hear, and I was glad: the fear in my voice had startled me. I told myself to get a grip and tried again. 'Alice? Are you here?' Better. The tremor was slight, nothing that couldn't have been attributed to the after-effects of sickness.

There was no reply. I exhaled, feeling the tension seep from my muscles.

I took the few steps along the landing to the bathroom. The door was open. There was a fresh towel folded on the side of the bath and a faint smell of lemon in the air: Alice must have cleaned up. I tried to feel grateful.

My eye was drawn to the other door on the landing, this one shut tight: the spare bedroom. The closed door had a sinister air. It occurred to me that I didn't know what time it was, or even what day. How long had I been asleep – or unconscious? Had Alice stayed with me? Had she slept in my spare bed?

I reached for the latch and it rose with a clang that echoed around the cottage. The door swung inwards and I stepped inside.

The room appeared untouched. The hill at the back of the house kept this part of the cottage in shade, and the green-tinted light that filtered through the window didn't reach the corners. The quilt my favourite aunt had made for me when she'd heard I was moving to Willowcombe was spread across the bed, undisturbed. The pile of books on the bedside table appeared untouched. A travel alarm clock ticked softly next to them, and I went over and picked it up. The numbers blinked at me: 6:30, but the little black lozenge sat next to p.m. With a shock, I realised that at least a day had passed.

My legs were beginning to feel weak again, and I turned back to the bathroom. By the time I'd showered and dressed, I felt more myself, and back in the bedroom I opened the curtains, made the bed and flung open a window to chase away the odour of the sickroom. There was no sign of my clothes from the day before.

I went downstairs slowly, gripping the rope as I descended. My handbag sat on the hallway floor, presumably where Alice had placed it when she'd found my keys. Everything else appeared just as I'd left it – the shoes next to the front door, the notepad on the hall stand with the scribbled reminder to buy washing-up liquid.

Coffee. Coffee was what I needed.

I padded into the kitchen and filled the kettle at the sink. Out in the back garden the light was starting to fade, and snails were at their twilight work, tracing silver lacework across the patio. I was about to turn away when a movement made me start: a flutter of white outside the back door. I leaned forward to try and get a better look, the rim of the sink pressing into my stomach, but there was nothing to see. I waited – perhaps it had been a bird? But then a breath of wind trembled over the grass on the hill and I saw it again, a flash of white fabric. It was the T-shirt I'd worn to the pub: Alice must have washed it and hung it outside to dry.

I took the key from its hook next to the back door and turned it in the lock. Outside, the evening air was still mild, the scent of honeysuckle sweet and heavy. Before me stood the concertina of the airing horse, my T-shirt and skirt hanging neatly on either side. In the middle section, hidden by the other clothes as though they were shameful things, were my bra and knickers.

I touched the T-shirt – warm and dry – then gathered up all the clothes and returned to the kitchen, dumping the lot on the table. For a moment I hesitated, then, hardly daring to look, I extracted my knickers from the pile. Thank God: there was no sign of anything to add to my humiliation.

'Are they dry, then?'

I let out a little shriek and dropped the knickers. Alice stood in the doorway, regarding me with cool amusement.

'Sorry, didn't mean to startle you. Just thought I'd pop by and see how you were feeling.'

'How did you get in?' My tone was harsher than I'd intended, and she pursed her lips.

'I took your keys when I brought you home. I thought someone should be able to check on you, in case you weren't well enough to get out of bed.' She looked down at the pile of washing accusingly. 'You really were terribly sick.'

'Yes, of course. Sorry. And thank you.' I was finding it difficult to string a sentence together. 'Thank you for bringing me home. And everything . . .' I trailed off.

'You really shouldn't drink like that, you know, if you can't handle it.'

I felt the blood rush to my face. 'I only had a couple of glasses of wine.'

'Well, it was more like three or four actually.'

'Not enough to make me sick.' Not sick like that, and not enough to make my heart race and my balance go; not nearly enough for that. What had been wrong with me?

'Well I'm sure you're right. You know your limits, after all.' She pointed at the washing. 'Do you want me to iron those for you?'

I shook my head. 'No, that's really kind of you, but you've done so much already. In fact, I think I need to go and lie down again, so . . .'

I smiled what I hoped looked like a friendly apology, but Alice's mouth was set tight and she didn't move. For a moment I wondered how long we could stand there like that, pretending everything was fine; but then she smiled too, the smile I liked, and I told myself to stop being ridiculous. She'd been kind. She'd tried to help.

'Of course, I'll let you go and get some rest. And perhaps you should get yourself to the doctor,' she raised a quizzical eyebrow at me as she turned to go, 'if you really don't think it was just the drink.'

I followed her to the door. A patch on the floorboards caught my eye: the scuff mark I'd noticed last night – I'd have to see if I could clean it off. It reminded me of something, and despite my wish to be rid of her, I had to ask the question.

'Alice?'

She turned around. 'Yes?'

'When we got back, where did you go?' She looked at me blankly. 'I needed the loo but I couldn't get up the stairs.' I laughed, trying to keep my tone light. 'I couldn't stand on my own – well, you know that. I . . .' another laugh, 'I ended up dragging myself up there! It felt like it took ages.'

'Oh dear, poor Lucy.' She held her head to one side, a slight pout of the kind you'd give to a toddler complaining they wanted ice cream. 'I just went to the kitchen. You said you wanted a glass of water. Don't you remember?'

Had I said that? I'd been thirsty, I remembered that much; and that taste in my mouth after I'd been sick. I might have asked for water. But how had it taken her so long?

As if she'd read my mind she said, 'I was only gone for a moment, you know. You must have got up the stairs quicker than you think. In fact, I wondered where you'd got to! I went into the living room, but there was no sign of you. So I checked upstairs and there you were on the floor of the landing.' She smiled again, showing her teeth. 'Dead to the world.'

I nodded, slowly.

'You were completely out of it. I'm not surprised things have got jumbled up. I had to help you into the bathroom, get you undressed—'

'Yes, thank you.' I cut her off, embarrassed. 'Thanks again – for everything.'

‘No need to thank me, Lucy.’ She turned back to the door and then stopped. ‘Oh! I nearly forgot.’ She fished in the pocket of her jacket. ‘Your keys.’

I held out my hand and she dropped them into my palm. I watched her leave, then closed the door behind her and rested my head against the wood as her footsteps receded down the path. Then I reached down and turned the key in the lock.

Chapter 6

The date has been creeping closer: Maggie has known it for weeks. It's the chill that descends as the evenings draw on, or the smell of woodsmoke from a distant bonfire, or the hay bales like enormous curls of butter scraped from the surface of the fields. It's some of those things, or all of them, that tells her the anniversary is drawing near.

She's prepared as usual, booking an overnight stay at a spa, telling David laughingly that she's going for her MOT. She's bought several new paperbacks, the kind with fluorescent covers with jaunty line drawings of wine glasses and high heels. Alongside them in her case is another book: *Jane Eyre*, which somehow they've managed to agree will be the first to be discussed at the book club. Now that she's volunteered to host the meeting, there'll be no getting out of reading it, though she's not a fan of eighteenth-century literature with its heroines who either sacrifice their happiness to dubious moral principles or are ignorant of their own desires to the point of wilful idiocy.

Still, she's never read *Jane Eyre*. Perhaps this one will be better.

She drags her case from the bed and pulls it across the floor, hoping the wheels won't leave a mark on the leather rug. Then it's down the curving staircase – 'reminiscent of the gentle curves of the surrounding Cotswolds landscape', as *Elegant Living* magazine once described it – trying to avoid the white walls on one side and the glass balustrade on the other. She could do with a hand, but David has long since left for the surgery. She was still in bed when he leaned down to drop his usual goodbye kiss on the top of her head, and she'd reached up to draw him closer, suddenly tearful. But he'd been in a rush and pulled away, giving her hair an affectionate pat and telling her he'd see her the next day. She had listened as the front door slammed and the sound of the car engine faded away, trying to ignore the loneliness that settled on her like a damp fog.

In the car, she turns on the radio, but they're playing country and western, a heavily accented woman's voice singing about how hard it is to be a woman. 'Too true,' Maggie says out loud and switches to the MP3 player. A tinny pop song blares out; just the thing. She puts the car into gear, gives a cursory glance over her shoulder, and pulls away.

Behind her, a small silver Renault eases away from the kerb and, keeping a careful distance, begins to follow.

* * *

Alice had to steel herself to go in when she first saw the Georgian facade of Armitage Hall, with its wide driveway and its globes of precisely clipped greenery either side of the front door. A handful of cars were parked outside: Maggie's Mercedes left at a careless angle nearest the entrance to the road, the others a mixture of sports cars and 4x4s she was sure hadn't seen a day's off-road driving in their lives. Everything screamed money.

The driveway continued beyond the house and she followed it around, hoping to find somewhere more secluded to park. Off to one side a few more cars had been left beneath the shade of some trees. The models were more modest than those at the front – presumably this was where the staff parked. Alice pulled in next to a Fiat Punto and got out, relieved to stretch her legs.

A sign at the corner of the building informed her that reception lay at the front of the house. She picked up her trolley case to minimise the noise she made as she crossed the gravel. It was unlikely anyone would pay her any attention, but Alice's instincts always favour discretion, and she's learned to listen to her instincts.

Doing so is what brought her here in the first place. She'd known as soon as Maggie's trip to the spa was mentioned that there was something more behind it. It had been that evening at the pub, Rebecca and Tom sniping at each other like spoiled children, arguing over where the first meeting of the book club should be held. Alice had listened, patient on the surface while the urge rose inside her to give them both the hard, stinging slap they deserved. Then Maggie had intervened, saying she'd have the meeting at her house but she had a lot on and they'd have to wait a couple of weeks to give her time to read the book. Tom had said, 'Couldn't you take it to the spa with you?' but as soon as the words were out he'd looked awkward, as if he'd said something he shouldn't have. Rebecca had butted in then, asking where Maggie was going, envy in her voice as she mused about how lovely it must be to be able to 'just drop everything and indulge yourself'.

Maggie had answered politely enough, but it had been clear that she wanted to change the subject, asking Rebecca how things were going with her baby clothes business. The distraction had worked, and when Rebecca was in full flow, Maggie had darted a sharp glance at Tom, who, thinking no one was watching, had mouthed 'Sorry' and given her a sheepish smile.

Alice had assumed that 'the spa' was code for something else, an affair most probably, and her heartbeat had quickened at the thought. A lie already. But then that wasn't surprising – these were Lucy's friends, after all. And where there were lies, there were secrets; secrets that could be used.

So she'd been surprised when she'd followed Maggie's car along the winding, tree-lined lane to Armitage Hall. It was an odd choice for an assignation, and Alice's curiosity had mounted as she entered the reception area.

A well-groomed brunette sat behind a mahogany desk, tapping away at a computer. Alice approached and fixed her with her best warm smile. 'I do hope you'll be able to help me!'

The receptionist looked up and blinked, then smiled herself as Alice launched into her story: she'd planned to visit the spa with a friend, Maggie Reeves, but she'd had to cancel when an important meeting had been scheduled at work. She'd been terribly disappointed because she knew that with Maggie's nightmare diary she'd never be able to reschedule, but then, hey presto! The meeting was cancelled at the last minute and she thought to herself, why not just head down to Armitage Hall anyway, surprise Maggie and see if they had a room free for the night? 'I was going to phone first,' she smiled again, half embarrassed to admit to her own foolishness, 'but then I thought, no: I'll put myself in the hands of Fate!'

The receptionist – Chloe, according to the badge on her jacket – was enjoying the opportunity to save the day. She tapped busily at her keyboard, then paused. A frown. 'No standard rooms, I'm afraid.'

'Oh dear, I did think it was a terribly long shot . . .'

But Chloe was jabbing at the keyboard again. 'Let's not give up too soon!' More typing, then an exclamation of satisfaction: the receptionist was beaming as though about to make all

Alice's Christmases come at once. 'Looks like today is your lucky day!'

Should she clasp her hands to her chest, or would that be too much? She decided against it.

'I've found you a superior room – that's one of the larger ones, and it's got its own balcony so you can sit outside if you like.' As if there were anything else to do with a balcony. Alice began to feel impatient. Maggie must have settled in by now and could come down at any minute.

'That's wonderful—'

'But I can go one better than that!'

The woman was like a game-show host, stringing out the big reveal. Alice raised her eyebrows in what she hoped was an expression of eager expectation.

'I can give you a room right next to your friend!'

And so here she is now, perched on the end of a bed with her ear pressed against the wall, listening to Maggie moving around next door. She wonders what it would have been like to come here together, if Maggie really were her friend. Would they have arranged to meet for coffee after they'd unpacked, looked together over the lists of beauty treatments, egging each other on to greater indulgence?

But no, that can never happen with Maggie; not with Rebecca either. They're Lucy's friends. They've allied themselves with her.

Alice shakes her head to clear her thoughts. None of that matters now. She's used to being on her own. She'd thought once that it wouldn't always be like that; but then Lucy came along and ruined everything.

She moves the pillow so she can get closer to the wall. Yes, she's used to being alone, but Lucy isn't. Alice is looking forward to seeing how she'll cope.

* * *

Maggie has decided against unpacking more than the red dress she's brought to wear to the restaurant, and her case lies open on the luggage holder near the door. The bedroom is comfortable and well furnished, with a grand old wardrobe of the kind that, if she were in a story, she might step through into another world. She'd like to do that, she thinks; not for good, just for today. Just until it's all over for another year.

She opens the French windows and steps onto a balcony overlooking the rear of the house, where a manicured lawn stretches to a distant line of trees. There's a small car park off to one side, and directly below, a patio provides a spot for guests to ignore the smoking ban. There are two of them down there now, identikit Home Counties blondes in white towelling robes and slippers, puffing away and looking over their shoulders every so often in a way that suggests they know they're breaking the rules.

Maggie herself gave up smoking not long after she met David. He'd been so sweetly determined to point out to her the error of her ways, running through the roll call of cancers before moving on to the risk of heart attack and stroke; then, with evident astonishment at her obstinacy, progressing to gangrene and amputation, and finally, with a last, desperate appeal to her vanity, premature wrinkling. She'd known it all already, of course, could have taken him through the list herself, her own father having been a chronic smoker who'd succumbed to emphysema at sixty-eight; but Maggie was a firm believer in the principle of something's-got-to-get-you-in-the-end, and she'd always enjoyed a cigarette. It was David's persistence that got to her eventually, his sincere belief that by smoking she was thoughtlessly, even selfishly, reducing their time together. She knew too that he hoped she would at some point change her mind about a baby, surmising that the prospect of a smoke-free pregnancy would be one more barrier to a determined smoker. She'd been touched that he cared so much, touched that he wanted a child with her, and, perhaps most of all, grateful that he accepted her decision without rancour when she told him firmly and finally that she simply wasn't cut out for motherhood. Giving up smoking had seemed like a small sacrifice towards repaying him for all that.

Maggie steps back inside, leaving the French windows open to cool the room. She takes a book with a fluorescent jacket from the top of her suitcase, then rummages further down until she finds the black-bordered cover of *Jane Eyre*. She lifts it out and examines it. A picture of a stern young woman stares determinedly into the middle distance: a self-sacrificer, without a doubt. Feeling only the tiniest bit guilty, she puts the book down again.

She pads from her room and heads for the pool.

* * *

Alice is starting to wonder whether she's made a mistake after all. She's been here now for ages and Maggie has done nothing of interest.

She'd waited in her room for almost half an hour before the sound of Maggie's bedroom door shutting had her flying off the bed, and she was almost in the hallway before she realised her mistake. The women she'd seen on her way from reception had all been wearing the spa uniform of towelling robes and slippers, but the set Chloe had given her still lay where she'd dropped them on the end of the bed. She'd stick out like a sore thumb wandering around in her own clothes.

By the time she'd changed, there was no sign of Maggie, and the thick white carpet muffled any sound. She took the stairs to the ground floor. At reception, Chloe was busy with papers and didn't look up as she passed.

She followed the signs for the treatment rooms, walking past glass-fronted doors with schedules of exercise classes in frames outside, and solid doors with numbers on them. If Maggie were behind one of those, she'd have no way of knowing.

The corridor ran the full length of the building, and at its corner she'd been faced with a choice: turn left in the direction of what a sign told her was a coffee bar and gallery, or take a flight of marble steps down to what was apparently the pool area. She paused for a moment and then turned left.

The coffee shop was brightly lit, with beech-veneered tables that gave it the corporate feel of a conference suite. A handful of women were scattered amongst them, but there was no sign of Maggie. At the end of the room, a single sheet of sloping glass took up most of the wall. Alice's heart leapt as she realised what it was: a viewing gallery, the perfect spot to keep an eye on whoever was in the pool below.

She took a seat at the edge, where she'd be able to duck out of sight if anyone chanced to look upwards. It took her only a moment to find what she was looking for.

Maggie was lying on her side on a lounger, propped up on one elbow and reading a book. A single swimmer sliced up and down through the water in an efficient front crawl. A few of the other loungers were occupied by guests, all women and most – unlike Maggie – paired up with friends.

That was over an hour ago, the Caesar salad Alice had ordered delivered, eaten and cleared away, and still Maggie lies there. She feels a stab of frustration: what is this all about? Why should this trip be such a secret if all Maggie is going to do is lie around reading? Yes, it's lazy and self-indulgent, but that wouldn't matter to someone like her.

Her jaw aches, and with an effort she stops grinding her teeth. She raises her second glass of orange juice to her lips while she watches Maggie, who barely moves and speaks to no one. It's all so ordinary, and yet . . . there is something, after all; something that nags away at her, something that isn't quite right. What is it?

She checks her watch again. Still Maggie lies there, staring at her book.

And then it comes to her. In all the time she's been watching, Maggie hasn't turned a single page.

* * *

The shower is good, hot and strong. The water bounces off Maggie's skin with a force that's almost painful. She's pleased she went for a swim, even though the tang of chlorine now fills the bathroom; it's stirred her from the lethargy that had crept over her while she lay at the poolside. She'd failed to lose herself in her book, her vision blurring as the words refused to make any sense, reading the same paragraph again and again, unable to retain its meaning. Eventually she'd given up without even realising she'd done so, staring at the same page while the rhythmic splash of a lone swimmer lulled her into a trance.

Later, when the swimmer had gone, the blank surface of the pool seemed to call to her. She slipped over its side making barely a splash and began to swim, enjoying the feeling of cutting through the water, the strength in her arms and legs. She was still young, she told herself, young enough for many things, if not for one.

When her muscles started to tire, she flipped onto her back and rested the nape of her neck against the pool edge, holding on with both hands as her legs floated out in front of her. Her eyes drifted up to where a long glass window overlooked the pool. She thought she caught a flicker of movement, but when she looked again, there was no one there.

Now Maggie pours a dollop of shampoo onto her palm and begins to scrub away the smell of chlorine from her hair. The suds run over her head and shoulders and down her body. She watches them stream over her stomach: still flat, or at least as flat as anyone has a right to expect at her age. She places her palm over it and strokes the skin, then tastes salt as the tears come and mingle with the shower water.

* * *

Tom has been expecting the call, though hoping it wouldn't come. He's spent the day at home hovering near his phone, for once having to disappoint a client who rang with a last-minute request. He had suggested another evening, but the client isn't the type to plan ahead, and Tom expects their tentative arrangement to be cancelled in a day or two. Still, this is Maggie, and he'd been sure, almost sure, that at some point today she would need him.

He picks up the phone on the second ring and holds it to his ear without speaking. The sobs come from another person, not the Maggie he knows, the Maggie with the dirty giggle who knocks back wine while burning dinner, who dances around his kitchen to Lady Gaga and cheats at the pub quiz. This Maggie is tired and lonely, worn out with the effort of every day that she looks at her husband and resists the suicidal longing to throw herself on his mercy and tell him what she's done.

'It's all right, Maggie,' he says, 'Just breathe now. It's all right.'

The words coming down the line are ragged and wet with tears. 'It was his child, Tom . . . his as well as mine . . . How can I keep it from him?'

And crouched in the corner of the balcony of Room 27 at Armitage Hall, Alice stays very quiet and thinks: *At last.*

Chapter 7

By the day after Alice's visit, I felt better. At first, her suggestion that I'd been drunk seemed ridiculous; surely a few glasses of wine couldn't have affected me that way. But the more I thought about it, the more difficult it was to come up with any alternative explanation. I hadn't been feeling unwell before, and apart from pinching some of Tom's crisps in the pub, I'd eaten very little that day that could have disagreed with me.

Perhaps the simplest explanation was the right one after all: perhaps the lack of food together with the alcohol and the warm day had been too much. The wine must have been strong, but it had been Tom's choice, and Tom's choices often were. And then there was the raging thirst – dehydration, the classic side effect of too much to drink. I groaned and covered my eyes with my hands: how had I let Alice, all of them, see me in that state? Surely I was old enough to have learned how to spend a quiet evening in a country pub without getting legless and having to be carried home?

I would have to go over there and apologise, take Alice some flowers to say thank you. I should do it now, get it out of the way.

With any luck, by the time we were together again, everyone would have forgotten about what happened.

I got up and went to the hallway to fetch my bag, then stood at the front door, chewing at my lip. Were flowers too much? Maybe it was better just to leave it. Besides, I had other things to do: the first meeting of the book club was in two days, and I still hadn't done the reading. It wasn't fair to the others not to be properly prepared. I put down my bag again with a feeling of relief.

I'd read *Jane Eyre* when I was a kid, too young to understand it and wanting only to impress my parents by strutting around the house with a great big hardback tucked under my arm. I was always the reader of the family – I'd had to do something, after all. Though two years younger, Nat was already adept at cello and tenor sax when I abandoned first the violin (my mother observing, 'It does sound worse than anything else when they're learning'), then the clarinet ('It's one of those instruments that really needs to be heard amongst others'). My parents had seemed more bewildered than disappointed; perhaps they thought it would be easier and less expensive to nurture the talents of their one gifted child, perhaps they were just grateful for the ceasefire on their eardrums. For my own part, I buried my nose in books and tried to suppress the feeling that I was a misfit, a gangly, tone-deaf ginger interloper in the midst of the Shaw musical geniuses.

I didn't remember much about the book, just a series of pictures, faded snapshots in my mind's eye: a little girl reading, hidden behind heavy curtains; a bundle of twigs cracking against the palm of a hand; a locked door, the handle twisting back and forth. They weren't enough for a book club discussion, and I dug out my copy and set about refreshing my memory.

For the first few chapters I read curled up on the sofa, every so often scribbling down a few words in a notebook balanced on the arm beside me. I noted the Gothic motifs and lodged away a few observations about the position of women in Victorian society. It wasn't until Jane had arrived at Thornfield Hall and met the enigmatic Edward Rochester that I started to feel the first faint stirrings of unease.

I tried to ignore them. How many stories, after all, had a woman fall in love with her married employer? I was nothing like Jane, and Richard was certainly nothing like Rochester – I'd seen Teletubbies more tortured. And more to the point, we'd never been in love, whatever I'd thought at the time. Still, I told myself I'd have to be careful; I'd never been part of a book club before, but I was pretty sure there'd be some discussion about the characters. I'd have to watch what I said, avoid the temptation to draw on my own experience. Maggie and Rebecca were both married – I didn't want them getting the idea I was some kind of home-wrecker.

That was what Liz had thought when she'd found out. My best friend and colleague at Waites – deep down I suppose I'd always known there'd be no way of keeping a secret from her for long.

We'd tried to be careful, Richard and I. At first, the attempts had their own kind of appeal: the stolen kisses in the stairwell, the elaborate excuses to work late when everyone else was sloping off to the pub. But as time wore on, the charm began to pall. I told myself not to pressurise him, not to turn into the nagging woman I was sure waited for him at home. Richard didn't criticise Melanie, not overtly, but he dropped hints, subtle asides that let me fill in the details for myself.

It didn't take Liz long to work out that something was going on. We lived together, after all. As the unexplained gaps in my movements began to mount up, she first hinted that I wasn't telling her something, then flat-out asked me what was going on. I kept as close to the truth as I could. I told her I was seeing someone and that he was married, adding that I couldn't give her any details as it wouldn't be fair to those involved. I saw her swallow the obvious retort to that bit of piety, but when she asked if it was anyone she knew, I had to get more creative – I knew she wouldn't let it drop if she thought it was someone at work. So I told her it was a guy I'd known in uni and met again recently through a mutual friend. The story satisfied her for a while, and apart from occasional, unsubtle attempts to pry into the state of my marriage-wrecking conscience, she let it go.

I don't know how long things would have carried on like that if it hadn't been for what we did that day. It was out of character; that's not an excuse – I know it doesn't make any difference – but it's true all the same. Perhaps it was the sense that we'd started to drift, that things weren't quite as exciting as they'd been before. Or maybe it was that Richard had seen me joking around with Dan the IT guy that morning and wanted to remind me whose property I was; that it was fine for him to go back to his wife every night, but woe betide me if I indulged in some half-hearted banter with the office flirt. Or perhaps it was just that he'd spent lunchtime in the pub – I could smell the evidence on his breath when he leant over my desk and asked if I fancied a spot of brainstorming over coffee. Whatever it was, when I said yes, I knew what he had in mind.

I followed him to the lifts, Richard standing with one casual hand in his pocket as we waited. I avoided his eyes as we stood there, keeping them fixed on the file I'd brought with me as a prop. Then the doors were opening and he held out his arm, gesturing for me to go first. The lift was empty, but as I moved forward, I heard heels clicking along the corridor, speeding up in an unspoken request to hold the doors. If whoever it was had called out, we wouldn't have ignored her, I'm sure of that – but she didn't, and I stepped inside and pushed the button to close the doors, unwilling to share the space with anyone else. The clicking stopped abruptly and Richard turned towards me.

He claimed afterwards that he hadn't planned to press the emergency stop button, that it must have happened as we fumbled around. He hadn't even realised there was a button that did that, he said – he'd thought that only happened in films. After all, what was the emergency that would ever necessitate stopping a lift? Would you be halfway down when you somehow learned there was an army of gun-wielding lunatics rampaging around the floor below? 'Unlikely on Tottenham Court Road, Lucy,' he'd said, grinning like a schoolboy. 'Even on a Monday morning.'

For the first few moments, it was exciting and urgent and hot. But then I started to worry that someone would hear us, that at any moment a voice would come over the intercom asking what the problem was. Then I saw the maintenance hatch in the roof and worried even more. I started to whisper to Richard that we shouldn't, but he told me to hush and put his hand over my mouth. I felt the hard ridge of the handrail pressing into my spine as he panted into my neck. I tried to twist away, but the movement made it worse. Richard's head was pushed up against mine and the stem of my earring was digging into the side of my neck. He mumbled, 'Lucy, Lucy,' and then it was over.

There were a handful of people in the lobby when the doors opened. I tipped my head forward and tried to hide my face with my hair, but Richard strode out ahead of me. 'You might want to take the stairs, people.' He grinned at me over his shoulder. 'I barely got out of there alive!' I heard a snigger and felt the heat rise in my cheeks. They'd think it was just Richard's sense of humour, I was sure; but then I looked up and saw Liz, her mouth hanging slightly open. For an instant our eyes met, and I knew. She'd put it all together.

For the rest of the week I barely saw her. I lay in bed listening to the shower running half an hour earlier than usual, and in the evening the door to her bedroom stayed shut. At work she no longer dropped by my desk to suggest lunch or complain about the latest unreasonable demand from Leery, her boss (real name Lawrie; his habit of dropping his gaze to chest height when addressing her had earned him his nickname). Part of me was grateful, but I missed her.

The news about the stuck lift had got around the office, and if Liz wasn't talking to me, there was no shortage of others wanting to share their own tales of lift-related horrors: it had shuddered alarmingly on the way to the third floor, it had gone up when it should have gone down, someone had stubbed their toe when it hadn't stopped in line with their chosen floor. 'And thank goodness,' said one of the interchangeable blondes from accounts – Kate? Karen? – 'it wasn't poor Matthew in there when it happened!'

We were sitting in a meeting room, twenty or so of us in a semicircle filling in a questionnaire headed 'Waites: the future now'. The aim, we all knew, was to identify unbelievers for the latest round of redundancies. I hadn't got past the first question: 'If Waites were an animal, what would it be?'

Kate or Kelly nudged me and cast a conspiratorial glance around the room. 'You know, Matthew! From payroll! Don't say anything to anyone, but he has the most dreadful claustrophobia. That's why he doesn't come to team meetings!' I nodded, wondering how long it had taken him to come up with that one. 'I mean, can you imagine? He'd have had hysterics!'

I nodded again. *What kind of animal . . .*

'And what if it had been someone with health problems? Someone who needed medication or something?'

They'd be expecting something powerful, impressive. A lion, perhaps? But no, too obvious.

'They could have got really ill! Or what if it had been someone who was pregnant?' Kate or Kathy's pitch had risen and one or two heads turned in our direction. I glanced at her paper. Beneath Question 1 she'd written 'Lion'. Inevitable, really.

'What if they'd got stuck and then *gone into labour*?'

A shark, perhaps? Too aggressive. It needed to be powerful, yet benign. An elephant? A few chairs along, a woman with brown hair was staring at us. I wondered what she'd put.

Kate or Kirstin appeared to be waiting for an answer. 'Yes, well, thank goodness it was only me. No claustrophobia, medical issues or pregnancy here.'

'I think you've been ever so brave. Honestly I do. But then,' she laid a manicured hand on my arm, 'it must have helped having Richard there with you.'

Was that a smirk? No, I was being paranoid. I looked across the room, but the woman with the brown hair had gone, slipped out somehow when I wasn't looking. I turned back to my paper and wrote 'Okapi'.

That should keep them guessing.

The gossip passed soon enough. It was Kate I had to thank – that was her name, after all; that Friday, when one of Waites's regular server failures wrote off a morning's work, she rang the head of IT to suggest he drink bleach before bursting into tears and fleeing the open-plan. There were problems at home, apparently. Waites had something new to talk about, and apart from Dan the IT guy humming 'Love in an Elevator' whenever he walked past my desk, the episode seemed all but forgotten.

I saw little of Richard over the following weeks, but the tension in the flat was becoming unbearable. Eventually I couldn't stand it any longer and went and knocked on Liz's bedroom door; but there was silence. She was out.

In the end I sent her a text – the coward's way, I knew, but at least I'd be making the first move. After a couple of exchanges, more friendly on my side than hers, she agreed to meet for lunch in a café near the office; I fervently hoped that being in a public place would make her less likely to shout.

We'd arrived separately, Liz just late enough to make me wonder if she was going to come at all. She took the seat opposite and glared down at her plate of pasta salad, stabbing at it with her fork in a way that suggested it had as much to answer for as I did.

I thought it best to come straight to the point. 'Look, Liz, I know you're angry I didn't tell you the truth—'

She held up a hand to stop me. 'How long's it been going on?'

'Not long . . .'

'*How* long? Days? Weeks?'

I swallowed. 'Three months, give or take . . .'

'For fuck's sake, Lucy!' Several heads turned in the crowded café. Liz glared at them. 'Yes? Can I help you?'

The heads swivelled back around, suddenly engrossed in their lunch.

'Three months.' She gave a humourless laugh. 'All that time and you never said a word . . .'

I said, 'I told you he was married.'

'Oh please, Lucy, don't even . . .'

'I didn't want to put you in an awkward position!'

Liz snorted. 'What, like seeing you post-coital with the director of finance, you mean?' She attacked another piece of pasta. 'In the office *lift*, Lucy? Christ, how tacky.'

I felt the heat rise to my cheeks. Maybe this had been a mistake. I should have given her longer to cool off, or at least suggested meeting somewhere further from work. I'd been scanning the room for people from Waites from the moment we arrived.

I tried again. 'I didn't plan any of this . . .'

'Well that makes it all right, then.' She pursed her lips. 'You know she comes to the office, right?'

I stared at her. 'Who?'

'Melanie, Lucy. His *wife*.' Liz was raising her voice again, but this time she caught herself. 'I can't believe you haven't seen her yourself. She's always popping in. What if she'd come in the other day while the two of you were *brainstorming* between the second and third floors?'

I felt the lead in my stomach. Did Richard's wife really come to see him in the office?

'Yeah. Well. You want to think about that.' Liz had the expression of someone who'd scored a direct hit and was finding it less satisfying than she'd expected. 'And what about the kids?'

I looked down at the slice of pizza I hadn't been able to touch. In horror, I realised that my nose was prickling and there was moisture in my eyes.

Liz put down her fork and leaned back in her chair. 'What were you thinking?'

The tears came then. At least I kept it together enough to avoid more head-turning. Liz softened the tiniest fraction and asked how it had started (which I edited) and whether I thought anyone else knew (no; and yes, I was sure about that).

It felt better talking about it. I think that's why I cried: it was the relief of finally being able to tell someone what was happening. And it was different afterwards, when we got back to the office, Liz giving me a final, friendly pat on the arm, ignoring Lawrie's pointed examination of his watch as she returned to her desk. I felt easier in myself. A problem shared, and all that. Having that one person who knows the thing that's worst about you.

And my time with Richard . . . our affair. That was the worst thing about me, the worst thing I'd done. I wasn't about to have it dissected for the entertainment of a book club. If the discussion moved on to the sanctity of marriage, I'd just shut up, claim I needed to go to the loo or something. No one would even notice.

At least that was what I thought then.

Chapter 8

Maggie drops the carrier bags onto the kitchen floor and swears as the wine bottles hit the flagstones. There are times, she feels, when lino would have its advantages.

Despite her best intentions, the shopping has been done at the last minute. She'd volunteered to host the book club thinking it would provide a distraction from the anniversary, something to think about when the day itself was over with; but in the event, work has been unexpectedly busy, Claudia finally agreeing the colour scheme for her study, and a tentative enquiry from the new incomer, Alice, which she has high hopes a little persuasion can turn into a significant project. She'd barely had time to get into Cheltenham to pick up some nibbles, and the selection at the supermarket wasn't all she'd hoped for. Thank God she isn't a competitive hostess – she'll leave that to Tom and Rebecca. In any case, there'll be plenty of wine. She'll keep their glasses topped up, and no one will notice that satay chicken isn't a bit 2009.

David has elected to make himself scarce for the evening, claiming it's all too literary for his tastes. For once, she'd have preferred him to make the effort: there's something about Alice's arrival that seems to have destabilised their little group. That evening in the pub had been downright uncomfortable before Tom turned up, and if he's late again . . . Hopefully the message she left him earlier will have done the trick. She'd wanted to talk to him after her return from the spa, part embarrassed, part grateful, feeling she ought at least to make contact before they saw each other amongst friends; but he hadn't answered his phone. She'd waited for the beep of his voicemail, then thanked him, making light of it by promising she'd break out a bottle of the good stuff at the book club, especially for him. 'Just don't be late this time,' she'd finished, only half joking. 'Your public needs you.'

Now she extracts the wine bottles, thankfully intact, and places them in the fridge. She hasn't even managed to finish the damned book; heaven knows she tried, but all that doom and gloom with the orphaned Jane was too much for her fragile mood. Still, she's read the introductory notes to her edition: a few key phrases repeated with confidence and interspersed with trips to the kitchen to refresh the canapés will surely be enough to get her through the evening.

She checks her watch, the silver Georg Jensen she fell in love with in Venice and that David had surprised her with on their last wedding anniversary. Still over three hours before people will start arriving: plenty of time to get ready. She scrunches the carriers into a ball and flips the lid of the bin. A triangle of shiny cardboard catches her eye, pushed flat against the bin liner. White letters disappear under a crumpled piece of kitchen roll. There's something familiar about them, and she reaches for a corner and fishes it out: a bag, heavy cardboard, with navy ribbon threaded through slots at the top. Maggie smiles as she reads the label: *XY*, and then in smaller letters beneath, *London*. David has been shopping again.

For most of their marriage he's shown little interest in clothes, cords and polo shirts forming the mainstay of his wardrobe; but over the last few months, there's been a change. The first time he appeared in a new pair of jeans, he'd looked so self-conscious that Maggie had had to suppress her laughter and, half surprised at the knowledge displayed by his choice of comparison, reassure him that no, he didn't look like Simon Cowell. Over the following weeks, the polo shirts had been replaced by T-shirts, the fit becoming tighter in a way that made her briefly wonder whether she ought to ask whether he fancied a night out at a musical. But David has always been unsmilingly heterosexual, and Maggie had at last concluded that he'd hit his mid-life crisis.

She folds over the glossy cardboard and thrusts it back into the bin. Mid-life crisis or not, she thinks, it's sweet that he's finally making an effort.

* * *

'Surely it's obvious that Jane's feelings for Helen Burns are more than platonic?'

Rebecca sits on the edge of the leather chair that would last approximately thirty seconds in her own home without Oscar trying to decorate it with felt-tip pen, and tries to look as if she's paying attention to the conversation. It's all so different from the way she would have done it: no welcoming cocktail or glass of Buck's Fizz, and the nibbles are straight out of a packet. The wine is good, though, she can tell, though she doesn't know as much about that kind of thing as Maggie does. Maggie had invited her to a tasting once, she remembers, at a smart hotel in Cheltenham. She'd have liked to have gone, but at the last minute she'd got nervous, worried she'd have nothing to say to Maggie's arty friends. She'd rung and told her Sam had a work emergency and couldn't look after the kids. It was a regular enough occurrence for Maggie not to question it.

Now Tom is holding forth – something about Jane Eyre being a lesbian, as far as she can tell, as if everyone else has to be gay just because he is. She lets the discussion wash over her as her eyes wander around the room. It's fashionable, certainly – Maggie is an interior designer, after all – but all those sharp edges and white walls would be no good with children. And could anyone really feel at home here? She tries to imagine David inserting his angular frame into a corner of the sofa, Maggie leaning over him as she hands him a glass of wine, kissing his cheek perhaps, then joining him, resting her head in his lap . . .

'Oh come on, Tom! The whole book is about Jane and Mr Rochester being soulmates!'

The exclamation rouses her from her thoughts. Lucy has swung around in her seat and is scanning the room for support. She'd been quieter than usual when she first arrived, but perhaps the glass of wine she's holding has done the trick. She should know better, really, after what happened at the pub the other night – and that was just the start of it, by Alice's account. Still, at least with the floorboards here, there won't be any lasting damage if there's a repeat performance. Rebecca frowns, thinking of her own living room carpet. Perhaps after all she'll do a non-alcoholic punch when it's her turn to host.

'Good grief, Lucy. Do you hear that clattering? That's the sound of Charlotte Brontë spinning in her grave.'

'I thought the most important theme was the rigidity of the class structure.'

'Oh come off it, Maggie,' Tom turns to her with a grin, 'we all know you only read the revision notes.'

Alice is flicking through her copy. 'I agree with Lucy.' She turns to a page marked with a scrap of yellow paper. 'Here, listen: "It is as if I had a string somewhere under my left ribs, tightly and inextricably knotted to a similar string situated in the corresponding quarter of your little frame."'

'Yes, exactly! That's Mr Rochester, isn't it? Talking to Jane just before he asks her to marry him.' Lucy's cheeks have taken on a pinkish tinge.

Alice closes the book again. 'But it's not a healthy relationship, is it?'

Tom snorts. 'What, are you saying his already having a mad wife locked in a tower wasn't a model for connubial bliss?'

'No, that's not what I meant.' Alice is staring at Lucy. 'It's the power balance: he's her employer, isn't he? He's the one in charge.'

Lucy examines her fingernails. The varnish on her index finger is chipped, Rebecca notices, a chink of bare nail showing through the dark plum. 'I don't think that necessarily follows.'

'Of course it does.' Alice's tone is unexpectedly firm. 'She relies on him for her living. How could they ever be equals?'

'But they are – that's why he loves her. Here, listen to this bit . . .' Lucy fumbles for her own copy.

'Oh, I know she *thinks* she's his equal! But she's kidding herself, isn't she? She knows in her heart that he doesn't need her. That's why she runs off into the storm . . .'

'Actually, I think you'll find she leaves early on a pleasant summer morning . . .' Rebecca spots her opening. She might have known that none of them would have read it properly.

'He's just using her.' Alice is bending back the cover of her book, her knuckles white. 'He betrays his wife, but it's Jane who has to leave her home, her job. She's the one who loses everything.'

'But she takes responsibility! She makes her own decisions and she does the right thing.' Lucy's flush has deepened.

'No, no, no!'

There's a catch in Alice's voice and Maggie shoots an anxious glance at Tom. 'Would anyone like another tempura prawn?'

'I don't mind if—'

'Don't pretend it's all right!' Alice's eyes are fixed on Lucy. 'Stop trying to pretend it's all right! She loses everything. She loses everything and she ends up all alone!'

The book springs from her hands and falls to the floor. For a moment everyone is still. Then a sob grazes the silence.

Chapter 9

I thought to begin with I was going to get away with it. I'd been the last to arrive at Maggie's, and apart from her holding me at arm's length and exclaiming that I looked '*Amazingly* human!' everyone seemed to have forgotten how our last night out together had ended. I allowed myself a single glass of wine, and by the time we started discussing the book I was able to nod along with Alice as she talked about Victorian values, convincing myself I liked her well enough, that I'd been imagining things after that night at the pub, my senses at fever pitch from dehydration.

I can't remember how it started. One minute everything was normal, and the next the atmosphere had changed. Alice was talking to me, her grey eyes fixed on mine as she said that Jane was stupid, that Rochester was the one in charge, that he was using her just because he could. I tried to plead Jane's case, knowing as I spoke the words that I was defending myself; but Alice's voice was shrill and she was leaning towards me, eyes wide with anger. I couldn't look away. I tried again to say how Jane, how I, had struggled to do the right thing, but Alice wouldn't listen. She was shaking her head and I could see tears welling in her eyes.

I couldn't stop looking at them, waiting for them to tip over the edge and roll down her cheeks. And then she said it.

She said I'd end up all alone.

Everything went quiet. No one moved. And then she started to cry.

The noise was horrible, loud, grating sobs. I should have tried to comfort her, said something or placed a hand on her arm; but I was like stone. I was suddenly sure she knew about Richard. I was certain she was going to tell everyone what I'd done.

It was Maggie who moved first, darting me a reproachful glance as she squeezed herself into the gap on the sofa. She pulled Alice into a hug, stroking her hair and shushing her as if she were a frightened kitten. I was getting in the way, so I stood and backed up a few steps, then stopped, unsure what to do next.

Words were coming from between Alice's sobs. I didn't want to hear them.

Maggie looked up and said, 'Lucy, get some tissues.' I didn't want to leave the room, but she was waggling her fingers in impatience, and I thought: *It doesn't matter. Let's just get this over with.*

The downstairs loo was along the hallway, and my feet echoed on the flagstones as I walked. I wondered what they were saying about me, whether they'd believe what Alice told them, what she'd say to convince them. Rebecca would be ready to judge me, I knew – that was just the way she was. But Maggie? Tom? Would they wait to hear my side of the story?

I wondered how Alice knew what I'd done, but it wasn't important. When I went back into that room, everyone's eyes would be on me, the mistress and the liar. I tried to tell myself that it shouldn't matter: people had affairs every day, and Richard was the one who was married, not me. But Rebecca and Maggie had husbands of their own – they'd see me as a traitor to the sisterhood, one of those women who betrayed her own sex for a man who couldn't be expected to know any better.

I pushed open the door to the loo and recessed lights flickered into life, casting a soft glow over the gleaming ceramics. The tissues were on a shelf and I grabbed them, the lights clicking off again as I left, as if I'd just stepped out of a fridge. It was only then, retracing my steps to the sitting room, that the obvious question forced its way to the front of my mind.

Why had Alice reacted the way she had?

I'd been so mortified at the idea of my dirty linen being aired in front of my friends that it hadn't occurred to me to wonder why my affair with Richard would have upset anyone but myself. And yet there was Alice, breaking down in floods of tears in front of a roomful of people she'd only just met. Whatever the reason for it, I thought, I'd find out soon enough.

I drew level with the entrance to the living room. The front door lay ahead of me and for a moment I considered simply carrying on, walking through it and down the path and along the road to my cottage without a backward glance or another word to any of them. I could pack up my things, drive back to London and forget I'd ever been there. I closed my eyes and took a deep, steadying breath.

I stepped into the living room.

Alice had stopped crying and was sitting on the edge of the sofa, rubbing at her wrists and wearing what was evidently intended to be a brave smile. Maggie had released her from her bear hug and was patting at her arm, while Rebecca had drawn up a chair to the other side of the sofa and was peering at her in fascination. Tom stood in front of the fireplace nursing an empty glass and shifting from one foot to the other, his eyes darting between Alice and the bottle of Hennessy on the coffee table.

I said, 'I've got the tissues,' and held them out, stiff-armed as a mannequin. Maggie took a couple and handed them ready-crumpled to Alice. She sniffed into them delicately.

'I'm so sorry, everyone.' Alice looked at Tom as she spoke, presumably on the basis that he seemed the most uncomfortable. 'I feel like such a fool.'

The others mumbled variations on the theme of 'Nothing to feel sorry for', but I couldn't speak. Alice was hugging herself loosely, her fingers tapping against her forearms. Next to her elbow there was a small scuff in the leather sofa, shaped like a miniature surfboard. I wondered if Rebecca had noticed. I bet she'd be able to recommend a cleaning product.

'And you especially, Lucy. Sorry for going off at the deep end at you like that.'

I gaped at her. Had I heard her right? I mumbled something non-committal.

Alice said, 'I feel like I owe you all an explanation.'

Maggie opened her mouth to speak and then closed it again, torn between politeness and curiosity. 'You don't owe us anything of the sort,' Tom cut in firmly, and I caught the flash of annoyance that passed over Rebecca's face.

'Thank you, Tom. You're all so kind. Really, though, I couldn't face you again if I didn't explain myself. Especially not when I was so rude to poor Lucy.'

I didn't like to hear myself described that way, but I didn't argue. Alice had stopped hugging herself and was settled back into the corner of the sofa, looking for all the world as though she were about to pick up her abandoned copy of *Jane Eyre* and begin reading to us aloud. The impression was so strong I almost felt I should sit cross-legged on the floor at her feet and wait for her to begin: 'There was no possibility of taking a walk that day . . .'

But Alice had a different story to tell.

Chapter 10

Tom stands in the shade of the willow, dabbing at his easel. The petals of the irises are beginning to crisp in the heat, and he's had to come out today to catch them before they pass their best. His mind, though, is on other things, returning time after time to the previous evening, the meeting of the book club. Something about it is bothering him; he's struggling to put his finger on what it is.

Everything had seemed fine to begin with, and he'd been pleased to see Lucy looking better after her departure from the pub. He'd felt vaguely guilty about that: perhaps he should have taken her home instead of Alice; he was her best friend in Willowcombe, after all. But he'd seen Matt, the Red Cow's more-than-attractive new barman, frowning as he watched Lucy stumble to her feet, and told himself he'd do better to try and repair her reputation with the staff of her local – and perhaps see if he couldn't get Matt's telephone number while he was at it. He'd succeeded in the end, on both counts; but by then he'd discovered that, notwithstanding his firm jawline and impressive biceps, Matt voted UKIP and still lived at home with his mum.

It's a shame, he reflects now with a sigh, that beauty alone is no longer enough. It must be a sign he's getting old.

He supposes he should be worried about Alice. It was she, after all, who'd been sobbing on Maggie's sofa. But that argument with Lucy – it had seemed personal somehow, for all they were supposed to be discussing the book. The way Alice had looked at her when she'd said Jane would end up alone . . . If it didn't seem so ridiculous, Tom would have said it was threatening.

The sun is getting stronger now and he checks his watch. Just gone one, legitimately time to stop for lunch. He stands and, considering for a moment, decides to leave his easel and paints where they are. He won't be long, and few people come that way.

Ferdy cocks an ear at his master's movement, then shakes himself to his feet and leads the way back home. 'Creature of habit, much,' Tom mumbles, not sure whether he means Ferdy or himself.

Away from the shade of the trees the heat is almost uncomfortable. Tom picks up his pace – the sooner he reaches his kitchen and a cold beer the better. Up ahead the stream curves in a gentle arc, stepping stones set into its bed at its narrowest point. A small post on the other side bears a sign, placed there in Aunt Lydia's time, informing inquisitive walkers that this is private property. As Tom rounds the bend, Ferdy lets out a couple of joyful barks and splashes across the water, planting his sturdy paws on the opposite bank and shaking himself vigorously.

A patch of lilac in the grass catches Tom's eye and he bends to inspect it. Milkmaids, Aunt Lydia had told him these flowers were called, and even now he can remember her voice as she pointed to the ground, her scent, wool and soap, mingling with the wet grass. His parents had been surprised when she'd left him the house and there'd been murmurs of discontent from shadowy relatives, but Tom had understood: The Gables was a magical place to Aunt

Lydia and she'd known he felt the same. To sell it would have been sacrilege, and to the horror and disbelief of his friends (and his dealer) he had packed his bags and exchanged his rented flat in Bath for this quiet, rambling old house in the Cotswolds.

A volley of barks brings him lurching back to the present and he straightens quickly, catching a glimpse of Ferdy's hindquarters tearing up the meadow towards the house. He must have spotted a rabbit; but then he barks again, and there's another noise – a low, harsh snarl.

Tom takes the stream in a single bound and runs towards the house. He can hear Ferdy's barking, frenzied now, interspersed with more of that diabolical snarling. It must be another dog, some mastiff or Rottweiler that's found its way into the garden. Ferdy's stout-hearted and Tom knows he'll try to defend his territory; but a cairn terrier will be no match for something that makes a noise like that.

From this direction he reaches the side of the house first, the meadow becoming lawn, then a gravel path that skirts the walls. There's no sign of Ferdy, but the barking is coming from the front of the building. He rounds the corner in a spray of gravel.

The sight that meets him stops him in his tracks.

Ferdy's fur stands on end, every muscle straining. His eyes are fixed on his adversary as he lets off another stream of barks and then – Tom would never have believed it if not seeing it with his own eyes – gives a long, guttural growl.

The woman in front of him is pressed against the porch, too terrified to move. Alice.

'Oh Jesus, Ferdy, no!'

Tom rushes forward and grabs the dog by the collar, pulling him away. He fishes for the front door key in his pocket – where the hell is it? But there's the spare, tucked out of sight behind a flowerpot on the windowsill. He snatches at it one-handed and forces it into the lock, Ferdy half throttling himself as he pulls against his collar. Then the porch is open and he pushes Ferdy inside, slamming the door shut with a force that echoes around the walls. The barks become desperate.

Tom turns to Alice. She's white-faced, frozen to the spot.

'Oh God, Alice, I'm so, so sorry. He's never done anything like this before.' He wipes sweat from his forehead. 'I don't know what the hell's come over him! Are you OK?'

She looks too traumatised to speak. *Please God*, Tom thinks, *don't let him have bitten her*. But there's no sign of any injury and her clothes are unruffled.

'Why don't you come in and let me get you something to drink.' He sees her eyes flick to the door and adds, 'It's OK, we can go in the back way. Ferdy can't get out of the porch.'

He leads her to the kitchen, Alice lowering herself unsteadily onto a bench. From the other end of the house Ferdy howls in distress. Tom picks up the kettle, then thinks better of it and reaches instead for the sloe gin. Alice's hands shake as he presses the glass into them.

'I don't really drink . . .' Despite the trembling, her voice is steady.

'But you've had a shock. It'll help.'

She holds out the glass, the tremor in her hand sending little waves across the surface of the liquid. 'I'd prefer some tea, if you have it.'

'Yes, of course. Whatever you like.'

From the front of the house, Ferdy's howls accompany the knocking of the geriatric water pipes as Tom fills the kettle. He crosses to the hallway and shuts the door.

'I really am sorry, Alice. Ferdy's normally a friendly little chap. I can't think what set him off.'

Alice shrugs. 'Dogs don't like me, I'm afraid.'

'He didn't hurt you, did he?'

She pulls back the sleeve of her cardigan. An angry red scratch stretches across her wrist.

'Oh Jesus, no, he didn't . . .'

'It's all right.' Alice fixes him with a cool stare. 'I'm not going to report it.'

Tom's throat is dry and he wishes he'd poured some of the gin for himself. He nods dumbly. 'Thanks. Thanks, Alice. That's really good of you.'

The sleeve of her cardigan is still raised. The red mark sits there like an accusation.

'Perhaps you ought to run that under a tap. I'll get you some antiseptic lotion.'

'It's fine, really. I've had my shots.'

'Even so, it looks sore . . .' Tom opens a drawer and rifles around: boxes of plasters, a pot of paracetamol, an old screwdriver. Where the hell is the antiseptic? A box of matches falls to the floor and scatters across the quarry tiles. 'Fuck!'

'Really, it's fine.'

'No, I know I've got some . . .' He swings open the door to the hallway and is greeted by another torrent of barks. A thud at the door shows that Ferdy hasn't given up his attempts to escape. What on earth is wrong with him?

In the tiny downstairs loo, Tom wrenches open the cabinet on the wall above the sink: a bottle of liquid soap, a spare loo roll, cotton buds. There, behind a rolled-up bandage, a flash of blue. He grabs the tube of lotion and heads back to the kitchen.

Alice is picking up the last of the matches. 'Here you go.'

'Thanks, I'll do you a swap.' The kettle starts to whistle, and as Tom turns to make the tea, he sees her lift the tube to her nose and sniff. He says again, 'I really can't apologise enough . . .'

'Please, there's no need. No lasting damage done.' He doesn't like that word, 'lasting', but her expression is innocent. 'Anyway, the reason I came is that there was something I wanted to ask you.'

'Oh yes?'

'Yes. I hope you won't think I'm being nosy . . .'

Tom murmurs in a way he hopes is encouraging, his curiosity rising.

'It's about Lucy.'

So there *is* something going on there. Tom keeps his tone neutral. 'It was good of you to take her home the other night.'

'Oh! It wasn't a problem. I'm only next door, after all.' A pause. Alice chews on her lip. 'She was quite sick, though.'

'Oh no, poor Lucy. Poor you! Did you have to clear it up?' Tom is suddenly thankful after all that he stayed at the pub.

'That wasn't the problem. The thing is . . . I really don't know how to say this . . .' She casts her eyes around the room. Down the hallway, Ferdy's howls have turned to whines that make Tom's chest ache. 'Do you think Lucy has a drinking problem?'

It takes a moment for him to register the words before he bursts out laughing. 'What, Lucy? Yes, I should think so! Doesn't do it nearly enough!'

Alice doesn't laugh. Her eyes are filled with anxiety. *Oh God,* Tom thinks, *we have a Puritan on our hands.*

'Sorry.' He collects himself. 'But no, Lucy doesn't have a problem with alcohol.'

'Are you quite sure of that?'

There's something in her earnestness that makes Tom pause. Again he feels a splinter of remorse: he left this woman, new to the village, to look after his sick friend and didn't even remember to ask whether she was OK. He changes tack.

'Why do you ask? Surely you can't think that just because of the other day . . .'

Alice shakes her head. 'No, no, of course not. We all overindulge now and again. But, well . . . this is going to sound silly.' She pulls at the sleeves of her cardigan and the red mark is out of sight again. 'It's just that she was so ill, and when I said something about how the wine had been quite strong she practically jumped down my throat.'

'That doesn't sound like Lucy.'

Alice sighs. 'I thought you'd say that. I've gone and put my foot in it, haven't I? I hope I haven't offended her.'

Tom gives another sympathetic murmur. Poor Alice: she's trying so hard to make friends. Lucy must have been feeling rough to have lost her temper like that, but it's not much of a welcome to the village – surely she remembers what it felt like to be the new girl.

'Anyway, it was probably nothing.' Alice shifts in her seat. 'I shouldn't say anything more.'

Tom catches the inflection in her voice. 'Why, what else happened?'

'No, I shouldn't say. Lucy would be upset. And anyway, you know her better than I do. If you're sure there's nothing to worry about . . .'

Tom frowns. The implied shift in responsibility has discomfited him. Perhaps, after all, it would be wrong to dismiss Alice's fears out of hand. He says, 'Why don't you tell me what happened? I'm sure there's a simple explanation.'

'If you don't mind, it would be a relief to talk to someone about it. And you and Lucy seem such good friends. You won't say anything to her, though, will you? I don't want her to think I've been gossiping about her behind her back.'

For a moment Tom hesitates; surely this *is* gossiping about Lucy? Perhaps it would be better to talk to her himself. But then she might react angrily, as she has with Alice; he could do without a confrontation. Besides, it's almost certainly nothing. He'll put Alice's mind at rest and have a quiet joke about it all with Lucy afterwards.

He smiles at her. 'No, I won't say anything to Lucy. I promise.'

* * *

Rebecca arches off the ground and drags the hemline of her dress over her bottom, the thin cotton offering some protection from the sun-baked bristles of the grass.

David's eyes follow her movement and he reaches over and lays his hand on her thigh. His heartbeat is returning to normal now and he knows they should leave; but her skin is soft and warm. He watches his fingers travel upwards beneath the fabric, pale against her tan.

She places a hand on his wrist. 'Davy, I've got to get back.'

He sighs. It is at times like this, about to step over the threshold into his other life, that he wants her most of all.

She rolls towards him and brushes a kiss against his lips. 'I wish we could go away again. Have some proper time together.' She pronounces it 'prrahper', forgetting to clip her West Country vowels as she always does after sex. He doesn't answer. The ball is in her court; she'll have to make arrangements for the kids. The absence of children from his own marriage had once felt like an aching void, but he admits to himself now that it has its advantages. He's already told Maggie that his research will require regular weekends away from home. She hadn't minded – perhaps, David tells himself, if she cared a bit more, made a bit more effort to spend time with him now and again, he wouldn't be here with Rebecca.

Rebecca's lips are against his again. 'I'll talk to Sam. Tell him I've got to go somewhere for work.'

'Again? He'll start to get suspicious.'

Her laugh is humourless. 'Not Sam.'

Her breasts are pressing against his chest. He can feel her nipples through her dress. He reaches up and pulls her closer to him, slipping his tongue into her mouth, enjoying the silky feel of her hair in his fingers. Maybe there's time . . .

'Ow!' Rebecca has elbowed him in the stomach in her haste to roll away. She's already standing, pulling at her dress. 'What the . . .?'

'Shh!'

The panic in her voice has him on his feet, fumbling at the buttons of his jeans. 'Christ, Rebecca, what is it?'

'I thought I saw someone – there by the bridge.'

They're tucked out of sight of the footpath, David has taken care of that; but if someone has heard something, has wandered off the beaten track . . .

'Shit! Are you sure? Did you see who it was?'

Rebecca looks at him with sudden displeasure. 'It wasn't Maggie, if that's what you're worried about.'

His jaw tightens. He hates it when she gets like this. 'I'd have thought that would worry both of us. What did they look like?'

'Fuck, David, I don't know!'

He bites down his annoyance. Clearly he's going to have to be the rational one. 'Well, was it a man or a woman?'

'I don't know! I just saw something move over by the trees.' She exhales a tremulous breath. 'I'm not sure what it was. Maybe a dog or something . . .'

David feels some of the tension ebb away. Anyone recognising them would surely have made a noise, an exclamation of some kind. He scans their surroundings again. Sunlight flashes on the surface of the stream, and near the bridge the trees cast their shade deep; but there's no sign of movement and the only sounds are the burbling water and the hum of insects.

Rebecca's imagination has got the better of her again.

He reaches out a consoling arm. 'That's probably what it was, just a dog.' She's unsure, still glancing anxiously at the bridge. 'And even if someone was there, they wouldn't have seen anything from so far away. The grass is too long for that.'

She looks up at him, big eyes, wanting to believe.

'It's fine, Rebecca. Everything's fine.' Honestly, sometimes it's like talking to a child.

She steps into the circle of his arms and he smells warm grass and sunshine in her hair. 'Sorry – I just get so nervous sometimes. I know what we're doing is wrong . . .'

It's a familiar refrain and one he knows how to handle. 'You deserve this. We both do. Everything you do for everyone else . . .' She nods and moves away from him again, smoothing her hair.

'I'd better go.'

'You're right.' He sighs, as he knows is expected. 'I'll wait here for ten minutes, have a last check around.'

He watches her go, her hips swaying self-consciously in the short summer dress. She takes a path away from the bridge, cutting a swathe through the tall grass to get back to the road. Once she turns and blows him a kiss over her shoulder, a Marilyn Monroe type gesture that looks practised. The artifice is oddly touching.

He checks his watch – he'll wait until she's well ahead before going back himself. It doesn't hurt to be careful. He'll head for the trees, stay in the shade and cool down. He's sure now there was no one there; it isn't the first time Rebecca has worried they've been seen, though they're always careful enough, parking in out-of-the-way spots or checking in separately to an anonymous Travelodge. The weekend he's booked in the upmarket hotel in the Lake District is an exception, but Rebecca had been getting restless, dropping hints that he was taking her for granted, that the charm of the slightly seedy locations they generally frequent was starting to wear off. He'd had to pay the deposit over the phone, no choice but to use his credit card. For a while it had worried him; but Maggie isn't the type to go through his paperwork. It's difficult enough to get her to look at her own.

He wonders sometimes whether there's a part of Rebecca that wants to be caught. He can imagine the drama of it all might hold a certain attraction for her, but he has no intention of finding out. He enjoys his time with her, is flattered by her interest – and God knows the sex has been a revelation – but he's not about to have his nose, far less his marriage, broken to relieve her boredom.

It's quiet beneath the trees. David looks back to where he and Rebecca lay – there's a shadow where the grass has been flattened but no one spying on them from here would have been able to identify them with certainty, and neither of them is the sort of person to attract suspicion.

He walks to the edge of the stream and looks in. The ground here is covered in small, flat stones, washed smooth by the water. He stoops and selects one, bending his knees and flicking his arm to send it skimming over the surface. It bounces twice and he crouches to search for another.

A shift in the air, a movement at the edge of his vision. He stands and looks around.

There's no one there.

He must have been more spooked than he'd thought by Rebecca's flight of fancy. He turns on the spot and peers between the trees, scanning the knotted trunks and gnarled branches that sag into the water. The bridge is on his left, a little upstream, and he walks to it and looks across. On the other side a stubbly meadow, the grass already mown, stretches to the brow of the hill. There's no sign of another soul.

He checks his watch – six minutes since Rebecca set off home.

The undergrowth rustles behind him. He jumps and spins around. Still nothing. It must have been an animal, a rabbit or a field mouse. He swears under his breath. Maybe his conscience is getting to him after all.

He turns again, a slow pirouette. A breeze ripples through the grass and the leaves tremble on the trees. Already they are changing colour: summer will soon be over. He looks at his watch again. Seven minutes. Seven minutes is plenty of time.

He sets off for the road, telling himself he's imagining the feeling of eyes on the back of his neck.

* * *

The pale green silk is nearly used up, but Alice knows there'll be enough to finish the grass. Then there'll only be the roses around the front door and the cross-stitch will be complete. The picture is called *Dove Cottage*, the same as the cottage Wordsworth lived in, but she's not sure if it's the same place. It's a pretty little house with a slate roof, but whitewashed, not like the golden stone of her cottage here. Maybe she'll find somewhere like it to live when she's finished in Willowcombe.

It went well today, at least after that dog was out of the way. Alice doesn't like dogs any more than they like her, and that beast of Tom's is a nasty piece of work. It will complicate things too, and she'd contemplated poisoning it before concluding that was more trouble than it was worth. The woman at the post office, Cynthia, has told her that Tom goes away often ('Always gadding about, that one'), so he must either take the dog with him or leave it with someone, kennels perhaps. Either way, there'll be opportunities enough without taking unnecessary risks. She can take her time, come and go as she pleases now that she knows where he keeps the key.

The dog had tried to warn her off, but she'd turned that to her advantage. It had hurt, drawing her nail across her wrist – she'd had to dig it in hard – but the mark had turned out just right, swollen and angry. Tom had been so worried she'd report his beloved mutt to the police that he was only too ready to invite her in, trying to ply her with that revolting gin or whatever it was, hoping, probably, that she'd get drunk and forget the whole thing.

He'd been the right choice, she'd seen that straight away: the kind of person who knew in his heart of hearts that he was self-absorbed but tried hard to believe he wasn't.

'Selfish,' she says aloud to the cross-stitch, stabbing the needle into the muslin.

It was always easy to persuade someone like that that they'd missed some important sign, a subtle cry for help from someone close to them – easy, of course, because that was so often what they did. He'd laughed at her at first, and she hadn't liked that, not one bit; but he'd come around quickly enough when she'd presented him with the evidence. Alice guessed that Tom had been around alcoholics before; there was none of that *Lucy isn't the type* nonsense. He knew how deceitful people with an addiction could be – his parents, maybe. Lots of posh people drink like fishes, don't they? Glasses of wine in the afternoon, trips to the Continent to stock up on boxes and boxes of the stuff. She's seen a documentary about it.

Lucy had made it easy for her too – it was always better to use the truth, and that silly comment about only having had a couple of glasses in the pub bore the authentic mark of someone sensitive about her drinking. And then there were the empty wine bottles stacked up in the pantry: if she'd only got around to recycling them when she should have done, Alice wouldn't have been able to collect them up and – reluctantly, of course, only because she was so terribly worried about her – store them in the boot of her car to show to Tom.

'Idle,' Alice remarks to her cross-stitch.

Of course, she'd had to buy more bottles to make it look sufficiently impressive, taking care to match the brands to the ones already in the kitchen. She could probably have found them all at Willowcombe Supplies, but she'd driven out to the supermarket outside Tewkesbury to be on the safe side. She'd tipped the wine down the sink, which was wasteful, but better than drinking it herself. The bottles she'd driven back to the bottle bank at the supermarket: at least the glass will be recycled.

As for Maggie and Rebecca, they're too close for comfort, she can see that already. She's watched Maggie going round to number 4 every day, eleven on the dot – tea and cake, probably, gossiping about the rest of them. Gossiping about Alice. She'll have to do something about it sooner or later, and already she has the beginnings of an idea. It's easy, after all, when people behave so badly, though you'd never imagine it of Rebecca to look at her.

'Like butter wouldn't melt,' says Alice.

She draws the last of the green silk through to the back of the muslin in a finishing stitch. The grass is complete, the amount of silk just right, as it always is. Now for the roses. She toys for a moment with choosing pink – it would look pretty against the grey of the cottage door and the white wall – but in the picture the roses are yellow. That's the truth and the truth is important. Lots of people these days tell lies without even thinking about it; her mother was one of them, so Alice should know. Alice only lies when it's necessary. Truth is important, but so is justice.

She threads the yellow silk through the needle. She taught herself how to cross-stitch – it's the kind of thing her nan should have taught her, the sort of good, wholesome pastime you'd expect would be one benefit of having been brought up by people a generation older than the ones who were supposed to have done the job. But her nan was a knitter, and knitting has never interested Alice. It's messy – all those balls of wool all over the place, coming loose and getting more and more straggly as they're used up. And then there were the jumpers and cardigans her nan made for her when she was young, dark green so she could wear them as part of her school uniform. How she'd longed for the plain, shop-bought jumpers in acrylic or lambswool that all the other girls wore. Instead her nan's homemade creations, with their lumpy, bumpy patterns and sleeves that always had to be turned up at the wrist, were yet another mark of her difference, something else for her classmates to snigger at and talk about behind their hands.

It doesn't matter now. A smile plays on Alice's lips as she pulls the silk towards her to complete another rose. Now she can wear what she likes and no one will laugh at her. Now she's the one in charge, even if they don't know it yet.

Perhaps when everything is settled she'll stay in Willowcombe after all. Maybe she'll persuade the owners of her cottage to sell it to her; renting is dead money, and it won't do to carry on like this. And when Lucy has gone, she might be able to get next door too, knock it through and make more space. She'll have the cash when the Pimlico flat is sold. Maybe she'll ask Maggie to help.

Her lips tighten: one thing at a time. She mustn't get carried away.

The last rose is complete. She draws out the needle and holds the embroidery frame at arm's length. Such a pretty scene. It would have looked so lovely on the wall of the nursery. The colours blur as her eyes fill with tears.

At first she'd wondered whether she should do something designed for children – fairies on toadstools or something; but she'd known her baby would love the little cottage with roses around the door. She would have pointed to it with a chubby finger and smiled up at Alice as she held her, knowing that her mummy had made it just for her.

A sob forces its way from Alice's chest. She turns over the embroidery frame, takes up the needle, and begins to unpick the roses.

Chapter 11

Sometimes I wonder whether I missed my chance, that night at Maggie's; whether if I'd been honest then, if I'd stood there and told my friends that I'd left my job because I'd had an affair with my married boss, Alice would have been satisfied.

She told us, you see, that she'd done the same thing. I'd got her the tissues and was standing there in Maggie's living room, waiting for it all to come out, and instead Alice said she'd had an affair with someone at work. Her story differed in the details, but the essentials were all there: a relationship with a man she knew was married, hoping he was going to leave his wife, eventually realising it wasn't going to happen. The same tale everyone's heard a hundred times – but Alice was saying she'd lived it, just like I had.

She'd stopped crying by then, but every so often she'd pause and sniffle into a tissue. Maggie was being sympathetic, but I saw the glance she flashed at Rebecca and knew she'd have something to say about it when they were alone. I barely opened my mouth. I didn't want to draw attention to myself, worried that if the others looked at me they'd be able to read the guilt all over my face. Once or twice Alice caught my eye, but if she was expecting something from me then I didn't see it. Perhaps if I'd handled things differently, if I'd taken her hand and told her she wasn't alone, that I knew I'd been selfish but I was learning from it – perhaps everything would have been different.

I suppose I'll never know.

It was the day after the book club and I was sitting at the kitchen table, my laptop open in front of me. In the previous hour, I'd typed three lines of my business plan, read them back and deleted them. I looked up from the screen and rubbed my eyes. From his position on the dresser, Ben from Manchester, August's Hunk of the Month, gazed at me with an expression that was probably supposed to be smouldering but instead looked faintly myopic. The calendar had been a Christmas present from my brother Nat, too horrible to display except that it made me smile.

August.

There was no escaping it: time was ticking. My redundancy money was dwindling, and I couldn't procrastinate for ever. I needed advice. It was time to try Tom again.

The front door of The Gables was closed as usual and I made my way around to the back, knowing by now that this was the way things were done in Willowcombe. As I rounded the corner, I felt in my pocket for the dog treat I always carried for Ferdy, waiting for the scuffle of paws on gravel. This time, though, there was no sign of him, and from somewhere inside I heard mournful barking.

Tom appeared at the kitchen door, a look of anxiety disappearing as he saw me. 'Oh, Lucy. Thank God it's only you.'

I decided not to take offence. 'Thank you – I think.'

But he was already turning back into the kitchen, beckoning

me to follow then shutting the door behind me. Something was up: Tom's kitchen door usually stayed open whatever the weather to let Ferdy wander in and out of the garden.

I took my usual seat at the kitchen table, clear except for Tom's copy of *Jane Eyre*. I held it up. 'Last night was more dramatic than expected.'

'Wasn't it just.' He opened the door to the hallway and Ferdy came bounding in with a woof. 'And not the only bit of drama we've had with our new incomer, either.'

I looked up with interest. 'Oh?'

Tom nodded to Ferdy, who'd pushed his wet nose into my palm for his treat, his tail wagging with a force that shook the rear half of his body from side to side. 'He tried to bite her this morning. Hence he's confined to quarters.'

I couldn't keep the disbelief from my voice. 'What, *Ferdy*?'

Tom grimaced. 'I don't know what came over him. He turned into a devil dog.' I laughed, then stopped as I saw his expression. 'It's not funny, Lucy. If he can change like that . . .'

I nodded. 'Sorry.' Tom was watching Ferdy, his expression a mixture of worry and puzzlement. A suspicious thought entered my mind. 'Did you actually see him do it?'

'What do you mean?'

'Did you see Ferdy go for her? For Alice?'

He sighed again. 'Yes. Thank God I did. If I hadn't been there to drag him away, heaven only knows what would have happened.'

The idea of Tom having to drag away the little dog sitting at my feet was ridiculous. 'She must have done something to him.'

'Really, Lucy, I love that you want to stick up for Ferdy – but what could she have done? She was just standing next to the front door. He had her *at bay*, for Christ's sake.' Tom shook his head in disbelief. 'And he must have jumped up at her before I got there, because she had a big red scratch all down her wrist.'

I started to say, 'Shc could have done that herself,' but then stopped. I was becoming absurd. Instead I said, 'So what happens now?'

'I honestly don't know. Alice said she wasn't going to report it.'

I hadn't considered the possibility that she would. The seriousness of what had happened began to dawn on me and I reached a protective hand down to Ferdy, who left off chewing for a moment and licked my fingers.

'Tom, you can't honestly think Ferdy's dangerous.'

'I don't know what to think. I've never seen him like that before.'

'Exactly. So it was a one-off.' I raised my voice as across the room the kettle burbled to a crescendo. 'Anyway, you can't keep him cooped up inside all the time just in case she calls around.'

It had come out with unexpected feeling, and he gave me a sharp look. 'You really don't like her, do you?'

I struggled for a reply that wouldn't make me sound petty. What did I have to accuse Alice of, after all? Taking me home when I was sick and washing my clothes. Yes, what a cow. 'It's not that I don't like her, exactly—'

He cut me off. 'It was good of her not to report Ferdy. Lots of people wouldn't have been so generous.' He put a mug on the table in front of me with a thud that sent a small tidal wave of tea slopping over the rim. 'And I would have thought that you'd have been a bit more welcoming, knowing what it's like to be new in the village.'

I stared at him, taken aback. I hadn't been unwelcoming to Alice. Had I? Had she said something to make him think I'd been unkind?

'Anyway,' Tom was taking the seat opposite me, 'I was pleased to see you looking better after our night at the Cow.'

There was something in the way he said it that made me defensive. 'I wasn't drunk, you know.'

I knew exactly how it sounded. Tom raised his eyebrows.

'I wasn't!' I took a gulp of my tea while he continued to study me, as serious as a headmaster. It was so unlike him that I found myself wanting to laugh again.

'Oh come on, Tom, it's not like you haven't seen me drunk before. Why wouldn't I just admit it if I'd been pissed?'

He didn't reply and the silence grew heavy. Then out of nowhere it came to me: ridiculous as it was, Tom thought I had a drinking problem. I could see in his face that I'd guessed right. Where the hell had that idea come from? Just a couple of weeks ago, he'd been happy to share his aunt's homemade gin in this very kitchen.

I felt my cheeks burn, and to my horror, moisture prickled at the corners of my eyes. I tried to get to my feet, but the bench was heavy and didn't move, hitting me in the backs of my calves and knocking me forward into the table. The thud sent Tom's coffee splashing in slow motion onto the wood. I mumbled an apology and headed for the door, muttering something about having forgotten to put the bins out.

Ferdy followed me, tail wagging. Tom was saying something, calling me back; I think he might have been apologising. But I didn't want him to see me crying, to have to add embarrassment to the playground insecurity of feeling that he was no longer my friend, that he and Alice had been talking about me behind my back.

I stepped outside, remembering to pull the door closed gently so that Ferdy, pushing his face into the doorway in his eagerness to run outside, wouldn't be hurt.

The path blurred in front of me as I set off home.

I know how it sounds: bursting into tears in someone else's kitchen over – what? A friend suggesting I could have made more of an effort with a new neighbour? That perhaps I'd had too much to drink on a night out? A night out, let's not forget, that had ended with my having to be virtually carried home by that self-same neighbour? You might think that this is hardly the stuff of high tragedy, that getting so upset over such things signifies a less than stable emotional state.

I wouldn't argue. When I sat in Tom's kitchen and felt the tears coming, I was appalled. It's not that I never cry – Liz had had more than her share of evenings with my snivelling through her stock of Kleenex – but this was different. It was a measure of how weak I'd become, how much my life in Willowcombe depended on the few friends I'd made. I couldn't bear for Tom to see that. I couldn't bear his pity.

Back at home, I poured a defiant glass of wine and sank into a chair at the kitchen table. The laptop sat there accusingly and I smacked the lid shut and pushed it away. Was Tom right? Was I being unfair to Alice? Was I so wrapped up in myself that I hadn't stopped to think how she might feel? I'd been like that when I was with Richard, after all. Too consumed by what I thought was love to care about the damage it would do, to worry about lying to my friends.

I squeezed my eyes shut. I wasn't going to cry again. When I opened them, my vision was blurred, but the tears didn't fall. Across the room, my image smiled back at me, the photo with my parents and Nat taken by some kindly passer-by on our last family holiday.

Of course. That photo.

Alice must have spotted it when she'd first come over. That was why she'd made that comment about 'parents like yours' at the pub. True, Mum and Dad didn't look much like their performing selves in the photo – that was partly why I'd chosen it in the first place – but they were surely recognisable to a careful observer. I remembered Alice's eyes darting around the kitchen, taking everything in – yes, she was a careful observer. Odd that she hadn't said anything at the time . . .

I should have felt better, but something was bothering me. I stared at the photo, trying to work out what it was. A memory tugged at the corner of my mind. I'd been sitting here this morning, trying to work. I pulled the laptop back into place and flipped up the lid. I looked up again. The four Shaws looked back.

I pushed the power button and waited for the screen to come to life. Across the room, my mother smiled at me, one hand trying to hold back her hair in the gusty winds of the British seaside. Then it hit me.

I shouldn't be seeing her.

I'd been sitting in the same seat that morning. When I looked up, I should have been staring straight at Mancunian Ben. Someone had moved the calendar and the photo frame. Someone had been in my home while I was out.

Something turned over in my stomach.

On the screen, the cursor blinked in the password box. Had they tried my laptop too? Had they rifled through my things, searching for a notebook with letters and numbers scribbled in the back?

I tried to tell myself I was being ridiculous. How would anyone have got in? I'd locked the door when I left the cottage. It had been locked again when I'd got back. I must be mistaken about the position of the calendar. It wasn't far away from the photo, after all. I'd thought I'd looked straight up from the laptop that morning, but I hadn't. It was as simple as that.

My eyes swept the room, looking for anything else out of place. Next to the calendar, a pile of unopened mail lay undisturbed. There was my jumper, draped just where I'd left it over the back of a chair. All the cupboards and drawers were firmly closed.

This was stupid. I had to stop worrying about phantom intruders and concentrate on what was real. I'd make some tea and then get back to what I should be doing: working on my business plan.

I filled the kettle and reached for the switch – and that was when I saw it. I froze, the hairs rising on the back of my neck.

Now I was sure of it: someone had been there. And they were sending me a message.

Chapter 12

'Well, I felt as awkward as arse.'

Rebecca looks down her Lycra-clad body and concentrates on the imaginary bowl of water resting on her stomach. This is the problem with coming to Pilates with Maggie – she always insists on talking through the sessions. It plays havoc with Rebecca's visualisation. *Out breath, two, three, four.* She says, 'I just thought it was odd. We hardly even know her.'

'I know – and don't you think that's sad?'

Rebecca curls her spine back slowly onto the floor. Vertebra by vertebra, the instructor had said, her Italian accent rolling around the syllables. She isn't sure her back is built for that kind of accuracy. She glances at Maggie out of the corner of her eye and immediately feels better: she isn't doing it properly at all.

'What, that we don't know her? She's only just moved in.'

'No!' Maggie's hiss carries across the tinkly music and the instructor shoots a disapproving look in their direction. 'I mean it's sad that she hasn't got anyone else to confide in.'

'We don't know that . . .'

'Why else would she break down in front of a roomful of near-strangers?'

Rebecca curls upwards again, concentrating on keeping her chin off her chest while she exhales. Honestly, how is she supposed to do this and carry on a conversation at the same time? The instructor is glaring at them now, obviously thinking the same thing.

'Besides, I'd never have had her down as the type.'

Rebecca feels something inside her go very still. 'What do you mean, the "type"?'

'Oh come on, Becs! She had an affair with a married man.'

Inhale, hold, lower back to the floor.

'I mean, I know she hasn't been here long, but I thought she was too proper for that kind of thing. Too classy.'

A flush rises in Rebecca's cheeks. Perhaps if she just stays quiet, Maggie will change the subject.

'I feel sorry for her, of course, but – oh for heaven's sake, I can't do this. My abs are killing me.'

And maybe that's why he doesn't want you any more.

The words flash into Rebecca's mind and she feels her flush deepen. What's wrong with her? This is Maggie, her best friend. How can she be thinking like this?

'And her boss, as well. I mean, how did she expect it was going to end?' Maggie shuffles into a seated position and wipes the back of her hand across her forehead. 'I thought this wasn't supposed to make you sweat?'

There's a pause. Maybe Maggie will move on now, talk about something else.

'I'll never understand these women who let them get away with it. I mean, she can't have expected him to leave his wife.'

'Maybe she didn't want him to.'

'Well that's all right then – as long as she's just colluding with the betrayal.'

Rebecca rests her head against the floor and tries to block out Maggie's voice. Somewhere behind her right temple a dull pain is starting to build.

'I don't know, though. I don't altogether buy it.'

The instructor checks her watch. It's large, made of rose-coloured gold, chunky against her slender wrist. A present from a lover, perhaps. A woman like her will have a lover, not a boyfriend or a partner, certainly not a husband. Rebecca watches her as she crosses the room and lowers the lights. The music changes to something involving pan pipes. Thank God, it's almost over.

'I couldn't help wondering . . .' Maggie's voice is thoughtful. 'I thought maybe there was something she wasn't telling us.'

'Like what?'

'I'm not sure. Like maybe he hit her or something. There's just something about her. She seems – I don't know, damaged somehow.'

Rebecca closes her eyes and lets the pan pipes wash over her. This is usually her favourite part of the class, the quietest time of the week, away from Ellie and Oscar and Sam. Even away from David. She feels a sudden stab of self-pity: they all place so many demands on her. And now her head is really starting to ache.

Next to her, Maggie lets out a long sigh. 'She must have self-esteem issues, anyway. You'd have to, wouldn't you?'

Rebecca holds her breath and waits for it to come.

'To keep hanging around like that at someone else's beck and call, knowing the sheets are barely cool before he's back with his wife. It must be pretty bloody awful.'

Her fingernails are digging into the palms of her hands. *Yes*, she thinks, *but there are some things that are worse.*

* * *

Tom picks up the red square of cardboard from the doormat and tuts. He'd only popped out for ten minutes to get the paper – it's as if the postman waited for his moment just for the satisfaction of filling in one of these stupid cards. He turns it over and inspects the details: too big for the letter box. He knows what it is.

In the studio he pulls open the drawer of his desk and lifts out his organiser, flipping through the pages until he finds what he's looking for. There it is, printed in the space for 6 August, tucked away in the bottom right-hand corner: *SC – 9 p.m.* As he'd thought, two days away, which is of course why he'd paid for next-day delivery. He stares again at the card, with its stern instruction to wait twenty-four hours before attempting collection. Aloud he says, 'Fuck that.'

Cynthia is at her station behind the counter when he arrives, decked out in a floral ensemble and pretending to be busy writing on a clipboard.

'Good morning, Mrs Sullivan, and may I say that is a particularly fetching outfit?'

She looks up with an expression of surprise that Tom knows is feigned. She uses that counter like a Martello tower, and he'd bet Aunt Lydia's Daimler she spotted him walking down the street at least three minutes ago. She probably knows what he's here for too.

'Good *afternoon*, Thomas. I think you'll find the little hand is well past the number twelve.'

'Good grief, so it is. I've been painting, you see. Quite lost track of time.'

Cynthia peers sceptically at him over her glasses. God, it's like talking to his mother. He almost expects her to ask if he's tidied his room.

'Is there something I can help you with?'

Tom tries out his most winning smile. 'I certainly hope so, Mrs

Sullivan. I'm afraid I was out when the postman called.' He holds up the red card, trying to inject the right mixture of humility and expectation into his voice. 'I was hoping it might be possible to pick up my parcel.'

Her face hardens almost imperceptibly. She's going to make him work for it.

'And may I ask whether you have read what it says on the card?'

Should he go for innocence or candour? 'Ah yes, I know it says I should wait twenty-four hours. The thing is, I was hoping the postman might have dropped it off already and I thought I could save you the trouble . . .'

Cynthia's hand moves to her glasses. It's a bad sign. The removal of the glasses signifies, always, an escalation in hostilities. He has to stop her, salvage the situation somehow. But what's this? The hand has paused, is dropping. Cynthia's lips curl upwards in what it takes him a moment to realise is a smile. Perhaps his charm has worked after all . . .

'Ah, Miss Darley! All done?'

Tom turns to see Alice standing behind him, a package wrapped in brown paper in her hands.

'Yes, Mrs Sullivan. Everything is so neatly organised back there, it only took a moment.' She smiles sweetly and holds out the parcel. 'Hi, Tom. I think this is yours?'

Tom has the momentary discombobulation of seeing someone he knows out of context, but then remembers his manners. 'Alice! This is unexpected. Thank you, you're a star.' He turns and beams triumphantly at Cynthia, who shoots daggers at him in return. 'So are you working here now?'

'Yes, just three days a week. Mrs Sullivan has been kind enough to let me help out until I find something more permanent.' Alice bestows another smile on her benefactress. 'I do so dislike being idle.'

'Quite so, Miss Darley. If only more young people followed your example.'

Tom lifts the parcel in salute. 'Well said, Mrs Sullivan. And now I must be off – I have a lot to do this afternoon.' Cynthia snorts.

'That looks interesting.' Alice points to the parcel. 'Have you been shopping?'

'Just some paints. I was running low on a few colours.'

'Oh really?' Alice's tone is innocent, but there's something about the way she's looking at him that he doesn't like. 'Do you have any favourites?'

'Well, not favourites as such, but there are some I use more often. Phthalo blue, for example – I use it to mix a lot of the greens.'

'I see, you must do. For the grasses and leaves, of course.' She is wide-eyed, as if this is the most fascinating thing she's heard all day. Perhaps it is.

'Yes, everyone thinks of the flowers, but for a botanical artist the stems and leaves are just as important.'

'Oh yes, I can see that. Some artists only use certain colours, don't they? It was Lowry, wasn't it, who used only five?'

He's surprised at her knowledge. 'Yes, it was. At least that's what the art historians thought until recently.'

'Oh? It's not true then?'

'Apparently not. He said it all the time, but now that there are so many fakes on the market, they've analysed more of the paintings they know are really his and it turns out he used more than five.'

'So it was a lie.'

'Well, a marketing device, perhaps.'

'No.' her tone is firm. 'A lie.'

'Didn't you say you had a lot to do, Thomas?' Cynthia's voice cuts through the thickened atmosphere.

'I did indeed. No rest for the wicked.' She snorts again and Tom can't help himself. 'Problem with your sinuses, Mrs Sullivan? I'd take an antihistamine if I were you. I hear the pollen count today is rather high.'

'You know,' Alice is looking up at him earnestly, 'I used to paint myself. Maybe I'll take it up again. Perhaps you can tell me where you buy your supplies?' She points to the box. 'The packaging is so – discreet.'

For a moment he holds her gaze. 'Edward Stimpson. They have a website.'

He feels her eyes on his back as he steps out onto the street.

Chapter 13

I can't remember how long I stood there in the kitchen, the kettle coming to a boil then clicking off again as I stared at the wall, thoughts racing through my head.

At first I was certain it was proof that someone had got into my house while I was at Tom's. I knew I'd have noticed if the corner of the fire blanket had been poking out of its cover before; and yet there it was, the little triangle of fabric dark against the tiles. Perhaps it sounds strange to be so sure about a detail like that, but the reason I have a fire blanket in the first place is the same reason I pay attention to it: it's important to me. And the packet was sealed all along the bottom with Velcro, just a black tab in the middle where you'd pull to release it. The fit was snug, everything designed to stay in place until needed. It wouldn't have come loose on its own, I was certain of that.

And then, as my breathing began to slow, I told myself not to be so stupid. No one else had been there. No one was sending me messages. I'd been mistaken about the position of the photograph, and as for the fire blanket – it hung on the wall near the back door. Maybe Alice had brushed past it when she'd hung out the washing the night she'd brought me home. Maybe I'd even done it myself. Either way, I just hadn't noticed it before. Surely I was past being paranoid about that kind of thing by now.

I was letting myself get carried away. It was a symptom of spending too much time alone. I tried to imagine myself thinking like this if Liz were here, interrupting her narrative of the latest gossip from Waites to tell her I thought someone had been creeping around my house because a photo frame had been moved.

Perhaps not.

I felt a sudden pang of longing for our flat in London, its cramped kitchen and the messy living room with the pile of free newspapers Liz always brought home and never put out for recycling. And Liz.

I should call her, I thought. It would be good to hear her voice again, catch up on how everyone was.

How Richard is, you mean.

But I ignored that little voice, tucked the blanket back into its holder, and reached for the phone.

'You know who I am. Leave a message and I'll get back to you if I remember.'

It was good to hear her voice, even the recorded version. I hadn't expected Liz to pick up – Willowcombe's unreliable mobile reception meant that these days I more often used the landline at the cottage, a number she wouldn't recognise – but I hoped she'd call me back when she got my message. Ten minutes later, the phone warbled on its stand and I grabbed it, already smiling.

'Lucy! Hello, stranger.'

I deserved the rebuke; I knew I should have made more of an effort to keep in touch since I'd moved to Willowcombe. Liz might have made no secret of her disapproval of my affair with Richard, but she'd never breathed a word about it to anyone at Waites; and when Richard's calls had become less and less frequent, his ability to get away from home for the night apparently ever diminishing, it was Liz who'd been my only confidante. Her advice had been of the cruel-to-be-kind variety, it was true; she didn't pander to my pathetic attempts to justify either Richard's behaviour or my own, and whenever I said anything particularly risible – variations on the theme of his wanting to leave Melanie but having to wait until the time was right – she'd give one of her snorts and shame me into silence. But she listened to me, tried to help me see what should have been blindingly obvious; and when at last, after a week of avoiding me at work, and when the mobile he'd bought for our calls went invariably straight to voicemail, Richard took me to a hotel bar and gave me the inevitable brush-off ('It's not fair to *you*, Lucy, to carry on this way'), it was Liz who'd brought home a bottle of vodka, a box of tissues and a startlingly brutal, if accurate, deconstruction of Richard's manners, morals and taste in clothes.

Now, brushing off my apologies in a way that made me think it was as well I'd made them, she asked me how I was settling into Willowcombe. I waxed lyrical about the charm of the cottage and the beauty of the countryside and the pub within walking distance (I didn't mention I'd probably never be able to hold my head up there again). I was so desperate not to admit that moving there might have been a mistake that I overcompensated wildly, extolling the virtues of the village until I realised with dismay that I'd painted a picture of such rural bliss that it would have been ridiculous to suggest I might drag myself away from it all for a soggy weekend in London. As I racked my brains for a way to backtrack, Liz came unexpectedly to my rescue.

'I was thinking of getting away myself, actually. Ivan's been doing my head in.'

Ivan was the latest of her boyfriends, a temperamental pothead actor whose work seemed to consist solely of 'immersive' pieces set in dilapidated warehouses in east London. He'd moved into the flat shortly after I'd left, and I gathered from her emails that Liz's motives had more to do with sharing the rent than hopes of domestic bliss. I couldn't see it lasting, but then who was I to judge?

I leapt at the opening. 'You'd be more than welcome to come and stay. It's only small, but the spare room is a decent size.'

'Cheers, hon. Would be good to get the smell of weed out of my clothes for the weekend. I swear Leery is about to stage an intervention.'

I laughed, and realised it had been days since I'd done that. I decided I had to ask. 'Liz . . .'

'No, Lucy.'

'No what? I haven't said anything.'

She exhaled. Only Liz could convey such a sense of exasperation with a single breath. 'I know what you're going to ask. You've got that voice.'

I felt my cheeks reddening. Thank God she was at the end of a phone line. 'I don't know what you're talking about.'

'Yes you do, don't take the piss. You were going to ask about Dirty Dick.'

It was her name for Richard. My fingers tightened around the receiver. I tried to speak, but realised with horror that if I did, I might start to cry.

'Look, Lucy, I'm telling you this for your own good: just forget about the guy. He's bad news.'

I nodded pointlessly. The silence stretched between us. Then Liz spoke again.

'Right, I wasn't going to tell you this, but maybe it's for the best. Just don't get upset, OK?'

Alarm brought my voice back. 'What is it? What's happened?' *Oh God, don't let him be seeing someone else.* The possibilities ran through my mind: there was that blonde woman in accounts, Helen someone; she'd always been flirting with him. Or maybe it was one of those French women from that magazine he'd been so keen to work with, someone chic with a name like Isabella or Élodie.

'He's been in an accident.'

I went cold.

'Lucy?'

'Is he OK?' My voice sounded small and far away.

'Yeah, yeah, he's fine.' Another pause. 'Well no, actually. He's in hospital. He's in a coma.'

My legs felt like they wouldn't hold me. I slid to the floor.

'Lucy, are you still there?'

My head was full of it: coma. *Coma.* I tried to form other words, but there was no room for them.

'He's OK, honestly.' She paused. 'It's not as bad as it sounds.'

The sentence pressed a switch in my brain. 'What the fuck do you mean, it's not as bad as it sounds?' I heard my voice scaling the octaves. 'You've just told me he's in a coma!'

And then the tears came. In a way, it was just like old times.

Liz talked to me through my sobs. It had been a car accident. One of Richard's tyres had burst and the car had come off the road. It was late at night and a quiet spot – no one seemed sure what he'd been doing there in the first place – and it had been several hours before a passenger in a passing vehicle had noticed the skid marks and the mangled foliage at the side of the road and had raised the alarm. Richard had broken several ribs and had a bad head injury. He'd been slipping in and out of consciousness when they found him, and the coma had been medically induced. The doctors said it was to give his brain time to repair itself.

'You can't see him, Lucy, you know that, right?' Liz's voice was unusually gentle. 'Melanie's there with him, and his parents.'

She didn't have to say it: I didn't belong there.

'Is he going to be all right?'

'They say he's got a good chance. He might not be . . . Well, it was a bad accident. He's lucky to be alive.'

I tried to ask questions, but there was a buzzing in my ears and I couldn't make sense of her answers. At some point I heard her telling me she had to go, and I must have said goodbye too, because then I was standing there, the phone silent against my ear.

The pictures ran through my head, but they weren't the twisted metal of his car, or Richard lying on a hospital bed covered in tubes. Instead, it was a memory: that day at Waites, our last time together, his smile as he turned and winked at me over his shoulder. I heard his laughter, his voice raised for his audience as he pointed back at the open doorway of the lift.

I barely got out of there alive.

I couldn't stop thinking about it. I'd be trying to wash up, surf the internet, write a shopping list – and then I'd find myself standing there, wondering how the accident had happened, whether Richard had woken from the coma and what it meant if he hadn't, whether I was right to stay away.

I tried to drown out the tiny, selfish voice that told me I'd had a narrow escape. I would have taken Melanie's place in a heartbeat for the desperate vigil by Richard's bedside, but what about afterwards, if and when he regained consciousness? When everyone else had gone and the long, lonely task of rehabilitation had begun . . . I wasn't sure I had it in me to deal with that. Perhaps it was a sign I hadn't cared for him at all, at least, not the way he needed now. I could only hope that Melanie did.

Desperate for a distraction, I reached for the novel we'd chosen for the second meeting of the book club: *Tess of the d'Urbervilles*. But of course, that's wrong, isn't it? We didn't choose that book; Alice did – though it didn't seem that way at the time.

We'd been at Maggie's, everyone trying to make polite conversation after Alice's story about the affair, pretending that someone bursting into tears and telling us their intimate regrets was an everyday occurrence, no more noteworthy than a sudden shower of rain on a hot afternoon, already forgotten. Someone raised the question of what we should read for the next meeting, and after a few options were tried out and discarded, we agreed on *Tess*.

So every time I found myself staring into space, I'd pick up the book and read for a while, trying to lose myself in the story. By the day before we were due to meet at Rebecca's, I'd almost reached the end. I hadn't enjoyed it much, and with only three chapters to go, I told myself I deserved a break. I picked up the small drawstring bag I'd packed earlier, slipped on my shoes and headed out, closing the door of the cottage softly behind me.

At the Old Forge I could see at once that Maggie was home, the windows on the ground floor flung wide open. I went around to the back and tapped at the door.

'Come on in!'

Maggie, I noticed, hadn't bothered to ask who it was. I wondered whether I'd ever feel that relaxed about visitors, but I knew the answer: not while Alice was next door.

I stuck my head around the door frame. 'Hi, Maggie. Have you got a minute?'

'Lucy! Yes, of course. Don't sit down – I was just going to take this out into the garden.' She dropped a handful of strawberries into the large jug of Pimm's on the table. 'Grab a glass and join me.'

I followed her out to the shade of an oak at the edge of the lawn. A table and chairs sat beneath it, and I thought: *This is the life. Making your own hours, sloping off on a Wednesday afternoon just because it's sunny and you can.* It was what I wanted for myself.

I told Maggie my idea, hesitantly at first, then with growing enthusiasm when she didn't laugh or tell me I was mad. I showed her the contents of the drawstring bag, removing the bracelets and pendants and earrings one by one, afraid to look at her as I laid them on the table. They were the pieces I was most proud of, those at least that I'd kept myself. Maggie inspected them carefully, holding them to the light. I took notes as she told me about market positioning and cash flow and tax. The more she talked, the more the idea became real. I told myself I had to try.

After a while, when the Pimm's had gone and we'd nibbled away the last of the fruit, Maggie said: 'You could have told me about your parents, you know.'

I stared at her, thrown. She smiled. 'Don't look so shocked. It's not a state secret, is it?'

'No, no. Of course not. It's just that . . .' I trailed off. 'How did you know?'

'Alice said something that night at the pub. I didn't catch it properly at the time, but when you were talking just now, I realised you reminded me of someone. And then your name . . . You don't mind me saying, I hope? I do think your dad's wonderful. And your mum too, of course.'

I assumed my practised expression of filial pride. 'Thanks.'

She picked up one of the bracelets and fastened it around her wrist. 'This one's my favourite, I think. It's the colours: just slightly more muted than the rest.' She held her hand out in front of her and turned it from side to side. 'You have to look at it more closely before you see how special it is.'

Something tightened in my throat, and it was a moment before I found my voice. 'Thanks, Maggie,' I said.

It was late when I woke the next morning, the day already sticky with heat. My optimism of the previous afternoon had vanished in the night, and it took every scrap of willpower I had to sit down at my laptop. I opened the search engine, moved the cursor to the search box and typed in 'starting a business'.

Two hours later, I had pages of notes, a list of books to buy and the beginnings of what promised to be a raging headache. In despair, I reviewed what I'd written. None of it made any sense. If I couldn't even get to first base on my own, what chance did I have of making a go of this? Perhaps I'd be better off sticking with marketing. Waites would give me a decent reference, Richard would make sure of that.

Richard.

The guilt hit me like a wave. How could I be sitting there thinking about my career when he was lying in a hospital bed, stuck somewhere between life and death? It came to me now that I didn't even know which hospital he was in. I had to find out: if I couldn't visit, I could at least call. Perhaps the nurses could tell me how he was.

I picked up the phone and dialled Liz's number, but it went straight to voicemail and I left her a message. Knowing Liz, she'd make me wait for her reply, imagining I'd calm down and she'd be able to persuade me out of it.

I was ashamed to think she might be right.

Chapter 14

Rebecca reaches for a cushion and punches it firmly in its centre before replacing it at just the right angle on the sofa. Later, she'll lay out the food buffet-style on the dining table so people can get up and help themselves; the book club will be meeting at seven for seven thirty, and they'll need something more substantial than Maggie's shop-bought finger food.

She surveys the living room with satisfaction. Everything is as it should be, clean and elegant – and with Sam and the kids at his parents until tomorrow, that's the way it will stay.

The book club is a good idea; funny how it took an incomer to suggest it. She only hopes the members have done the reading this time. After all, if she has managed it, a mother of two children and with a business to run to boot, there's precious little excuse for any of the others. Organisation, that's the key: measuring out the time for ballet and football, shopping and cooking, birthday parties and spelling tests. It's how she has to run her life.

Her mind wanders to Maggie, the way it does so often these days. Maggie, who won't have read the book and won't care either. Who'll just turn up and make everyone laugh and then go home again, back to her white-walled palace with its granite worktops and designer sofas. Back to David.

She thinks back to the text she received from him earlier today: *I want to feel ur hot cunt around my cock.* He likes to shock her with his language, and from anyone else she'd find it repellent; but somehow from David – intelligent, cultured David, with his knowledge of wine and current affairs – it's different, thrilling. She'd gone to the bathroom when she'd felt her phone vibrate in her pocket and read the text twice with her back against the door, feeling herself grow wet. She'd replied quickly, as he liked her to – *Imagining you there now* – then deleted both messages. Ellie and Oscar laughed up at her from the screen and she shoved the phone back into her pocket, not sure whether the churning in her stomach was excitement or shame.

He's promised to take her away for the weekend soon. She's going to tell Sam she's attending a seminar on brand management, and David has already made his excuses to Maggie, telling her he'll be staying in London for meetings. They've decided on the Lakes; this time, she fervently hopes, staying somewhere nice. David is ever so slightly overcautious when it comes to the use of his credit card. Rebecca had dropped a subtle hint to that effect the last time he'd taken her to a roadside hotel, where he'd paid in cash and remarked on the excellent value of the bed and breakfast package. She sincerely hopes he's picked up on it.

The oven timer pings and she heads for the kitchen to check the parsnip crisps.

* * *

'Aren't you even the slightest bit curious, darling?'

David doesn't raise his head from the *Telegraph*. 'Not even slightly.'

'But she really is an enigma. Such a quiet little thing but a veritable home-wrecker, by her own admission. You'd never imagine it to look at her.'

'Hmm.'

'She was absolutely distraught, you know. Cried buckets all over the sofa.'

He looks up. 'I hope she didn't get mascara on the leather.'

'God, David, are you for real? No, she didn't. I checked.'

He knows she won't have done. With a sigh, he unfolds himself from his seat at the table.

'Anyway, she knew who you were.'

'Really?' He crosses the room to inspect the sofa. 'Well, I am the local doctor.'

Maggie smiles to herself. He really is pompous sometimes. 'No, I don't think that was it. She said she'd seen you out and about. How did she put it? On a nature walk, apparently.'

He leans over and peers at the leather. 'Where was she sitting?'

'Just there. Yes, she said she'd seen you checking out the local wildlife.'

'Well, there's nothing here, thank God.'

'Yes, I told you I'd checked. So you didn't speak to her, then?'

'Maggie, I have no idea what the woman is talking about.' He straightens and put his hands on his hips. 'I haven't been on a nature walk in twenty years.'

She applies a last coat of lipstick, perfect as always without the aid of a mirror, and heads for the door. 'Right you are, then. Don't wait up.'

'Aren't you forgetting something?' He points to the coffee table.

'Oh Christ, yes – she'd have my guts for garters.' Maggie brushes past him and picks up the copy of *Tess of the d'Urbervilles*.

* * *

Tom already knows who it is when the knock comes at the door. He'd grabbed Ferdy by the collar and wrestled him into the hallway when the barking and snarling started, just managing to pull the kitchen door closed without catching the little dog's snout. He can hear him now, jumping up madly and throwing himself against the wood. He'll have to get her out of here quickly or Ferdy will end up hurting himself.

'I've caused a commotion again, haven't I?' Alice holds out her hand. A dog treat sits in the middle of her palm. 'I thought I'd bring a peace offering.'

'Thanks, Alice, there was no need to do that. Ferdy's the one who ought to be making peace.' He takes it from her and places it on the kitchen counter. 'So, are you all set to dissect *Tess*?' She looks confused. 'The book club. I was just about to head over to Rebecca's.'

'Oh yes, of course. I wondered what you meant for a moment!' She ducks her head, suddenly shy. 'I came to check you were coming, actually. I was a bit embarrassed – you know, after last time . . .'

'Well, no need to be.' Tom keeps his tone brisk. On the other side of the door, Ferdy's barking is becoming hysterical. He'll have to take him to one of those pet psychologists if he keeps this up. 'I think we'd better be off.'

'Yes, absolutely – don't want to be late!' Then, pointing to the treat on the kitchen counter, 'Aren't you going to put that in his bowl? Not very hygienic leaving it there.'

Their eyes meet for a moment. There's something not quite right about Alice, Tom thinks; maybe Ferdy doesn't need a psychologist after all. 'No,' he says aloud. 'I'll give it to him when he's behaving.'

He locks the door and pockets the key. If anyone asked, he wouldn't be able to explain it, but there's suddenly one thing he's sure of: the only place he's putting that dog treat is the bin.

*

Lucy is already at Rebecca's when they arrive, and Tom sees her raised eyebrows as he enters the conservatory with Alice. He tries to send her a look that says, 'Don't ask me, she came over to mine'; but she's already looking away, talking to Rebecca. Perhaps he should find an opportunity for a quiet word, let her know he's changed his mind about Alice, that he understands now, in a way he can't put into words, why Lucy finds her – what had she said? – cold. It's the right word, or almost. He'd have gone for 'unsettling'. But it's going to be difficult to share confidences tonight – Rebecca has them on a schedule. She's already told them, passing out some kind of cocktail with a physalis on a stick, that they'll be allowed half an hour for conversation before food is served, 'and the literary discussion will commence after the starter'. Better to make amends with Lucy over lunch; they haven't done that for a while.

He takes the seat next to hers. Lucy's glass, he notices, is already empty. Perhaps she arrived early.

Alice is chatting to Rebecca, admiring her 'beautiful home'. Her first visit, then, though surely it's weeks since she moved into number 1. Odd that it's taken Rebecca so long to issue the invitation. She's making up for it now, though, enumerating her trials over the building of the conservatory. Then, 'We had to do no end of work when we moved in. Shall I give you the grand tour?' They disappear off in the direction of the kitchen-diner.

'Thank God she's got rid of the kids for the evening.'

The relief in Lucy's voice makes him laugh. 'So they're out, are they?'

'Sam's taken them to the grandparents. Ellie's all right, I suppose, but Oscar – he's just such a little . . .'

'Shit? Yes, isn't he? Last time I saw him, I was out with Ferdy, and Oscar kept trying to pull his tail when he thought I wasn't looking.'

'God, really? There's a future serial killer right there.'

She's looking tired, he thinks. The dark circles under her eyes stand out like bruises against her redhead's skin. Yes, he'll take her to lunch, ask her straight out about the drinking.

A loud knock at the front door interrupts his thoughts, and Lucy scrambles to her feet. He starts to say, 'Don't . . .' but she's already on her way, calling, 'Don't worry, Rebecca, I'll get it.'

Maggie, of course: he can hear her greeting Lucy with exaggerated air kisses, then footsteps on the stairs. Rebecca's on her way, but it's too late: Maggie's already entered the living room without having been handed a cocktail from the silver tray, and instead of having her jacket removed for her and spirited away, she's slung it on the back of a sofa. One look at the set of Rebecca's jaw as she re-enters the room confirms that her choreography has been upset. She is not amused.

Tom suppresses a sigh. He's fond of Rebecca, really he is, but she can be a wearing host.

* * *

It's a nice house, nicer in its way than Tom's or Maggie's. Alice feels more at ease here. She can imagine her own cottage looking something like this, though there isn't room for a conservatory, which is a shame. Rebecca has children too, of course, so the furnishings are practical as well as sophisticated – removable covers on the sofas and chairs, shiny blonde wood that can be wiped clean easily. Yes, there are ideas here she can use.

Rebecca was showing off as they walked around the cottage, but Alice hadn't minded. She'd liked looking around and it had given her the chance to plant a few seeds for the evening ahead; unnecessary, probably, but it's important to take your chances when they come. *Don't look a gift horse in the mouth*, her nan would have said. So she'd oohed and aahed over the children's bedrooms, the pink duvet with the unicorn on the girl's bed, the Spider-Man coverlet on the boy's, telling Rebecca how she hoped to have children of her own one day, how proud she must be, how motherhood was the most special gift in the world. Rebecca had lapped it all up.

The homosexual, on the other hand – Tom, she reminds herself – is becoming a disappointment. He hadn't been anywhere near as grateful as he should have been when she gave him that biscuit for his horrible dog, hadn't even asked her how her wrist was. It was fine, of course, she always healed quickly; but she'd put a clean bandage over the spot so he couldn't have known that. For all his airs and graces, he could do with learning some manners. And she hadn't liked the way he'd looked at her as they were leaving his house either. Suspicious. There was no other word for it.

He's sitting next to Lucy now, talking quietly and every so often breaking into laughter. He can't have said anything to her yet about the drinking. It's a shame: Alice had hoped by now to see the first cracks appearing in their little clique. Still, she's pleased to see he's keeping a surreptitious eye on Lucy's wine glass, noting how often she reaches for the bottle. The idea is there. And there's plenty of time yet.

'Right, everyone,' Rebecca stands and claps her hands twice, calling them to order. 'On to the main business of the evening: *Tess of the d'Urbervilles*, the most famous of the novels of Thomas Hardy. And I hope,' looking hard at Maggie, 'that we've all managed to give it the attention it so richly deserves.'

Maggie grins at her over the rim of her wine glass. 'Absolutely, Becs. Me and Tess, we're like that!' Alice watches in astonishment as Maggie crosses her fingers and giggles. Can she really be this obtuse?

The conversation starts slowly. Rebecca comments that *Tess* is far shorter than *Jane Eyre* – 'Over a hundred pages less'

– and Alice thinks she may be about to say something about the structure of the story; but instead Tom points to her e-reader and says, 'I don't know how you can even tell with those things,' and the discussion turns again to whether it's possible to enjoy the reading experience with anything other than paper and ink. Then someone suggests they compare page numbers in the various editions, and Alice has to check her own copy along with the rest, forcing herself to stop grinding her teeth long enough to call out, 'Just two hundred and eighty-six in mine!', nauseous at the banality of it all, imagining getting up and walking down the hallway to Rebecca's pristine cloakroom, vomiting her Camembert and cranberry parcel with rocket and pomegranate salad all over the white porcelain.

Just be patient, she tells herself. *Wait for the moment.*

It's Lucy who eventually creates the opening; Alice couldn't have asked for more. She says, 'It reminds me of *Jane*, in a way; just how different everything was for women then. How restrictive.'

Alice gives just the slightest of steers. 'Oh, I agree. Women had no power at all – no one could argue that it's like that now.'

Tom nods. 'That's the problem, I think, with those attempts to try and "update" classic novels.' He forms the quote marks with his fingers in the air. She hates people who do that. 'Of course you still care about the characters – that's what good writing is all about – but they behave the way they do because of the context they're in. They're products of their time. We all are.'

'So true.' It's Lucy again, ever the faithful sidekick. 'They're always doing that with Shakespeare. I remember seeing a production of *King Lear* set in the 1930s with gangsters and molls. They put Gloucester in a straitjacket instead of stocks, and all the time the dialogue was going on about his wooden prison!'

They're getting away from the point, and Alice tries again. 'It's hard to imagine now how it must have been for women then. No control over anything, not even their own bodies.'

Lucy is nodding. 'Yes, you're right. If Tess got pregnant today, she'd have so many more options. The whole story would have to be completely different.'

It's like a switch has been pushed on Rebecca. Alice knows it as soon as she opens her mouth: it's going to be perfect.

'What do you mean, "options"?'

'Well, you know . . .' Lucy has picked up on the ice in Rebecca's tone. She looks sideways at Tom, as if for backup. 'She wouldn't have to keep the baby.'

Rebecca draws herself upright. 'I hardly think that's a sign of progress. As a mother, I find today's casual approach to abortion frankly horrifying.'

Lucy opens her mouth and then shuts it again, and it's Tom who replies. 'I don't think anyone's suggesting people are casual about it.' Alice sees his quick glance at Maggie. Her eyes are cast down, studying an imaginary loose thread on the hem of her top.

'Really? I have to disagree with you there.' Rebecca looks over and Alice gives her the subtlest of nods. 'It's just too easy now. Women aren't careful. They think it doesn't matter, that they can just head off to Mary Stoops, or wherever, and cut off those little *lives*.'

Maggie looks up. 'I don't think it's easy at all.' Her voice is quiet, so quiet that perhaps Rebecca doesn't hear.

'And you know what's even worse? It's as if the fathers don't have any right to a say. Half the time these women don't even tell them!'

Alice couldn't have scripted it better. With an effort, she stops the smile that's twitching at her lips. Rebecca is looking around at her guests, daring them to argue.

Maggie stands, her face pale. She says, 'I'm sorry, everyone, I'm going to have to leave. I think I've got a migraine coming on . . .' And before anyone can say another word, she's gone, the sound of the front door closing echoing down the hallway.

Chapter 15

It was three days before Liz returned my call, and in the meantime, I'd left her another two messages, each time practising before I picked up the phone, trying to infuse my tone with just the right level of concern – not giveaway casual, nor *Single White Female* manic. I must have succeeded, because she was in a conciliatory mood when she called. Either that, or she'd been practising too.

'They won't tell you anything, Luce, honestly. Even Elaine couldn't get any info out of the nurses.'

This was a blow. As Richard's PA, Elaine combined cast-iron determination with an air of authority that no one, not even the partners, had been known to refuse. If she hadn't managed to get information on Richard's condition over the phone, the chances of my succeeding were non-existent. Still, I wasn't going to give up that easily.

'At least let me try. I could say I was his sister or something.'

'Lucy, even if you *were* his sister, they wouldn't tell you. They've got rules about this stuff – it's patient confidentiality, isn't it? They take it really seriously.'

'Or I could come myself. Melanie can't be there every second.'

There was a long silence. I gave in first.

'Liz, I just want to see him. Nothing else. I just want to know he's being looked after.'

She measured out her words, deliberately patient. 'And what would you say? It's immediate family only on ICU. Who would you say you were?'

'Well, like I said, a sister. I could say I'd been away – abroad somewhere . . .' Even to my own ears, it sounded feeble.

'And what happens when they tell Melanie that Richard's long-lost sister has paid him a visit? How long do you think it would take her to put two and two together? Do you really want to do that to her, Lucy? Now, of all times?'

My hand tightened around the receiver. I couldn't answer.

'Look, I'm not going to tell you where he is, Lucy. I'm sorry, I'm just not. It wouldn't be fair to anyone.'

I tried to summon up some righteous indignation – who was Liz to decide what was fair and what wasn't? But part of me was relieved: in truth, I wasn't sure I wanted to see Richard either. I wanted to have *seen* him, to have done my duty; but I wanted it over, not to have to look at him lying in a hospital bed, tubes everywhere, machines beeping and puffing and sliding up and down the way they did on TV.

She sighed. 'OK, I'll tell you what I'll do. I'm going to take a few days off next week and I'll come down for a long weekend. You can show me around St Mary Mead . . .'

I laughed in spite of myself. 'I didn't know you were a Miss Marple fan.'

'Everyone's a Miss Marple fan. So like I say, you show me around your manor and I'll bring a bootful of booze and we can get pissed and commiserate over my crap love life, for once. And before I come down, I'll go and see Richard – give you a first-hand account. Deal?'

It was the best I was going to get. 'Deal.'

It wasn't until she'd hung up that it dawned on me that Liz wasn't part of Richard's immediate family either.

Since my conversation with Maggie, I'd spent as much time as possible hunched over my creaking laptop, reading articles and ordering books that promised to make my new venture a sure-fire success. I'd even put together an outline business plan and had a shortlist of company names, promising myself that as soon as I'd chosen one, I'd get some cards printed (and keep the receipt – by then I'd learned the phrase 'tax-deductible expense').

It was good to feel busy again. And though I knew it wouldn't be easy, for the first time since I'd come to Willowcombe, I felt there was some direction to my life.

I tried to ignore my anxieties about Alice. I did my best to keep out of her way, and it seemed she was doing the same: she hadn't come to the cottage since I'd been ill, and I'd seen her only at book club meetings or when we passed from time to time the way neighbours do, catching sight of her over the garden fence as I returned home laden with supermarket carrier bags ('Have to dash – frozen veg!') or about to turn into the driveway to The Gables as I drove past (a wave of the hand, bright smile plastered over my face, wondering how much she was seeing of Tom and whether they'd been talking about me behind my back).

Stop worrying about Alice, I told myself. Just be polite when you see her, as friendly as you'd be to any of the villagers. You don't have to be best mates. You just have to live next door to her.

It was this new, more mature version of myself who welcomed Tom when he came round to invite me to the pub for Sunday lunch. It was the day after Rebecca had hosted the book club, and I was more than ready to swap my planned omelette for the Cow's roast and trimmings. As I sat opposite Tom, reaching around the roast potatoes for the bottle of red, my last disastrous evening there seemed like a long time ago.

'This is nice,' I said imaginatively.

'Yes, isn't it? Thought you could do with fattening up.'

I picked up the wine. 'Shall I be mother?'

I'd deliberated as I stood at the bar over whether to order alcohol, but in the end decided it was better to pretend to have forgotten that conversation in Tom's kitchen. Perhaps I'd misread what he meant. After all, he hadn't directly accused me of being a raging alcoholic; and it wouldn't have been the first time I'd imagined things lately. Now he pushed the dish of potatoes to one side, making it easier for me to pour.

'I had another visit from Alice yesterday. That's why we arrived at Rebecca's together.'

'So are you and she bosom buddies now?' I tried to keep my tone light, but didn't quite pull it off.

'I wouldn't put it like that.'

Something in his voice made me look up. He was frowning at his plate. He said, 'I'm sorry about what I said the other day.'

I wasn't sure how to respond. Were we even thinking of the same conversation?

'When I implied that you hadn't been very nice to Alice.'

'Did she tell you I hadn't been?' I heard the petulance in my voice and wanted to kick myself.

'No, Lucy, she didn't.' There was something very stern about the way Tom used people's names sometimes. 'I just wanted to say . . . I think I know what you meant. About finding her difficult.'

I waited, but he'd picked up his knife and fork and showed no sign of saying anything more. I toyed with asking him what had changed, with telling him about the photo frame and the fire blanket; but I knew how it would sound. Besides, I didn't want to waste another conversation with Tom on the subject of Alice.

The rest of the meal passed in mostly comfortable conversation. Once Tom stretched out to top up my glass and I stopped him, placing my hand over its rim with a laugh, saying I had things to do that afternoon. I wanted to make the point, you see. For a moment he looked as if he was going to say something, but he evidently thought better of it. *Message received and understood*, I thought.

Later, over coffee, I told him about my plans to start a business. His response wasn't what I'd hoped for.

'It's really hard, you know. It's not enough to have talent. Actually making money is more difficult than you'd think.'

I was torn between feeling flattered that Tom thought me talented and patronised by his low opinion of my business sense.

'I realise that, Tom. I know I'll have to work really hard . . .'

'People don't want to pay for craftsmanship these days. They're just as happy with mass-produced crap.' The bitterness in his voice took me aback. I started to reply, but he was talking again. 'How long does it take you to make a piece of jewellery? Those earrings – they're yours, right?'

'Yes . . .'

'How long?'

'I don't know – a couple of hours, maybe.'

'You have to know, Lucy. You have to know *exactly*. You have to price your time and your materials, your overheads.'

I knew all this. I wanted his encouragement, not buckets of cold water. I said, 'I do understand that – I'm not completely naïve. Anyway, you make it sound as if it's impossible, but you've made a go of it. And Maggie and Rebecca.'

'Rebecca plays at running a business. She has Sam to support her. She's probably losing money, not making it.'

'Well, you and Maggie then. Maggie's successful, isn't she? And you, you make a living from your painting.'

He didn't answer and too late I realised how intrusive I was being. I didn't know anything about Tom's finances. How did I know whether his paintings brought in enough to live on? That big house and the stately old car were, he'd told me, inherited. He obviously came from money. Perhaps there'd been more liquid wealth to go with the house and the Daimler; perhaps his parents provided some kind of financial cushion.

I'd been presumptuous. I hurried to undo the damage.

'I mean, I don't know, obviously. I know it's hard for artists . . .' I took a deep breath, ready to reveal my own hard-luck story. What did it matter now? Maggie and Alice knew who I was already – it was only a matter of time before the rest of the village found out. 'My parents are musicians.'

I expected him to want to know more, but instead he said, 'You shouldn't take me as your role model.'

'I'm not! That's what I'm trying to say. I know it's hard. I saw my parents struggle before they got their breaks. Dad had to work two jobs, normal jobs, I mean. It was the same for Mum – well, as much as she could around looking after me and my brother.'

It was a relief, telling him something true about my past. I wondered why I'd been so wary of sharing it; it seemed silly now. I kept going, telling him about our tiny flat, my parents taking crap jobs that paid by the hour so they could get to rehearsals or auditions while one or the other of them stayed with me and Nat. 'So you see,' I finished, 'I do know what it's like. I know that people have to do all kinds of things to pursue their dreams!'

It was a corny enough note to end on, but the sentiment was

sincere. I looked at Tom, eager to see that he'd recognised I was serious.

He looked as if I'd slapped him.

For a moment, neither of us spoke. I couldn't understand what I'd done. I'd thought I'd offended him by suggesting he had it easy. Had I now offended him by suggesting his painting wasn't successful?

He said, 'Are you trying to tell me something, Lucy?' He sat very still. A nerve was twitching in his cheek.

And then something shifted and I saw the tension leave his body. He sat back and passed his hand over his mouth, rubbing his fingers against the light stubble on his cheeks.

'I'm sorry, ignore me.' He flashed his sailing-catalogue smile. 'I just wanted to be sure you realised what you were getting into.'

I smiled back, pretending his answer made perfect sense.

Chapter 16

It was a week after Alice lost her virginity that her grandad died, suddenly and straightforwardly. The doctors said it was a massive stroke, nothing anyone could have done. Two months later, with a minimum of fuss, her nan followed him. They said it was her heart, and perhaps it was, but Alice knew the real reason: her nan hadn't wanted to stick around with just the two of them rattling round the house like a couple of dried-up peas in an old tin can. Her grandad had always been the one who made things all right, who didn't mind when Alice didn't have a lot to say, who never worried whether she made friends or not. It was he who'd oiled the cogs of their household, and without him, she and her nan rubbed roughly against each other, awkward and out of kilter.

She supposed that the funeral was sad, but her grandad had been a popular man and afterwards their flat was filled with old men in their Sunday best, smelling of tobacco and stale beer. Her nan had twittered around them like a small bird, offering plates of sandwiches filled with ham and tinned salmon. After they'd gone, Alice had helped her to wash up, and when the last plate had been put away, they sat at opposite sides of the kitchen table and she watched her nan cry silent tears onto the oilcloth. After a while, she thought she should put her arm around her, so she got up and walked around the table – but her nan had reached out and taken her hand, giving it a squeeze and then releasing it with what, while ever so small, was unmistakably a push. So Alice had gone to her room and lain on the bed, looking up at the ceiling and wondering how long the council would give her to move out after her nan followed her grandad into the ground.

It was a surprise to discover that the flat was hers after all. There had been some money, it transpired, her parents' life insurance, and her grandparents had used it to buy their home from the council, 'To give you a bit of security, like,' as her uncle Bertie had put it. The girls at Waites had been by turns congratulatory and envious, telling her that Pimlico property was worth a fortune and she should sell up and find somewhere of her own, 'away from all the memories'.

But Alice didn't mind memories, and though over the weeks she cleared away some of the relics of her grandparents' lives the big wooden spoon with 'Wife Beater' printed on the handle, the salt and pepper pots shaped like a cat and a dog that her nan always left out on the kitchen table – many of them she left where they were. This was her flat now; they were her choices.

She'd become a regular at the Manx by then, and she'd seen him once or twice since that night. He didn't acknowledge her, suddenly intent on his pint glass whenever she walked past, and one or two of his friends would elbow him and snigger; but she hadn't really cared. A couple of the Waites girls, torn between attempted sensitivity and a desire for gossip, had asked her what had happened but lost interest when she failed to supply satisfactory details. So she'd been surprised when, sitting there one evening, watching Lissa flirting with a long-haired Australian from the IT department, she'd heard someone next to her clear his throat and looked up to see him standing there, holding out a glass filled with something clear.

'Vodka and lemonade, right?' He looked pleased with himself.

She nodded, and he seemed to take this as an invitation to sit down, long limbs dangling over the edges of his seat. He was wearing a black T-shirt with some kind of picture on the front, too faded to make out what it was. The neckline was stretched from wear.

'I haven't seen you about for a while.' He couldn't meet her eyes as he said it. She toyed with a flat contradiction but decided to say nothing. When she sipped her drink, she noted he'd bought a single measure of vodka. The pause between them grew.

He picked up his own glass and then put it down again without drinking. 'You here with your mates, then?' He gestured with his head towards Lissa, and Alice nodded again. It was clear he was struggling for anything else to say. She thought about getting up and leaving, going back to her quiet flat and watching TV. She'd started a new cross-stitch, a picture of a basket of flowers with a kitten sitting next to them. She could probably finish the bow around its neck before going to bed.

He was watching her from between long locks of black hair. It was dyed but thick, and she saw that his skin was surprisingly good, smooth and white. It came to her then, as clearly as if someone had spoken the words into her ear. She said, 'Yes,' and when he just nodded, thinking she was answering his question, she said it again and reached for his hand as she stood. He looked up at her, puzzled, then, 'Oh, right. Right,' and took a last gulp of beer as he got to his feet and followed her to the door.

His flat was as she'd remembered it, a narrow hallway with

grubby paintwork and doors all on one side. They went straight to his room, Alice following as he stumbled into a chest of drawers and switched on a table lamp.

'Shit, sorry, I meant to tidy up. I mean, not that I thought . . . you know.'

He swept a pile of magazines and clothes from the bed onto the floor, then pulled the duvet across. It wasn't straight – a big triangle of navy fabric dangled at the foot of the bed, while next to a pillow Alice could see a smaller triangle of crumpled sheet beneath. She sat down and he sat next to her as she'd known he would, covering the sheet so she wouldn't have to look at it. He opened his mouth to say something else, and she leaned across and placed her lips on top of it. A second later he was sticking his tongue into her mouth, more like her nan stoking the fire than a washing machine this time, his hands inside her top, fumbling at her bra. When she lay back on the bed, he tried to get up, reaching no doubt for his wallet or the bedside drawer; but she pulled him on top of her and said, 'Don't, it's OK,' and when he looked uncertain she said again, 'It's OK,' knowing he'd believe it without her having to tell a lie.

He lay on his side next to her when it was over. Her hands rested on her stomach and he reached across and brushed the back of one of them with his fingertips, almost as if he knew. He asked her if she wanted a cup of tea and she said no, she had to go, and got up and dressed quickly. At the door he stood there in his T-shirt and boxers and said, 'Look, this is a bit embarrassing now, but . . . I'm Rob.' He smiled at her. 'And you're Emily, right?'

She smiled back, thinking: *He has straight teeth. That's good too.* And then she left.

In the office the next day Lissa said that the barman at the Manx had confessed to Shane in IT that they watered down the beer. 'He tried telling him they all do it! Honestly, Shane said it was a disgrace and they should be reported. So we're all going to the Jugged Hare from now on.'

Alice nodded and agreed that was the only thing to do.

* * *

Maggie walks along the lane to the main road, enjoying the feel of the sun on her face. She's always loved this walk, loved the Old Forge from the moment she set eyes on it. David had been surprised but pleased, expecting her to object to an old building in, as he put it, 'a village full of old fogeys like me'. She'd laughed and told him he was a young fogey – 'Well, youngish, anyway' – and that she loved him for it; and she'd immediately seen the potential in the house's lime-washed walls and mullioned windows, engaging an architect and wearing down the planners with sheer force of will until they allowed her to open up the interior and let the light come flooding in. It's every bit as beautiful now as she'd imagined, every bit as stylish and unique. She can't imagine ever wanting to leave.

At the end of the lane she turns right onto the main road towards Mellingford Cottages. Rebecca's house, number 4, is the first to be reached from this direction, and she can see the white lines of the conservatory jutting out at the back. It wouldn't have been her choice, but Rebecca's tastes have a tendency towards the suburban; and they certainly need the extra space with the two kids. As she nears the gate, she catches a snatch of a lyric sung in a male voice: 'That's what makes you byoo-ter-ful.' So Rebecca is in.

She'd been in two minds about coming, wondering at first whether she'd be able to face her after what she'd said; but Rebecca wasn't to know how hurtful she'd been. Perhaps if she understood what it had taken for Maggie to do what she did, how she was still being punished for it, she'd feel differently. Either way, it's best to put it behind them. That's why she's come to see Rebecca now, to make things up to her before she has the chance to interpret that sudden departure from the book club as some kind of personal slight.

She pushes open the gate and walks down the weedless pathway to the front door. Rebecca, she knows, listens to music while either cleaning or baking – she hopes it's the latter. She raises her hand to the knocker and raps out the little rhythm she always does – tap, tap, ta-ta tap. The music stops.

Maggie looks over the fence at number 3 as she waits for Rebecca to come to the door. The roses in the Fosters' garden are in full bloom, and she wonders if Madeleine would notice if she snipped off a few for the hall table.

The door stays shut. What's keeping Rebecca? Maggie lifts her hand to knock again, and then pauses. The music has stopped and there's no sound of movement inside. She waits a few seconds more, then lowers her hand and turns back down the path. On the other side of the gate she follows the road towards the high street, keeping close to the hedge as she rounds the bend just past number 1. When she's far enough away to be obscured from the cottages, she stops and waits, straining to listen. At first all she hears is a blackbird singing from the hedgerow, and she's about to chide herself for being paranoid when it comes, faint but just loud enough to make out the words: 'You don't know-oh-oh, that's what makes you byoo-ter-ful!'

She bites her lip. Maybe Rebecca is busy, mopping the floor or something similarly inconvenient. Still, it isn't like her to ignore the door; surely she could have explained that it wasn't a good time? The thought follows unbidden: *unless she doesn't want to see you at all.* But no, that's ridiculous, surely. There's no reason for Rebecca to feel that way. She'll go and see Tom, ask him whether she said anything last night to indicate she'd taken offence.

She turns into the narrow road that slopes gently upwards to The Gables, the low grass in the middle parched almost white in the heat. The house rises up before her, all golden Cotswold stone and ivy; but the image of rural tranquillity is shattered by the frenzied barking coming from inside. As she listens, the barks turn to snarls, then there's a loud thud, like something heavy hitting a door, and more barking.

Maggie hurries towards the house. Has a dog got in and attacked Ferdy? Where's Tom?

There's another crash and she breaks into a run. A piece of gravel lodges inside her shoe and she swears as it cuts into the arch of her foot, but she doesn't stop. The door to the porch is shut. She calls out as she reaches for the handle, 'Ferdy! I'm coming, Ferdy!' The door won't budge. She tries again, but her fingers are sweaty and useless, sliding over the metal. She grabs at her top and wraps her hand in it, this time managing to get a purchase through the fabric. She pushes hard.

It must be locked.

Another thud echoes from the house, then a long, heartbreaking howl. For a moment, Maggie freezes, but then her brain kicks into gear: the back door.

She turns and runs around the corner of the house, straight into something that knocks the breath from her body.

'Ferdy really doesn't like her, does he?'

Tom grimaces. 'That would be something of an understatement.'

'I couldn't believe it was him making that terrible racket. I thought you had the Hound of the Baskervilles in here at the very least.'

Tom looks down at Ferdy lying on the kitchen floor, his head on his paws. 'Well, at least it seems we've narrowed down the cause. He was OK with Lucy when she was here, and he's happy enough with you. Were you waiting long?'

Maggie dabs at the cut on her foot. 'Only five minutes or so. I thought I'd hang around for a bit and ask you to patch me up. Anyway, I wanted to check that Ferdy was all right. Maybe he doesn't like Alice's perfume. Is that what it is, Ferdy?' Ferdy looks up at the sound of his name and wags his tail. 'There, he's such a sweetie. You wouldn't hurt anyone, would you, darling boy?'

'I wish she wouldn't come over. She knows what he's like with her.'

'Maybe you have an admirer.'

Tom pulls a face. 'Do grow up, Maggie.'

She laughs. 'Touchy. She said she wanted to borrow a screwdriver – though why she'd come up here instead of going next door and asking Lucy, I don't know.'

'Maybe she tried. We were having lunch at the Cow. Still, she could have tried Rebecca. I bet Sam's got a screwdriver for every occasion.'

Maggie inspects the cotton wool, not meeting his eyes. 'Perhaps Rebecca wouldn't answer the door.'

'What?'

She sighs. 'There's something up with her. I went to see her earlier, and when I knocked, she turned off the music and pretended she wasn't in.'

'Maybe Sam was home and wasn't in the mood for visitors.'

'It was One Direction.'

'Ah.' Tom opens a drawer and pulls out a blue and white tube of lotion. 'Here, put some of this on. You don't want it to get infected.'

'Did Becs say anything last night? After I'd gone, I mean.'

'I wouldn't worry about it.' She notices he hasn't answered the question. 'You're OK, though?' He meets her eye and nods; he knows better than to ask about her non-existent migraine. 'Good. Just make sure you're extra-enthusiastic next time she's regaling you with Elsie's latest ballet triumph, and she'll forget all about it.'

'Ellie, Tom, her daughter's called Ellie.' But Maggie is grinning in spite of herself. Then, 'She was rather abrupt when I saw her. Alice, I mean.'

'Oh?'

'Hmm. And you know, she's a sturdy little thing, too, for all that she looks as though a stiff wind would blow her over. I ran right into her and it knocked me for six, but she stood there as if nothing had happened at all.'

'She was probably in shock.'

'Thanks, Tom, very flattering, I'm sure. Anyway, she looked a bit . . . well, shifty. And she couldn't get out of here fast enough.'

'She probably wanted to get home and bandage her cracked ribs.'

Maggie rolls her eyes. 'I'm telling you, it was odd. If it hadn't been for Ferdy going nuts in here, I'd have half wondered whether she hadn't been trying to break in.'

'Oh come on, that's ridiculous.'

But Maggie has caught his glance down the hallway. 'What is it? Spit it out, Tom, you're making me nervous.' And strangely, she is; the hairs on her forearms are standing on end. 'What happened?'

'Nothing. It's nothing.' He rubs his hand across his mouth. The gesture is uncharacteristically uncertain. 'It's just that when I came in, Ferdy had managed to get himself stuck in the snug.'

Maggie stares at him. 'How on earth did he manage that?' Tom doesn't reply. 'So that must have been what all the banging was; he was trying to get out.'

They sit in silence for a while. Then, 'Do you like her, Maggie? Alice?'

'Yes. Yes, of course I do.' A pause. 'She was very kind to Lucy that night she was ill.'

'Yes, she was, wasn't she?' His voice has dropped. 'And she's been very good about Ferdy. She could have caused a lot of trouble over that scratch on her wrist.'

Maggie looks straight at him. 'You'll keep him away from her, won't you, Tom? Ferdy, I mean. For both their sakes.'

Tom glances back down the hallway to where the door to the snug stands open, as it always does.

'Yes. Yes, I will.'

* * *

Tom watches from his studio window as Maggie limps down the drive. He should have offered her a lift, but the feeling of unease that crept up on him when she joked about Alice trying to get into the house has been growing, and he knows that, however foolish he's being, he won't be satisfied until he's checked.

His desk looks as it always does: the pots of brushes and pencils; the laptop, half open as usual; even the small white cup with the sticky remains of his morning espresso. He presses the power button on the laptop and waits as it hums into life, presenting him with its usual request to enter his password. He leaves it and opens the drawer beneath. His organiser sits innocently in the centre and he lifts it out and leafs through the pages, uncertain what he's looking for. He puts it back and reaches under the desk for the waste-paper basket. A ball of crumpled brown paper lies at the bottom: the packaging of the parcel he collected earlier. He'd told Alice it had contained paints; well, he has plenty of unopened tubes to support that story. He replaces the bin and heads for the stairs.

The wardrobe door in the blue bedroom is closed tight – and why, after all, had he imagined anything different? He skirts the edge of the bed and stands in front of it, the mirrored front reflecting the doorway and a sliver of the landing beyond. He looks over his shoulder, but there's nothing there.

He opens the wardrobe and bends down to reach for something at the bottom, reproaching himself for letting his imagination get the better of him. The plastic carton takes up most of the space and his knuckles scrape against the wood as he pulls it out and lifts it onto the bed. It has grown heavier recently, but Sebastian, his most recently acquired client, has very particular tastes. Tom snaps open the lid.

Everything appears as he left it. One at a time he lifts out the items, turning them in his hands, a slow smile on his lips as he remembers using them. Nothing is out of place. He's being paranoid.

He replaces them in the box. Last in is the latest addition, the black rubber mask with tubes through the holes where the nostrils go. He hadn't been sure about trying breath control, but Sebastian was so earnest in his entreaties that he's decided to capitulate. He hasn't told him that, of course – Tom has to maintain the illusion that he's in charge – but he's looking forward to their next appointment and revealing his newest purchase.

He slides the carton back into the wardrobe and pulls a blanket from the top shelf to lay on top. As a disguise it's probably useless; but he feels better for having put it there all the same.

It's late that evening when the phone rings in his studio, the second line with the number only a select few have been given. The timing is irritating, but it's an occupational hazard: for many of Tom's clients this is the easiest time to reach him, after family or flatmates have gone to bed. As he stands at his desk, no one overhearing him would detect any change from the warm, relaxed tones he always employs with his clients; but as the conversation continues, he pulls out a chair and sinks into it, passing his hand over his brow, then his lips, then his brow again. Eventually he says, 'That's wonderful, I'll see you then,' and lets the phone drop to his side while his chest rises and falls in deep, calming breaths and he stares at the red zero on the answerphone. After a while, he reaches out and presses a button.

A stern female voice intones, 'You have no new messages.'

But Quinn had left him a message, he's told him so, a graphic one; had been even a little hurt that Tom had not responded. Perhaps there's a fault with the machine. Or perhaps Quinn simply dialled the wrong number without noticing. Maybe even now an elderly spinster is listening in horror to his Home Counties tones describing precisely what he's going to do to Tom when he next sees him.

Tom tries to tell himself it doesn't matter: whatever has happened, the message is gone. He looks around the studio again. Not a thing out of place, not so much as a paintbrush. It's the same in every room. He's being ridiculous – for why would anyone bother to search his house?

But the answer comes all too quickly: a wife. A wife who's found out about her husband's extracurricular activities, who's even now searching for evidence to boost her divorce settlement.

Alice? Could Alice be that wife?

Tom remembers her tears at the book club meeting, those horrible gasping sobs, sandpaper across the surface of his brain. She'd said she'd had an affair with a married man; but there'd been something not quite right about the way she'd told them – like she was watching for a reaction. Perhaps it was her own husband who was having the affair. Or perhaps she was the mistress of one of his more colourful clients, someone stringing along a wife and girlfriend while seeing Tom to service his more specific requirements: Leo, maybe, or Alastair.

He casts his mind back over their meetings, searching for some sign of animosity; but there's nothing. Alice barely seemed to register his presence at the book club meeting. If anything, it was Lucy she'd shouted at. Tom hasn't warmed to Alice – he can be honest about that to himself at least – but she's never been anything but friendly to him.

No, Alice has nothing to do with this. It's Maggie who's put that idea into his head, but it makes no sense. The lost answerphone message was simply a glitch in the technology, or the product of Quinn's imprecise dialling. Nevertheless, he'll be careful, even more careful than usual. And he'll watch for – something. Anything amiss.

And the next time, if there is a next time, he'll change the locks.

Chapter 17

I'd been looking forward to Liz's visit. I wanted to see her, of course, and I wanted to find out how Richard was; but more than that, I needed reinforcements.

I'd been to see Maggie a few days after the book club and found Alice there, hunkered down at the kitchen table for all the world as though she lived there herself. Maggie looked upset – her eyes were red and there was a box of tissues in front of her – but it was clear neither of them was going to tell me what was going on. I left them to it, pissed off that after I'd confided in Maggie I apparently wasn't good enough for her to do the same.

I tried to pretend it didn't matter, that I wasn't at war with Alice, that nobody had to take sides; but I was doubly glad that Liz was coming to stay.

I'd been watching for her from the living room window, and I heard the battered Beetle chugging down the road a few moments before it came into view. She pulled up behind my car and was stepping out in almost the next second, all bright red lipstick and bleached blonde hair, wearing a polka-dot dress and waving. I threw open the door and had to stop myself breaking into a run down the path, for the first time in weeks not worrying about making a noise, about whether Alice was home, about whether those cold grey eyes of hers were watching from a window.

Liz was wrestling a giant carpet bag from the back of the car, and when I got to her, she pulled me into a one-armed hug, then pushed it into my hands as she reached back inside.

'Oh fuck it!'

I was laughing without knowing why.

'The bloody Ben and Jerry's has defrosted!' Liz turned back to me holding a carrier bag. Something white and sticky was dripping from one corner.

'Please tell me you didn't drive all the way from London with a carton of ice cream in the back of your car.'

She looked at me as if I was demented. 'Of course not! I bought it at Reading services.'

Besides the dripping bag there were four bottles of wine in a cardboard carrier – trust Liz to make sure the alcohol arrived safely – and an oversized shoulder bag from which a pair of hair straighteners and a bottle of mineral water were trying to escape. I led the way back up the path, Liz exclaiming at the prettiness of the cottage in just the way I'd hoped she would.

We went straight to the kitchen to dispose of the mess, and Liz ran her hands under the tap while complaining about the traffic on the M4. I reached for the kettle, but she stopped me and demanded a tour.

It was the first time I'd shown anyone around the cottage since Nat had visited soon after I'd moved in. I took my time, pointing out the fireplaces, and the ancient cistern in the bathroom, and the deep windowsill in my bedroom where I could sit in a nest of cushions and look out past the road to the river and the fields beyond. I enjoyed showing off the small, square rooms with their bits of furniture. Here, I realised, it didn't matter that I was only renting; this was my home, in a way the flat in London had never been. Alice wasn't going to change that.

Back in the kitchen, I was about to fill the kettle when I caught sight of Liz's raised eyebrows. I put it back on its stand and retrieved some wine glasses from the cupboard instead.

'That's better.' Liz went to the fridge and found the bottle of supermarket white I'd stored there in readiness. 'Ah, the old Sauvignon Plonk! That's a relief. I was starting to worry you'd been getting into bad habits.' She nodded towards the back door. 'Anywhere to sit outside?'

For the first time since she'd arrived, I felt a prickle of unease. 'It doesn't get a lot of sun at the back.'

Liz shrugged. 'Fine with me. I'd rather look at it than sit in it anyway.' She watched with a lopsided smile as I unlocked the door. 'I thought village life meant leaving your doors open?'

I tried a laugh in place of an answer and stepped outside. A quick glance over the fence showed no sign of Alice, but her kitchen window was open. I set the glasses on the patio table and took the seat furthest from the door, where I could keep an eye out for one of her stealthy appearances.

Liz poured us each a generous measure of wine, and tipped her head back to take a long draught. She replaced the glass on the table, a bright red crescent imprinted on its rim like blood. Then she said, 'Go on. Ask me.'

'Did you see him?'

'I told you I would.'

I decided not to remind her she'd claimed only immediate family were allowed in. 'And?'

'He's still in a coma. They say the swelling's going down, though.' She saw my confusion. 'The swelling to his brain.'

I nodded, tried to find something to say.

'They can't tell at this stage how much damage there's been.'

I blinked rapidly. 'How does he look?'

I saw Liz bite back the obvious reply. She studied her glass for a moment, then looked up at me. 'Peaceful, Lucy. He looks peaceful.'

I nodded again. There was so much I wanted to ask, but every question seemed stupid. What did any of it matter? But still, still . . .

'Where did it happen?'

'What?'

'You said it was a car accident. Where did it happen?'

'I don't know. Some country road somewhere, that's all I heard.'

'And he was on his own?' I needed to imagine it. If I could imagine it, I could believe it.

'Yeah. It was late, dark. You know what those winding little roads are like. He was probably going a bit fast, misjudged the bend . . .'

'And no one knew what he was doing there?'

Liz studied her fingernails, studiously silent. I said, 'Does Melanie think that too? That he was meeting some woman?'

She sighed. 'Christ, Lucy. How would I know what Melanie thinks about anything?'

'But that's what you think.'

She sounded tired. 'We both know what he's like.'

We sat in silence for a while. I lifted my eyes to the fence, but there was no sign of movement in Alice's garden. I wanted to ask Liz whether Richard had been seeing anyone else, how long it had been after I'd left before he'd begun flirting with someone new; but I managed to stop myself. I knew how pathetic it would sound.

It wasn't right to do this to Liz. She'd taken time off work, gone to the hospital for me, driven hours across the country to see me. I should make the effort to be more of a host. No, not that: more of a friend.

I forced a note of jollity into my voice. 'Wasn't I supposed to be commiserating with you this time? How are things with Ivan?'

Liz wrinkled her nose and reached for the wine. 'I'll need a top-up for that.'

We finished the rest of the bottle and opened a second while we talked. There was no sign of Alice, and after a while I forgot to keep glancing across at the fence. I'd planned to take Liz to the Cow for dinner, but the wine made us lazy, and when hunger finally hit, we went inside and toasted endless slices of bread instead, slathering them with butter and jam and eating at the kitchen table.

It was good to focus on someone else for a while; I even found myself – hateful person that I was – grateful for Liz's problems with Ivan, welcoming the chance to dispense my own advice for once. Not that she needed it: Liz isn't the kind to put up with any sort of crap for long, and it was clear to me, if not to Ivan, that he was already toking away at the last-chance saloon. Every time I found myself about to tell Liz something about Alice – Alice in my house, or Alice shouting how I'd end up alone, or Alice cosying up to Maggie – I stopped the words before they'd formed in my mouth and swallowed them. Every time it felt like a small victory, almost a spell: *Alice isn't important. Alice doesn't matter.*

By the time I climbed the stairs to bed, I felt more relaxed than I had in weeks. I got undressed while Liz used the bathroom, and lay down while I waited to hear the creak of the door telling me that she'd finished and I could go and clean my teeth. There was a fine crack on the ceiling and I followed its line to the window, letting my eyes drift downwards to where the milky moonlight floated through the gap between the curtains.

I closed my eyes and slept.

*

The next day was grey and drizzly, so I abandoned my plans to show Liz around the village on foot. Instead we drove to Tewkesbury, where she spent a contented hour rummaging through charity shops for what she called 'vintage finds'. She emerged triumphant with two scarves and a crocodile-effect handbag with a broken clasp. 'Six fifty for the lot! You wait,' she said, flapping a navy scarf like a matador, 'if the rest of the outfit looks the part, everyone will think this is Hermès.'

When Liz started to flag, we stopped at a café for tea and cake and then made our way back to the car. Liz had bought a pile of postcards and sat scribbling while I watched the rain splashing on the windscreen. A tall, dark-haired man in skinny jeans that were too young for him strode across my field of vision, his arm outstretched towards a black car parked alone in the corner. Its rear lights flashed as the doors unlocked with a chirrup, and he got in quickly, no doubt eager to be out of the rain. I listened for the rev of the engine, but there was nothing: perhaps he was waiting for someone.

'Are we anywhere near the cheese-rolling here?'

'The what?' I looked over at Liz. She was adding her own teeth marks to the lid of the bitten biro she'd found in the glove box.

'They roll cheese down some enormous hill somewhere, don't they? It's a West Country thing.'

'Erm . . . no idea.'

'Like welly-wanging.'

'I'll take your word for it.' A blonde woman in vertiginous heels was trotting through the car park, taking the same trajectory as the man in skinny jeans. Her face was buried in the collar of her jacket, but there was something familiar about her.

'And thumb-wrestling. Or something to do with thumbs, anyway.'

'I think you're the one who should be living in the Cotswolds, not me. Where do you get all this stuff?'

'Oh, you know . . .' She was writing again, big loops on her *y*s and *g*s, the pen digging firmly into the cardboard.

I looked back through the windscreen as the door on the passenger side of the black car swung shut. So the blonde woman was with Skinny Jeans.

'There – fabulous.' Liz replaced the lid on the pen with a flourish. 'That's the first postcard I've written in about ten years.'

'Who's the lucky winner – Ivan?'

'No, Mum. She'll love it – she's always complaining you can't stick text messages on the fridge.' She was chewing the pen again. 'Though perhaps I should send one to Ivan too. He'll think it's fabulously retro . . .'

The black car was still immobile. It was a new Mercedes, I saw now: expensive and boring. A solicitor, perhaps, or an accountant.

'Done!'

I looked down at the postcard in Liz's lap. Scrawled across two lines were the words *Wish you were here!*

'Is that it?'

'OK then . . .' She grinned and wrote something else. 'There!' She'd added at the bottom: *Wash up before I get back.* I laughed as I watched her stuff the rest of the postcards into their paper bag. 'Bet he doesn't, though.'

The windscreen had started to mist over and I switched on the heaters, watching as they breathed clear patches into the fog. Through one of them I saw the back of the Mercedes rocking gently.

'Is that . . .?' Liz was leaning forward, scrubbing at the screen with the palm of her hand. I peered through the clear space at the bottom of the glass. There was no doubt about it: the boot of the car was moving rhythmically up and down. 'Jesus! In the middle of the day!'

I grinned. 'I'm not sure if I'm outraged or jealous.'

'Both. Definitely.' Liz pressed her face close to the glass, but the rear window of the Mercedes had steamed up and there was nothing to see. 'And a Merc too. Rich *and* horny.'

'Yeah, but bad taste in clothes.'

'Did you see them?'

'Mm. He was wearing skinny jeans.' Liz raised an eyebrow. 'Too old for them, though.' Something scratched at my mind as I said it.

'What about her?'

'Leather jacket, ridiculous heels.' *I'd seen her before.*

'Thought as much. They're having an affair.'

'What? You don't know that.'

'I bet you. He's trying to recapture his youth, she wants to believe she's still desirable.'

I tried to feel indignant. 'Not everyone—'

'Shush! We're reaching a climax . . .' The back of the car was rocking more violently. 'Oh yeah, baby, give it to me, yes, yes, yes!'

She'd timed it perfectly, the boot of the car stopping its see-saw motion with her final exclamation. I couldn't help myself: I rested my head against the seat and howled.

'Well, hell, Lucy,' Liz spluttered through her own laughter. 'There I was thinking you'd moved to some sweet little village full of grannies making scones, when all the time you've been living in a *den of vice*!'

I reached for the ignition. 'Right, belt up. That's enough dogging for the day.'

'You realise that if we go now, they'll think we've been watching them.'

'They'll be too busy basking in their post-coital glow to even notice.' I put the car into gear and started to move away. 'Shit!' I'd stalled it. The damned thing was always temperamental in the wet.

Liz's voice was muffled as she hid her face in her hands. 'You were saying?'

I grappled with the gearstick and turned the key again. The engine gave a *hrrr-hrrr-hrrr* sound. Liz groaned and I suppressed the urge to tell her to shut up. I forced myself to release the key. Stop, breathe, count to three. There was no sign of movement in the Mercedes. I turned the key once more; the engine wheezed and died again.

'Oh for fuck's sake . . .'

Liz started to giggle. 'That's what I love about you, Luce, you're so discreet.' She peered through the lattice of her fingers. 'Oh Christ . . .'

I looked up. The driver's door of the Mercedes was opening, one denim-clad leg emerging into the rain.

Liz giggled again. 'Oh shit, Lucy, he's going to invite us to join in.'

'Shut up, Liz!' I turned the key again. *Please, please, just fucking start.*

This time, with a final reluctant cough, it did. I threw the car into first and tugged the wheel to the left, away from the Mercedes and towards the exit. The tyres squealed on the wet tarmac, as melodramatic as a TV cop show.

'Nice.' Liz twisted her neck to stare through the back window. 'There's our Casanova.'

But I kept my eyes focused on the road ahead. I'd suddenly realised who that blonde head had reminded me of, and I was quite sure I didn't want to see who she was with.

Chapter 18

Alice shuts the door of the bathroom behind her, forcing the noises in her throat down, down where they won't be heard.

It had gone perfectly. She should never have doubted herself.

She'd been worried at first about the delay in visiting Maggie. She'd planned to go round straight after the book club, strike while the iron was hot; but she'd heard Tom arranging to meet Lucy for lunch the next day and knew he'd be out of the house for at least an hour. It was too good an opportunity to miss, so Maggie would have to wait.

She'd made sure she was the last to leave Rebecca's, planting a few ideas with her host before saying goodbye: how strange it was that Maggie's migraine had come on so suddenly, what a shame that the evening had been cut short when Rebecca had gone to so much trouble. She'd seen Rebecca's annoyance and hoped it would be sufficient to keep her from accepting any apologies until Alice could get to Maggie and move things along.

In the event, it was Maggie who had seen *her*, and much earlier than she'd expected. She'd had a narrow escape at Tom's. If she'd been less flustered, she could have taken the chance to have a quiet word there and then; but it wasn't the way she'd planned it and her mind was too busy working out excuses to leave much room for improvisation. Still, Maggie had seemed to buy that story about needing to borrow a screwdriver – though really she should have realised Tom was the last person Alice would have asked for something like that. Well, almost the last.

She'd spent the rest of the afternoon rehearsing her lines, running through every possible reaction until she was sure she was ready. The next day she'd gone to call on Maggie, wearing her warmest smile and telling her she'd popped by to see how she was feeling. 'You must have thought I was so rude yesterday! I was so anxious about my washing machine leaking all over the floor that I forgot everything else.' She tipped her head to one side and regarded Maggie closely. 'I've had migraines myself – I know how awful they can be.'

And as she'd said the words she'd seen it: the flicker of awareness, the tiniest wrinkle in Maggie's brow. She'd known then that she was right: the migraine had been another lie. She'd smiled again and waited, as though she had all the time in the world.

It was awkward, keeping her standing there on the doorstop, and after a few seconds Maggie had caved and invited her in. Alice accepted her offer of coffee and they sat in the kitchen at the oak table Alice knew would have cost more than all her own furniture put together, making polite conversation. Twice she caught Maggie's eyes flicking to her watch when she thought she wasn't looking. The third time it happened it was almost eleven o'clock and Alice was ready to take her cue, putting down her cup and turning its handle so that it was precisely parallel to the edge of the table. 'I'm keeping you,' she said, and stood to go.

Maggie rose too. 'Sorry, Alice, you must think me very rude. It's just that I'm due at Rebecca's. We always meet for coffee around now.' She flashed an apologetic smile. 'Becs is a stickler for punctuality!'

'Oh? Are you sure?' Maggie, already halfway to the door, turned and looked at her. 'It's just that I saw her on my way over, and she was getting in the car.'

Maggie's smile had fallen the tiniest fraction. 'Oh well, she was probably nipping out for a sec.'

Alice shook her head. 'She said she was going shopping.'

Maggie was almost too easy to read. Alice thought that if she'd stayed very quiet she could have heard the thoughts flitting through her brain, shrill whining sounds, like gnats around a light bulb. Why was Rebecca going shopping when they were due to meet for elevenses? Was she pissed off that Maggie had left the book club early? Did she really think she should have stayed there with a raging headache? Or had she seen through her excuse?

Alice had smiled sweetly at her then. 'So does that mean you've got a bit more time after all?'

She'd stayed for almost another hour, watching Maggie struggling to make conversation. She could have yawned with the effort of it all; but it was necessary to leach out the time, ensure that Maggie wouldn't change her mind and decide to head over to Rebecca's, just to check, or to leave a note, or to do anything that would spoil things before they'd even got started. 'That would throw a spanner in the works,' her nan would have said; and for a moment Alice had heard the words as clearly as if they'd been spoken in her ear, and seen it, a big, heavy, shiny spanner sitting on the table between them, the kind that if she brought it crashing down would send shards of that expensive oak splintering into the air, ends as sharp as stakes.

Maggie had looked relieved when eventually Alice had risen and said that she'd best be getting on. She would need to do better, she knew, but for now it was enough.

The next day, she was knocking at the door at ten to eleven, telling Maggie she wanted to engage her services to redecorate her sitting room and bedroom and mentioning in passing that Rebecca was 'out and about again, no sign of her car'. She saw Maggie suppress her frown, telling herself, no doubt, that something unexpected must have come up to interfere with their regular engagement; but when Alice offered to drop by the next day to talk through ideas for colours and fabrics, Maggie didn't object when she said she'd be there at eleven.

That afternoon she'd driven to Cheltenham and bought interior design magazines and a lemon drizzle cake. After supper, she'd sat at the dining table, flicking through the pages, circling the pictures she liked. Perhaps after all she'd go ahead with the project when everything else was done, keep the little cottage and really make it hers. But then she'd turned the page to a feature on nurseries, complete with cribs and cot blankets with sprigs of flowers on them; and she'd had to bite down hard on her fist to stop herself from crying out. She crossed the room and unhooked the Monet print that hung on the wall between her cottage and number 2, then went to the kitchen and took the longest, sharpest knife she owned from her knife block and carried it back to the dining room. She raised her arm and stabbed the plasterwork where the print had hung, dragging the blade down the wall and then pulling it back and stabbing again, over and over. Afterwards, she rehung the print over the ruined wall and threw the knife in the bin, then went to the kitchen sink to wash the blood from her hand where the blade had slipped into her flesh, and applied antiseptic lotion and a bandage.

The next morning she unwrapped the lemon drizzle cake and put it on a plate, covered with a clean tea towel. She removed the bandage from her hand; it would only draw attention. Then she went to Willowcombe Supplies and bought flowers, pale pink peonies, just like those she'd seen in one of the magazines.

She arrived at the Old Forge at eleven on the dot, holding out the flowers and the cake to Maggie as she opened the door: 'Just a recipe I wanted to try out – I warn you, I'm not much of a cook!' She'd chosen her expression carefully, practised it in the mirror until she was sure it was right: the look of someone who had bad news and wasn't sure whether she should share it. At first she saw Maggie trying to resist the temptation to ask; but when the coffee was made and the cake cut, and Alice was pushing it around her plate refusing to make eye contact, Maggie's curiosity had got the better of her.

She said, 'Are you all right, Alice? You don't seem your usual self.'

Alice liked that, the idea that she had a usual self, and that Maggie thought she knew what it was; but she suppressed her smile and put down her fork, turning it so that the handle aligned with the edge of the table. She said, 'I knew you'd notice if I came. I told myself you'd be too perceptive not to pick up on something.'

She thought it might have been overdone, but Maggie was too curious to detect the false notes. 'I don't want to pry, of course. But if you'd feel better talking to someone about it – whatever it is . . .'

'You're very kind.' A pause. 'Oh dear, I do feel rather uncomfortable about this.' Alice had produced a box of tissues from her handbag and placed it on the table. They were man-sized, infused with some sort of balsam. They'd been difficult, actually, to fit in her bag; but they were unmissable, and a bit of priming could work wonders. She continued, 'It's just that you obviously don't know what she's been saying . . .'

'Rebecca?'

'Well, yes. And I have to say, Lucy too.' Alice kept her gaze on the grain of the table. *Let her think she's prising it out of you.*

'What do you mean?'

'The other night, when you left . . . Rebecca said she thought you'd been behaving oddly lately. That you weren't being altogether honest with us – well, with her.'

'What? My head was killing me, I couldn't help that.'

'No, not about that. She said she thought you'd been keeping secrets.' She watched for the reaction – yes, there it was. The flicker of consciousness. 'She said you used to talk about everything together, but every time she saw you now it felt like you were keeping something from her. She said it was putting up a barrier between you.'

But now there was disbelief in Maggie's expression. Alice realised she must have got something wrong. Was it out of character for Rebecca to be so perceptive? But Maggie had a guilty conscience – she should be ready to believe she'd been found out. She must have used the wrong words then. The reference to a barrier, perhaps; too metaphorical for Rebecca.

She said, 'Well, that was the gist of it, anyway. She probably didn't use those exact words.' Yes, that was better: the disbelief replaced by worry. 'And Lucy agreed. I don't know if I should say this, but it was almost like Lucy was egging her on.'

Maggie was frowning. Was she upset with Rebecca and Lucy, or did she just think Alice was troublemaking? Time to up the ante.

'And then Lucy asked Tom whether he knew what was going on.'

There was a moment's silence. Then, 'What did Tom say to that?'

Alice let the seconds drift past. For a moment she thought she might just sit there quietly, her expression pinned in place, until Maggie begged her to tell her what she knew. But there'd be no begging. Not today, anyway.

She shrugged. 'Tom? Well, he didn't say anything, of course. I think he felt as awkward as I did.'

Maggie's sigh of relief was almost audible.

It had been easy after that. Maggie had offered her another drink, and when Alice had finished embroidering her account of Rebecca's probing questions, the coffee was replaced by wine and they moved on to other topics. Alice touched lightly on her failed affair; there was nothing, after all, like gossip about your fictitious love life to inspire another woman's confidences. Besides, convincing Maggie she'd been the first victim of the book club might be important later, if suspicions started to be aired. When Maggie had finished sympathising, Alice moved them smoothly on, asking how she had met David, about his job, their hobbies and friends.

Maggie had talked freely, Alice gathering up the little details she scattered through her anecdotes, storing them away for the time when they might be useful. In return, she sowed some seeds of her own: how difficult it must be to maintain a marriage alongside successful careers, the importance of trust when your partner had to spend so much time away from home. She watched for the cues, pressing here and there when she saw she'd struck a chord, letting her eyes well up as she said how much she envied Maggie her happy life with David, every so often reaching out to top up Maggie's glass. She hadn't thought she could do it – she'd never had much luck getting people to like her – but there was something about Maggie that made her easy to talk to, even if she had a script to follow. And then, miraculously, when Alice was holding forth about how wonderful it must be to have someone with whom you could be completely honest, knowing they wouldn't judge you, the tears had finally filled Maggie's own eyes and traced black lines down her cheeks.

Maggie hadn't explained about the pregnancy – that would have been hoping for too much – but it didn't matter. She'd cried and Alice had comforted her, pretending to think she was upset that Rebecca and Lucy had been talking about her behind her back. Rebecca, she'd said, must have her own problems to imagine that Maggie was keeping things from her; that if anyone asked *her*, it was Rebecca who seemed to be hiding something. She didn't give Maggie the chance to ask what she meant – she'd let that question fester for now – just shook her head and said, 'I'm sure we all have our secrets.'

It had been only a few minutes later, Maggie still red-eyed and fragile, when Lucy had arrived bringing her own bunch of flowers. She'd been taken aback at seeing Alice there, that much was clear, and her questions about whether Maggie was feeling better sounded insincere after Alice's careful groundwork. In the end, she'd got the message that she wasn't wanted and left with a face like thunder. How Alice had loved to see it! All puckered lips and impotent fury as she told them she'd show herself out.

She's gone now, and Alice had excused herself right away. The bathroom door is safely locked behind her and she's as far away from it as the room will allow. She picks up one of Maggie's fluffy towels and buries her face in it, giving in to the laughter that shakes her whole body and makes her gasp for breath. After a while, when she can't stop, she bunches the towel in her hands and stuffs the end of it into her mouth until her chest is burning and her eyes are streaming and she hears a high-pitched *hee-hee* sound and knows she won't laugh any more. Then she pulls it from her teeth and sits on the floor with it in her lap, waiting while her breathing slows and the tremors still. At the sink, she washes her face and hands, letting the cool water run over the pulse points at her wrists, over their map of blue and purple veins. She dries them on the towel, now smeared black with mascara, damp with tears and saliva. Then she folds it carefully and places it back on the rail, the stains on the inside where no one will see.

* * *

Maggie opens the fridge and scans the shelves in despair. A wedge of Camembert, half a punnet of furry strawberries, a jar of marmalade. She's barely gone out over the last few days, and David clearly hasn't done any shopping either. She considers heading to the supermarket, but that would mean a drive, and the thought of the brightly lit aisles and screaming toddlers is enough to bring on an actual migraine – karmic retribution, probably, for the one she invented.

Still, she tells herself, it had been more like pre-emptive action than an actual lie: if she'd had to keep listening to Rebecca's sanctimonious crap, a migraine would have been inevitable sooner or later. She'd made the same excuse to David when she got home and headed straight up the stairs. He'd come up soon afterwards with a glass of water and some heavy-duty painkillers, padding quietly around the bedroom picking up her clothes from the floor. Maggie had lain very still and pretended to be asleep.

She debates ringing him now and asking him to buy something on his way home – but then remembers that he's working late again. It's a shame, especially as he's going to be in London this weekend. She'd offered to go with him but he'd told her he'd be up to his ears and would feel guilty leaving her to roam the city on her own. She hadn't pressed the point. It was the way he'd always been, the flip side of what she loved about him: his seriousness, his commitment to succeeding at whatever he put his mind to.

She's always known that he wouldn't have enjoyed being a father, whatever he'd thought once. It wouldn't have suited him to have to divide his attention, unable to give everything either to his work or to his relationship with his child. Their marriage is different: it's Maggie who shifts and bends and moulds herself to whatever time he gives her. It's never felt like a sacrifice – she has her friends and her business. She's never found it difficult to be flexible.

The pregnancy, arriving three years into their marriage, had been a shock. She'd never paid close attention to the timing of her periods, and it wasn't until she'd been putting a new box of tampons into the bathroom cupboard and noticed that the one already on the shelf had barely been used that the slow, creeping suspicion had started to dawn. She'd stood there, trying to remember the last time, what she'd been doing; and when she remembered feeding the vending machine in the loos at the restaurant they'd gone to for her sister's birthday, she at first refused to believe it. Her sister had been an April baby – it was then halfway through June.

She hadn't waited, hadn't wasted time pretending she was just late. She'd driven to Cheltenham that afternoon, picking the largest and most anonymous chemist's, buying some nail varnish and cotton buds and then, oh so casually, a pregnancy test. She'd peed on the stick in the loos of a department store along the road, her mouth dry and her heart pounding as she waited for the lines to appear. By the time they did, she knew what the result would be, had remembered with sickening clarity the bout of food poisoning that had had her running constantly to the loo, nullifying, she now realised, the effectiveness of her pill. She was already crying tears of anger at her own stupidity when the two pink lines formed in the window.

She gave herself a week before she made the appointment, needing to be sure that she'd considered everything. She tried to imagine continuing the pregnancy, giving birth, the arrival of a small, helpless creature who would change every aspect of her life, who would depend on her utterly. The thought horrified her. Each night as she lay on the sofa, her head in David's lap, listening to him talk about his day, the patients with imagined ailments and poor personal hygiene, the idea he'd started to formulate about getting back into research, she'd asked herself if she should tell him. But how could she, when she knew what he'd want, and she couldn't, wouldn't go through with it? He would leave her when she refused, and though he'd never admit it, even to himself, lying there alone in the cold nights afterwards he'd wish she'd never told him.

So when the week was up, she'd made the appointment, telling David she was spending a few days with friends, people he didn't know well and wouldn't ask about her visit. When it was over, she returned to her hotel room and took it in turns to cry and drink and sleep for three days. Then she travelled back to an empty house, and when David had called and said he was sorry, surgery had overrun and he was going to be late, she'd told him that it didn't matter at all, and yes, she'd had a lovely time, but she was pleased to be home.

It was rare now that she thought about it at all. She'd been barely nine weeks into her pregnancy, the only thing that had been removed a tiny collection of cells, no bigger than a grape. She hadn't wanted it and she couldn't mourn it. But when the first anniversary came, she'd been surprised by the memories that had washed over her – not of the pills or the nausea or the blood, nor even the blank days in the hotel room afterwards, someone knocking on her door, asking her if she was all right; but of kissing David goodbye as she left, of him standing outside the house waving her off and telling her to say hi from him to Nita and Dev, of the way he'd laughed at her on her first night back when she told him that Nita's cooking was even worse than her own. Remembering those things, the urge to tell him the truth had been so strong that she'd stood in the bedroom with her hands pressed against her mouth, as if the words would escape if she gave them the chance. She'd left the house, calling to David that they needed more milk, and hurried down the road, not knowing until she'd turned into the lane to The Gables that she was going to see Tom.

Telling him what she'd done had saved her marriage, she was sure of that. He hadn't judged her the way she knew Rebecca would have done. He'd just listened and asked her gentle questions over cup after cup of hot, sweet tea, which he'd put into her hands and told her to 'drink up' as if she were a child with the flu. And on each anniversary after that – three of them now – she'd called on him to pour out the words she could never tell another living soul. He was her pressure valve, the person who took her secret, the one so heavy it almost dragged her to the ground, and lifted its burden from her marriage, lightly, easily, because to him it weighed nothing at all.

It's a pity, she thinks now as she closes the door of the fridge, that Tom doesn't seem to like Alice. He hasn't said very much – he'd told her once that as a gay man it was an unpardonable cliché to bitch about other people – but it's clear that the business with Ferdy has got them off on the wrong foot. Of course, she herself hadn't been sure of Alice at first; though it's difficult now, after she's been so kind, to remember why that was. But Alice has picked up on Tom's feelings, asking Maggie delicate questions about his likes and dislikes, trying, she's sure, to find a way to make things right. She'll talk to Tom about it – it's the least she can do.

In the meantime, she's hungry. She collects her keys and heads for the door.

* * *

Rebecca is sitting on the floor of the bathroom. She spends so much of her time here now, she thinks to herself, perhaps if she and Sam ever get divorced it will equip her to cope with the broom cupboard she'll doubtless find herself living in.

But no, there'll be no divorce. She loves her children; she loves Sam too, in spite of what people would think if they ever found out what she's done (not that they will – she and David are far too careful for that). It's just that she needs something more, something for herself. Someone to see her as more than a wife and a mother, the person who always remembers the homework diaries and the PE kits, who irons Sam's shirts and darns his socks. Well, not darns his socks, obviously – no one does that these days.

There's no reason for this, this anxiety that's started to dog her, the feeling that try as she might she can't shake: the feeling that Maggie suspects something.

It had started that day in the fields. They shouldn't have been there, so close to home, out in the open like that, but she couldn't resist him and the danger was part of the thrill. She knows that David didn't take her alarm seriously, and at the time she'd allowed herself to be reassured by his confidence; but she's found herself returning to that moment time and again in the days since, feeling someone watching her, scanning the shadows beneath the trees where, really, anyone could have stood unseen. Not Maggie, of course – she might suspect something, but she can't know for sure; but perhaps someone who's dropped hints, said just enough to put the idea in her head. Maggie hasn't been the same with her since, Rebecca's sure of it. On the night of the book club she arrived late and left early, claiming a headache, barely even saying goodbye.

Perhaps she should have answered the door when she'd called round the next day. Maggie had probably heard the music and figured out she was being ignored; but she'd been cleaning up after the book club and wasn't in the frame of mind to be interrupted by someone who hadn't been able to get away from her fast enough the day before. And as Alice had said, that supposed migraine had come on all too suddenly.

Still, she hadn't expected it to be the start of an estrangement, and the next day she'd set out the cups and plates as usual – but eleven o'clock had come and gone with no sign of Maggie. It's been the same story every day since. Rebecca had even baked banana bread because she knew Maggie loved it, though frankly she could have taken or left it herself. Even now, a small slice she's saved from Sam's lunch box is tucked out of sight in a Tupperware container at the back of a cupboard, awaiting Maggie's arrival. It will only last another day or two.

The phone in her hand vibrates gently and she taps the screen. She's already deleted her own message, and David's reply sits there alone: *No chance – M fine w me.*

That word – 'fine'. It covers a multitude of sins. She wishes she could see Maggie and David together, judge for herself. The phone buzzes again and she feels her cheeks redden as she reads the message.

From downstairs comes a thud and a muffled 'Shit.' She'd asked Sam earlier to move his briefcase from the hallway, but he obviously didn't and has now tripped over it. The sequence repeats itself with boring regularity – how he's capable of doing something so stupid more than once baffles her. His voice travels up the stairs: 'Becs, we're out of milk. I'm off to the shop.' There'd been a full two pints earlier – he's given in to the kids and made them hot chocolate before bedtime, despite her warnings about sugar levels and preservatives.

She doesn't answer, and a moment later she hears the click of the front door closing behind him. She looks down at the screen of her phone: *Can't wait for next w/e. Want to get u wet in the Lakes.* She selects 'Delete all messages' and goes to the sink to splash water on her face.

* * *

The bell over the door of Willowcombe Supplies jangles as Maggie pushes it open. A bored-looking girl with acne looks up from behind the counter and mumbles, 'All right?' around her chewing gum. She's probably the daughter of the owners, nepotism being the lifeblood of Willowcombe's economy. Maggie gropes for a name – Libby, is it, or Lizzie? – then settles for a smile and heads to the back of the shop.

The cramped shelving units form a narrow aisle to the chiller cabinet, which hums away in its own microclimate of cool air and the faint, sweaty odour of soft cheese. As always, it holds a selection of local produce alongside the branded tubs of spread and generic packets of processed meat: bacon and sausages from one of the farms outside Little Sowerbury, cloudy apple juice in big glass bottles, cling-filmed blocks of mature Cheddar. Maggie stares at them, waiting for inspiration.

Behind her, the door jangles again and muffled voices sing-song from the front of the store. Maggie selects some cheese – its shape is satisfyingly regular; cuboid, she thinks, turning the word in her mind. She'll get an onion and some eggs and make an omelette, and if she's lucky there might be a lettuce and a few tomatoes in the racks near the windows.

'Mags! I thought it was you.'

She recognises the warm West Country vowels immediately. 'Hi, Sam. Just popping in to get some provisions.' She holds up the block of cheese in evidence.

'Same here. The kids have been at the Nesquik again.' He reaches past her for a carton of milk. 'Don't tell Becs!' He's grinning, tapping the side of his nose, and Maggie finds herself smiling back. Obviously Rebecca hasn't told him she's *persona non grata*.

'Do you know if she's coming to Pilates this week?' She keeps her tone casual.

'You know Becs. I can't keep up with her.' He gestures for her to go ahead of him, and she walks to the end of the aisle, where the eggs are kept. 'She's off again this weekend, some conference or other.' There's a note of irritation in his voice – he'll be child-minding, no doubt. Maggie tries to look sympathetic. 'How about you? Poor old David still burning the candle at both ends?'

'Hmm. Well, keeps him out of mischief.'

There's only one box of eggs left – that's what comes of shopping in Willowcombe at the antisocial time of 6.26. She picks it off the shelf – no obvious signs of damage, and with the cheese in her other hand it's too awkward to check. She should have taken a basket.

'Is he still doing his research thing? That fund whatsit?'

'Yes, he loves it. Think it's turning me into a work widow, though.' She hears the edge to her voice and hurries on. 'He's away this weekend too, actually. A whole pile of meetings.'

Sam puffs out his cheeks. 'Who knew academics worked so hard? There was none of that weekend nonsense when I was at uni, I can tell you. Here, do you want me to take those for you?'

He keeps up a steady stream of chat while the girl behind the counter rings up their shopping and eyes him from beneath spidery lashes. He's good-looking, Maggie supposes, in his way: tall and blonde, with his rugby-player physique that only the slightest bulge around the top of his shorts indicates might one day soon turn to fat. Just the kind of man she'd have picked out for Rebecca.

They walk back together as far as number 4, Maggie formulating her excuses for not going in; but it doesn't occur to Sam to ask. He waves to her as he opens the gate, telling her he'll say hi to Becs for her, not noticing she hasn't asked him to. Not noticing, Maggie sometimes thinks, could be an Olympic sport for some men.

Back in her kitchen, she unpacks the shopping and takes a mixing bowl from a cupboard. It's only when she opens the carton that she discovers that, despite the unblemished cardboard, the tops of two of the eggs are smashed to smithereens.

* * *

The restaurant is small, intimate, the kind of place Tom wouldn't have chosen so close to home. Quinn, though, had been insistent, telling him he wanted to celebrate what he called their 'anniversary'. Tom suspected what he had in mind; it made him nervous and he'd suggested going further afield, to Cheltenham perhaps. But Quinn has to work – he always has to work – and couldn't afford the time.

Anyone else, Tom might have refused; but it's an anniversary after all.

He studies Quinn across the table. In the subdued lighting the last ten years seem to have left hardly a mark on him: a little heaviness around the jaw, perhaps, the hairline just a fraction higher. He wonders what changes Quinn sees in him. Would he still have lusted after Tom the way he looks now, begged him as he did that night? Everything might have been different. It's a curious idea but he has no regrets.

They'd been drunk, of course, lying on the floor of Quinn's room, the cheap carpet of the student halls tacky where it touched their skin, laughing hysterically at something, he doesn't remember what. Tom knew by then that Quinn wanted him, had felt his eyes on him, singling him out amongst their group of friends, taking chances to brush past him at the bar, touching his hand as he passed him a drink. He liked him, liked the attention, but Quinn wasn't his type. He knew that at some point he'd have to bring the matter to a conclusion, give him some subtle but unmistakable sign that it was never going to happen; but their friendship wouldn't survive Quinn's embarrassment and Tom had been in no hurry. So when Quinn rolled towards him and placed his meaty rugby player's hand on his thigh, he moved away laughing, pretending it was a joke. He expected Quinn to laugh too; but instead he raised himself up on one elbow, looked Tom squarely in the eyes and said, 'I'll pay you.'

Tom had stared back at him as the seconds stretched out between them. He started to laugh again but was stopped by Quinn's grave expression. He said again, 'I'll pay you, Tom. I'm serious.' And before Tom could process the words, Quinn's tongue was in his mouth and, against all expectations, his body was responding.

He hadn't had sex with him for the money, whatever Quinn had thought. It was his quiet determination that had impressed him, his desire. He'd told him that since, and Quinn had laughed and said, 'Right. I don't recall you giving it back, though!' And it was true. Afterwards, when they'd got dressed and Tom was about to leave, Quinn had stopped him, pressing some crumpled notes into his hand. For a moment, he'd considered refusing them, but then Quinn had grabbed him and kissed him again, hard, his hands on his arse, and Tom, knowing that he would ask him again, and that he'd say yes, thought: *It's better this way.*

Now, Quinn raises his glass of champagne. 'Feels like we should have a toast. What do you think – to us, and all who sail in us?'

And Tom raises his own glass and says, just a little more quietly, 'To us.'

It's dark by the time they leave the restaurant, the sharp edge to the night air a warning that summer will soon be over. The street is deserted and the laughter and music of the restaurant cease abruptly as the door closes behind them. Quinn glances around, then grabs Tom's hand, pulling him down the street, panting and laughing.

A few yards further and an alleyway – oh God, hasn't he always known there'd be an alleyway? – opens to their left, its velvety blackness spilling onto the pavement. Another quick glance, Quinn's breath in his ear, warm and beery, a metal door cold against his cheek, the rip of foil, the sharp, sweet pain.

Afterwards, they walk to Tom's car and Quinn waits while he unlocks the driver's door. For a moment, Tom fantasises that this time he'll just get in and drive away; but when he turns to say goodnight, Quinn drops a last hasty kiss on his lips and there they are – the dry, sharp edges of the folded notes pressed into his hand. Tom finds his automatic smile and steps into the car, the money already inside his jacket. In the rear-view mirror he watches Quinn's back recede down the street, his head down, leaning into each step. He starts the engine and pulls away.

Five full minutes pass before a pair of headlights appear like yellow eyes in the darkness and a silver Renault eases itself onto the road behind him.

Chapter 19

I'd volunteered to hold the next meeting of the book club at my place before Liz had said she'd visit, but it seemed rude to make her spend an evening with people she didn't know talking about a play she'd probably never seen. I'd thought about postponing, but when I'd mentioned the idea to Tom, he'd pulled a face and told me to prepare myself for Rebecca's wrath.

'Rather you than me. She'll have agreed child-minding detail with Sam – you know what they're like.'

I did. I'd heard Rebecca and Sam discussing arrangements before: Sam playing five-a-side on Saturday afternoon in return for Rebecca going to the hairdresser on Thursday evening; a golf trip with the boys balanced by a weekend seminar on marketing; pub quiz matched with school reunion, paintballing with tennis. Every activity was recorded, weighted, marked up on the marital tally sheet. Just thinking about it exhausted me.

I'd bottled it, of course; but now the day of the book club had arrived and my friends would be turning up at seven expecting food, drink and an evening moralising over *An Inspector Calls*. Not, I reminded myself, that Rebecca was in any position to moralise: that expensively highlighted hair ducking into the Mercedes had been hers, I was sure of it. I wondered who she'd been with, but perhaps it was better not to know. Maybe I should drop her a hint to be more careful, but there was unlikely to be a chance to get her alone at the book club. Besides, if I confronted her, I was sure she'd deny it.

Right now, I had more pressing problems. I had to come clean to Liz.

'I wondered why you'd been revisiting GCSE English.'

We were sitting in the living room and she nodded at the book on the shelf in the alcove. It had been there since the previous evening, when I'd given up on the romcom Liz had chosen to reread the opening and final few pages while Jennifer Aniston interrupted someone else's wedding to confess what a horrible, selfish person she'd been.

'I can put it off. Honestly, it's not a problem.' I heard the lack of conviction in my voice.

Liz shrugged. 'Don't worry about it. It'll be nice to meet your friends.' She unfolded herself from the sofa and crossed the room to the bookshelves. 'Even that neighbour of yours you don't like.'

I gaped at her. I thought I'd barely mentioned Alice, replying to Liz's questions about who lived next door as briefly as possible before steering the conversation on to other topics. I'd been sure I'd given nothing away. Evidently I was wrong.

'Alice?' I said, trying for nonchalance. 'I do like her.'

Liz gave one of her snorts. 'Yeah, course you do.'

I didn't want this conversation now, not when in a few hours Alice would be sitting in this very room. Here in my home for the first time since she'd stripped me of my clothes and left me sick and unconscious while she'd – what? I stopped myself. Done my laundry? Dropped by to check I was feeling better?

I got up and went to the kitchen, mumbling something about making a start on a chocolate mousse.

'I can understand it, you know. It's because you feel threatened.'

I turned to see Liz leaning in the kitchen doorway, my copy of *An Inspector Calls* in her hands. I decided not to answer.

'She's the new girl and she's muscling in on your friends.'

I opened a drawer and picked out something at random. 'Come on, Liz, we're not kids. Anyway, I'm the one who introduced her to everyone.'

'Exactly. And now you wish you hadn't.' She nodded at my hand. 'I don't think you'll need that for chocolate mousse.'

I looked down: I was holding a potato peeler. I sighed and dropped it on the table. 'OK, you're right. I can't stand her.'

It should have been a relief to say the words out loud, but instead they hung there, misshapen and wrong. Liz was about to reply, but I cut her off. 'No, I didn't mean that.'

'You're allowed not to like people, Lucy.'

'But that's not it.' I searched for a way of explaining. 'It's just that there's something about her.' Liz had folded her arms, and bright pink fingernails drummed against one elbow. I said, 'She watches me.'

'She what?' The fingernails went still.

'Alice. Sometimes when we're all out together, I'll turn around and I'll catch her looking at me. You know, really staring.'

Liz gave an uneasy giggle. 'What, do you think she fancies you or something?'

'Don't be stupid.' I'd snapped at her and Liz's face went hard. 'Sorry. I'm sorry.'

'There's no need to be a bitch about it.'

'Sorry,' I mumbled again. I looked up at the clock – four hours until they were due to arrive. Until Alice was here. My hands were cold.

Liz said, 'You worry too much about what people think.'

'I'm not imagining it.' My voice sounded flat; I wouldn't have believed me either. I waited, but Liz didn't reply, so I tried again. 'Alice watches me. It's weird.'

I took the kettle and filled it at the tap. I said again, weighing out each word, 'She watches me.'

Liz met my eyes and held them. She nodded. 'Then I'll return the favour.'

Chapter 20

Everyone always says how thick the walls are in these old cottages, but it's surprising how the sound carries when you sit quiet and still. Alice can hear them now, the rumble of voices through the wall of the kitchen, rising and falling, punctuated now and then by the thud of a cupboard door or the clink of utensils. They must be getting the food ready for tonight. It won't be like that when Alice has her own guests, Maggie perhaps, or Rebecca. She won't let them wait on themselves. She'll make them sit down with a glass of wine and they'll watch her as she moves around the kitchen, thinking how capable she is, how lucky they are that she moved to Willowcombe.

But there's still so much to do. And first she has to get through tonight.

She's not sure whether she'll be able to eat anything. The thought of it, swallowing food that woman has handled, makes her want to gag; but they'll notice if she doesn't. Still, she was practised at that kind of thing once, knew all the tricks of spitting into tissues or mugs, even buying tops with elasticated cuffs so she could push food from her plate up her sleeves when her nan wasn't looking. It hadn't been pleasant, the sliminess next to her skin; but there were only so many times she could say she'd eaten a big lunch at school, or that she'd gone to the chicken shop on the way home. She's past all that now, of course, though she keeps an eye on her weight all the same: it doesn't do to let things slide.

She'd worried about what he'd think, that first time; whether he'd be put off by her fat thighs or the curve of her belly, which, no matter how little she ate, was never completely flat. But he hadn't seemed to notice at all; and then, when some months had passed and he'd appeared at her side at the Manx and taken her home again, she concluded that her imperfections couldn't have mattered that much. He'd even tried to see her once or twice after that. Lissa had said she'd seen him in the Manx and he'd asked after her; and one evening as she came out of Waites he'd called to her from across the road, pretending it was a chance encounter and asking her for a drink. She'd turned him down, of course, knowing there was no point. He'd leave her in the end; people always did. And she'd got everything she needed from him by then.

She'd known almost at once that it had worked. She could feel it, the warm, sweet spark of life; and though she'd read somewhere that all foetuses started life sexless, she had known too, with absolute certainty, that her baby would be a little girl.

She had wondered what it would feel like to be a mother. She'd been only seven when her own had left her, killed alongside her father when the new car they'd picked up ten minutes earlier collided with a lorry. Alice had been invited to a birthday party that afternoon – her best clothes were already laid out on her bed – and her mother had promised she'd be back in plenty of time to take her. Whenever a person told a lie, a bit of their soul turned to dust, that's what her nan said, and Alice wondered if the bigger the lie, the more of your soul you lost. Her mother's lie had been so big and black that if that were true, there'd be nothing of her soul left at all, just a pile of dust lying there in the road. And how was Alice supposed to meet her again in heaven, like her nan had said she would, if there was nothing left of her to go there in the first place?

Her nan and grandad had tried their best, she knew that. They talked about her parents often, her nan claiming it was important to 'keep their memory alive'. But their memories weren't anything like Alice's. They pretended Alice's mother was just like other people: 'Yvonne would do anything for anyone,' they said, and 'Yvonne was as good as gold.' After the funeral, when her grandmother was filling up black plastic bags with shoes and clothes and bathroom things, Alice had asked for the book from her mother's bedside drawer, the one with her drawings in – the big eye, and the lady with her head chopped off, and the man who had snakes instead of hands. They weren't nice pictures exactly, but looking at them Alice felt closer to her somehow, as if she knew what she was feeling when she drew them.

Her nan had just pursed her lips and pretended she didn't know what she was talking about.

In the end, Alice decided it didn't matter. What was the point in memories, real or not, when the people you were remembering were dead? Her parents had left her, and sooner or later her grandparents would do the same. Alice wasn't stupid: her nan and grandad were old, and old people died. What was the point in loving people when sooner or later they always left you alone?

She'd known she would never leave her own daughter. She simply would not allow it to happen. She lay in bed at night, her hands on the smooth curve of her belly, and whispered to the little life inside that she would look after her, that they would never be separated. She used the words that she'd never used to another person. She told her that she loved her.

She considered going to the doctor, but the idea of it scared her. She'd seen the things they did on television: squirting gel on the mother's stomach, putting some instrument there so they could point at the baby on a screen while the machine made funny noises like when you put a seashell to your ear. She didn't want other people pointing at her little girl, telling her she was too small or too big, or not in the right position. Her baby didn't need any of that. And though it scared her sometimes, she was determined: she would do this, all of it, on her own.

At work she was careful not to give herself away. She knew she was supposed to tell her manager, and part of her would have enjoyed telling Lissa and Jenny. But they would have had too many questions, guessing at who the father was (they would have guessed right, of course), asking how he'd reacted to the news. She could see it all: there'd be a return to the Manx, all the girls staring over at him while he tried to ignore them, one of them – Lissa probably – third drink in, getting up and going over to tell him what she thought about men who fathered children and didn't even give the mothers the time of day. And what if he decided he wanted to see the baby; what then? She was hers, only hers. It was unthinkable.

Alice watched what she ate carefully, didn't drink. She made excuses not to go to the pub, knowing that the others would surely notice a sudden abstinence from alcohol. They didn't seem bothered when she said no, and after a while they stopped inviting her at all. She only minded a little; there were more important things now.

And day by day she looked in the mirror, standing sideways on and raising her top, watching her bump grow. It had been such a slow, gentle process; if anyone else had been looking, they probably wouldn't have seen any change at all.

* * *

'So – who'd like to start with a synopsis?'

Rebecca scans the sitting room expectantly. It's too small, really, for this many people. Lucy would have been better to have kept them all in the kitchen. It's what Rebecca would have done, and she'd have made a virtue of it: stuck some candles in empty wine bottles and played soft music in the background, created a little Parisian bistro in the heart of Willowcombe. Still, you needed vision for something like that.

She catches Tom's eye. It's clear he's about to make some objection, and she stops him with a glare. 'After all, Elizabeth won't have had a chance to read it.'

'It's Liz. And I have, actually.'

Rebecca smiles brightly. Lucy certainly has some odd friends. This Liz person looks like some kind of fifties throwback, with her bleached hair and red lipstick; and she's sure that when she reached for her drink she caught a glimpse of a tattoo on the inside of her wrist. Rebecca doesn't approve of tattoos. They look cheap at any age, but how much worse in a few years, discoloured ink on wrinkly skin? It's a sure sign of someone who doesn't think ahead.

'Well then, perhaps you'd like to summarise the story to get us started?'

'Sure – anything to secure my place as honorary member of the village book club!' If Rebecca didn't know better, she'd have said Liz was being sarcastic. 'So, as the title suggests, an inspector calls. It's a family he calls upon, quite well-to-do, all a bit pleased with themselves.'

'Not like any of us, then.' It's Maggie, and there's a sharpness to her tone. Rebecca wonders who it's aimed at.

From his station at the other side of the room, Tom raises an eyebrow. 'I certainly hope I'm not like any of those people.'

'Ah, but that's the point, though, isn't it?' Liz turns to him with a smile. 'None of them realises what they're doing.'

'We should finish the synopsis before we get on to the character analysis.'

'That's right, Becs, you keep us on the straight and narrow.' Maggie's voice is cold, and Rebecca looks at her in surprise.

Liz continues, ignoring them both. 'So the inspector tells them that a young woman, an actress, has killed herself by drinking disinfectant.'

'She wasn't an actress, was she?' Lucy says. 'I thought she worked in the factory the father owned?'

'Oops, yep, that's right. Sorry – I didn't read it cover to cover.' Rebecca suppresses a sigh. Is she the only one who takes this seriously? 'Anyway, the inspector starts asking questions, and it turns out that all of the family have had something to do with the dead woman, Eva Smith, in one way or another. The dad sacked her, and the daughter got her fired from another job, and the son got her pregnant and then abandoned her. And the mother was the worst of all, though I can't remember why. Anyway, they've all wronged her.' Liz pauses. 'To be honest, I get a bit hazy after that. In the end, we find out she isn't real.'

'Bravo!' Maggie claps her hands. There's a flush on her cheeks.

Tom says, 'You know, it's funny, that's the way I remembered it too. It doesn't actually end like that, though.'

'Doesn't it?' Liz sounds unconvinced. 'But doesn't the inspector leave and then they all start talking about how strange it is that they haven't come across him before, when the dad knows all the local bigwigs?'

Lucy nods. 'Yes, that's right. And one of them – the son, isn't it? – goes out and asks a policeman, and he tells him there's no one by that name in the force.'

Rebecca sniffs. 'And that's how you can tell it's a period piece. You'd never be able to just go outside and find a policeman these days.'

'That's right! The world's going to hell in a handbasket, Becs!' Maggie leans forward and a droplet of wine swings over the edge of her glass and onto her arm. 'Sorry, Luce. I caught it, though.'

Rebecca says, 'Don't you think you ought to slow down?' Her voice is sharp, and she sees Lucy look from her to Maggie in alarm.

Tom clears his throat. 'It's got a double twist. Quite modern, really.' Maggie is staring at Rebecca, but Tom carries on, pretending not to notice the tension. 'They all conclude that the inspector is an impostor and he's been telling them a tall tale.'

'It's like *Friday the 13th*!' Liz smiles triumphantly around the room.

'What?'

'Er . . .'

'We're supposed to be talking about books . . .'

'The double twist. You know, when you think it's the ghost of the dead boy killing all those annoying teenagers, but it turns out it's his mum, and then right at the end when the only survivor is floating in a boat and you think it's all over, the boy's corpse comes out of the lake and *gets her*!'

'Hmm.' Tom studies Liz over his wine glass. 'Well, yes, I suppose in a way . . . So they've all decided that the inspector isn't real and some of them have learned their lesson, and some of them haven't—'

'No, some people never learn.' Alice speaks quietly, but there's something in her tone that makes Tom stop. She waves her hand. 'Sorry, carry on. I was just thinking . . .'

'Yes, carry on, Tom,' Lucy mutters. 'At this rate we'll get to the end of this synopsis sometime in 2064.'

'And then the phone rings and it's the police calling to tell them there's been a suicide after all and an inspector is on his way to talk to them.'

Rebecca nods. 'So just as they think they've got away with it, it looks like they're going to get their come-uppance after all.'

'And here endeth the lesson.' Lucy gets up. 'Anyone for a top-up?'

* * *

Alice watches Lucy circulate with the bottle. She has to be careful, mustn't let her catch her staring. She has to join in, act normally, even though she can feel the heat of the gaze from that woman across the room, the one in the spotty dress.

Why is she here? She's spoiled everything. She might not have recognised her yet, but she's working on it, Alice can tell. She's seen her stealing glances when she thinks Alice isn't looking, trying to work it out. But she won't panic: she's come too far to do that now. She huddles deeper into the corner of the sofa and tips her head forward so that her hair falls in a curtain across her face; there's no need to make it easy for her.

From his seat near the fireplace, Tom is holding forth as usual. He's managed to get the only armchair in the room – hardly gentlemanly, but by now she knows not to expect any better. He's saying something about the play being moralising, as if that's somehow a bad thing. To her astonishment, Rebecca agrees.

'I mean, it's obvious we're all supposed to think what dreadful people the Birling family are. But honestly, I don't know what it is most of them do that's really that bad.'

'Oh come on, they're an awful bunch.' Lucy has finished her circuit and is standing in the middle of the room, empty bottle in hand. 'And you can't seriously be telling us you don't agree with the premise.'

'It's all a bit dull, though, isn't it?' Maggie is looking to her for agreement, and for a moment Alice has to focus hard to keep from screaming at them all. 'Having to sit through an hour and a half of someone else's dinner party just to make the point that people should be *nice* to each other.'

The woman in the spotty dress is still staring at her. She can feel her eyes like flies crawling on her skin. She twists further away and holds her hand to the side of her face.

Tom says, 'I couldn't agree more. John Donne did it better in a few lines: "No man is an island ..."'

Rebecca is talking again, saying something about how it's all very leftie, and what's so terrible about Mr Birling saying that people should look after themselves and their families before anyone else. She should have expected it, of course, that these people would think that way, that they wouldn't have a clue about the damage they did going through their stupid, selfish lives without seeing anything around them. And now Lucy is replying, and she can scarcely believe what's coming out of her mouth.

'It's not just that, though. It's about people being responsible for each other. How if you don't act with good faith, if you don't care about your impact on other people, the results can be far worse than you ever intended. It's like a chain reaction.'

Tom shifts in his seat. 'If anyone starts talking about butterflies and hurricanes, I really am going to need another drink.' He squints at his glass. 'And I haven't finished this one yet.'

Alice feels the flush rising to her face and closes her fist around the tissue in her hand. It's damp from the wine she wiped from Maggie's sleeve, and the fibres shred beneath her fingernails.

'And where does that sort of thinking get you anyway?' It's Rebecca again, her West Country lilt just edging to the surface. 'You can't go around second-guessing everything you do, just in case somewhere down the line something bad happens. People have to take responsibility for their own decisions.'

'That's my point ...' Lucy tries to interrupt, but Rebecca is getting into her stride.

'I mean, you could just as easily argue that the woman who died brought it all on herself in the first place. If she hadn't made trouble by organising that strike at Mr Birling's factory, she wouldn't have been sacked.'

Alice squeezes her fist harder around the tissue, and then releases it again. Some of the fibres have worked their way under her nails, and she runs her thumb beneath them, watching the flakes fall to the floor. They lie there on the oatmeal carpet, fat little crescents of white, like maggots.

The voices rise and fall around her, but the pressure is building inside her head and it's getting harder to make out the words. She should leave, say she's feeling ill. That's what Maggie did last time, so no one can complain.

They will, though. They'll talk about me after I've gone.

Lucy is speaking, her voice raised, arguing with Rebecca. How ironic that she should be the only one to understand. Except that she doesn't, of course. Not yet.

It's getting hot. Alice's palms are clammy around the tissue. She should get up, put it in the bin before anyone notices the mess she's making.

'Alice?'

The woman with the spotty dress is standing in front of her. It *is* her, she's sure of it now. The yellow-white hair, the red lips. A thick black line of make-up sweeps up from the corner of each eye. It makes her look like a cat.

'Alice?'

She has to say something. She forces a smile while she searches for the words, but it doesn't come out right and the woman takes half a step backwards. Alice feels the panic flutter in her chest: she can't afford this now, not with this one.

'Do you need a glass of water?' The woman is frowning, three lines forming a downwards arrow on her brow. 'You look a little flushed. It is warm in here.'

What's her name? She'd been too flustered at Lucy having brought someone from London to the village to concentrate on the introductions, and now she can't remember it. She tries a smile again, playing for time. 'I'm fine. Thank you.' The corners of the woman's lips have turned upwards in reply, but those lines are still there on her forehead.

'Are you sure? I can get you something if—'

'No, really. Thank you, though.' How stupid that she can't remember her name. She stares at the black eye make-up. Those little flicks at the edges, she remembers those. She was a gossip, she recalls, can picture her back there, her way of walking, a voice that carried, and a big laugh, raspy at the edges. A red coffee mug. The faint smell of cigarettes.

She can feel it coming back to her.

High heels on tiles.

Yes.

'Honestly, I'm fine.' And now she is. 'Thanks, Liz.'

'OK then.' The lines on the woman's brow have gone and she's smiling, relief tinged with a lingering uncertainty. 'Well, I might get myself some water all the same. I think this wine is going to my head.'

She turns away, the spots on her dress swinging before Alice's eyes.

'Alice?'

The breath stills in her chest as Liz turns back to her. She should have realised it wouldn't be that easy.

'Have we met before?'

Alice surveys the room, weighing her answer. Near the fireplace, Tom is tipping back another tumbler of whisky, the lamplight throwing golden darts into the liquid. Maggie stands next to Lucy, swinging around her glass of wine as she talks, for all the world as if she hasn't already spilled it twice. Rebecca has vanished, presumably to the bathroom.

She meets Liz's eyes and holds them as she speaks. 'I don't think so. I've been told that before, though.'

'Told what?'

'That I've got one of those faces. People think they know me.' Across the room, Maggie is pointing to Tom, who shakes his head in response. Alice allows herself to breathe. The three of them are too wrapped up in their own conversation to be paying attention to this one.

'Where was it you said you lived before you came here?'

She hadn't. Has Lucy been talking about her? 'London.' Then, seeing the question forming, 'Pimlico.'

'No, I don't know Pimlico.' As if Alice had suggested she should. Why won't she just go away?

'Yes, well, like I said – I've got one of those faces . . .'

'Work, then? What did you do? In London, I mean.'

Perhaps she should just tell her. Why not, after all? It wouldn't mean anything. Just a coincidence to exclaim over then set aside. This woman is nosy, that's all. Alice should just give her something, drop her a morsel of information and send her on her way.

'You don't like questions, do you, Alice?'

It's like a slap. 'What?'

'You don't like people looking too closely.' The spots slide to one side and Alice feels the pressure as Liz lowers herself onto the arm of the sofa.

She tries to laugh. 'I'm not sure I know what you mean.'

'I thought Lucy was being paranoid, but she's right. You've been watching her all evening.'

This isn't right. This isn't how it's supposed to go.

Alice says again, 'I don't know what you mean,' but her voice is flat, a bad actress rushing her lines. Liz shifts her weight and the fabric of her skirt brushes Alice's hand. She tries to lean away, but the sofa is too soft, cocooning her, and instead she tips her head forward again, hiding her face behind her hair.

Liz's voice is a whisper. 'I know I know you.' She leans closer, trying to peer into Alice's face. There's a vibration in the air and the smell of cigarettes intensifies as fingers reach for her hair.

No.

She grasps Liz's bony wrist. 'I don't like to be touched.'

Black-rimmed eyes widen. They're brown, Alice sees now, the colour of mud. She releases her, but Liz's hand stays there, frozen in mid-air.

Alice glances back towards the others. Tom has left his seat and Maggie is leaning into him, one hand on his arm. Her wine glass lists precariously in the other, but Lucy is laughing at something and none of them seem to notice. They don't notice anything; she should have realised that by now.

She turns back to the mud-coloured eyes. 'I'm sorry, I need my personal space.' Liz stares back, and for a second Alice holds her gaze before releasing her, feeling something inside unlock and slide away.

Liz blinks once, twice, and then she's on her feet, backing off. Alice resists the temptation to follow. She watches as Liz stumbles backwards and Tom catches her and swings her around in one easy motion, telling Lucy her carpet is doomed. Their eyes meet again but Liz looks away and laughs, loud and fake, pretending she's fine.

Alice counts to ten and gets up to leave.

Chapter 21

Liz saw it from the start: she knew Alice was hiding something.

I'd noticed her talking to her. I'd tried not to let it bother me that it seemed that after everything I'd said, the two of them were getting on – pardon the unfortunate pun – like a house on fire; Liz draped over the arm of Alice's seat, chatting away as if she'd known her for years. At one point it even looked as though they were whispering together; but then Maggie had almost thrown her wine over me for the twentieth time and Tom was spinning an unlikely yarn about a strip joint he'd once visited because it claimed to cater to intellectuals (motto: *Veni, vidi, veni*), and when I looked around again, Alice was on her own and Liz was coming over to join us.

No: that's not right. That's not how it was.

Liz was backing away from Alice – that's what it looked like. She bumped right into Tom and jumped as if she'd been burned. He grabbed her arm to steady her and she spun around and I saw her face.

She looked terrified.

Tom saw it too. The shock showed in his eyes and he dropped

her arm; but then Liz looked at him and blinked and it was gone. Whatever it was that had frightened her, it was over, just like that, so quick I could almost have believed I'd imagined it. She laughed and said something about how she was sorry for having thrown herself at Tom, and he laughed too, and Maggie said, 'Nice to know I'm not the only one having trouble staying upright,' and we all smiled at each other and pretended that nothing had happened.

They left not long afterwards – Rebecca first, saying something about the kids, Tom offering to walk her home because he knew she expected it even though she was only two doors away. Maggie and Alice followed a few minutes later. I watched them, arms linked as they went down the moonlit path, Maggie swaying gently with each step.

My throat tightened, seeing them like that. I remembered my own return home with Alice, her arm around my waist, her fingers digging into the soft flesh below my ribs. I imagined them walking down the quiet, dark lane to Maggie's cottage, footsteps echoing on the worn tarmac . . . Suddenly I couldn't bear it.

'Maggie!' I was on the path before I realised what I was doing. She tried to swing around, clumsy with wine, and would have fallen if it hadn't been for Alice's hand on her arm.

'Looocy!' She grinned at me. 'Whassit?'

'I, er . . .' Alice was staring at me, a half-smile on her lips. I had no idea what to say.

''Ave I forgotten something?'

'You can stay here if you like.' One of Alice's eyebrows arched in surprise. 'I mean, easier for you, isn't it, than walking home in the dark?'

'S'fine! Jussa shorr walk.' Maggie blew me a kiss, and Alice dodged neatly to avoid her out-swung arm.

'But the path is so uneven . . .' I groped for something to make it sound less ridiculous. 'You don't want to turn your ankle in those heels.'

Maggie looked down at her shoes. 'S'fine, Lucy! I'm like Carrie whassername . . .'

'Don't worry, Lucy.' Alice's eyes glittered in the dark. 'I'll look after her.'

Her smile was cat-like, and I felt a chill like a knife blade over my skin. When I tried to speak again, my throat was dry. They were walking away, Alice pausing to fasten the gate, holding onto Maggie's elbow with one hand to keep her steady. Suddenly I wanted to be indoors, the thick walls of the cottage between us.

They were the other side of the fence now, two heads silhouetted in the moonlight. Alice turned towards the house, and even from a distance I could see the silvery light reflected in her eyes. 'You don't need to worry, Lucy. Really. You know I'll take care of her.'

They were almost out of sight around the bend in the road when her final words floated back to me on the cool night air.

'Just like I took care of you.'

'Jeez, Luce, no need to slam the door like that!'

Liz stood in the doorway to the sitting room, two empty wine glasses in each hand.

'Sorry, wind caught it.' I was already reaching for the front door key, dangling on its piece of cord from a nail hammered into the plaster. The single lock I'd found an endearing sign of country living when I first moved in all at once seemed naïve and inadequate. I told myself I'd buy a couple of bolts when I next went into Tewkesbury.

'Everything all right? You look a bit . . .' Liz tailed off and I glanced up. I could have asked her the same question: she was pale beneath her make-up and I could see the effort it was costing her to keep her voice light.

'Fine.' I guided the key towards the lock, trying to ignore the tremor in my fingers. 'Just a bit tired.' The key skittered over the wood and I tried to laugh. 'Too much wine.'

When I turned around, Liz had gone. A clink of glass and porcelain came from the kitchen.

I collected an armload of crockery and followed her, passed her plates one at a time for the dishwasher. I said, trying for normality, 'You know, Mum never lets me load her dishwasher. She always says I do it wrong.'

Liz straightened and turned to face me. 'You can't stay here, Lucy.'

I felt myself go still. 'What do you mean?'

She was trying to avoid my eyes, but I could read the tension in the set of her shoulders.

I said, 'What happened tonight? I saw you talking to Alice. She said something, didn't she? I saw you; you looked . . .' I didn't want to say it. *You looked scared.*

She didn't reply, and suddenly the cottage seemed very quiet. I thought: *Maggie's out there with her now, alone in the dark.*

Liz said, 'I think you should stay away from her.'

I tried to laugh. 'Yeah, well, that's going to be tricky, what with her living next door and all.'

'I'm serious, Lucy.' She paused, as if unsure whether to say more. Then, 'I think I've seen her somewhere before.'

Somewhere in my memory something shifted. 'Alice?' I said stupidly. 'Where?'

Liz shook her head. 'I don't know. I can't place her. But I tried to ask her about herself and she kept trying to change the subject.' She glanced around, as if checking no one was listening. I should have found it funny, but I didn't.

She said, 'We know her, both of us. I'm sure we do.'

The next day I tiptoed around the kitchen as Liz packed, trying not to make any noise that might carry through the walls to number 1. I kept my anxiety buttoned up tight as I watched her drain the last of her tea and shrug her shoulders into her jacket. She picked up her bag and pulled the car keys from her pocket, and I kept the smile plastered to my face as I followed her down the path and out to the Beetle that it seemed had arrived only moments before. I pretended everything was fine as we hugged goodbye, and as I waved the car around the bend, and as I walked back to the front door, keeping my eyes straight ahead, and as I shut it firmly behind me and turned the key in the lock.

Then I walked into the kitchen and checked that the back door was locked too. And when I'd done all of those things, I sank down at the kitchen table and clasped my hands together to stop them shaking.

Who was Alice? What did she want from me?

I hadn't recognised her, I couldn't pretend I had. And yet I'd known there was something familiar about her all the same, something that caught at the edge of my memory. That fitted somehow – Alice belonged at the edge of things, slithering around in the shadows; a movement you caught out of the corner of your eye, but when you tried to look at her directly, there was nothing to grasp onto, nothing that would stick.

If Liz thought she'd seen her before, the connection must be in London. Alice had moved to Willowcombe from the capital, she'd said as much. I tried to remember what she'd told me, but the details shifted out of focus. Somewhere near the centre, I thought – Bayswater? Kensington? But if it had been anywhere I knew myself, surely I would have noticed and remembered.

Unless she'd been lying.

Liz had recognised her and was sure I knew her too. That pointed to Waites. Had Alice worked there? I cast my mind back over the teams: the other publicists I discounted immediately – I knew them all well, or well enough that I'd have recognised her if Alice had been amongst them. Accounts or IT, perhaps? Maybe HR? I realised I could barely remember any of them: over five years I'd worked there, and I couldn't recall more than a handful of people. What did that say about me?

It hadn't always been that way. I used to have lots of friends at work – or at least, lots of people I could chat with in the kitchen and join for a drink at the end of the day. But that was before Richard. Before I'd started to refuse the invitations to the pub in the hope that he'd find some excuse to work late and we'd slope off to the hotel around the corner from the station. Before I preferred to go home and spend the evening waiting for my mobile to ring in case he wanted to whisper down the line, telling me how much he wanted me; or later, to say he was sorry that he hadn't been able to see me, but Melanie was getting suspicious; or later still – the death knell, the same excuse I'd heard him use a hundred times to her – that work was just so busy, he really couldn't get away.

The idea came to me in a rush that made me catch my breath: was it possible that Alice was really Melanie?

Why hadn't it occurred to me before? If my new neighbour really did know me, she must have moved in next door for a reason. And who would have a better reason than Melanie? Who else had any reason at all?

But it still made no sense. I might never have met Melanie, but Liz had. She would have recognised her. And besides, Richard's wife was at his bedside, waiting and praying for him to wake from his coma. She wouldn't just up sticks and travel halfway across the country, leaving the kids behind while their dad hovered on the edge of life and death. No mother would do that.

Think.

Alice didn't like me. I'd known it from the moment she'd turned up on my doorstep, the coldness in her eyes before it was masked by her smile. Perhaps she *knew* Melanie? Maybe she was a friend or relation? Or perhaps Melanie had sent her? Was this all some kind of revenge?

That night I'd been ill, my heart thundering in my chest. I'd sat next to Alice at the pub. Could she have put something in my drink? Where had she been when I was dragging myself up those stairs? Did she follow behind me, watching silently as I crawled along the floor?

And the things in the cottage that had been touched, moved; small things I could explain away, yet important to me – the photo of my family, the fire blanket that was more like a comfort blanket. The actions had felt deliberate, *targeted.* They'd felt like Alice.

Even Ferdy knew it. Ferdy, who I'd never seen so much as growl at anyone else. Maybe he'd jumped at her and maybe he hadn't; but Tom had seen him snarling at her, trying to keep her from his house. What was it he'd said? That he'd never seen him like that before. Ferdy had felt it too. The thing that everyone else tried to ignore and cover up with coffee mornings and book club meetings.

There was something wrong with Alice.

She was there now, I was certain of it. I could feel her presence, a dark, malevolent thing behind the walls. A blight on my home.

A low buzz made me start: my phone was vibrating on the table. I grabbed it to stop the noise. It was a message from Liz: *Nightmare fucking traffic. Move back to London!* A second later and another buzz. I jabbed at the screen and another speech bubble appeared. *Will look through pics when home x*

Liz had promised to go through the photos on the Waites staff directory to see if there was one of Alice. I tapped back: *Thanks. Drive carefully xx*

I waited but the phone stayed silent. The traffic must have started moving again.

I felt a surge of gratitude to Liz for taking up the cause. I wasn't alone any longer, worrying that I was losing the plot. Liz was sure she knew Alice. She was going to try to find out how.

I put the phone down and reached for the laptop. There was one thing, at least, it should be easy to check.

I stared at Facebook's familiar blue and white screen and typed in her name. To my surprise, there was just one result: but the photo wasn't anything like the woman who had moved in next door. This Alice Darley was older, with greying hair and a flinty expression. She lived in Swansea and worked in a solicitor's office. She liked Marks and Spencer's home insurance. She didn't like people who ate with their mouths open.

I tried 'Darly' instead, but the page gave up, an algorithm somewhere offering me instead random Alices from around the world.

I deleted 'Alice' and reinserted the 'e' in Darley. Just three results. The home insurance lover, Carl from Winchester and Liv Darley (Fraser) in Portsmouth. I clicked on Liv and the screen flicked obediently to her page. She was about the right age, but that was all. I peered closer. Perhaps if she lost some weight, dyed her hair . . . But no. It wasn't her.

I told myself that not everyone liked Facebook. I tried Twitter, then LinkedIn, finding another photo of the woman called Liv but no one else. Then I turned to Google. Nothing.

Alice Darley was invisible.

I chewed at the skin at the side of my thumb. Waites. The answer had to be at Waites.

The website was useless, only a few suitably glamorous account managers deemed worthy of a photo. In desperation, I turned to my phone. I wasn't much for snapping away on nights out, but now and again when the drinks had been flowing someone would have grabbed the nearest phone to record the moment for posterity. The Waites drinking groups were interchangeable: maybe Alice had been amongst them.

I flicked to the gallery. There was that guy from IT I'd had a passing thing for – Dan, that was it – one arm around me, the other stretched into the foreground in a way that indicated he'd been holding the camera. He'd kissed me later that night, hot and heavy against the wall outside the loos, his hands up my top and his erection digging into my stomach. I'd been so drunk I could barely stand, and Liz had interrupted as he'd almost persuaded me into the disabled loo, steering me out of there by the shoulders and making me drink a glass of water.

I tapped at the screen.

Some girl I didn't know pulling a stupid face at the camera, tongue lolling out and eyes screwed up, presumably telling the world what an EXCELLENT TIME she was having.

A guy in a Rolling Stones T-shirt raising a bottle of beer.

A girl in a pink vest top that showed too much cleavage.

Two girls. Three girls. Another guy.

Who the hell were these people?

I kept scrolling through, but I already knew it was hopeless. There was no sign of anyone who looked like Alice.

I gave up on the photos and tapped out another text to Liz. *Let me know when you're home.*

But she never did.

Chapter 22

Alice closes the lid of the toolbox. She likes the way it snaps into place, the little catches clipping into the grooves. It wasn't cheap, but it's worth paying a bit extra for quality. She'd bought the contents separately on the same basis, eschewing the starter sets and selecting just the right items for the job. They had all come with guarantees too: Alice allows herself a smile as she pictures the face of the man in the DIY store if she tried to return them because they hadn't done the trick. But that won't be necessary. It's only bad workmen who blame their tools, that's what her nan always said. Alice isn't a bad workman.

She pushes the toolbox into place at the back of the cupboard under the sink. It won't be needed for a while.

She flicks on the radio and waits for the traffic reports.

* * *

Rebecca pulls out her phone again, just in case she's missed an alert. Perhaps she shouldn't have sent that message to David. She knows he doesn't believe that Maggie suspects something. The last time she raised the possibility he'd almost bitten her head off.

She looks down at her words on the screen: *Something's up with Maggie. Has she said anything?* It was sent eleven minutes ago, and still no response. She bites her lip. Should she leave it?

She taps out another message. *Looking forward to the weekend xxx*

David can ignore it all he wants, but she knows something's up with Maggie. She'd barely spoken to her all night at Lucy's, except to make some snarky remark. And then, spending all her time with Alice. Alice! Who's nice enough, of course, but still an incomer with the London dirt barely off the soles of her shoes.

She must be suspicious, surely. What other explanation can there be?

But David has said no, and surely he should know. It wasn't like Maggie, he'd said, to have ideas like that and not say anything. She can't imagine it either. Maggie is always so direct. *Too* direct, sometimes. And what she'd said about Alice having an affair . . .

She won't think about that.

The timer pings and she pulls a batch of honey and oat cookies from the oven. Elevenses with Maggie might be a thing of the past, but she knows someone else who'll appreciate her baking, someone who's seen Maggie's behaviour and might have their own theories about it.

Ten minutes to cool and then she'll take them round.

The garden looks OK from a distance, but you can tell close up that Lucy doesn't know what she's doing. The hollyhocks need staking and there's a clump of borage in the corner of a bed that will spread like wildfire if it's not uprooted quickly. With only the Fosters between them, she'll be finding the stuff sprouting through her own lawn before she knows it, and it can give kids the most horrible rash.

With an effort, Rebecca swallows her irritation. She needs to keep Lucy on side for now; if the borage is still there at the weekend, she'll go and pull it out herself. Lucy probably won't even notice.

'Hi, Rebecca!'

The voice from the other side of the fence makes her start. Alice smiles at her over a basket of carnations and snapdragons. 'Just picking a few for the table. All this lovely sunshine has been so good for the flowers!'

'I was just thinking the same thing.' Rebecca points at the borage. 'The weeds too, more's the pity.'

Alice's laugh tinkles away and Rebecca thinks: *She has such a lovely smile.*

'I see you've been busy too.' There's a pause in which Rebecca's mind races through the possibilities. Then Alice points towards the Tupperware. 'Baking, is it?'

She looks down at the container to hide her relief. 'I thought I'd bring some cookies around for Lucy. Say thank you for last night.'

'Sounds lovely.'

'Well, it's not easy catering when you're not used to it.'

'I'm sure she'll love them.' Is it a hint? Does Alice want to join them?

'They're honey and oat.'

'Delicious.'

'All natural ingredients.'

'Always the best way.'

Does Alice ever blink? She must do. Rebecca must have missed it. 'Well, I . . .'

'Yes, you go ahead. I'll just . . .'

'Oh! Why don't you join us?'

'Oh no, I . . .'

'There's plenty to go around!'

'But they're for Lucy.'

Rebecca laughs. 'Oh, she won't mind! Why don't you put those in water and come on over.'

Is it rude to invite someone into another person's home? But no, they're neighbours, after all. This is what village life is all about.

Rebecca raises her hand to the knocker as Alice disappears inside her cottage, leaving the door open behind her. She smiles: she already fits in so well.

Lucy takes an age to come to the door. Rebecca can hear her crashing about in one of the bedrooms, then running down the stairs. Surely she can't still be making the bed at this hour? Finally she appears at the door looking pale, her red hair drawn back in a messy ponytail. Rebecca summons a bright smile and holds out the Tupperware.

'I come bearing gifts!' She sweeps past her and heads for the kitchen. 'Don't bother shutting the door, Alice is coming over in a sec.'

'What?'

'Alice, Lucy.' Rebecca takes a deep breath and pretends she's talking to Ellie. 'Alice. Is. Coming. Over. I just saw her in the garden.'

Lucy has followed her in and is standing in the doorway. 'What, my garden?'

'Well, no, *I* was in your garden, and Alice was in hers. Obviously. Wakey wakey!' Rebecca picks up the kettle and empties it out – stale water in the bottom, just as she'd guessed. 'I brought you cookies.'

Lucy has taken a few steps into the front room and doesn't look around as she speaks. 'Er, thanks . . .'

'Well, are you coming to help? You do the tea and I'll put these on a plate.'

But Lucy is at the front of the cottage now, walking to the window and then backing up again. Rebecca sighs and gets the cups herself. They've been put in the cupboard the wrong way up: she'll have to rinse them.

'So is she coming over now? Alice?' Lucy is at the window again.

'Yes, she was just putting some flowers in water. Why don't you come and sit down. You're like a . . .' Rebecca gropes for an appropriate simile. Dog with a bone? No, that's not right. 'You're very restless this morning.'

Lucy returns to the table. Her skin is pale against her black T-shirt: perhaps she's overdone it with the wine again. Maybe coffee would have been better, but Rebecca knows from experience that Lucy only has instant.

'So, has your friend left? I didn't see her car.'

Lucy takes a seat. 'Yes, she had stuff to do this afternoon. Her mum's coming over.'

Rebecca brings the cups to the table and pulls out a chair. She'll pour Alice's tea when she arrives. She doesn't like to re-boil a kettle, but it's the lesser of two evils to keep it nice and hot. 'So what did she think of our book club?'

'Great, great . . .' Lucy's eyes are on the doorway.

'I thought you managed us all ever so well.' She hadn't, of course, but there's no harm in buttering her up.

No reply. She really must be hung-over.

'And those little empanadas were delicious!' Out of a packet, of course. She'd seen them in M&S the other week.

Still no response. Rebecca glances at her watch. This is getting her nowhere. Should she just ask her now, before Alice arrives? Or would it be better to wait and ask Alice too? No. Better handled one to one. Just in case the answer isn't one she wants to hear.

'Actually, Lucy, I had something to ask you.' She tries to make it casual but doesn't quite pull it off: across the table, she's finally got Lucy's attention. She takes a steadying breath. 'Have you noticed anything wrong with Maggie?'

'Wrong with her? I'm not sure what—'

'Well, not wrong as such. More . . .' Her fingers tap out a staccato rhythm on the tabletop as she searches for the word. 'Off.'

'In what way?'

'Oh, you know . . .' But clearly Lucy doesn't. She's staring at her blankly. Perhaps it's better just to leave it. 'It's probably nothing.'

But she's piqued her curiosity now, she can see that. It's amazing what a whiff of gossip can do.

'She's been OK with me.' A pause as Lucy picks her words. 'I did think she was a bit snippy with you last night.'

'Snippy?'

'You know, sharp. Abrupt.'

'I know what snippy means.' Rebecca stops herself from adding *thank you*. 'I meant, why did you think that?'

'Well why did *you* think she'd been off with you? She just seemed annoyed a couple of times. I mean, she was laughing, but she seemed cross all the same. I can't remember specifics. Sorry.'

A silence falls between them. The clock on the wall tick-ticks into it.

Rebecca pushes the plate across the table. 'Want a cookie?'

'No, I'm good, thanks.'

Definitely hung-over. What a waste of her baking. 'So she hasn't said anything to you, then?'

'No, sorry.'

Rebecca isn't sure whether she's disappointed or relieved; but then a movement over Lucy's shoulder makes her look up. 'Oh hi, Alice. We'd almost given you up.'

There's a crash. Lucy's mug is on its side, hot tea pooling on the table, and Lucy is on her feet lunging for kitchen roll.

'Good grief, Lucy! What's wrong with you this morning? You've been like a . . . like a cat on a hot tin roof ever since I got here!' There. She knew it was something to do with pets.

Alice reaches over to right the mug and shoots Rebecca an amused glance. 'Just as well I wasn't here earlier – we might have drenched our next read.' She holds up a book. 'Tom's choice, I'm afraid. Not really my kind of thing, but I suppose it's different at least.'

Rebecca takes the slim paperback from her hands. '*Fanny Hill*? Never heard of it.'

'Really?' Lucy has stopped dabbing at the table and is staring at Alice, something not altogether pleasant in her expression. 'Tom chose that? For the book club?'

Rebecca reads from the cover. '"Memoirs of a Woman of Pleasure". Good grief – is that what it sounds like?'

'I'm afraid so. I haven't read it, but the blurb gives you an idea.'

'And Tom chose it?'

'Yes, Lucy! Alice has already told us that.' Rebecca flicks through the pages. 'But really, what was he thinking?'

Alice shrugs. 'It's of historical interest, I suppose.'

'Is that your copy?' Lucy is pointing at Alice.

Alice hesitates for the briefest of moments. 'It is.'

'Handy that you had it already. Especially when you told us a minute ago that you hadn't read it.'

There's no mistaking the challenge in Lucy's voice. She's glaring at Alice, the sodden kitchen roll clutched in her fist. If she keeps squeezing like that, it's going to drip all over the floor.

'Don't *you* have any books you haven't read, Lucy?' Alice laughs, warm and pleasant. Like sunshine on water, Rebecca thinks. 'Funnily enough, that's how Tom came to pick it.'

'Oh? And how was that?'

'He saw it on my bookshelf and I had to confess! I picked it up at a charity auction as part of a job lot of books, you see. I always thought I should read it – it was one of the earliest books to be banned, wasn't it? – but somehow I never got around to it. Tom said that made it a perfect candidate for the book club.' She smiles at Lucy. 'It *is* stretching the definition of a classic, I agree.'

Lucy's glare falters.

'Well, I don't want to interrupt you, ladies. I just thought I'd pass on your assignment.'

Rebecca reaches for the plate of cookies. 'You're not interrupting a thing! Is she, Lucy?' She'll show Alice that at least some people in Willowcombe know the meaning of courtesy. 'Take one of these and join us for a cup of tea.'

But Alice is turning to go. 'That's very kind of you, but I should get on.'

Well, who can blame her? If Rebecca hadn't already plated up the cookies, she'd have had a good mind to take them away again. She rises to her feet. 'Actually, I'd better go too. Ellie's got a fancy dress party tomorrow and I need to finish the snout on her Peppa Pig costume.'

She waits for Lucy to protest, or at the very least to comment on the ambition of the costume – surely few mothers would be so daring – but Lucy's eyes are on Alice and she doesn't seem to have heard her. Rebecca collects her container with a sigh and follows Alice out.

At the door, she turns. Lucy's hand is already on the latch, the door half closed before they've barely stepped onto the path. Rebecca says, 'I can see you're not yourself this morning. Maybe next time, a couple of glasses of water before you go to bed . . .'

She blinks as she finds herself staring at the panelling of the door. And then from the other side comes the unmistakable sound of the key turning in the lock.

Chapter 23

That stupid book.

I may have been slow on the uptake, but just the same I knew there was something wrong with what Alice had said. I mean – Tom? It wasn't that he'd have had any problem recommending a bit of historical porn – I could imagine him finding it funny to get Alice and Rebecca reading about 'white shafts' and 'enormous machines' – but *Fanny Hill*? No. Altogether too bawdy for Tom's tastes.

I was all set to go over there to ask him about it; but then Alice had been so convincing. When I asked her why she had her own copy already, she didn't even blink. Everything was so plausible. And that passing reference to Tom having seen it on her bookshelf – I'll be honest, it got under my skin. I didn't like the idea that he was popping next door, oh so chummy, when he knew I didn't like her and he'd as good as said he felt the same. And now apparently he'd been colluding with her, choosing what to read for the book club *she'd* suggested in the first place.

So though I was almost sure Alice had been lying for some weird reason of her own, there was always the chance that she wasn't. I couldn't bear the idea of storming over there, telling Tom how fucked up she was, only for him to give me one of his disappointed looks and tell me that of *course* he'd suggested we read *Fanny Hill*, and why on earth did I think that Alice would make up something so utterly mundane?

After Alice and Rebecca had left – Alice looking as if butter wouldn't melt in her mouth and Rebecca making a parting shot about my rampant alcoholism – I went back to the kitchen and proved her wrong by pouring myself a generous vodka. It burned my throat and somehow that was good, cleansing. I took another gulp, then crossed the room and pressed my ear against the wall between my cottage and Alice's. Faint sounds of running water and metal clinking against china: Alice was washing up. And I was listening at the wall. Which of us was the nutter?

But that was what Alice did: she made sure she looked like the reasonable one. I remembered the day she moved in, when she'd appeared at my door and caught me nosing at her belongings. She'd thrown me off balance – deliberately, I thought now – letting me know she knew what I'd been doing and then smiling, putting me at ease until her next attack. She did it so easily, one moment the vulnerable new girl, the next implying that I was spying on her, or that my garden was a mess, or that I drank too much. And never coming right out and saying it. Always staying the right side of the line so I could tell myself I was being paranoid.

Who was this woman? Why was she here?

There was a thud as Alice's front door closed. Of course: it was Tuesday, one of her afternoons at the post office. For several minutes I stood there, chewing at my lip, trying to decide whether I was losing the plot. Then I headed for the back door and stepped onto the patio.

The grass on the hill behind the garden was yellow from the heat, but here, next to the house, it was as cool and shaded as always. I glanced across at number 3. The fence was too high to see much, but it didn't matter. The Fosters only ever came down at weekends and their cleaner came every other Thursday. There'd be no one there today.

Alice had trimmed the jasmine along the top of the fence, but on my side, long, white-flowered tendrils still bobbed gently in the breeze. I pulled up a patio chair and positioned it against the edge of the flower bed. Gingerly I placed one foot on the seat. Nothing creaked. All the same, I pulled the chair closer to the house and steadied myself with a hand against the wall before stepping up.

Slowly I straightened and looked into Alice's garden.

Everything was neat and orderly. The paving slabs, the same golden stone as the walls of the cottages, were freshly swept. Three terracotta pots formed a triangle in one corner, filled with plants in full flower. I didn't know the names, but I recognised them as the type the garden centre had recommended after my first choices had sickened and died in the shady spot. My own versions had flourished for two days before being devoured by slugs and snails. Alice must have used poison.

Diagonally opposite, at the back of the courtyard, a tree with delicate purple leaves rose from another pot. The third corner housed a small green box with a padlock, presumably for garden tools, and in the fourth, closest to my lookout point, sat a pretty wrought-iron table and two chairs.

It was all exactly as it should have been. And what, after all, had I expected? A telescope trained on my back windows? A mysterious pile of soil marking the burial site of who knew what?

The back door was shut and I told myself I wouldn't have tried it anyway – even if all that jasmine hadn't made it so difficult to get a foothold on the fence. There was a pane of glass in the top half, but all I could see was the reflection of the garden. I stepped down and moved the chair further along the flower bed, hoping that changing the angle would improve matters. If I leaned in close to the fence . . .

Now I could just make out something white and flat – a tablecloth. The layout of the kitchen must be similar to mine then, space for a table and chairs near the back door. I peered closer, shadows and reflections shifting as my eyes made sense of the shapes. The table seemed to be clear except for a low, round object I couldn't make out – a dish, perhaps – and what might have been a box with a handle on top. A toolbox, or a sewing box maybe.

I clambered down and pulled the chair back to the table. What was I doing? What had I learned? That Alice kept her table covered with a cloth and wasn't prone to clutter. I was behaving like an idiot.

I sat down and rested my head against the stone of the house. It was rare these days to be able to enjoy the back garden without worrying that Alice might appear. A gentle breeze played across the hill, setting the grass to whispering like the sea. I closed my eyes.

When I awoke, the afternoon had cooled and the stiffness in my neck told me I'd slept for some time. I checked my watch: 4.30. Alice would be closing up soon, extracting some final snippets of gossip from Cynthia before she made her way home. And here I was, napping away the afternoon when I should have been working on jewellery designs, or my business plan, or even just starting this week's reading.

I went inside and flicked the switch on the kettle. I had a copy of *Fanny Hill* somewhere, I was sure of it. I'd bought it in my teens at a church jumble sale, of all places, dragged there by my mum in aid of some good cause or other. The old dears on the stall had had no idea what they were selling to a thirteen-year-old girl, but a quick flick through the pages had assured me it was well worth my twenty pence. I'd read it in bed, thrilled and horrified, reaching beneath the covers to find my own 'seat of pleasure'. I'd been such an innocent. Most thirteen-year-old kids these days had probably seen everything *Fanny Hill* had to offer in glorious Technicolor, courtesy of YouTube.

I leant against the counter while I waited for the kettle to boil. The kitchen was fairly tidy, but the pile of junk mail in front of Nat's calendar would need sorting out soon before it toppled to the floor. I'd inadvertently got myself onto a mailing list somewhere and now poor Mancunian Ben was barely able to see past the catalogues for kitchen gadgets and trays with cushions under them.

I froze. Something was wrong.

Seconds passed as I stared. The kettle bubbled to a crescendo then clicked off. Outside, a bird warbled a brief snatch of song. A rustle of wings. Breeze through the grass.

I crossed the floor to the dresser. An arm's length away, I stopped.

The calendar was in its usual place. The pile of junk mail appeared undisturbed. The pens and the elastic bands and the scrap of paper with the start of my shopping list were all as I'd left them.

I bent forward, peering at the calendar.

Ben had gone. In his place, James from Preston belatedly announced the arrival of September.

I drew a shaky breath and backed away. The edge of the table struck my hip, hard, and I stumbled, grasping at a chair to stay upright. I sank into the seat, my eyes fixed on the picture.

I hadn't changed it. I knew I hadn't.

Alice. Alice. Alice in my house.

I held onto the edge of the table and forced myself to breathe.

The calendar might have been like that for days. I hadn't noticed before, but so what. Here it was, well into the month, and I hadn't thought to change the page. That was evidence enough that I barely glanced at it.

It could have been Liz. I tried to picture it: Liz picking it up and sniggering at the silly pictures, idly turning the page with one red fingernail.

But no. *No.*

If she'd noticed the calendar at all, Liz would have said something. She couldn't have resisted the temptation to tease me about something so godawful. But then perhaps I hadn't been around when she did it. Maybe I'd been in the shower, or I'd had to run out once for milk. Perhaps by the time she saw me it had slipped her mind.

I pulled out my phone. She should be home by now, probably tearing around trying to Febreze away the smell of Ivan's pot before her mum arrived. I tapped out a message:

Did you change the month on my calendar?

I looked at the words and then deleted them. They sounded OCD. I tried again.

I see you preferred James from Preston to Ben from Manchester! :)

Exclamation mark and smiley face. Christ, I was such a people-pleaser. I pressed send and waited. Nothing. Liz was busy.

Now that the shock was ebbing away, my brain stirred into life. It didn't need to have been Liz. It could have happened at the book club meeting. Anyone could have wandered into the kitchen if they'd felt like it and flipped the page. I could have been busy with the food, or perhaps they'd taken out a plate or a glass when I was in the other room. Or any one of a hundred other scenarios.

I would have laughed if I hadn't felt so stupid. What the hell had got into me?

I crossed to the dresser and picked up the calendar. James from Preston was blonde, blue-eyed and boy-band-ready, shirt unbuttoned to show a honey-coloured six-pack. Not my type at all, but then the same had gone for January through August, as Nat would have known perfectly well. I missed him, I realised. I should try to get home more often, see Mum and Dad too. Maybe I'd drive up there one weekend, the end of the month perhaps. I checked the dates: the 27th fell on a Saturday.

And then I saw it.

The calendar fell from my hands, catching on the pile of junk mail and sending it cascading to the floor. I stared at the mess. The calendar had landed to one side, face down. I bent and reached for it, gripping a corner between my fingertips. I turned it over.

There it was. Drawn in the corner of the square marked 25. Something red.

To anyone else it might have looked like a teardrop inside a teardrop. But I knew what it was.

It was a flame.

There's a reason I don't light the fire in the sitting room. There's a reason I have a fire blanket in the kitchen. There's a reason I would never, ever leave my hair straighteners plugged in.

On 25 September 2013, at a little before midnight, I was in the queue for the loos at the Midnight Cowboy, a nightclub in Leeds with a fine line in cheesy pop. I'd left my friends at the bar, drinking tequila slammers and flirting with a bunch of Geordies. We were two days into a hen party for a marriage none of us gave more than even chances of lasting the year, and we were all very, very drunk.

The ringing when it came was ear-bleedingly loud, cutting across the music. At first I thought it was another track, but then the music stopped and the ringing kept going and a girl behind me said, 'Some loser's set off the fire alarm.' My head was hazy from the tequila and at first no one moved and I thought: *I'm not leaving now, I need to pee.* But then something changed and people were pushing and shoving and a girl stepped on my foot with her high heel, right on the instep, and someone else slammed into my back, and there was screaming and I realised I could smell smoke.

The lights didn't go up. They should have done, but they didn't. I couldn't see where I was going, but it didn't matter because there were people all around me, the tang of sweat and panic, and I couldn't do anything except let myself be carried along by the crowd. I tried to push my elbows to the side, to give myself room to breathe, and I remembered firefighters coming to my school and singing a song about there being air on the floor; but there was no room, no room, and I'd be trampled if I tried to drop down, and the smell of the smoke was getting stronger, and still the coloured lights were flashing, lighting up the faces all around me, green and red, open mouths and beads of sweat.

I twisted my head to look for my friends, but I couldn't tell which way the bar was, and there were bodies everywhere, a sea of them. I lifted the hem of my top and pressed it over my mouth, and I could hear people coughing and my eyes were streaming and I knew it was the smoke that killed you, but God, I was so frightened of the flames. I was pushing now too, and on my left a woman stumbled and fell. I reached out, tried to grab her, but the bodies kept moving forward. I opened my mouth to scream at them to stop, and smoke filled my throat.

I gasped for air, clawing at the shape in front of me, no longer caring about the woman who'd fallen, no longer caring about anything but getting out of there. I had to get free. I had to breathe.

I pushed again, but my vision was blurring and I wasn't sure any longer where the door was. I tried to turn, but bodies pressed in on every side. My chest burned and in my head a voice whispered: *This is it.*

And then there was a shove against my back, and my feet were moving, and suddenly – dear, sweet Jesus – there was air on my face and the body in front of me wasn't there any more. I felt my knees buckle and someone caught me by the elbow and sat me on a wall with something around my shoulders and tears running down my face.

I was one of eighteen people treated for smoke inhalation that night. One girl cracked a rib in the crush (was she the one I'd seen fall? I never did find out) and one guy had concussion from an ambulance reversing into him, winning hands-down the prize for the most ridiculous injury. No one died, which goes to show that even when you think things are pretty fucked up, there's always the potential for them to get worse. That's the lesson I tried to take from it anyway. That and make sure you know where the exits are at all times.

We came home the next day. None of us wanted to stay any longer. Cat, the girl who was getting married, took it as an omen and broke off the engagement, so at least some good came of it. For a while I had dreams about it: I'd wake in the night, heart racing, and have to go downstairs and check that everything was OK, feeling for heat with the back of my hand against the doors before opening them. I made my parents get another smoke alarm so there was one downstairs as well as up; it went off every time someone burnt the toast, which was often, but they were treating me with kid gloves and not even Nat complained.

For the first couple of years afterwards we'd phone each other on the anniversary. Nothing was ever arranged, but somehow between our group of friends we'd check in on everyone who'd been there, make sure we were all OK. We didn't talk about what had happened – no one wanted to relive the details – but we knew we all remembered it and that was enough. Eventually the calls hadn't seemed necessary any more; sometimes we exchanged messages on Facebook and sometimes we didn't, and that was OK too.

But I never forgot the lessons.

And now this. This doodle.

I knew it was Alice. The sneakiness, the passive aggression, the way the drawing was tucked into the corner of the date of the anniversary, tucked away just like Alice herself. Of course it was her. She must have snuck out to the kitchen during the book club meeting. But why? Was she letting me know she knew something about me, like she'd done when she referred to my parents? Was I supposed to feel powerless because she knew about my past while I knew nothing about hers?

I felt a surge of anger. Who cared about Alice's past? There was nothing she knew about me that wasn't public knowledge. The fire had got a few column inches in the press at the time, Mum and Dad's minor celebrity adding a bit of gloss; anyone could have found out about it if they'd looked.

I stooped and picked up the flyers and the catalogues. I'd put them out for recycling. Then I ripped out the page for September from the calendar, tore it into confetti and added it to the pile. Alice wouldn't make me get rid of a gift from my brother, but there was no way I was going to stare at that drawing until the end of the month.

The 25 September had been marked in my mental calendar for so long, it never occurred to me then what Alice meant. It should have been obvious, but I didn't get it. I didn't get it at all.

*

I planned to have it out with her. No more asking other people's opinions, no more worrying what she'd tell my friends, or if they'd take her side instead of mine. I'd wait for her to come home and then go straight over there, catching her off guard, asking her what she thought she was playing at. I stood at the window watching for her, rehearsing what I'd say.

Nothing sounded right. If I accused her of trespassing, I'd sound unhinged – she'd been here at my invitation only the previous evening. If I told her I knew she'd drawn on my calendar, I'd sound like a toddler complaining that someone had played with her toys. I could picture it, Alice standing there with that smirk of hers, pretend-bemused: *Goodness, Lucy! Why would you I imagine I'd do such a thing?*

I started to lose my nerve. I told myself I'd give it another ten minutes and if Alice hadn't come back it would be a sign I should leave it alone. Six minutes later I realised I was going to do that anyway, and sloped into the living room to try to numb my brain with teatime TV. I skipped through the channels and settled on a quiz show populated by middle aged men in short-sleeved shirts. The host was asking, 'What comes next in the sequence: Herbert, Jefferson, Walker . . .'

I pulled my phone from my pocket. Still nothing from Liz.

The shirts were conferring. Presidents, surely, it had to be something to do with presidents. 'I'll have to hurry you . . .'

Maybe I should call her. Share what had happened. I started to dial and then remembered – she was with her mum. It could wait.

The leader of the shirts said, 'Clinton,' and the shot switched to the other team. Wrong, then. On the screen, a smooth-faced man with thick glasses was jiggling in his seat, just about managing to stop himself from sticking his hand up. I bet everyone hated him at school.

I selected the photo gallery again. Maybe I'd missed something. Girls in pub. *Swipe.* Girl in pub. *Swipe.* Boy and girl in pub.

'Hussein!' yelped Smooth Face. I snorted. No way was that right.

Here was one taken in the office. Someone had suggested Waites take part in a charity fund-raising thing involving wearing pyjamas to work. Liz was standing next to her boss, Lawrie/Leery, wearing satin PJs with a print of watermelons. Where did she find those clothes?

The host purred in appreciation. 'That's right! They're all second names of presidents of the United States!' *Oh come on.*

Lawrie's pyjamas were pale blue cotton, reminiscent of hospital scrubs, the creases down the front suggesting they'd been bought new for the purpose. As ever, his eyes were fixed on Liz's cleavage. It was a miracle she'd managed to put up with it all these years without punching him.

They were on to the next question, Smooth Face still glowing with pride. 'What comes next: laconicum, caldarium, tepidarium . . .' Something to do with the periodic table? Christ, these were hard. Maybe I should make myself feel better and switch to *The Chase.*

I looked again at the photo. I hadn't centred it very well. Liz and Lawrie were too far to the left and I'd caught another girl almost out of shot on the right. She was wearing mint flannel pyjamas, a surprising choice for the fashionistas of Waites. Perhaps she was trying to channel Granny Chic.

It was Smooth Face again. 'Frigidarium!' The host beamed. 'And would you like to explain the connection?' Of course he would; he looked like he was about to come all over his buzzer. 'They're Roman baths, in order of temperature.'

Where the hell did they find these people?

I swiped left. A group photo this time, but my motivation for taking it was obvious: Richard was standing in the middle, no pyjamas ('Sorry, guys,' sly wink, 'I sleep naked'), but his jacket was off and his shirt collar unbuttoned to show he was all for taking part. Liz had escaped Lawrie and was flanked by a couple of girlie junior account managers, blonde and tanned, wearing slippy little PJs with spaghetti straps and lace trim. I'd watched Richard giving them the eye earlier. A few guys from accounts, where pyjamas apparently meant shorts and T-shirts; Dan from IT smiling straight at me and probably hoping to get his hands on my tits again if he played his cards right.

And off to the side again was the girl in the mint pyjamas. She'd tried to duck out of the photo by the look of it, but a spotty girl in a SpongeBob SquarePants nightshirt (what was it about the concept of 'pyjamas' that was causing so much difficulty?) had her by the elbow and had pulled her into shot. She was looking down and her hair had fallen across her face, but there was something about the way she stood . . .

I peered closer. Yes, it could be her.

The hair was the wrong colour, dark instead of light brown, and long instead of Alice's neat bob. But the turn of her head, that long neck, the thin lips . . . I zoomed in, hoping to find some telltale sign. I couldn't see any jewellery, and her hands were obscured by the body of the man in front of her. I swiped left again, but found myself looking at a photo of Nat pointing at a cupcake. It had been taken in the tea shop the weekend he'd stayed with me. I'd reached the end of my London photos.

I swiped back again, stopping on the photo of Liz and Lawrie. The girl in the mint pyjamas was at the very edge of the picture but looking at the camera; or looking at me? Perhaps she'd thought she was out of shot. That long hair, though. It was still getting in the way, her fringe dropping over her eyes. Could Alice ever have looked like that? I zoomed in again, but it was impossible to tell.

Tinny applause from the television broke my concentration and I stabbed at the remote control. Quiet settled over the house.

I turned back to the photos, meticulous this time, searching the background of each one for the girl with the long brown hair. But there was nothing. If it was Alice, she hadn't been caught on camera again.

I swiped back to the photo of Liz and Lawrie and attached it to a text message. I needed a second opinion from Liz. I tapped out: *Girl on the right = weirdo neighbour?*

Then I sat back and waited.

Chapter 24

Nine weeks had passed since that night at the Manx, and Alice was busy.

She stood in the doorway of the bedroom that had been hers until her grandmother died and she'd swapped it for the larger room at the front. She'd always kept it neat and tidy, but it had never really felt like it belonged to her. It felt hollow now with all the furniture gone, her footsteps echoing on the bare floorboards. But it wouldn't be that way for long.

She bent and dipped the paintbrush in the paint. Primrose, it was called, one of the paler yellows from the patchwork of shades on the far wall. She hadn't been sure of it at first. She'd stood there with the sample pots lined up at her feet, biting her lip while she peered at one colour then another, trying to imagine what they'd look like covering the whole room. She'd wanted to check with someone, wondering if Lissa or Jenny would come around if she asked them. But no, they'd never done things like that, even when they were supposed to be friends. Anyway, how would they know what Laura would like? It was Alice who was her mother. She was the best judge.

Now she felt the doubt like a cold breath on the back of her neck. Would her own mother have known what Alice liked? But of course, she'd had Alice's father to help. They'd always had each other. And if they'd cared about Alice, they would never have left her.

Her grandmother's voice came into her head: *That's enough of that, Emily. Honour thy father and mother.* Alice took a breath and forced the hands that were halfway to covering her ears back to her sides. Her grandmother was gone. She didn't have to listen to her any more.

She reached out and stroked the paintbrush down the wall. The yellow looked bright and cheerful against the dingy cream of the old paint. Another brushstroke, then another. Each one covered up a little more of the cream. It would be gone soon. Everything would look different.

Later, with the first coat drying on the walls, she collected her coat and bag and headed to the shops. The afternoon was flat and grey, but when she emerged from the tube at Oxford Circus, the store windows glowed with electric light.

She'd already researched the furniture she was going to buy: the cradle that transformed into a bed for when Laura got bigger; the chest of drawers with the baby changing table on top. She'd read all the reviews, but she wanted to see them before she committed, make sure of the quality.

Inside the department store, tinkly music was playing. Alice let it wash over her as she inspected the directory: baby and child, third floor. It was busy, the weekend shoppers out in force. At the foot of the escalators a crowd had formed, and she stretched her hand in front of her, keeping a space between her bump and the thronging bodies. She saw a woman shoot her an odd look, but ignored her.

The furniture section was at the back, and she threaded her way through racks of baby clothes to get there, pausing now and then to take a sleeve or collar between her fingers, marvelling at their delicacy.

Nearby, a clutch of women were picking up bibs and socks, comparing the embroidered motifs. 'Oh look, Hannah, aren't they gorgeous!' An older woman held up a hanger to a younger one, who turned to inspect it at arm's length. Her coat shifted, and Alice saw the bulge of her stomach.

'Lovely, Mum, but I think we've got enough.' The woman called Hannah gestured towards the bags littering the floor. 'I've already spent a fortune today.'

Hannah's mother smiled as she tucked the hanger under her arm. 'I'll just get these. You can never have too many bibs.'

For a moment Alice hesitated, but then her feet were moving of their own accord. The woman looked up as she approached, the smile still in place. She looked kind, Alice thought.

'Excuse me,' she said. 'I hope you don't mind, but I couldn't help overhearing what you were saying. About the bibs.'

'Oh, right.' The woman laughed. 'Well that's one thing about new babies, isn't it? The washing machine is always on!'

Alice's brow crinkled in a frown. 'Is it? I don't know.' She glanced down at her stomach. 'It's my first one, you see. I'm not sure what to get.'

She saw the woman's smile fall a fraction and knew what she was thinking: *Why is she asking me? What kind of person doesn't even have a friend to go shopping with for baby things?*

'I've just finished work,' she improvised. 'I thought I'd try to get some bits and pieces, but I don't really know what I'm looking for.'

'Well, it's never too early to start.' The woman's eyes flickered to Alice's stomach. 'When are you due?'

The question surprised her, but she supposed this was the kind of thing people asked. No one had asked her anything about

Laura until now. How could they? This woman was the first person to know she existed. This was her daughter's introduction to the world.

Alice felt something bubbling inside her. It was an unfamiliar sensation, but her mouth broadened in a smile as she told the woman she had a while to go yet but she wanted to make sure everything was perfect. And suddenly she was telling her about the primrose paint that was low in chemicals, and the woollen carpet she was going to buy, and the baby clothes made only of natural fibres.

They were still talking as Hannah and the other women moved away, and Alice followed along with Hannah's mother. She had so much to tell her, so much to ask, and she could see she was just as excited about Laura as Alice was herself. They passed the furniture section on the way to the tills, and Alice pointed out the chest of drawers with the changing table on top. Hannah's mother agreed it was a very sensible idea.

And all the time there was that feeling bubbling away inside her.

Hannah's mother paid for the bibs, and Alice looked around for signs to the café. They could get something to drink while they arranged when they'd next meet up. Perhaps they could come back here, look at the prams. Alice had narrowed it down to a couple of options, but a second opinion would be useful. It was a lot of money, after all.

Hannah and her friends were waiting at the end of the till – perhaps she should invite them for a coffee too? She could compare notes with Hannah, find out whether any of the others had children. She turned to ask Hannah's mother what she thought, but she was walking past her, heading straight for Hannah and her friends. They started to move away and Alice began to follow, thinking it was a mistake, that Hannah's mother hadn't realised she wasn't with them; but then she saw her turn, one hand raised in a half-hearted wave. 'Nice to meet you!' she called back over her shoulder. 'Good luck with it all!'

And then Alice realised: Hannah's mother was just like all the others. She wasn't really interested in Alice. She didn't really care about her. She didn't care about Laura either.

With an effort, she unclenched her fist. The palm of her hand was warm with blood where her fingernails had cut the flesh. She laid it on her stomach, wanting to protect the little life inside. 'It's all right,' she whispered. 'You've got me. We've got each other.'

She couldn't feel the bubbles any more. The feeling had drained away. Now that it was gone, she thought she knew what it was, the name to give the unfamiliar sensation. She'd feel it again, she told herself: when Laura was born and it was the two of them together.

She'd feel happy.

Alice sips from the china cup. She's had to order already so they won't kick her out: the tea shop gets busy in the afternoons, and she supposes they have to cater for the tourists however much of a nuisance they are. Gem, the woman at the counter, had been apologetic and said she didn't like to rush local people, and Alice had smiled at being included in that description and replied that she didn't mind at all. Which she didn't. It isn't Gem's fault Tom has such appalling timekeeping.

It's a sign of bad manners. Imagining he's more important than anyone else, that his time is more precious than hers. Alice feels the heat rising and takes a breath. Not much longer now, and he'll find himself having to make more of an effort if he wants to keep any friends at all. Lucy won't be amongst them, though.

She lets her gaze travel around the shop. Most of the people here are day-trippers; you can spot them a mile off – cameras and maps, waterproof jackets and those Velcro sandals they all seem to wear. Her own grandparents would never have visited somewhere like this: the trips they'd taken had been to the coast, places like Margate and Ramsgate, her grandad knotting a handkerchief on his head to keep off the sun, just like one of the men on the postcards they used to sell in the little shops on the front. Alice had never liked those postcards.

This is different, though. The kind of place she'd have liked to come before, if only she'd known it existed. Quieter. Genteel. It's funny the way things work out: if it hadn't been for that woman, she might never have realised she wanted to live in the Cotswolds. In Willowcombe itself, in fact. Now she can't imagine living anywhere else.

That's why things have to be done properly. She doesn't want the rest of them harping on about how terrible it was, and if only *Lucy* had been here to see this, and what would *Lucy* have said about that. They have to see her for what she is. They have to understand they should never have been her friends.

Of course, she'll have to be subtle. Lucy has her suspicions, that's clear. And you have to be careful about exposing people's lies: things don't always turn out the way you expect. She's not having the other three ganging up on her, cutting her out when they should be thanking her for telling them the truth. So there'll need to be a bit of – what do the newspapers call it? – collateral damage. Create a little distance between them all, just for now. It's unavoidable, and besides, they deserve to be punished too. Not as much as Lucy, but they've lied all the same, and big lies at that. She can't just let that go.

A figure appears at the door: seven minutes late, which she supposes by his standards counts as prompt. She waves to Gem and orders him a latte.

* * *

Tom would have preferred to meet in the pub – would have preferred, in fact, not to meet at all, but there's something about Alice that's difficult to say no to. He'd been surprised when she'd called to arrange coffee, hadn't even realised that she had his number; but if it keeps her from sending Ferdy into a frenzy by visiting the house, he isn't going to complain.

He made sure his organiser was stowed away in his desk before he left, and he's double-locked the back door too. Tom has never subscribed to the notion that one shouldn't lock one's doors in the country – the city doesn't have a monopoly on dodgy characters – but he's been especially careful since the episode with the answerphone. There's probably an innocent explanation, but it doesn't hurt to be cautious; and halfway down the drive he'd turned and scrunched his way back to the front door, giving it a firm tug to make sure that it too was locked.

He hopes Alice doesn't want to talk about Lucy again. He'd kept his eye on her at Rebecca's and again last night. She'd had a few glasses of wine, but no more than the rest of them, and considerably fewer than Maggie. If she has a problem, she's hiding it well; though Tom has enough experience to know that alcoholism and duplicity go hand in hand. Either way, it's none of Alice's business, however good her intentions. If she raises the subject again, he'll – politely, of course – tell her so.

The tea shop is as full as he'd expected and it takes him a moment to locate Alice at a table towards the back. The day is baking hot – ridiculous for September – and it will be even stuffier there, away from the door. Why hadn't he persuaded her to go to the pub?

She waves at him and he threads his way through the tables.

'I got you a latte. I hope that's OK.'

Tom smiles and takes the seat opposite her, thinking: *Dear God, surely she could have chosen something cold?* 'Thanks. Everything all right?'

It sounds abrupt to his ears, but Alice doesn't seem to notice. 'Oh fine, fine. I just wanted to give you this.'

He takes the book from her hands with a grimace, and Alice laughs. 'I told Lucy you wouldn't approve, but she was quite insistent.'

'*Fanny Hill*? Don't tell me this was her choice?'

Alice nods. 'She said it was historically significant.'

'It's eighteenth-century porn.' A man in a cagoule at the next table looks up with interest. 'Well, I suppose that counts in a way.'

'Those who do not learn from the mistakes of history are bound to repeat them.'

'Isn't that Santayana? Misquoted?' A flush speckles Alice's throat. He's annoyed her, though God knows how. He says, 'It's actually "Those who cannot remember the past are condemned to repeat it." Although he said it in Spanish, of course, so there's some flexibility in translation.'

A tight smile. 'Thank you, Tom. I'll remember that.' Alice picks up the menu. 'In any case, Lucy seemed to think there would be some lessons for us in the text.'

Tom raises an eyebrow. 'Not likely, I wouldn't have thought, unless she's planning on turning our book club into a swingers' group.' The man in the cagoule looks over again and nudges his wife.

Alice is still studying the menu. 'She seemed to think you'd know what she meant.'

For a moment he thinks he's misheard her. Then the buzz in the tea shop fades away as the words sink in.

Alice looks up. 'I was debating getting a scone, but I think I'll pass. There's no point eating if you're not really hungry, is there?' She leans towards him and reaches for his arm. 'Are you all right, Tom? You've gone quite pale.'

He draws back. 'Bit of a headache. I think I've had too much sun.'

'Would you like a glass of water? You really don't look well.'

'It's fine. Sorry, Alice. I'm just not . . .'

She waves to the woman at the counter. 'Gem, could we get a glass of water over here?'

He knows if he looks up that the man in the cagoule will be staring at them. They'll all be staring at him if this gets out. How the fuck has Lucy found out?

'Honestly, it's fine.' He looks over at the woman behind the counter and forces himself to smile. 'I'm good with the coffee, thanks.' She swivels on her heel, flapping a tea cloth in a way that suggests she doesn't have time for this kind of thing in the middle of the afternoon rush.

He turns back to Alice. 'So what else did Lucy say?'

She tips her head to one side. 'About the book?'

'About why she thought I'd get it.'

'I thought you'd know.'

Is she deliberately evading the question? Tom shrugs. 'No idea, I'm afraid.'

'Well then.' Alice pushes back her chair. 'I must be on my way. I just wanted to give you that – no, don't get up. You look like you should stay put for a few minutes. And you should get a glass of water. It's much better at hydrating you than coffee.'

She collects her bag from beneath the table. She's leaving and still she hasn't answered his question. Tom holds out the book. 'Don't you want to keep this?'

'No, you take it. I'm going into Tewkesbury tomorrow. I expect I'll find a cheap copy somewhere.' She's almost at the door when she turns, her voice carrying over the hum in the shop. 'Don't worry, Tom. I'm sure we'll all find out what Lucy meant at the next meeting.'

He watches her leave, the sting of bile at the back of his throat.

* * *

Maggie looks down at the cardboard box in her hands and musters a suitably grateful expression. 'Thank you, David. That's really . . .' she struggles for a word, 'practical.'

He takes it from her. 'Well, now you've got that book club of yours, I thought it would be easier than having to order books from town.'

'We're reading the classics, David. They're not exactly difficult to find.' She catches his expression and hurries on. 'But this is more convenient, of course.'

He extracts the e-reader from its polystyrene bed and holds it out to her. 'The power button is there on the bottom, look. I've already programmed in your details.'

God, she hates these things. They're so soulless. Still, he means well, and it's been a long time since he's bought her a gift for no reason. She gets up and leans over the back of his chair, putting her arms around him and burying her face in his neck to smell his familiar scent.

Except that it isn't familiar. She pulls back. 'What aftershave is that?'

She feels him stiffen. 'I didn't notice. Some stuff I got for Christmas. From your sister, I think.'

'No, she bought you that jumper, remember. The one you said looked like a cat had been sick on it.'

'Well I don't know.'

She smiles to herself. Even after all their years together, he's still self-conscious about his small vanities. 'I prefer the Cartier stuff.'

'I'll bear that in mind. Look, do you want me to show you how this thing works or not?'

Maggie pats his shoulder and returns to her seat. She's spent all afternoon on the Sissinghursts' study, trying to talk Claudia out of American oak for the flooring – which surely anyone could see would turn the whole look from urban-industrial to New England pastiche – and she'd been looking forward to a long bath and an early night. A thought occurs to her. 'Is it waterproof?'

'For heaven's sake, Maggie, it's an electrical appliance!'

Oh well.

She watches as he runs his finger over the screen, letting her mind wander as he points here and taps there. He loves teaching her things, whether she knows them already or not. Most of the time she finds it endearing, though she'd never have imagined marrying a man like David. Of course she'd never actually thought she'd marry at all, her own parents' relentless cycles of passion, acrimony and sulking making a less than convincing case for the benefits of matrimony. Most of her boyfriends had been brooding, arty types, prone to sitting up all night smoking Camel Lights and debating philosophy. One or two had lasted longer than a few months, but none had ever made her wish to give up her independence for a shared life.

Not until David.

They'd met at an art gallery, at a show being given by a friend of a friend. She'd seen him standing alone in front of a painting, a tall, tweedy figure, all angles, his shoulders hunched as he peered at the canvas. An academic of some kind, she'd assumed. The painting he was staring at had been one of her favourites, layers and layers of dark grey and burgundy with a trail of three-dimensional structures rising up through its centre like a spine. There was something incongruous about the two of them together, and she'd gone over to ask him what he thought of it.

He'd started when she'd spoken and turned to her with furrowed brow, as though she'd set him a particularly difficult maths problem. Then he'd swivelled back to the painting and squinted at the rectangle of white cardboard pinned to the wall next to it. He said, 'It's called *Being from nothingness, part two*.'

Then, when he realised she was waiting for something more, 'It's not really my kind of thing.'

She'd smiled, enjoying his honesty. 'I love it. It's a bit creepy, though, I grant you. Aggressive almost. Bone through flesh.'

He'd looked at her then in a way that was far from academic and the words had hung in the air between them, suggestive in a way she hadn't intended. She'd found herself blushing – she, who hadn't blushed for a decade – and had hurried off, pretending she'd seen someone she knew across the room, feeling his eyes on her as she walked away.

It was much later that evening when he'd found her again and asked her out. She'd been surprised by his directness, and surprised too when, two weeks and three dates later, he'd taken her to bed and proved to be a passionate and attentive lover. Her friends expressed doubts at the match, but they didn't see what Maggie saw. David was ambitious and serious-minded, traits she found she admired; but what she fell in love with was the way the lines in his brow disappeared when she made him laugh. By the time he asked her to marry him, she didn't have to think about her answer.

In the years since, their lovemaking has settled into a comfortable if infrequent routine; their jobs are demanding, and David's research consumes so much of his energy it's hardly surprising that he rarely responds to her overtures. These days she waits for him to make the first move when he isn't too tired or distracted by the events of the day.

Now he's holding the e-reader out to her. 'It's pretty straightforward.'

'So even I should be able to use it.' But she smiles to show she doesn't mind. 'I think Rebecca has one of these. I'll ask her to help me if I get stuck.'

'I would have thought you can manage to work it out if Rebecca can. That reminds me . . .' He shuffles in his seat and examines a spot on the wall behind her head. 'I ran into her this afternoon.'

'Oh? Did she come into the surgery?'

'No, I'd just gone out for a coffee.'

'I didn't think you had time for that kind of thing.'

'Well, anyway . . .' He shuffles again, and she thinks in surprise: *This is what they mean by looking shifty.* 'She told me they'd settled on the book for your next meeting. I've put it on here so you're ready to go.'

She leans across and kisses his cheek. He really is the sweetest man.

* * *

Tom scrapes at the surface of the paint with a palette knife, watching the colours morph and separate. There's an alchemy to this, transforming the surface of the canvas to shade and texture, more satisfying than the chemistry of pills and powders to which his younger self had turned. For once, he's pleased with what's taking shape on the canvas. The colours are vivid, the proportions true. Quinn lies there before him, his chunky, rugby player's arse to the heavens, head turned to the side on an outstretched arm, surveying him from beneath one half-closed eyelid. Even now, the painting partly finished, his essence is there: the swagger and the humour and the lust. It's his best work. How can it be right that he'll never be able to share it?

But Quinn is married now, the father of two small boys with their mother's blonde hair and his own relaxed charm. Tom sees them together from time to time, assembled by one or other of their shared friends, summer barbecues in leafy west London gardens or afternoons in pubs near the river. He likes Fiona, a robust, horsey-looking woman with a raucous laugh, but suspects that the feeling isn't mutual. She was friendly enough when they first met, but on learning that Tom didn't hunt, shoot or play rugby, she'd plainly been at a loss to understand why he'd exiled himself to the Cotswolds, or what he and her husband had in common; and when a girlfriend had joined their group and asked Tom whether he'd found himself a 'nice young man' yet, he could almost hear the cogs turning in that equine head. A shard of ice had entered her eyes then, and it hadn't melted since.

Tom puts down the palette and turns the easel to the wall.

If any of this gets out, Fiona will be the least of his problems. His father, a rampant homophobe, will disown him on the spot. As for his mother . . . He passes a hand across his forehead. His mother will do whatever his father tells her to.

He returns to Alice's words, as he has so many times already. Perhaps he's mistaken her meaning, or perhaps Alice is the one who's mistaken. It isn't like Lucy, surely, to pass on veiled messages – and through Alice, of all people. Much more likely that something has been lost in translation.

The air in the study is treacly, slowing his brain. He needs to get out.

Outside the day has darkened, pewter clouds trapping the heat of the earlier sunshine. Ferdy trots ahead of him down the path, pausing every few moments to snuffle at the grass. There's no sign of life as he passes Mellingford Cottages, the windows and doors shut though the cars parked in front indicate the occupants haven't gone far. Perhaps Rebecca is at Maggie's; though judging by the display the previous evening, there's been some kind of argument there. Tom has no desire to involve himself in it: whatever the cause, they'll patch it up in time. Maggie isn't the type to hold a grudge, even if Rebecca is.

Here's the junction with the lane leading to Maggie's house. For a moment he toys with turning into it, kicking off his shoes and curling up in one of Maggie's cloud-like sofas, telling her everything to the accompaniment of a glass of something red and heavy. After all, he's kept her secret all these years; perhaps it's time to ask her to return the favour.

But no. Maggie is the giver of confidences, he the recipient. That's just the way it is. And no matter how hard she'd try not to, no matter how unshockable she considers herself, he knows she would judge him – not for the thing itself, but for all the years he's listened to her guilt and shame without confiding his own; for the implicit lies in response to her questions about his relationships and the explicit ones when she's asked – in that blunt way of hers – how a watercolour painter in a small village makes enough to live on. The shock would be one from which their relationship would never recover.

They round another bend and the stone walls of St James the Elder rise up on their left. Tom pushes open the lychgate and breathes in the damp, sweet scent of cut grass and rotting leaves. There's no one else in sight, so he lets Ferdy off the lead and ambles after him, reading the inscriptions on the headstones as he goes. A few carry names that are familiar to him, relatives of the longer-established village families, Sullivans and Wainwrights and Josephs.

He's in the older part of the cemetery now, the stones lopsided and beautiful, green with lichen, here and there a praying angel or a crucifix. He wonders whether any of the people in these graves are still remembered, and if so, whether it is with love or anger or regret. Or have all those who knew them now themselves passed to dust and ashes? How will it be for him?

His jaw tightens. He won't just be remembered in the village if this gets out; he'll be notorious. He can imagine how it will be: Cynthia Sullivan, her eyes bright, leaning across the post office counter, pulling the flesh from the bones of his reputation like a carrion crow.

His hands are shaking.

He sinks down on a kerbstone. Christ, how he wishes he hadn't given up smoking. He'd kill for a cigarette. He takes a deep breath instead, and then another.

No one knows. How can they? He's always been so careful.

Except that time in Tewkesbury.

The memory hits him like cold water. He'd known, hadn't he, that he shouldn't have met Quinn there, known he'd want one of his danger fucks to celebrate their anniversary. He'd known and he'd done it anyway. What if they'd been seen?

Stupid stupid stupid.

His hand curls into a fist.

But Lucy? She's his friend. And she isn't some innocent. If Lucy had seen something, would she really have been so shocked that she couldn't bring herself to talk to him about it?

Perhaps. Perhaps if she'd seen Quinn press those notes into his hand. And if she really is sending him a message with her choice of book club material, that's exactly what must have happened.

His fist smashes into the kerb, pain splintering through his knuckles and up his arm. He swears and presses his injured hand into his armpit. At his feet, Ferdy whines, chocolate eyes on his face. Tom reaches down and caresses his head, and Ferdy whines again and licks his hand.

He tells himself again: *It could be nothing.* What if he storms over to Lucy's, demanding she tell him why she chose that book, and she doesn't have a clue what he's talking about?

He mustn't panic. If Lucy's found him out, if she feels she needs to tell their friends, so be it. He'll deal with the consequences. And if she hasn't, if this is all – please God – the product of his own fevered paranoia, he'll count his blessings and never, ever take any kind of stupid risk ever again.

He gets to his feet and starts to retrace his steps, but Ferdy has caught the scent of something in the other direction and Tom lets him have his way; he'll make a circuit of the cemetery and then head back.

If he'd turned back along the path, he might have seen the inscription on the headstone with the weeping cherub. He might have paused to read it, feeling a fleeting pity for the little girl who died in the Year of Our Lord 1863, aged just six years old. Life was hard back then, he might have thought, for William and Henrietta who lost their beloved daughter. And then hc might have felt the breath catch in his throat as he read the name beneath, telling himself it was coincidence while knowing that it wasn't.

Alice Emily Darley.

Chapter 25

I read *Fanny Hill* cover to cover. And I knew there was something wrong.

I couldn't think why Tom had suggested it. At first I told myself it didn't matter, but as the day of the next meeting approached, the anxiety began to grow. I had a feeling, hard to put into words, that nothing good would come of it. It felt like the book club was tainted. Every time we met, something seemed to go wrong: Alice bursting into tears, that stupid argument about abortion. There'd been nothing so dramatic when I'd hosted, it was true; but then I remembered Liz backing away from Alice, telling me afterwards that she'd recognised her from somewhere.

It felt like it was building. That if we met again, something bad would happen.

I tried to tell myself I was being ridiculous; but then I'd find myself staring into space, making connections I wasn't sure what to do with. Alice had likened herself to Jane Eyre. Could Maggie have seen herself as Tess of the d'Urbervilles? Had that been the reason for her sudden exit? Perhaps she'd had an abortion, or knew someone who had, and Rebecca's remarks had struck home.

It would explain the sudden cooling of their friendship. And if that was right, was one of us supposed to recognise ourselves in the inspector, or perhaps the family he called on? And now Fanny Hill. Who was the 'woman of pleasure'?

I tried again to contact Liz, but her phone was going straight to voicemail and I left another message to add to her collection. I sounded manic but I didn't care. I needed to know what she'd found out about Alice.

In a bid to stop myself staring at the phone, I decided to call on Maggie. I'd ask her about registering as self-employed and perhaps sound her out on missing the next book club meeting, see how it was likely to go down. Alice would be working at the post office, so there'd be no risk of running into her there again. I took my mobile with me – Maggie's house got better reception than mine, and perhaps Liz had sent a text that hadn't got through.

My head was full of thoughts of Alice as I walked down the lane to the Old Forge, but at the sight of the car in the driveway, I forgot all about her. It was a black Mercedes, showroom-new.

The car I'd seen bouncing up and down in the car park in Tewkesbury.

A picture flashed into my head: blonde hair, chic jacket, high heels clicking across the wet tarmac. It might have taken me a moment to recognise her, but it was Rebecca. Rebecca, with her homemade biscuits and her spotless kitchen and her organic cotton children's wear.

I stood in the middle of the lane, my mind racing. Had it been David wearing those skinny jeans? Did Maggie know? Was that why she'd been sniping at Rebecca at the book club? Why Rebecca had been bringing me mid-morning cookies and asking whether I'd noticed anything wrong with her? But it didn't make sense. If Maggie had found out, I could imagine her practising her golf swing on David's car – or Rebecca's, for that matter – but contenting herself with sarky remarks? No, that wasn't Maggie.

I might have turned back then, gone home to mull it all over; but at that moment Maggie emerged from the house with two empty wine bottles for the recycling bin. She saw me and waved.

'I see you've spotted David's new baby.' Maggie nodded towards the car and rolled her eyes. 'He claims it's more fuel-efficient than the Audi, but you know what men are like. Any excuse to trade up to a newer model.'

Her words hit me like a fist, but there was no sign that she'd meant anything by them. I stared at her stupidly while she turned and headed for the kitchen, calling back over her shoulder to ask if I wanted coffee. My mind racing, I followed her past David's study, strains of a Bach concerto coming from behind the door. Photos of the two of them sat in their usual place on the hall table: whatever Rebecca had done to upset her, Maggie didn't know the worst of it.

I tried my best to behave normally, asking my rehearsed questions and nodding mechanically as Maggie replied with what was probably good, solid advice if I'd actually been listening to it. After a while I pretended to have what I needed and said goodbye. At the door, I turned as if struck by a thought and said, 'Are you still planning to go to the book club tomorrow?'

Maggie laughed. 'Wouldn't miss it for the world. I've actually read this one!'

'I was thinking I'd pass.' I shrugged. 'Not sure I've got a lot to add to the conversation.'

Maggie wrinkled her nose. 'Tom will never forgive you if you mess up his seating plan. You know he's almost as bad as Rebecca about that stuff.' She placed a heavy hand on my arm, bracelets jangling on her wrist. 'Anyway, we'd miss you.'

I felt suddenly protective of her. How dare that husband of hers be shagging around behind her back? And how dare Rebecca, two-faced cow that she was, swan around playing domestic goddess while betraying not only her own family but the woman who was supposed to be her best friend? And yes, I know – pots and kettles. But at least Melanie wasn't my friend.

I wondered if I should tell Maggie what I'd seen. In a place like Willowcombe, it was bound to come out sooner or later. I could tell her the bare facts, draw no conclusions – perhaps it hadn't been David's car after all, or perhaps it had been borrowed by a colleague – and leave it to her to decide what to do about it.

And Maggie would say, 'Thank you so much, Lucy, for letting me know. I'm really grateful for your honesty.'

Maybe not.

I said, 'I'm not sure that the book club was such a good idea.' She raised an eyebrow, and I struggled on. 'It's just that we always seem to have some kind of drama, don't we?'

'Do we?'

'Well, there was that thing with Alice the first time . . .'

Maggie's smile hardened a fraction. 'She was upset, that's all. People are allowed to get upset.'

I nodded as if I were sitting on a dashboard. 'Oh, of course, of course. But then there was the discussion about *Tess* and, well, you know, Rebecca going all pro-life . . .'

'Well, everyone's entitled to their own opinion, I suppose.' But her fingers had tightened on the door frame. She said, 'Look, Lucy, I wouldn't worry about any of that. It's not a big deal. And your evening was fine – no drama there.'

Except you spending the whole time needling Rebecca. And Liz backing away from Alice like she was a rabid dog.

I forced a smile that felt like it was splitting skin. 'You're right. And I wouldn't want to come between Tom and his seating plan!' I turned to leave. 'I'll see you there tomorrow.'

As I reached the end of the drive, I turned back to wave, keen to leave the impression that none of this had been of the least importance; but Maggie had gone.

I took a last look at the black Mercedes and headed for home.

I was almost late getting to Tom's, and the noise from the kitchen told me everyone else was there already. I'd considered ringing with an excuse – a headache (already taken) or some kind of plumbing emergency – but everything I came up with rang hollow, and after the conversation with Maggie, I knew she at least would see right through it. In the end, I'd driven to Tewkesbury to buy some posh chocolates for Tom, dug out a dress from the dwindling supply of outfits that hadn't yet seen Willowcombe's nightlife, and set off with the uplifting thought that it was best to get it over with.

The back door was wide open, and Tom spotted me as I approached.

'Lucy! Come on in. No, of course you're not late. Have a glass of wine – I'd offer you a tot of Aunt Lydia's special, but I think we'd better save that for the *après-lecture*!' His face contorted in a stagey wink.

I made to take the glass from him, but then I saw his hand. An angry bruise spread from the knuckles almost to the wrist. He saw me flinch.

'Yes, gruesome, isn't it? The cord has gone on one of the sash windows. As I discovered when it fell on my hand.'

'Jesus, Tom, how heavy are your windows?'

'Oh, you know these old houses . . .' He wouldn't meet my eye.

I held out the chocolates. 'I didn't trust myself to choose a wine that would pass muster.' It had been intended as a joke, but something had gone wrong with my voice and it came out sounding sarcastic. I hurried on. 'I got these from that little place in Tewkesbury, you know, next to that restaurant, what's it called . . .?'

Oh Jesus, what had I said now? Tom's smile had vanished and he was staring at me as though I'd crawled out from under a stone. I said, 'I should have brought wine. I can always pop back home—'

He cut me off with a laugh and a shake of his head, and there was the old Tom again. I told myself I was imagining things.

'Where's Ferdy?'

He grimaced. 'He's having an evening with the Williamses.' He saw my question. 'They've got the farm further along. I thought it was best . . .' He gave an infinitesimal nod in Alice's direction.

She was talking to Maggie, their heads close together. Rebecca was standing to one side, trying to look absorbed in an old map on Tom's wall.

Tom followed my gaze and sighed. 'Come on. I think we'd better go and rescue her.'

It was stuffy in the kitchen, despite the open doors, and it was a relief when Tom ushered us into the room he called the snug. It was cooler there, evidently a side of the house not reached by the sun, and when Tom bent and switched on a couple of table lamps, they suffused the battered old chesterfield and wingback chairs with a gentle glow. Everyone sat down, and the split in the group that had been so obvious in the kitchen seemed to soften and blur.

Tom picked up a copy of *Fanny Hill* from the side table next to his chair, and like an orchestra obeying a raised baton, we reached for our bags and withdrew our own.

'An e-reader!' Alice pointed to the device in Maggie's hands. 'I thought you preferred paper and ink?'

Rebecca looked pleased. 'They really are ever so convenient. When did you get it?'

‘I didn’t.’ For a moment it seemed as if Maggie would say nothing more, but then she relented. ‘It was a present from David. Apparently I need to join the twenty-first century.’

Had Rebecca’s face betrayed the slightest flicker at his name? I couldn’t be sure.

Tom cleared his throat. ‘Ladies, as host this evening, I absolutely forbid any further discussion of format. No comparison of electronic versus paper, no font size or page counts. Tonight we are going to focus on proper topics for a book club discussion. One,’ he counted on his fingers, ‘structure; two, plot; three, characterisation; and four, style.’

He glared at us with mock severity and I found myself smiling. Perhaps this would be all right after all.

Alice had taken the spot on the sofa next to Maggie, and I watched her from across the room as the conversation flowed, hastening to agree with everything Maggie said, ready to supply an example to support every observation. I almost expected Maggie to reach across and pat her on the head. *Good Alice! Clever Alice!*

I could see that Rebecca didn’t like it either. She kept glancing in their direction, a puzzled look on her face that made me wonder whether she and Maggie had exchanged less-than-flattering opinions of Alice in times past. Then I wondered whether they’d done the same about me, and wished I hadn’t.

With an effort I brought my attention back to the discussion. Tom had been true to his word and had navigated us past structure and plot and on to characterisation. Rebecca was saying something about there being too many characters, and Tom was trying not to laugh. I looked over at Alice. She was perched on the edge of the sofa, her hands folded in her lap. As if on cue, she spoke, ignoring Rebecca’s comment. ‘But the subtitle is interesting, isn’t it?’ She tipped her head to one side on that long neck. ‘*Memoirs of a Woman of Pleasure*. I’m not sure that’s what Fanny is.’

‘In what way, Alice?’ Tom had been tense earlier, I’d thought, but since we’d started discussing the book, he’d seemed to unwind, leaning back in his chair and stretching out his legs.

‘Well, it seems to me that she’s really more of an instrument for other people’s pleasure.’

I snorted and tried to cover it with a cough. Alice swung towards me. ‘You don’t agree, Lucy?’

There was something about the way she said it that pushed my buttons. Or maybe it was just that I was fed up of hearing her voice, her half-baked opinions regurgitated from a GCSE revision guide; or the way she was cosying up to Maggie, as if no one would remember that a few weeks ago she’d been all over Rebecca, begging for a tour of her ‘beautiful home’, salivating over the washable fucking seat covers.

I said, ‘No, actually, I don’t.’

‘Will you tell us why?’ *Us.* As if everyone else agreed with her. I met her eyes and she smiled, sugar sweet with a hint of teeth.

‘Just that that’s exactly the kind of anti-sex bullshit dressed up as feminism that really pisses me off.’ I heard Tom’s intake of breath, but I was getting into my stride. ‘I mean, it’s as if a woman can’t be allowed to enjoy sex! She has to be someone’s victim, or she’s being used, or she thinks she’s happy but she isn’t really, or she’s using sex as a way of covering up some terrible void.’

I looked around the room. The others looked interested, I thought.

‘I mean, no one would be trying to spin that line if Fanny were a bloke.’ I drew a breath. ‘Why can’t she just enjoy a good shag?’

Alice had drawn back in her seat, her mouth a prim ‘O’ of horror. Rebecca was bent over her e-reader, apparently intent on the text. Sitting like that, her body blocked my view of Tom. I wonder now whether things would have worked out differently if I’d been able to see his reaction.

Maggie raised her glass with a grin. 'And amen to that.'

Another moment and Alice said, 'We can see you have strong opinions about this, Lucy!' That fucking *we* again. 'But surely, most prostitutes are women. I'm not sure imagining Fanny as a man is very relevant.'

'That's not the point. I'm talking about her motivation.'

'But you said, what if she were a man?'

Christ, she was annoying. 'I'm just saying we wouldn't be having this discussion. People expect men to enjoy sex.'

'So are you saying that a male prostitute wouldn't have to deal with any social consequences?'

'Of course I'm not!'

Alice pressed a finger to her lips as though suppressing a smile. There was something about it that made me uneasy. She swivelled on her seat, her knees pressed tightly together. 'What do you think, Tom?' That tinkly laugh. 'As our sole male reader?'

'Actually, I think we should bring this to a close.' He got to his feet and I looked up at him in surprise. 'I need to attend to the cooking, I'm afraid.'

Rebecca said, 'But we haven't done the last one yet. What was it? Style.'

Tom looked at me and a vein throbbed beneath the skin at his temple. 'I'm sure Lucy can take charge. She seems to have plenty to say tonight.'

He left the room, glass in hand. Into the silence Maggie said, 'Don't worry, Lucy, he's been funny all evening. I think it's his time of the month.'

Alice sat and smiled, sugar sweet and a hint of teeth.

Tom stayed in the kitchen while we tried to keep the conversation going, but there was only so long we could recite descriptions of genitalia, and by the time he summoned us to the table, we'd moved on to agreeing the book for the next meeting: *Madame Bovary* by Flaubert. I'd never read it, but it had been Maggie's suggestion, and Rebecca and Alice had seemed happy enough with the choice when she'd assured us that there wouldn't be a single 'stiff staring truncheon' in sight.

We were ushered into the dining room, the first time I'd seen that part of the house, candlelight glinting off the crystals of the chandelier above the table. I tried not to fixate on all those little points of light, the way it would just take a careless arm to turn them into something different, wild and angry. The grandeur of the room was unsettling, reminding me that Tom came from a different world to mine, one about which I knew almost nothing. He moved around on silent feet, depositing before us amuse-bouches of something pink and foamy in small glasses, conversation replaced by murmurs of appreciation and the tinkle of cutlery. The empty glasses were whisked away and the starters presented, Tom receiving the compliments as his due, Rebecca weighing the silverware in her hand with reluctant approval and struggling to conceal her annoyance that he'd trumped her evening with an extra course.

I tried to engage Tom in conversation, first about the meal then the paintings on the wall, how often he'd visited the house when his aunt lived there; but he answered me with monosyllables, refusing to meet my eye. He was quieter with the others too, I thought, and when we were ensconced in the snug once more and sipping at his excellent coffee, he made no attempt to hide his yawns.

Rebecca was the first to take the hint, the decision no doubt made easier by the meaningful glances and whispered asides being exchanged constantly between Maggie and Alice. She rose from her seat, handbag clutched in front of her, claiming that she needed to make sure the children were in bed and Sam had done the washing-up. There was a brief, awkward silence as we each computed the permutations of who would walk her home and who would stay. I saw Tom resigning himself to make the offer and got to my feet before politeness forced him to it.

'I'll come with you, Rebecca. I should get back myself.' No one asked why, and a childish disappointment stabbed at my insides. Maggie and Alice raised their hands in farewell, Maggie's right and Alice's left in perfect synchronicity. Rebecca saw it too and laughed, a hard, brittle sound. She said, 'I'll see you two BFFs at the next one,' and stalked out with me trailing in her wake.

At the door, she air-kissed Tom's cheeks and stepped out into the night. I turned to him to say goodbye, but his face was set in an expression of such fury that I took a step backwards. He reached for my arm and pulled me towards him, his fingers pinching the soft skin above my elbow. I said, 'Tom, what . . .' but his mouth was next to my ear and I felt hot breath and spit as he spoke.

'I don't know what the fuck you're playing at, Lucy, or how you found out; but if you breathe a word to anyone, *I will fucking end you*.'

He released me and I stood there shaking as the door closed in my face.

Chapter 26

Alice settles herself at the kitchen table and picks up the embroidery hoop. She'll do a bit of cross-stitch before bedtime, just to settle her mind.

The book club meeting had gone better than she'd dared hope – but, she reminds herself, it had come close to unravelling. Too close by half. She must learn from that; she can't afford to make another mistake.

The risk she'd taken in the tea shop with Tom had been stupid, but her anger had got the better of her. How dare he patronise her like that, with his 'flexibility in translation', his posh-boy sneer? He had no idea who she was, what she'd endured, what she could do to him if she chose. So she'd flung out the line a little further than she'd intended, and had been rewarded by seeing that sneer wiped right off his face.

It had been a satisfying moment, but afterwards had come the doubts, the realisation that she might have pushed him to confront Lucy alone, that it might undo all her careful preparations. She'd imagined the conversation: the angry accusations, the shouting, the denials that at first he wouldn't believe; then Lucy, 'But Alice told me *you'd* suggested the book'; the silence as they looked at each other, putting together the pieces.

By the time she'd got through the door of the cottage, her mouth was flooded with saliva and she'd run to the bathroom to be sick, holding onto the edge of the toilet seat and heaving until her stomach ached. She'd been due at the post office that afternoon, but when Cynthia answered the phone and heard her voice hoarse from vomiting, she'd accepted her excuses with no more than a sorrowful observation that Cyril would have to pick the runner beans by himself.

She'd spent the rest of the day at her dining room window, peering around the edge of the curtain, waiting for Tom to appear. Her nan's voice ran through her head, making it difficult to think. *Temper, temper, Emily. Temper, temper.* She said aloud, 'Shut up,' and dug her fingernails into the skin on the inside of her wrist.

Eventually she'd heard the footsteps. She went cold all over then, knowing even before she saw the flash of white shirt against the hedgerow that it was him. But his eyes were fixed on the ground and his pace didn't slow. The dog was with him. He was just taking it for a walk.

She'd allowed her breathing to ease while she made sense of it all. Tom hadn't called at Lucy's. He wasn't going to ask her why she'd chosen that book. Now that she was calmer, she thought she understood: he was incapable of believing he was really in danger. Someone like him, he'd been getting away with things all his life. Why imagine that was going to stop now? No, he'd be telling himself not to jump to conclusions, that no one could know his dirty little secret. He'd think he'd been too clever, too discreet. He wouldn't believe that she, quiet, stupid little Alice, with her *misquotes* – she'd curled her nails into her wrist again then – could have found him out.

So he'd wait for Lucy to make the first move. And Alice had seen to it that she did.

In the end, tonight had been easy. There were even unexpected bonuses: Lucy telling Tom that she'd bought those chocolates next door to the restaurant where he'd met his – what did they call them? – his *trick*; that was a real stroke of luck. Alice had snuck a look at Tom's tight, pale face and almost expected him to order them all out of there on the spot; but he'd composed himself, still hoping, no doubt, that he was seeing things that weren't there. So she'd had to bide her time and help things along when the moment came. But it had been so simple! He and Lucy could hardly have been real friends in the first place if he was so ready to believe she was going to give him away. No honour amongst thieves, that's what her nan would have said.

And now everything is almost ready. She's laid the groundwork with Maggie, a gentle hint here and there. In truth, it's been harder than she'd expected – Maggie is resolutely uncurious about her husband's whereabouts – but Alice has persevered, nurturing the idea that Rebecca has her sights on him. It's touching, really, that it hasn't occurred to Maggie that the attraction might be mutual: Rebecca is a good-looking woman, if you like that kind of thing (which David clearly does). Perhaps Maggie thinks she's too common for David's tastes – anyone can tell that accent is put on – or maybe she thinks he's above infidelity. Whatever the reason, she's going to get a rude awakening soon enough. She won't be sorry about missing those coffee mornings after that.

It wasn't part of the plan to begin with, but she's found the rift between Maggie and Rebecca strangely satisfying. All she'd wanted at first was to create enough disharmony to avoid them sharing notes, ganging up and talking about her behind her back; she'd had enough of that kind of thing at school to know how it can go. She's come to like Maggie, though, for all that she's done a terrible thing. She has to be punished, that's unavoidable – but when that's done, it will be nice to have her to herself. What was it Rebecca had called them? BFFs. She'd looked it up on the internet when she got home; it means 'best friends forever'. She's never had a best friend before.

But it's important not to get distracted. It's Lucy who's to blame for Alice being alone, Lucy who has to know how it feels to lose the people you care about. She has to suffer.

Maybe she can persuade Rebecca it was Lucy who told Maggie about the affair. She can imagine how Rebecca would react to that. Or get Maggie to think Lucy knew about it and has been laughing at her behind her back? Yes, that might work.

Alice pulls the needle from the fabric. Just that little bit of grass to do next to the gateposts, and then she'll start on the roses. She looks longingly at the pink silk; but no. The roses are yellow. You can't change things just like that. She would have taught her little girl that when she was older. She would have explained to her how important it was to tell the truth, and her curls would have bounced as she nodded and looked up at her mummy with big brown eyes, understanding that it was an important lesson.

Alice's hand strays to her stomach and rests there. That will never happen now, and that's another thing that can't be changed. But truth isn't the only thing that's important. There are other things too.

Things like justice.

* * *

Maggie emerges from the cupboard with a mixing bowl in her hand. 'This will do, won't it?'

Tom nods. 'Anything you don't mind having dog slobber in.'

She fills the bowl at the tap and places it in front of Ferdy, who wags his tail and bends his head to slurp the contents. Next to him, Tom sits at the island on a stool that was a one-off commission from an up-and-coming designer Maggie discovered at Camden Market. She takes a moment to enjoy the aesthetics of the image before taking a seat next to him.

'Everything OK? You're looking a bit peaky, if you don't mind my saying so.'

Tom rakes his fingers through his hair. 'Just stuff. You know.'

'Do you want to talk about it?'

He shakes his head. 'Not really. But thanks.'

Ferdy finishes lapping at the water and sinks onto the floor, settling his head on his paws with a snuffle.

'So . . .'

'So.' A pause, then a sigh. 'Sorry, Maggie, I'm not the best company today.'

'Who said you ever were?'

He smiles then. 'Thanks. Again.'

She should be comfortable with silence, that's what David is always telling her. *There's nothing wrong with just sitting quietly now and again. It doesn't have to mean anything's the matter.* But there *is* something the matter with Tom. She'd seen it last night when he snapped at Lucy, and he'd been out of sorts for the rest of the evening, barely taking part in the conversation.

She tries again. 'It was a lovely meal last night.'

'Hmm. You and Rebecca seemed a bit strained.'

It throws her. 'Why do you say that?'

'You weren't talking much, that's all.'

Maggie grimaces. 'We weren't the only ones then.'

Tom is silent. This is ridiculous. She has to tell him. 'It's been a bit awkward with Becs since I found out.'

'Found out what?'

'That she's got a thing for David.'

She'd expected surprise, shock, maybe indignation, more likely that he'd find it funny. But he just sits there, avoiding her eyes. She says, 'So you knew.'

'Not really.'

'What does that mean?'

He speaks slowly, measuring his words. 'Just that I always thought they seemed to get on well. Considering they're so different.'

'What, that Becs is as thick as two short planks, you mean?' The bitterness in her voice comes as a surprise. 'So do you think she's making a play for him?'

He's studying the view through the window. It's started to rain, fat drops splattering the glass. 'I wouldn't say that exactly.'

'Then what?'

'You should talk to David, Maggie. He's the one you should be asking about this.'

The rain is getting heavier. Perhaps the Indian summer is coming to an end after all. She says, her tone flat, 'Are you telling me there's something going on?'

'No, God no! I'm just saying that if you're worried, you should talk to him about it. Get his side of the story.'

She doesn't like his choice of words, but Tom's lips are set in a tight line and she knows she'll get nothing further from him. And he's right, of course: she should ask David if Rebecca has tried it on with him, find out precisely how angry she needs to be. The things Alice has told her about are no more than flirting, after all: batting her eyelashes at him in the post office, touching his arm and giggling. Knowing David, he hasn't even noticed.

She decides to change the subject, but Tom has got there first. 'So what did you think of the choice of book for last night?'

'Exhausting. I'm too much of an old lady for that kind of thing. What on earth possessed you to choose it?'

Tom holds up his hands. 'Good God, it wasn't me. I just supplied the food. I was only sorry that catering duties meant I missed some of the literary criticism.'

'Well you didn't miss much. We compared engines and truncheons for a bit and that was pretty much it.' She laughs at his look of relief. 'Goodness, Tom, if I'd known how much you cared, I'd have gone and stirred that crab thing for you myself.'

'Now there's an offer.' He picks invisible lint from his shirt. 'Nothing else, then? No interesting observations on influences or motives?'

'Nope. You were there for the juiciest bit, when Alice and Lucy had their little contretemps. I don't think those two really get on, you know.'

'You might be right there.' Tom gets to his feet. 'Anyway, I should be off.' Ferdy scrambles up and leads the way to the door.

'Maggie?'

'Yes, Thomas?'

'What made you think I picked that book?'

She shrugs. 'I don't know.' But then she remembers. 'Alice told me.'

'Alice said that? Are you sure she didn't say Lucy?'

'No, Tom, my memory's not that bad.' She laughs at him. 'There's no need to get defensive. It wasn't that awful.'

But he's fastening the lead to Ferdy's collar and doesn't reply.

* * *

Rebecca grabs the last sock from the line and runs inside. Typical of her luck, and when it was nearly all dry too. She's barely set the laundry basket down when Ellie's shriek has her dashing for the living room.

'For God's sake, what's the matter now?'

Ellie is sitting on the floor, her face pink and crumpled in distress. On the sofa, Oscar lies with his feet on the cushions, the picture of innocence.

'Mummy! He, he . . .' Tears and snot are running down Ellie's face. It's the kind of thing you could never say, thinks Rebecca, but sometimes it's hard to remember that you love your children.

'For God's sake, Oscar, what have you done to her?'

'Nothing!' His outrage is pitch perfect. 'And you blassamed, Mum! You told us not to blassam.'

He means blaspheme, but she's in no mood to find it funny.

'I was watching *Peppa Pig*!' Ellie has controlled herself enough to form a sentence. 'And he turned it over!' She points at her brother with a trembling finger. 'And he won't give me back the 'mote!'

Rebecca screws up her eyes and tries to pretend she's somewhere, anywhere else. For God's sake, can't she leave the room for five minutes without Armageddon descending? And where the hell is Sam?

'Oscar, give me the remote control.'

'But Mum—'

'Now!'

They both jump at her tone. She jabs at the buttons and Peppa trots back across the screen. 'And I don't want to hear another peep out of either of you!'

She storms out with the remote control in hand. At least that will buy her a bit of peace until the bloody programme is over. At the bottom of the stairs, she stops and listens: there it is, just as she'd guessed. The faint hum of the extractor fan. Sam is in the bathroom, probably hunched over one of his comics – sorry, *graphic novels*. Christ, how she hates that! Locked in there for hours, something unmentionable festering in the pan, God alone knows what germs being spread on the pages of those stupid comics, ignoring everything else. Leaving everything to her, like he always does.

She's filled with a sudden rage.

'Sam!' No answer. '*SAM!*'

Nothing. Tears prick at her eyes and she dashes them away with the back of her hand.

No. This isn't how it's going to be. Not tonight, when she has orders to assemble and the proofs of the spring catalogue to approve, and when she still has to nag Oscar about his homework and get Ellie's ballet kit washed and dried for Monday.

A clear, tempting thought forms in her mind. Fuck it. Just fuck it all.

The remote control clatters on the floorboards. Rebecca steps over the batteries that are rolling down the hallway, snatches the car keys from their hook, and slams the front door behind her.

* * *

The sound reverberates in the open air. Three doors along, Alice rises from where she's been kneeling at her flower beds and watches Rebecca storm down the path, car keys dangling from one hand. Her phone, she notes, is already to her ear.

Chapter 27

I didn't march right back and bang on the door until Tom opened it, demand to know what was going on. I didn't cause a scene.

I kept remembering his face, the way he'd looked at me as I'd stood on that doorstep. I'd never seen him look at anyone like that. I wouldn't have imagined he ever could, laid-back, easy-going Tom. But he'd looked at me like I was vermin. Like I needed to be exterminated.

I didn't think he'd listen to anything I had to say. I had no idea what I'd say anyway. All I knew was that, whatever it was, whatever he thought I'd done, it was her. It was Alice. Somehow she'd laid a trap for me and I'd fallen right into it.

That night I lay in bed replaying the conversation in my mind, trying to remember what we'd been talking about before Tom flounced off to the kitchen. I must have said something to upset him.

And I'd known it was coming, hadn't I? Known that something was going to happen at the book club meeting, because something always did.

Because it was the book.

The idea was like an electric shock, jolting me upright in bed. Tom hadn't suggested we read *Fanny Hill*. A bawdy period romp? I'd known it was rubbish as soon as Alice had said it. So why had she lied?

Why had she wanted us to discuss that book?

I dredged my memory. We'd starting talking about the structure, but no one had had much to say about that and we'd moved quickly on to plot. I hadn't had much to contribute; I'd been more interested in watching Rebecca's puzzled glances at Maggie and Alice on the sofa, trying to work out how Alice had usurped her place as Maggie's best pal.

Alice. It was Alice who'd made me say something. She'd been talking about Fanny; that was right, the 'woman of pleasure' thing. Trying to make out that she was some kind of pawn being used for other people's kicks, like she couldn't make her own choices, like she wasn't important enough to have her own motives. She'd said something similar when we'd been talking about *Jane Eyre*: that Jane was being used by Rochester. It had got under my skin then, and it had had the same effect that night.

Just like she'd known it would.

I'd given her the reaction she was looking for, hadn't I? I'd climbed right up onto my high horse, banging on about sexual double standards, saying no one would have a problem with Fanny shagging around if she were a man.

If she were a man. Oh Christ. If she were a man like Tom.

And Alice prodding away with those comments that didn't quite make sense, that didn't quite follow what I'd said but were close enough so that you wouldn't notice the gaps unless you were looking for them.

Alice, with her head tipped to one side, that smile playing on her lips. *Are you saying that a male prostitute wouldn't have to deal with any consequences?*

Oh for the love of God. How had I been so blind?

Good-looking, charming, witty Tom with no sign of a boyfriend, no mention of any exes. Tom, who took such good care of himself. Tom, always late back from who knew where, some flimsy excuse that we all knew wasn't real. Tom, with his big house and his fine wines and his old but expensive-to-run car. Tom, who'd got so prickly that time I'd suggested I could make it in business because he supported himself through his art.

For fuck's sake, Lucy. Watercolours of wild flowers sold in Cotswolds gift shops? What had I been thinking?

Poor Tom.

But no, that wasn't fair. He wouldn't want my pity. And maybe he didn't need it either. Maybe he enjoyed his work, like Fanny. What did I know about it? What did I know about anything? I'd been so naïve, thinking this sleepy little village with its tea shop and its tourists was in some kind of parallel universe, untouched by the realities of life elsewhere. That people here didn't love or hate or fail with the same passion and despair that they did in the city. That they didn't have to make ends meet.

And yet it *was* different here. Things were harder to hide. How did Tom find his clients? How did they find him?

It wasn't important. All that mattered was that she'd worked it out. Clever, quiet, watchful Alice. Somehow she'd worked it out, and she'd found a way to use it against me. Because for some weird, fucked-up, unfathomable reason, it didn't matter what secrets she found out about Tom or anyone else. Because it wasn't them she was out to get.

It was me.

I scrabbled on the bedside table for my phone and it came to life, filling the room with cold blue light and casting shadows into the corners. Contacts, Liz, message. I tapped at the screen.

Call me. Please. I need to talk about Alice.

I'd pressed send too soon. I followed the first text with a second.

As soon as you can. It's important xx

The alerts would probably wake her; I knew that Liz kept her phone next to the bed. She'd be annoyed at being disturbed, but that couldn't be helped. I needed her.

The steely light of dawn was creeping in at the window before I fell asleep, the phone still silent in my hand.

I woke after just a few hours, head aching and skin hot, not rested but unable to stay in bed. I checked my phone: still nothing. There was a loose, queasy knot of anxiety in my stomach and for the first time I wondered whether Liz was all right. It had been two weeks since she'd gone back to London, and I'd heard nothing from her, not even a short line to say she couldn't talk now but would be in touch soon. Even by Liz's easily distracted standards it was odd. Then again, I had to admit I'd hardly been the most reliable communicator since I'd moved to Willowcombe. Perhaps it was a bit rich to expect Liz to respond immediately now that I needed her.

I should try something different, email her at work. If she was ill, someone might have set up an automatic reply; and if she was fine and just too wrapped up in other things to respond, it would get her attention.

It wasn't until I was stepping into the shower that I remembered that today was Saturday. Perhaps she was having a lie-in. She'd see my message, pick up on the urgency and get in touch later. I just had to be patient.

The morning dragged. I checked my phone every few minutes, knowing that it wasn't on silent, that it had plenty of charge, that I hadn't really heard a faint electronic tinkle. Not sure whether

I was more irritated with Liz or myself, I dragged out my boxes of beads and buttons from under my bed, telling myself to do something productive until she called. I sat at the kitchen table selecting colours and textures, remembering Tom's admonition that I needed to know exactly how long it took me to make each piece. I would aim for one bracelet and one pair of earrings in an hour; one bracelet and one pair of earrings, and Liz would call.

She didn't.

I tried ringing her again, but it went straight to voicemail and I hung up in disgust. I sent another text: *Have I done something to piss you off? Please, please call me.*

I went out.

The air was thick with heat. I kept my eyes straight ahead as I walked down the path, but I could feel Alice watching me from her window, her gaze burning into the back of my head. Watching. She was always watching.

The village was too small. Eyes everywhere. I had to get out.

My car was parked at the side of the road. There was no shade, and the heat when I opened the door took my breath away; but I didn't stop even to lower the windows.

I drove.

The road opened up in front of me and I switched on the radio. For a moment I considered driving all the way to London, turning up on Liz's doorstep and showing her the photo of the girl with the brown hair. Perhaps if Liz recognised her, this would all start to make sense. But then the music was interrupted by a traffic report, and a sympathetic-sounding woman told me that there'd been an accident on the M4, and that roadworks were causing tailbacks in both directions on the M25; so at the junction I turned right instead of left, and took the road to Cheltenham.

I returned with five things that day: three of them were a copy of *Madame Bovary*, an application form for a small business loan, and a crisp white card from an adviser at the bank with strong hands and a sensual mouth that made me remember how long it had been since I'd had sex. I had coffee in a big, bright department store, and walked along pavements and looked in windows and went into shops and picked things up and put them down again and no one, *no one* looked at me. No one knew who I was. No one cared.

Afterwards, I sat in the car and put the key in the ignition but didn't turn it. It was better here, away from Alice. I could think.

I reached into the carrier bag on the passenger seat and pulled out the book. The cover showed another woman in period costume, this one even more melancholy than Jane Eyre. I turned it over and read the back: *Emma Bovary is beautiful and bored, trapped in her marriage to a mediocre doctor and stifled by the banality of provincial life.*

What did Alice have planned for us this time? For it was Alice who'd persuaded Maggie to suggest it, I had no doubt of that. Alice who'd selected the book to match the secret. Alice pulling the strings, manoeuvring us into position, waiting for the moment to reveal all, feeding off the misery and anger like the vampire she was.

Marriage to a doctor suggested Maggie; but Maggie didn't seem bored or stifled. And she was devoted to David, speaking with pride of his work and never appearing to notice that he had more than a little of the quality of a stuffed shirt. I read more: *longs for passion and romance . . . fantasies . . . debt . . . adultery.*

Adultery.

I should have realised. If even I had worked out what was going on between Rebecca and David, Alice would have sniffed it out in a heartbeat. How long had she known? Was it before she'd wound her tentacles around Maggie? Was that the purpose? So she could get close enough to whisper in her ear, a little hint here, a sly observation there?

Maggie wasn't stupid. She wouldn't have responded well to tittle-tattle. But the solicitude of a concerned friend? Yes, that was the way that Alice would have played it. *I didn't know whether I should say anything . . . it's probably nothing . . . I know that if it were me, I'd want someone to tell me . . .*

But she hadn't done it yet. Maggie and Rebecca's friendship had cooled ever since that argument over *Tess of the d'Urbervilles*, but surely they wouldn't have been sitting in the same room, managing to maintain a civil conversation, if Maggie actually thought Rebecca had been shagging her husband. And yet there was such distance between them now, the two women whose daily meetings and gossipy girl-talk I'd once so envied. How had Alice done it?

That argument. Another book club meeting. Another stage set by Alice. Abortion. Rebecca railing against its evils, Maggie quiet and pale, leaving early with the migraine she'd forgotten about by the time I called to see her the next day.

Maggie had had an abortion. And somehow Alice had found out about it.

I wondered if David knew. Maggie's reaction suggested not; but perhaps the baby hadn't been his. A youthful indiscretion, perhaps, or an affair. God knew, everyone seemed to be having those. And then Alice had been at Maggie's almost the next day, ready to drip a little more poison in her ear. I didn't need to imagine what she'd said: I'd seen the results. The cancelled coffee mornings, the catty asides, Maggie and Alice ignoring Rebecca like a couple of schoolgirl bullies.

And when the book club next met, it was going to get a whole lot worse. Unless I could find a way to stop it.

By the time I got back, the shadows had lengthened into evening and a spectral moon looked down on Mellingford Cottages. I cut the engine and sat there in the gathering dusk. Perhaps for once I should do the watching.

Alice's car was in its usual spot, and the dim light that spilled from one of the ground-floor windows indicated that she was in the kitchen at the back, the door to the dining room standing open so that the light passed through. I got out of the car and shut the door quietly, then winced at the beep-beep that confirmed it was locked. But nothing stirred at number 1.

It was just a few steps to the silver Renault, and in a moment I was staring in at its bare seats and empty footwells. I don't know what I'd expected to see, but it was sales-room clean, not so much as a sweet wrapper to give a clue to the personality of its owner.

But I knew as much about Alice's personality as I wanted to. I was looking for something else.

The glove compartment. People kept documents in their glove compartment, didn't they? Detectives were always doing that on TV, looking around shiftily before ducking into the passenger seat, pulling out a handful of papers, eyes widening as they found some crucial piece of information. I checked over my shoulder – no sign of another soul. I felt for the door handle and tugged.

For a moment there was nothing; then the shriek of the alarm split the air. I jumped, swore, spun on my heel. Alice stood in front of me.

I felt sweat break out on my brow. How the hell had I missed her? What had she seen?

She was raising her arm; there was something in her hand. She was going to hit me. I couldn't move; but then her hand jabbed the air and the alarm fell silent.

She smiled at me, eyes glittering in the shadows. 'Hi, Lucy.'

I stepped back. 'I was just . . .' I cast around, desperate for the lie. My eyes fell on the car door. 'It looked like it wasn't shut properly. I thought I'd just give it a slam.'

She didn't move. 'That was kind of you.'

I tried to smile. 'But it was locked after all. Obviously.'

'Obviously.'

'But better safe than sorry. Ha ha.'

'Oh yes, always.' She drew out the *s* at the end, *alwaysss*.

'Well, I'd best be getting in . . .' I sidestepped around her and she twisted her head to watch me. There was something serpentine in the movement. I shivered.

She drew back her lips in a grin that showed teeth. 'Looks like the evenings are getting cooler at last. Goodnight, Lucy.'

I didn't trust myself to answer, just raised my hand and scuttled to the door. And when I'd locked it and peered out of the very edge of the window as I drew the curtains, Alice had gone, just as silently as she'd appeared.

I told you I bought five things that day in Cheltenham. The other two were door bolts.

Chapter 28

Alice sits at the table, staring down at the paper in her hands. The envelope had been folded before being stuffed through the letter box, and a crease runs through the centre of the message scribbled on its back. Just twenty words, but what damage they had almost done:

> *Lucy – I'm so sorry about last night.*
> *Please call me when you get back.*
> *We need to talk about Alice.*
> *T*

The paper shivers gently and she puts it down and clasps her hands to stop them shaking. It had been too close. Too close by half.

She'd almost decided there was no need to wait any longer. She'd watched Tom walk past the cottages the day after the book club meeting, first in one direction and then the other, that stinking mutt pulling at his lead. He'd glanced up both times but his pace hadn't slackened. When by the next morning he still hadn't turned up at Lucy's door, she'd considered ringing Cynthia with an offer to make the most of the Sunday closing by tidying up the stockroom; after having phoned in sick, she knew she needed to make amends. She'd been about to make the call when something, some unknowable instinct, told her to wait. She'd put the phone down then and returned to her seat near the window.

Lucy had been out when he arrived. That had been lucky: Alice had seen her getting into her car, accelerating off as if she were on a racetrack instead of a quiet country lane, with who knew what cyclists or walkers or tractors around the next corner; so when Tom had appeared in his expensive jeans and his expensive shoes and his crisp, expensive shirt, Alice hadn't had to rush out to intercept him, hadn't had to do anything at all except sit quiet and still and watch.

He'd strode up the path as if he meant business, and Alice had thought at first that he planned to finish what he'd started when he'd walked Lucy to his door after the book club. She'd followed them then, of course, telling Maggie she was going to the toilet – the loo, as she'd learned to call it – waiting just inside the doorway to the kitchen, where she could see him lean down and say something into Lucy's ear as she left. It had taken only a few seconds, and even her hearing hadn't been quite sharp enough to pick out the words; but the shock on Lucy's face had said it all, and when he'd slammed the door while she was still standing there looking like an envelope without an address on it, Alice had had to turn away quickly and scuttle down the hallway to the bathroom before allowing the laughter to burst from her belly. Maybe now he was coming to tell Lucy how disgusting she was, how he didn't want to talk to her ever again; how if she tried to tell anyone what she knew, they'd never believe her; that he'd make sure everyone thought she was a vicious, lying gossip.

She'd heard him knock at the door and wait and knock again, then watched him turn and register the absence of Lucy's car. He'd started to walk back to the gate, but then appeared to think better of it, stopping in the middle of the path and drawing out his phone from his pocket. He looked at the screen, then replaced it again – the signal in the village must have been experiencing one of its regular lulls. More rummaging in his pocket and a crumpled piece of paper emerged. He leaned on the door to write, then folded the paper in half, not stopping to read it through, and shoved it through the letter box.

After he'd left, she'd gone into the kitchen and reached into the coffee jar for the keys she'd had copied while Lucy had been sleeping off the little something she'd slipped into her drink. The back door was safer, but the fence was awkward and there'd be no need to explore this time. Just a quick glance at the note, check everything was as it should be, and she'd be gone. So she'd taken the front door key and walked swiftly up the path to number 2.

Another mistake. She should have taken both sets of keys.

She'd opened the door and closed it again while she unfolded the note, so that to anyone passing she'd appear to be waiting for her knock to be answered. And then she'd read the message and the words had danced on the paper and she'd felt the blood rushing in her ears, and she'd sunk to her knees, right there on the doorstep where anyone could have seen her. She'd thought she was going to be sick, and she'd pressed her hand to her mouth, and then she'd heard the sound of an engine and known it was Lucy coming back.

For a second she'd frozen, and wild thoughts had swum through her head, thoughts of ending it all right there, a hand on the back of Lucy's neck, the quick, hard crunch of bone against steering wheel; a rock to the skull, hair matted with hot, sticky blood; pressure on her throat, watching her eyes bulge and her mouth work as she squeezed the life from her. And then the engine had died and at the last possible moment her limbs had come to life and she'd half jumped, half rolled to the side, hiding in the shadows behind the hollyhocks, waiting for something, anything that would give her a chance to escape.

And Lucy had obliged. Alice had hardly been able to believe her luck when she'd seen that furtive glance over her shoulder, the long stare that slid from Alice's cottage to her car. It had been obvious what she was going to do, and while her nose was pressed up against the car window, Alice had crept down the path on silent feet. Lucy was so busy spying that she didn't hear the faint squeak of the gate that had made Alice freeze in horror; and when she'd seen Lucy's hand reach out to the car door, she'd known what she should have known all along: it was going to be all right. It was going to be all right because Alice was the servant of truth and the bringer of justice, and her will was the will of the universe, and nothing would prevent it from being done.

Lucy had looked so shocked when she'd caught her out that Alice had almost laughed in her face. She wouldn't try anything like that again. Not that it would have done her any good: Alice hasn't brought anything with her that would give her away. All she needs are her memories, and they're there all the time whether she wants them or not.

For a while, they'd tormented her. She'd wake in the night, tears streaming down her face as she saw again the crazy angles of the stairs, her useless hands stretched out in front of her, the unforgiving concrete rushing up to meet her face. And the emptiness had ached in the pit of her stomach and she'd curled over like the small life she'd lost and wound her hands around her middle and wept so hard she'd almost choked. She'd begged to forget her memories then, hollow-eyed and stick-limbed, unable to work, her excuses becoming less and less plausible until one day she'd had the letter offering her money to go, a 'goodwill' payment, they'd called it, and she'd wondered in desperation what she would do now, what she could ever do again with all these pictures in her head that wouldn't go away.

It was then that she'd realised: the memories were a gift. They were there to remind her what had been stolen from her. That the thieves had to be punished.

The next morning, she'd got up, showered and dressed. She brushed her hair and went to the station and caught a train and walked into the office, the place where she was sure she'd find a way to make them pay.

As for the memories, she knows they'll fade eventually, when her work is done. The time is getting closer now.

She takes a last look at the envelope before pulling at a corner. It rips slowly, a long, thin, satisfying shred with Lucy's name at the top. She crumples it into a ball, puts it in her mouth, and feels the words die between her teeth.

* * *

Tom fiddles with his mobile phone. It's rude, he knows, but he has to have something to do with his hands.

His mother says, 'He's pleased you came, you know. He doesn't show it, but he is.'

Tom nods, eyes on the screen.

She says, 'He just finds it hard to . . . You're so different, the two of you.'

There are creases around her eyes. He should come home more often, be a bit more help. He says, 'What has the doctor said?'

'Oh well, you know what they're like.'

He nods again. 'And you? How are you managing?'

She ignores the question. 'It's easier for him with your brother. That's all it is. He can talk to him about the business. You never . . .'

'I know. It's OK, Mum.' He reaches out and takes her hand, feeling the bones move beneath her paper-thin skin. 'It's OK.'

Later, he sits on the bed in the room where he slept as a child. His posters and drawings are long gone, replaced by toile de Jouy wallpaper and an embroidered bedspread before his first year at university was out. He draws the phone from his pocket: still nothing from Lucy. Well, he shouldn't be surprised after the way he's behaved. He should have known better than to believe Alice; there's something wrong with that woman, he's sure of it now. He doesn't know what she's up to yet, but he'll find out soon enough.

In the meantime, a few days away will do him good, give him some perspective and Lucy a chance to calm down. He'll make it up to her when he gets back, and between them they can decide what to do about Alice.

* * *

Rebecca strokes the wiry hair beneath her fingers. Sam's chest is smooth, a squishy layer of fat starting to form over the muscles there. David is leaner, the hairs dark against his pale skin. She curls her fingers into them and tugs gently.

He kisses the crown of her head. 'I should go.'

The morning light filtering through the polyester curtains has turned everything a flat shade of beige. Maggie would probably have a name for that colour. Rebecca rolls away from him onto her back.

'Rebecca, don't be like that. Last night was great, but I can't do this unplanned. I don't want her getting suspicious.' A pause as he hears how it sounds and adjusts his syntax. 'I don't want to hurt her. Neither of us does.'

She turns and looks at him. It was his eyes she'd noticed first, she remembers. Silly and romantic, but true all the same. They'd been in the garden of the Old Forge, where she'd escaped when the combination of the wine and the open fire at Maggie's dinner party had got too much. Somehow she hadn't been surprised when he'd followed her outside, taking the chair next to her without speaking, the two of them sitting there in the dark while electricity danced over the surface of her skin. She can still remember the look in his eyes when he turned towards her, alive with intelligence and interest. And so what if the interest had been more in how she'd feel moving beneath him than what was going on inside her head? It was more than she'd had from Sam in a long time.

They'd kissed that night, nothing more, but back at home, lying next to her husband, she'd barely slept. She tried to tell herself that it didn't matter, that they'd both had too much to drink, that telling Maggie would cause needless hurt when it would never happen again. In the morning, she'd made breakfast and packed lunches while her brain hummed and her fingers trembled, sick with nerves that at any moment Sam would read her betrayal in the brightness of her eyes or the flush in her cheeks. But he noticed nothing.

When Maggie arrived at eleven for their regular coffee and cake, Rebecca had barely been able to look at her. She'd bustled around the kitchen while Maggie had chatted about the previous night, her sore head, the commission she was working on. It was hard to believe it was that easy; that all she had to do was let her talk, and Maggie wouldn't notice anything either.

It was another two days before David called around. As soon as she opened the door, she knew what was going to happen. He'd looked at her and she'd felt real.

She isn't sure how she feels any more.

She says, 'Maggie's already suspicious. I keep telling you that.'

He sighs, and she knows what it means. He's bored of this conversation. He thinks she's being paranoid, or else that if

Maggie is upset with her, it has nothing to do with him. Perhaps he's right. But something has happened, she knows it. She can see Maggie now, giggling away with Alice, the two of them whispering in corners. What kind of way is that to behave, after all their years of friendship?

David shifts his weight in the bed, about to get up. She rolls back to him and swings a leg over his hip, easing herself on top of him, pressing her nipples to his chest the way she knows he likes.

'Rebecca . . .'

But she pushes her tongue inside his mouth to make him stop. Let Maggie whisper and giggle with her new friend: she doesn't need to let it upset her. She just needs to feel real.

It's late when they leave the Travelodge.

They stand in the corner of the car park, still able to smell one another beneath the synthetic citrus of the shower gel. Their cars are parked as far apart as possible, David's just inside the entrance from the slip road, Rebecca's in the row closest to the door. Both are far, far too easy to spot on the half-empty tarmac.

David slips one hand under Rebecca's buttocks and the other into her hair, tipping her face up for a final kiss. From beneath the trees that form the perimeter, too faint for either of them to hear, comes the crunch of a camera phone.

Chapter 29

I'd had a restless night, and in the morning I was up early, ready to fit the door bolts; I wanted more between Alice and me than a single lock. Ten minutes later, a flimsy piece of paper covered in unintelligible diagrams and arrows spread out before me, I found to my dismay that I didn't have the right drill bit.

I should have gone out to get one there and then, but the truth is I'm rubbish at DIY: my chances of making things worse by drilling a useless hole or managing to split the wood were high. I told myself I'd find a handyman to do it; at least then I'd have the comfort of knowing the job was done properly. Tom had given me the number of someone he used when I'd wanted a new shower screen installed, and it was still on the pin board in the kitchen. I called it straight away, but no one was there so I left a message.

I spent the rest of the day wondering whether to go and see Tom. I was sure by then that everything that had happened at the book club, all the threats and anger, had come from Alice. Should I try to explain, hope it sounded plausible enough to at least make him pause and consider; or would it only make matters worse, adding an attempt to blacken the character of an innocent bystander to my list of supposed crimes?

In the end, I decided to go. I'd tell Tom that Alice was out to get me; that whatever he thought I'd done, I hadn't, and that whatever he'd done, I didn't care. I'd tell him that before the night of *Fanny Hill* I hadn't had a clue how he got his money, and I wouldn't have been any the wiser if he hadn't given the game away himself; but it was his own business and no one else's and I would never, ever breathe a word of it to another human being.

I knew I didn't have any kind of evidence about Alice to back me up (thanks for nothing, Liz). I knew Tom might not be prepared to listen to a word I had to say; but he was my first friend in the village, my best friend even if I wasn't his, and I had to try.

Alice's car was in its usual place, but I could tell she wasn't home when I left the cottage: I couldn't feel her watching me as I walked down the path. I contemplated trying her car door again; but the alarm would be on, and besides, if there'd been anything of any use in it before, she would have moved it by now. And what was I looking for anyway? I didn't have the first idea.

It was hot again, too hot for September, and I felt the sweat on the top of my lip as I turned into Tom's drive. The gravel crunched underfoot and I wondered how long it would be before I'd be crunching back down it again, whether I'd have regained a friend or lost him for good.

I rounded the corner and stopped in my tracks, suddenly cold in spite of the heat. A figure moved in front of the porch, neat brown hair, grey cardigan.

Alice.

I made to turn and leave, but it was too late; she was raising a hand in greeting. I waved back, dread gnawing at my stomach as I walked towards her. What had she been saying to Tom this time?

She said, 'He's not home, I'm afraid.'

I glanced over her shoulder: there was no sign of his car.

A smile twitched at Alice's lips. 'Go and knock if you don't believe me.'

I wasn't going to contradict her. Instead I said, 'So what are you doing here?'

The words and their tone were rude, but Alice just looked at me with her odd little smile while the seconds dragged by. I felt the sweat beneath my arms and wondered if she could smell it.

Eventually she said, 'He's away for a few days. I was just dropping by to water the plants.'

Tom had asked her to do that? She was watching for my reaction and I refused to give her one. 'But what about—'

'Ferdy's with the Williamses. He doesn't like me much, I'm afraid.'

'I heard he attacked you.'

'Oh, that was nothing.' There was something about the way she said it, like she was telling me a secret. She smiled as she saw me take it in, two rows of sharp little teeth. I made an effort not to take a step back.

She gestured at the path. 'Shall we go?'

I hesitated, but what choice did I have? Alice talked as we went, but I looked straight ahead and stayed as far from her as the path would allow. She didn't seem to notice. She was saying something about how it was good that she'd seen me, that she'd been planning to drop by, something about dates, arrangements, postponing . . . I heard the words 'book club' and forced myself to concentrate.

'It's such a pain, but I haven't really got a choice. It was the earliest they could do and you can't leave death-watch beetles. They can eat right through the timbers.'

I struggled to find my way back to the conversation. 'Death-watch beetles?'

'Yes, in the roof. They're going to fumigate the whole place. I'll have to move out for a few days . . .'

Oh God, no, don't ask to stay with me . . .

'So I'm afraid I'm going to have to bring the book club forward a week – this Friday instead of next. I've checked with the others and it's fine with them. Does it work for you?' She gave me a sidelong look. 'You'll still have a few days to do the reading.'

I felt the heat rising up my face. Of course, I didn't have the demands on my time that she did: Cynthia's A4 envelopes wouldn't stack themselves. I swallowed and kept my voice even. 'I think I can manage that.'

We'd reached the road. I'd tell her I needed to go to the shop; but she was turning towards the high street herself, saying she had errands to run. I watched her go in relief.

I suppose I should have known then that she was lying. Deathwatch beetles that didn't make trouble in any of the terraced cottages but Alice's? But it seemed like such a small thing, meeting one week instead of the next. I didn't stop to think about it. I didn't stop to think about the dates.

It's a long read, *Madame Bovary*, long and depressing. I paced myself, pausing after a chapter or two to work on my business plan, or more often to stare at the TV. I didn't like the heroine, a farmer's daughter trapped in a loveless marriage to a mediocre doctor. She gets into debt and has affairs and finally ends it all with a dose of arsenic. She's supposed to be romantic, but I thought she was selfish and unkind. I guess it takes one to know one.

She was supposed to be Rebecca, of course. It was Rebecca who was the adulterer, whose secret was going to be exposed when we all sat around Alice's table. I wondered how Alice was going to do it, and what would be left of my group of friends when she had.

On the day of the book club I was up early, nerves stretched like elastic. The heat was stultifying and I opened all the windows, desperate for a breath of air. The shade at the back of the house offered no relief – the warmth seemed to radiate from the ground, rising up through the floorboards and muffling sound. I drifted from room to room, plucking my clothes from my damp skin, unable to settle to anything. Once I heard the whir of the vacuum cleaner as Alice prepared for her guests. I couldn't have borne it, but the heat must have suited her: good weather for the cold-blooded.

In the afternoon, I tried to call Liz, knowing even as I dialled the numbers that there would be no reply. I waited for her usual message, but it had been replaced with something different. I gnawed at my bottom lip as it played, and when it was finished, I hung up and dialled again, listened, put down the phone and stared at it as if it might bite.

This user's mailbox is full and cannot accept any messages at this time.

I got to my feet and walked into the kitchen. I stood at the open back door and tried to breathe. I walked back to the living room. I stared at the spines of the books on the shelves there. I picked up the phone and dialled again. The same strangely modulated voice repeated its message.

Where was Liz? What had happened to her?

My knees were weak and I sat on the floor. I wouldn't panic.

There was a problem with her phone, that was all. It had probably started days ago. That was why she hadn't been in touch. All her contacts were on her phone. She was probably in some chain store right now, berating a spotty kid, demanding he sort it out on pain of death. She'd probably never even got my messages.

I'd email her, use her address at Waites, where she'd be bound to see it. She obviously didn't have any news about Alice, but that didn't matter. I knew she was fine, of course she was, but it wouldn't hurt to ask her to reply even if she was busy. Just so I knew for sure. Just so I could put that niggling little worry to bed.

I tapped out a short message, including the numbers for both my mobile and the landline at the cottage, and pressed send. As long as she didn't have the day off, Liz should be in work for an hour or so yet. I googled jewellery sites while I waited for a reply. There were too many results, page after page of professional-looking stores, specialists in gemstones or precious metals, arts-and-craft types, personalised design and elegant packaging. I clicked back to my inbox before despair had a chance to take hold.

Nothing.

I snapped shut the lid of the laptop, irritated with myself. Liz was away from her desk, or too busy to look at emails and hadn't noticed the message. It was ridiculous to sit there waiting for a response. And it was so fucking *hot*. What business did it have being this hot in September?

A shower. I'd go and take another shower, wash off this uneasy feeling. I pulled the ground-floor windows closed, checked the door was locked and climbed the stairs.

That evening I was ready early, the sense of foreboding so strong that I began to believe that the reality couldn't compare. I sat in the living room and waited until I heard Alice's front door open and close twice, two sets of greetings muted by the lifeless air, then I walked through the rooms checking that everything was shut up tight. The cottage sighed in the heat. I collected my copy of *Madame Bovary* and a bottle of wine and locked the door behind me.

I heard footsteps on the road as I walked through Alice's garden. The stride was long, masculine. Tom.

I will fucking end you.

I quickened my pace and knocked at the door. Behind me the gate creaked open and I knocked again.

'Lucy, we need to talk—'

The door swung open. 'Lucy! No need to take the paint off. Rebecca thought we were being raided!' Maggie's smile as she opened the door was skin-deep, and it wavered over Rebecca's name. She pulled me into a brief hug. 'And there's lovely Tom!'

I ducked under her arm and into the hallway; I wasn't ready for another one-to-one with Tom. Maggie was stepping back to let him in and I kept going, into the space Alice used as a dining room and then through to the kitchen at the back.

There was a strangeness to that room that for a moment I couldn't make sense of. I stood there, looking around, trying to work it out. The shelves were empty, there was no clutter on the table. There was a kettle, a toaster, a tea towel on a hook, a plate of nibbles on the worktop – and yet none of it looked real. There was nothing personal, nothing to give a clue to the identity of the person who lived there. It was a stage set in a low-budget TV series.

I looked for the circular thing I'd seen when I'd peered through the glass of the back door, but whatever it was, it had gone.

There was a movement at the door and Alice stood there, her face arranged into a smile. I thought: *She's just like her home – a facsimile of real life.*

She came forward with her arms outstretched, and for a second I thought she was going to try to hug me; but instead she reached for the bottle I was gripping with both hands.

'Welcome, Lucy. Shall I take that from you?'

I pushed it at her and backed away. A sudden, clear picture of Liz doing the same flashed through my mind. The words were out of my mouth before I could stop them. 'Do I know you, Alice?'

The confusion in her eyes was gone in a moment, replaced by that cool, glittering gaze. She laughed. 'What do you mean? Of course you do! We're neighbours.' She held up the wine bottle and pretended to peer at its contents. 'You haven't started early, have you?'

'I don't mean from here. I mean before . . . Did I know you in London?'

She had gone very still. 'Why do you say that?'

'Liz said you looked familiar.' The tremor in my voice was slight enough to miss.

'I get that a lot.' Alice smiled again, quick and tight. 'I must have one of those faces, I suppose.'

'So we couldn't have met then? Not before you came here?'

'Oh, well I don't know about *couldn't*. All kinds of things *could* have happened.' The smile was still there, but the tips of her fingers were white where they gripped the wine bottle. 'And most of us go around with our eyes shut, don't we? We hardly notice who's around us.'

The playfulness had gone from her tone. She took a step towards me and it was as much as I could do to stand my ground.

'But you don't recognise me, do you, Lucy? And we've been living next door to each other for two months.' She took another step, and this time I couldn't help myself. My heel struck something hard as I retreated, and a sharp edge dug into my back: the kitchen counter.

I shrugged, tried to keep my voice level. 'You know how it is when you see someone out of context.'

She stepped closer, just an arm's length away now. 'Maybe you should take a closer look.'

Another step and we were almost touching. I smelled a mixture of perfume and fabric softener. She lifted her face towards me, and when I looked into her eyes the hatred there took my breath away.

She said, 'Don't worry, Lucy. It'll come back to you,' then turned, picked up the plate from the counter and left the room.

I stood there, my hands clutching the edge of the worktop, waiting for my breathing to slow. From the living room I could hear the rumble of voices welcoming the arrival of food. I pulled my phone from my pocket, but there was nothing, no call or message from Liz. At the top of the screen, a cross flashed next to the symbol of a telephone mast: no reception. The village had turned its face again from the rest of the world.

I breathed in once, twice. I had a landline next door. Less than two minutes from here I could have the receiver in my hand. There was no need for alarm. I should join the others, let the evening take its course; and if by Monday I'd heard nothing from Liz, I'd ring the switchboard at Waites and ask to be put through to Lawrie. As his PA, Liz would probably screen the call, but if she didn't, I'd tell him I was worried about her and ask him to put her on. She'd be cross with me, but too bad. I had to know she was OK.

From the living room I heard Maggie call my name, asking me to bring more wine. I collected a couple of bottles from the worktop, and walked back through the darkened hallway.

I felt the atmosphere as soon as I entered the room.

Alice sat at one end of a small pale-grey sofa, Tom at the other. A lone dining chair stood opposite, and at right angles to them both, a pair of matching armchairs faced each other. On one, Rebecca shuffled in her seat, eyes on her lap as she picked at the hem of her summer dress; on the other, Maggie sat bolt upright watching her, hands flat against the armrests. Alice darted sidelong glances between them, the shadow of a smile playing on her lips.

Maggie looked up as I came in and I saw that the skin on her throat was mottled pink and cream. 'There you are! I'll have the red.' Her hand trembled as she reached towards me. Perhaps Tom had seen it too, because he stood and took the bottle from my hands.

'Shall I be father?'

'Always so helpful, Thomas!' The acid in Maggie's voice stopped him in his tracks, but she waggled her glass at him. 'Top me up.'

'Do take a seat, Lucy. Here, let me take that from you.' Alice was on her feet again and I held out the second bottle to stop her from getting too close.

'White, anyone?'

There was no answer. I looked around for a seat, but there were only two options: a foot above everyone else on the solitary dining chair, or squeezed on the sofa between Alice and Tom. I chose the chair.

Tom cleared his throat, apparently as keen to get on with it as I was.

'So, *Madame Bovary*.'

He talked about Flaubert, reminding us that this was his first novel, that it had been prosecuted for obscenity on publication, 'Like our last book, in fact.' I felt his eyes on me then, but I'd opened my copy of the novel at a random page for just such moments, and kept my own gaze fixed on the paper. From time to time Rebecca and Alice chimed in, and after a few minutes I added some bland remarks, not wanting to draw attention with either silence or wit.

Maggie barely spoke. From my position, seated between her and Rebecca like a net cord judge at a tennis match, it was hard to watch her without being noticed; but every so often, when the others were engrossed in their conversation, I chanced a glance in her direction. Most of the time she was staring at Rebecca, hostility etched so sharply into her features that I half expected Rebecca to raise a hand to shield herself.

There was no question about it. Maggie knew.

It was Alice, of course, who helped things along, needling, prodding, easing the conversation down the path she'd laid for it: 'I don't think anything can justify an affair' (eyes dropped in mock humility). 'I thought once that it could, but now I know I was just being selfish.' 'Emma's husband loves her, doesn't he? And she humiliates him.' 'Everything she does is to satisfy herself. She doesn't care who else she hurts.'

And Rebecca flushed and squirmed on her seat, her repeated attempts to change the tack of the conversation subverted by Alice at every turn.

I began to wonder if Alice's confession had been real. For someone who claimed to be filled with remorse about her own affair, she didn't seem to have any problem lingering over the topic. And there'd been something wrong about those tears on Maggie's sofa, the way she'd shouted at me. Had she been trying to draw me out? Had she found out about me and Richard like she'd found out about Rebecca and David? Was I supposed to be Jane Eyre?

Perhaps Alice knew Melanie; maybe they'd met through the connection to Waites. Maybe they were friends, and Alice was here on her orders to spoil the new life I was trying to build for myself.

Even as the thoughts ran through my head, I heard the narcissism: *all this to punish me?* But what other explanation was there?

I tuned back into the conversation. 'I think some of the symbolism is important.' Rebecca's voice carried an edge of desperation. 'The hat, for example . . .'

Tom took up the thread. 'You mean the hat Charles wears to school as a boy?'

Rebecca opened her mouth to reply, but Alice broke in again. 'Charles is such an interesting character, isn't he? I think it's really fascinating that Flaubert made him a doctor.'

From the corner of my eye, I saw Maggie shift in her chair.

'I mean, surely as the daughter of a farmer, that's a higher-status husband than Emma could ever have hoped for.'

Tom had felt it too, the charge in the air. His eyes flicked to Maggie and then to Rebecca.

'What do you think, Rebecca?' Maggie's voice carried across the room, cold and clear. 'Do you think a doctor would be quite the catch?'

I saw the colour drain from Rebecca's face. For a moment she was silent, considering, I suppose, whether to attempt to brazen it out; but a look at Maggie's expression must have told her it was useless. She got to her feet. 'I think I should go.'

'I'm sure you do.' Maggie stood too. 'Can't have everyone hearing what a slut you are, can we?' The wine glass trembled in her hand. 'I wonder what Sam will say when he finds out you've been fucking my husband.'

There was a second's perfect silence. Tom sat slack-jawed in horror: clearly this was news to him. From the other end of the sofa Alice watched Rebecca and Maggie with mild interest, as though they were characters in a soap opera.

I thought: *Please, Rebecca, please say how sorry you are.* But instead she straightened her shoulders. 'I don't think this is the place to discuss this.'

A crack like a gunshot split the air, and I spun towards the sound. Blood dripped slowly from Maggie's hand onto the carpet. A single, evil shard of wine glass protruded from her fist.

I said, 'Maggie . . .' not sure what words were coming next; but Tom was on his feet, reaching for her. She spun on her heel.

'And you! *You!*' She raised the hand with the glass. 'Don't you even speak to me! Don't you *dare* speak to me!'

He shrank away from her, the shock written across his face. *Surely,* I thought, *whatever Alice has told her he's done, she must see that she's lying. She must see that Tom doesn't know what she's talking about.*

And then Alice's quiet voice slipped through the room. 'How could you, Tom?'

'How could I what?' He swung to face her. 'I don't know what the fuck you're talking about!'

'I trusted you, both of you.' Maggie's voice was raw.

Tom said, 'You have to be joking if you think *I've* been fucking David,' and I almost giggled at the absurdity of it all.

'Oh come on, Tom.' Alice again, smooth as silk. 'You know what you did.'

'I'm afraid I haven't got the first fucking idea.'

'After all these years . . .' Maggie swivelled back to Rebecca, pointing at her with the glass. 'And *you*, you *bitch*, you can just stay exactly where you are.'

Rebecca froze halfway to the door.

'Always playing the innocent, little Miss Perfect, with your fucking baking and your Pilates. Trying to get yourself nice and tight for him, were you?' She laughed, loud and shrill.

I said, 'Maggie, please . . .' but she didn't seem to hear.

'I bet you were. You'd have to, after two kids.'

Two spots of colour flamed high on Rebecca's cheeks. 'David never had any complaints.'

Maggie had moved before the final word had died on the air, launching herself across the space between them, the glass in one clawed fist. I finally came to life and threw myself after her, grasping at her clothes, an arm, whatever I could reach.

Someone screamed – perhaps it was me – and I felt a hot, sharp pain across the palm of my hand; but I had Maggie now, the edge of a sleeve, her arm, and I held on for grim death.

She didn't even look at me.

My muscles were burning and I didn't think I could hold her

for long, but then Tom was there, grabbing her around the waist, lifting her feet from the ground and turning her away. I watched Maggie struggle in his arms; but he was strong, and even in her fury she was no match for him. Gradually she became still as sobs racked her body, bringing tears to my own eyes. Was this what Melanie would have been reduced to if she'd ever found out about Richard and me?

Maggie sank to her knees and Tom sat on the floor behind her, cradling her against his chest as she wept. I looked back at Rebecca. She was standing motionless, her face pale, staring at Maggie. I reached out and placed a hand on her arm. 'Go. Go now,' I whispered so that Maggie wouldn't hear.

She started at my touch. My hand had been cut, I saw now – I'd left a bloodstain on her sleeve. For a moment she just looked at me, but then she crossed to the door, giving Maggie and Tom as wide a berth as the room would allow.

From the hallway came the soft click of the front door shutting. Maggie raised her head at the sound and pulled away from Tom. 'Get away from me.'

'Maggie, I didn't know—'

'Just fuck off, Tom!' He recoiled, and Maggie scrambled forward on all fours, reaching for the seat of the armchair like it was a life raft. I watched as she pulled herself to her feet, and as she turned back to the room, her eyes fell on me. 'Lucy!' She pointed with the glass, the end red with my blood. 'Did you know that bitch was screwing David?'

I tried to respond, but no words would come. Maggie threw me a look of disgust. 'Oh, I get it.'

'Maggie, I—'

'I bet you thought it was really funny. I bet you were just laughing your arse off.' She was pacing now, side to side, tapping the glass against her thigh. 'Coming round to my house, asking for my advice, and all the time you *knew.* You knew what was going on and you didn't say anything!'

I stayed silent. I wouldn't try to justify myself.

Tom stretched out his hand. 'Maggie, just put the glass down. You're hurting yourself.'

'As if you care about that.' Alice, alert as ever for her cue.

'And what the fuck is that supposed to mean?' He looked from Maggie to Alice. 'Come on, spit it out! What am I supposed to have done?'

Maggie said, 'David's left me. Is that what you wanted?' Her voice was flat now, the anger gone.

Tom's jaw had dropped, but he recovered quickly. 'I'll say it again: I don't know what you're talking about.' He spun to face Alice. 'This is your doing, isn't it? What lies have you been feeding her?'

But Maggie was still speaking. 'You were the only one who knew. You were the only person I ever told . . .'

'Maggie, I've never, I would *never—*'

'Why now, Tom? If you were going to tell him, why wait all this time?'

He looked at her in disbelief. 'David knows about the baby?'

So I'd been right: there had been an abortion.

I looked across at Alice, still sitting on the sofa. Her face showed the same expression of polite interest, as if they were talking about holiday plans or getting a new kitchen. She knew all this already.

Tom was ashen. He said, 'Maggie, I'm so, so sorry.'

'You're sorry? You end my marriage and you're fucking *sorry*?'

'That's not what I meant . . .'

Maggie was crying again, her words breaking between the sobs. 'He said he could have forgiven . . . forgiven me . . . anything else . . .'

So Maggie really had been Tess. That was why she'd got so upset at Rebecca's comments about abortion. She'd terminated a pregnancy herself. A pregnancy that apparently Tom had known about but David hadn't. But how the hell had Alice found out?

Tom said, 'I didn't tell him! Why would I do that? I can't believe you'd think I'd do that!'

Alice moved between them, so quick and silent I hadn't realised she'd left her seat until she was there, placing her hand on Tom's arm. He flinched as if burned.

'I think it would be best if you left now.'

He turned to face her, and over her shoulder I met his eyes for the first time. The dislike I'd seen there as I'd left his house had gone. In its place was understanding: he knew now what Alice was. He opened his mouth to speak, but Maggie cut him off.

'No more.' Her voice was tired, her anger spent. 'Just leave me alone. Please, all of you, just fuck off and leave me alone.'

Alice stared at us, eyebrows raised, sure she wasn't included in that request. For a moment Tom didn't move; but then he turned on his heel and left the room. There was nothing to do but follow him, but by the time my shaking legs had carried me out of the front door and onto the path, he was almost out of sight along the road.

Back home, I sank into a chair at the kitchen table and sat there without turning on the lights, wanting to be invisible. My hand stung but the bleeding had stopped, and next door all was silent. They were still in the living room, perhaps, Alice taking the opportunity to reinforce her lies, convincing Maggie that the rest of us were laughing at her, betraying her. Well, there was some truth to the betrayal, after all.

I held my head in my hands, massaging the skin at my temples. I'd been so stupid. I'd seen Willowcombe as an escape, a sanctuary where I could forget the person I'd been and invent a new one.

But it had never been that; not even in the earliest days, when I'd been so desperate to make friends, to become part of village life, hiding who I was and what I'd done. And then Alice had arrived, and the veil that had covered my secrets, all our secrets, had been ripped away and everything had changed.

I wondered whether it could ever be the same again.

I raised my head to see a green light blinking at me through the darkness. The answerphone. My mouth went dry.

Liz.

And I knew. The moment I saw that flashing green light, I knew. Something was very, very wrong.

Chapter 30

Emily had always liked churchyards. They were so still and peaceful, and that smell: cut grass and evergreens and beneath it something else, something she suspected other people didn't catch, a secret scent she shared with the foxes and the rabbits and the crawling things under the ground.

Dust and ashes.

She was tired now, and it had seemed natural to come here. She knew it wasn't likely that Lucy would recognise her if she saw her on the train back to London – she was so self-absorbed she probably wouldn't notice if Emily sat opposite and stared at her for the whole journey – but still, there was no need to take unnecessary risks. So instead of making her way back to the station straight away, she'd followed the road past the cottage with the 'To Let' sign, and when she saw the spire rising from behind the trees she knew that this was somewhere she could rest and wait.

It hadn't been as easy to follow Lucy as she'd expected; none of this had been easy. It wasn't like it was on TV. Back at Waites she'd been taking her time, trying to plan everything out, the only thing getting her out of bed in the morning – on the days when she got out of bed – the burning need to make Lucy pay for what she'd done. But then one day when she'd gone into the office Lucy hadn't been at her desk; and when she wasn't there the next day, or the days after that, she'd realised with a sick feeling in the pit of her stomach that she'd left for good. He'd got rid of her, probably. That was the kind of thing he'd do. And Lucy deserved it, deserved to lose her job; but she deserved much worse than that, and how could Emily make sure that she got it now?

In the end, she'd been lucky: no, not just lucky. She'd been patient, and she'd kept her eyes and ears open. Luck was no good if you weren't ready to take advantage of it. She'd kept an eye on that girl, the one Lucy was friends with, timing her trips to the kitchen to coincide with hers, pausing near her desk every so often in case she dropped some useful hint about where Lucy had gone, where she lived, anything she could use. She'd considered trying to make friends with her so she could just come right out and ask – but Emily wasn't good at making friends. Still, as the days passed and her desperation grew, she'd started to think she might have to try; but then she'd got the bit of luck she needed.

She'd gone to check the pigeonhole for the admin pool. Management always circulated the press cuttings through internal mail, and now and again there'd be a signed contract or an invoice to pick up. It was a thin batch that day, nothing of interest, and she was about to return to her desk when she saw it.

There, in the section for outgoing mail: an envelope addressed to Lucy Shaw.

She'd felt the blood rush to her head and for a moment the words swam on the paper; and then she'd stretched out her hand and tucked the envelope beneath the pile of cuttings. Back at her desk, she slipped it into her handbag, and for the rest of the morning she felt it there, like a heartbeat. It grew louder, more insistent as the hours passed, until she got up from her desk and, mumbling that she wasn't well, stumbled from the office. The other girls rolled their eyes as she left and she knew they'd be talking about her when she'd gone, but she didn't care.

Back at her flat, she took the envelope from her bag with trembling fingers. The glue was stuck fast, but the address showed through a plastic window instead of being typed on a label. She wouldn't need to try to steam it open, better simply to replace the envelope afterwards.

The letter was short but it confirmed what she'd already guessed: Lucy had been made redundant. It informed her that a payment – and here she blinked at the figure: three times as much as she herself had been offered – would be deposited in her account by the end of the month.

Emily didn't like to remember how she'd been back then, when she'd found out that Lucy had walked away with all that money, rewarded for everything she'd done, everything she'd taken from her. She'd had to wear long sleeves for the best part of a month afterwards; but it didn't matter, because she had the address.

She didn't bother going back to Waites after that, but she no longer found it difficult to get up in the morning. Now she was out of bed before dawn, sitting in her car across from Lucy's flat by 7 a.m., her eyes trained on the windows, watching for any movement. She hadn't known then what she was going to do, had even entertained the notion of just following her down the street and plunging a carving knife into her back, right up to the hilt, so that the sticky blood ran over the handle and pooled on the ground. But she'd known somehow that that wouldn't be right. It would have left her feeling short-changed.

So for weeks, whenever Lucy had left the flat, she'd followed her, not sure what she was hoping to see. She kept a careful distance as she tailed her around supermarkets, or sat in the corners of cafés or pubs watching meetings with men and women she didn't recognise, eavesdropping on their banal conversations. Richard was never there: it was clear the affair was over. Everything it had cost, everything it would cost them still, and they'd just discarded each other like a pair of old socks.

And then one day as she'd watched Lucy leaving her flat, closing the front door behind her, she knew something had changed. There was something different about her, about the way she walked, a half-pace swifter, looking straight ahead. A sense of purpose.

Emily had followed her down the street, and after a few minutes she saw her hurry down the steps to the tube station. She kept her distance as she went after her, eyes trained on the black leather jacket, the flash of red hair. The station was busy, the human smell of sweat and cheap perfume clogging her senses; but she kept her head, and when Lucy caught first one tube and then another, Emily was behind her.

At Paddington, she'd stayed close as Lucy walked to the concourse and boarded a train. She'd felt the panic rising again then, not knowing where she was going, not having her own ticket to follow; but she'd stood next to the barriers and watched her stride down the platform, past three carriages, then four, before she turned and stepped inside.

The electronic board told her the train was going to Bristol, leaving in four minutes. She ran back to the machines to buy a ticket, jabbing at the buttons, unable at first to make sense of the questions it was asking her; but eventually she had the ticket in her hand and was pushing past the loiterers near the gates, hearing a man say, 'Steady on, love,' as she ran onto the platform.

She'd had to get on at the nearest door and walk to the right carriage as the train eased its way out of the station. It was half empty and she spotted Lucy easily enough, her nose in a magazine.

The seat behind her was free, and Emily slid into it, listening as the conductor told Lucy to change at Bristol, and that she would need to walk across the platform for the train to Ashchurch. She'd started to panic then, worried that she had no ticket for the second leg of the journey, and she'd made up an elaborate story for the conductor about an urgent phone call and needing to change her plans; but it hadn't been necessary. The train to Ashchurch had been almost empty and no one had appeared to check her ticket.

When they'd disembarked, Emily had watched from the ticket office with her heart in her mouth as Lucy walked towards the single taxi at the rank before passing behind to another car. She pretended to check her phone while she heard the introductions take place, the driver, a man, confirming he was from somewhere called Linnells and inviting Lucy to call him Kev.

She listened, desperate for a clue as to where they were going, hoping the taxi driver wouldn't get fed up and either approach her or leave. But Lucy was getting into the car now, into the back seat as if the man were a chauffeur. She wondered what the cabbie would say if she told him to follow that car, like they did in films. Laugh at her, probably, ask her what she was doing. Maybe refuse. Maybe report her to the police.

The car door slammed, and she stood rooted to the spot. But then she heard Lucy ask how far; the window must have been open. She could just make out the voice of the man, Kev, as the engine started up. 'To Wilcome? Only ten minutes. Very handy for . . .'

His voice was carried away as the car passed. She looked up in time to see white lettering on the black paintwork: *Linnells Homes and Property.*

She'd misheard, of course, Kev's West Country accent mashing together the syllables. But it was close enough for the taxi driver to work out where she meant, and he'd dropped her off on what he called the high street, she having no better address to offer. She'd hoped to catch sight of the black car again, but the roads were too twisty to see far ahead and her own driver was slow, keeping the meter ticking for as long as possible.

She wandered up the high street but there wasn't much to see: a post office, a pub, a café, some kind of village store and a couple of shops selling tea towels and Cotswolds fudge. Her grandad had liked fudge; but he was gone and there was no one else to buy it for now. There was no sign of Lucy.

Here and there a narrow side street branched away from the main road, and at the first few junctions she turned into them and investigated; but every time the buildings thinned out quickly and she hurried back to the high street, fearful of wasting time. After a while the shops were replaced by a short terrace of houses, doors opening straight onto the street, and then by a grass verge edged by trees and hedgerows. The lack of buildings was disconcerting, and after another couple of minutes she'd stopped and turned around again, certain she was going the wrong way.

It had been a souvenir shop that had come to her rescue. She'd gone in to ask whether they had a map of the village, and the old man behind the counter had laughed and said she wouldn't need one of those. His eyes had crinkled behind his glasses when he'd said it, so she hadn't minded; and when he'd asked where she was looking for, she said she'd heard there was a cottage being rented out and had hoped to take a look, only now she'd lost the address. She'd expected him to wrinkle up his nose and tell her that there were lots of places to let, or that she'd better check with the estate agents; but instead he'd nodded and said, 'That'un'll be the Harvey place. Mellingford Cottages.' And he'd gone to the door with her and pointed down the road, back in the direction she'd been walking before her nerve had failed, and told her it was only five minutes and to be careful of the traffic: 'Them lorries shoot round them bends summat criminal.'

She'd set off again, and when a few minutes later she rounded a corner and saw the black car parked at the side of the road, the white lettering on its paintwork glowing in the sunshine, she could almost have cried in relief. The house for rent was number 2, a board outside bearing the name *Linnells* in the same flowing script that decorated the car. It was a pretty little place, golden stone softened by a front garden filled with flowers. Too pretty for Lucy.

Now, sitting in the churchyard, Emily wondered why Lucy was here. The village didn't suit her, this woman who had affairs with married men, who wore leather jackets and tight jeans and had sex in lifts. But Emily had punched the number of the estate agent into her phone all the same, and perhaps, after all, she'd begun to understand. Lucy had been paid off and there was no sign of another job. Maybe she'd decided to start again somewhere new, somewhere people didn't know what a selfish, wicked slut she was. Maybe she thought she could walk away from everything she'd done, as if none of it mattered. As if there wasn't a price to pay.

Emily realised that she was muttering. She did that sometimes when she was angry, or just thinking hard. It was one of the reasons people thought she was weird. Not here, though. She looked around the churchyard. The only souls here were long past caring whether she muttered or not.

For the first time she focused on the gravestone at her feet, her eyes seeking out the dates. They were the most interesting things about graves: how many years did this person live? And behind it, the other question, the one everyone was really interested in: will it be longer for me?

This one had been young, just six years old. Emily supposed she should find that sad. It was the kind of thing her nan would have shaken her head over, dear-dearing as if she cared. But what was the point of that? She didn't know this child. She'd died over a hundred years ago. And what did it matter anyway? Some people lived to eighty or ninety; others didn't make it past a few weeks. That was just the way things were.

And then she saw the name.

Alice Emily Darley.

The words danced in front of her. *Alice Emily. Emily Alice.* Her name, or almost, and she knew it was a sign. She was supposed to come here. She was supposed to see this.

And she knew what she had to do.

Chapter 31

The message was brief; the caller had forgotten to identify himself, leaving just a number and a request for me return his call 'any time, don't worry how late'. I refused to analyse what that meant. I picked up the phone and called straight back.

It was answered on the second ring, but it took me a moment to recognise the voice, cracked with tears. I had to strain my ears to make out the name: Lawrie. Leery. Liz's boss.

My knees buckled and I slid to the floor, hardly able to breathe, feeling already the shape of what was coming. His words slid over each other, making no sense and perfect sense – *accident . . . tyre . . . so fast, nothing she could have done.* He was still talking, but I cut across him. 'Which hospital?'

He said, 'Lucy, I don't know . . .'

'Someone will do.' I groped for names, people who'd have a better grip on the situation than Lawrie, but I couldn't remember any. 'Can I speak to HR?' But it was almost ten o'clock at night; no one would be there.

He said again, 'I don't know . . .' and I got to my feet, impatient, thinking I would cut him off, call around the hospitals myself;

but he'd gone silent and the blood seemed to slow in my veins. He took a shaky breath and tried again. 'I don't know how to tell you this, Lucy. She's gone.'

And I wanted to ask 'Gone where?' but he was sobbing now, this man I barely knew, and then I understood; and the floor tilted and I thought: *Well, I suppose they had worked together a long time, he'll be lost without someone to make his coffee, that's so horrible, what a horrible thing to think, he cared about her, he misses her, I don't even know when it happened.*

She's dead. Liz is dead. Dead. Dead. Dead. Dead.

Lawrie was apologising for crying, saying it had been such a shock, and after everything with Richard . . . He stopped abruptly. I registered dimly that I should say something, tell him I knew about Richard. I tried to speak, but nothing came out.

He cleared his throat. 'The funeral is on Tuesday. I'm sorry, no one thought . . . I know it's short notice.'

Four days. I took a breath, swallowed, took another. I said, 'Where is it?' My voice sounded far away.

'I'll send you the details. We've got your email address on file, haven't we?' I heard someone speak quietly in the background. 'Well, I should go.'

There was nothing else to say, but I couldn't bear to put down the phone and be left alone in the silent cottage. I swallowed again. 'Thanks for . . . Thanks.'

Lawrie snuffled. 'It makes you think, doesn't it? First Richard, now Liz. Bloody cars. We can't live without them. We forget how dangerous they are.' A pause. 'Lucy? Just check your tyre pressure before you set off, won't you. It's a long way. And if Liz . . . if Liz had . . .'

His voice cracked again and he choked a goodbye before hanging up.

I stared down at the phone in my hand. Liz was gone. She was *dead.*

I ran up the stairs, but my knees were weak and I only just reached the bathroom in time. My stomach clenched, and I threw up until there was nothing left but saliva and stomach acid.

I lay on the floor shivering, the sweat cold on my forehead. Something stirred in a recess of my mind, but I felt too sick to work out what it was. I rested my head against the tiles and closed my eyes, trying to concentrate. There was a connection, I could feel it. Something important.

The car accident. That was it. *Another one*. Two accidents in the space of three months. The people at Waites I was closest to, one in a coma, the other – the word felt heavy and alien – dead.

And Alice. Alice, whom Liz had recognised, Alice who'd moved into the house next door, who'd claimed the village as her own and shattered old friendships as if they'd been made of glass. And days after she'd met her at the book club, Liz was gone, gone before she could remember how she knew her. Gone where she could tell no one her secrets.

And now here I was again, throwing up in my bathroom, just like I had that night. The night Alice had drugged me.

Because Alice was responsible for all of it, I was sure of that now. Liz's death, Richard's accident. What was it Liz had said about the night he'd crashed his car? I dredged my memory. That he was in some out-of-the-way spot, that no one had known why he'd been there. She'd implied he'd been meeting a woman.

Could it have been Alice? Had he been cheating on me as well as Melanie? I didn't want to believe it, but it was possible. All Richard's easy charm; why imagine I'd been the only one? And when he'd lost interest, I'd told myself that it was the stress of being unfaithful, that he'd found it too painful to continue. I'd been so blind! He'd already moved on to someone else.

Or then again, perhaps he'd been seeing Alice before me.

Oblivious as I'd been, that might have been how it was. Maybe he'd ended things with her; maybe she blamed me.

Whatever the sequence, it didn't matter. Alice had found out that Richard had been two-timing her, or that she'd been dumped for someone else, or else that she was just the latest in his line of affairs. It all boiled down to the same thing: she wasn't special, any more than I was.

So she'd taken her revenge.

Somehow she'd caused the accident and left Richard for dead. Maybe she'd been in the car with him. They could have argued, Richard had been distracted or she'd grabbed the wheel and the car had come off the road. Perhaps she'd been able to walk away, pretend it had nothing to do with her.

Could it have been like that? An accident? A failure to get help rather than a deliberate act?

But no, not with Alice. Everything about her was deliberate. She didn't improvise. She would have planned it, lured him out into the middle of nowhere and parked on a blind bend, or stood in the road, made him swerve and crash. Or she'd cut his brake cables, his foot stamping uselessly on the pedal as he hit the corner.

The pictures flashed through my mind and I squeezed my eyes shut, trying to stop them.

And then Liz. Beautiful, sarcastic, kind, stroppy Liz, whose voice I would never hear again. She'd said something to Alice, that night I'd hosted the book club. She'd hinted that she knew her, and Alice had thought she was going to be exposed. Exposed before she had the chance to finish whatever she'd come here to do. So she'd had to take care of Liz. A crash on the roads was common enough, and after Richard, she knew it could work; why not try it again?

A voice in my head whispered: *This is madness. People don't do things like that.*

But Alice did.

I'd seen how she manipulated people. I knew what she'd done to me, creeping into my home in the guise of helper, watching me crawl on my hands and knees, humiliating me.

I held onto the toilet seat and pulled myself upright. My stomach ached and my legs were weak and I had to fight the urge to lie down again on the floor. But she was close; there, on the other side of the wall. A woman with glittering eyes and a smile that made you forget what she was.

I'd stayed too long, pretending I could win this battle. There was no time now to rest. I had to get out.

On the landing I stared at the blank square of darkness that was the doorway to my room, considering whether to pack some clothes; but the fear was taking hold of me now, icy fingers on my skin, and instead I made for the stairs, forcing myself to take my time on my shaking legs. My handbag lay at the bottom and I reached inside to check that my purse and keys were there.

I froze, every hair on my body pulling at my skin. She'd been there. I could feel her.

I stood, straining my ears for any sound. All I heard was the soft tick of the water pipes, the groan as the timbers gave up the heat of the day. But she'd been in my home, I knew it. I could smell her, there beneath the old stone and soot of the cottage: perfume and fabric softener.

I crossed to the living room door and pushed it open. Everything was as I'd left it: the empty cup on the coffee table, the squashed cushion on the sofa. I turned and headed back across the hallway.

At the entrance to the front room, I stood watching the moonlight cast shadows across the floor. Then I reached for the light switch and the shadows fled.

My eyes roamed over the armchair by the window, the

bookcase, the hearth in which a fire had never been lit. Nothing was out of place. I breathed deep and there it was again: the faintest odour of something sickly sweet. The ghost of Alice's scent.

Only the kitchen remained. I walked to the doorway, reaching for the switch the moment I stepped over the threshold. I heard the blood rushing in my ears but I kept my movements slow, deliberate as I walked to the back door and tugged at it.

It was still locked, just as it should have been.

I let out a shaky breath. And then I saw it.

There on the kitchen table was a book, face up so I could read the title: *An Inspector Calls.*

I stared at it, unable to move. It wasn't my copy.

Alice. I must have forgotten to lock the door and she'd let herself in while I'd been upstairs. Had she somehow known that I was out of the way? Or had she just not cared?

Seconds passed while I stood there, numb with fear. And then something clicked into place and I ran to the front door and stabbed the key into the lock, twisting it with such violence I should have broken it; but when I pulled the door to check that it was locked, it opened and I slammed it shut and twisted the key again, not caring how loud it was. There was no advantage to subtlety now: Alice had come into my home and left a calling card. She had declared herself.

I went back to the kitchen and stood panting at arm's length from the table. The book sat there, pretending innocence. Something had been placed between its pages: a couple of inches of plain white paper protruded from the top edge. A note.

I didn't want to pick it up. I didn't want to touch something that she'd touched. It was an unclean thing, there in the heart of my home. And yet I couldn't stop myself. I had to know what it said.

I stretched out my hand and brushed my fingertips over the cover. I told myself: *It's just a book.* I picked it up.

It was an old edition, perhaps the one Alice had used when we'd discussed it at the book club. I tried to remember. That had been the night I'd hosted the meeting, the night Liz had joined us. The only night there hadn't been a connection between the text we were reading and a secret one of us had been keeping.

But perhaps there had been a connection after all. Perhaps the note would explain what it was.

I slipped my finger between the pages and found the place that had been marked. There was something written in pencil in the margin, but I didn't look at it, not at first. My eyes were drawn to the piece of paper. It wasn't a note. Nothing had been written on it at all. But a line of printed text ran along the longer edge, and next to it was a logo, a large navy-blue 'W'.

I knew what it was. I'd seen hundreds of them.

It was a compliments slip from Waites.

The girl in the photo on my phone. Different hair, different clothes. Perhaps even a different name. But it was Alice. She'd worked at the same place I had, gone every day into the same office. I must have seen her around. Liz had known she was familiar the first time she'd seen her. And yet I'd lived next door to her for two months and I'd never seen it. What did that say about me? Was I really so blind?

I put the compliments slip on the table and turned my attention to the page that had been marked. The paper was rough, cream shading to brown at the edges. Two vertical pencil lines had been drawn alongside a portion of the text. The speech belonged to the inspector:

> the time will soon come when, if men will not learn that lesson, then they will be taught it in fire and blood and anguish.

Next to it in small, neat handwriting were written two words:

Time's up.

Something cold settled over me and a single thought filled my head: I had to get as far away from Alice as I could.

I put down the book. I went to the drawer where I kept my utensils. I selected the knife with the longest blade.

In the hallway I collected my handbag. My front door key was still in the lock, the key ring dangling beneath. I turned it and stepped outside.

The only light came from the kitchen, softened through the open door to a dim glow that seeped onto the ground beneath the window. Alice's house was in darkness. There was not a light to be seen from the other cottages. The dying hollyhocks swayed in the breeze, shifting shades of indigo and grey. In the distance, a barn owl screeched.

I stood motionless, my eyes adjusting to the dark, the scent of honeysuckle in my nostrils and the still-warm air cloying against my skin. I felt for the car key and gripped it between my fingers, the counterpoint to the knife in my other hand. I would be quick.

I left the shadow of the house and ran, half crouching, to the gate. It squeaked as it opened and the noise set my teeth on edge; but I pulled it closed again, enduring another squeak so it wouldn't swing and whine. My car was in its usual position on the other side of the road. I looked back at the cottages. There was no sign of any movement, but I waited, holding my breath, counting silently to five while I peered into the darkness. Nothing.

I stayed low as I crossed the road, but when I reached the car, Lawrie's words rang in my ears. *Bloody cars. We forget how dangerous they are.* Could Alice have done something to *my* car? He'd told me to check something . . . I scrambled for the memory. Tyre pressure.

I never checked my tyre pressure, didn't even know how to do it. In London's crawling traffic it had never seemed important. I clenched my fists, the keys digging into the palm of my hand. It hurt, and I deserved it.

I crouched by the front wheel. The tyre looked fine, but what did I know? I'd have a look at the others, and if I couldn't see anything wrong, I'd take the risk. I couldn't spend another night separated by only a wall from Alice. I'd drive carefully, find somewhere to stop where there'd be other people. A service station, maybe. I'd stop and I'd stay awake, and in the morning I'd find a garage and get the car checked out.

I shuffled around to check the wheel on the passenger side. From there the car would hide me from anyone leaving the cottages. And that was when the smell hit me.

Petrol.

I knew what she'd done straight away, knew it with terrible certainty; but still I moved around the car on bent knees, checking the tyres, hoping against hope that I was wrong, pretending the dark stain on the road could have been left by another vehicle. But when I climbed behind the steering wheel, shutting the door swiftly behind me to cut out the interior light, when I put the key in the ignition, and turned it and heard the engine cough, and saw the red light blinking on the fuel gauge, I couldn't pretend any longer.

I wasn't driving anywhere.

Chapter 32

It had been a busy morning and Lissa was in a bad mood, nursing a hangover and complaining about everything: her computer was too slow, the office was too hot, what kind of idiot sent letters without putting a name on the envelope? Emily knew from experience that it was best to keep out of her way when she was like this, and she waited until Lissa was back from an extended lunch break before heading out herself. She brought her own sandwiches – the ones in the shops were so expensive, and full of calories – but she always left the office at lunchtime. She didn't like people seeing her eat, and besides, a bit of exercise and fresh air were good for the baby.

She walked down the corridor to the lift. It seemed designed to keep people waiting as long as possible, and there were a couple of people standing outside the doors now: that tall girl with the red hair, and the finance director, Richard someone. A mechanical ping carried down the corridor: for once, Emily would be in luck if she hurried.

She picked up her pace as Richard and the girl disappeared into the lift, his hand on the small of her back. The gesture was familiar, affectionate; she'd store it up, mention it to Lissa if she was still in a bad mood later. Emily wasn't interested in gossip, but it would be useful if Lissa needed a new target for her bitchy remarks.

Her shoes clattered in the corridor as she made for the lift. They'd hear her coming; she wouldn't need to call out to them to hold it for her. She was almost there when she saw the girl inside turn and reach for something. The doors slid shut.

They'd gone. The girl must have pressed the button to close the doors. They'd deliberately left her behind.

Emily felt the anger bubble in her chest. So she wasn't important enough for them to wait for her. Her time didn't matter. She could just hang around for another ten minutes waiting for the lift to come back because obviously she didn't have anything better to do.

Her nails were digging into her palms and she forced herself to unclench her fists. Let them go. People like that were always the same, always selfish. She didn't have to let it concern her. There were more important things. Her hand moved to the swell of her stomach, so slight that only she knew it was there. Stress wasn't good for the baby. She'd just take the stairs.

Alice smiles as the engine of Lucy's car splutters again and dies. It won't be long now before she returns to the cottage. She lets the curtain fall and steps away from the window.

It's neat that the anniversary has fallen when it has. As if it's meant to be this way. She's spent a long time planning this, how to get the time she needs to make Lucy understand. That's important: there's no point punishing someone if they don't understand what they've done. Lucy has to know why she deserves what's coming to her.

It's important too that the punishment fits the crime. It hadn't worked out quite the way she'd planned with him. With Richard. He was supposed to have died. At the speed he'd been going, he really should have done. That's the problem with road accidents: too many variables. Different cars, driving styles, hazards. It's unpredictable. And there are trade-offs to be made: no one would know that you've let the air out of someone's tyres, but you can't be sure of the outcome. The tyres might burst when they're driving slowly, or on an open road with room to contain the skid, or they might not burst at all. She'd thought long and hard about whether it was right for the girl, for Liz. It had been the hot weather that had swung it in the end: so easy for tyres to blow in weather like that, and there was no sense in looking a gift horse in the mouth. Still, she hadn't been sure it would work, not at all, not right up until that moment when she'd heard the traffic report with the news of the accident, the fatality closing a section of the motorway.

Then again, if you wanted to be certain of your results, you risked detection. With Richard, she'd taken that risk, ducking out the back of the country inn where they'd met, pretending she was going to the loo and hiding in the shadows to pour oil on his brake pads. He'd been furious when she'd returned and told him the reason she'd insisted on meeting: that she knew about his affair. He'd thought she was threatening to tell his wife; that she was going to blackmail him! Well that's the kind of thing you have to expect from a person like that. But then she'd explained what he'd done, he and Lucy, what they'd done to her, and the fury had drained away. He'd pretended to be sympathetic, but she could see that he still didn't understand. He'd thought he could buy his way out of it, promising her a promotion, a pay rise, not comprehending that he could never buy back what he'd stolen from her. She could see the calculations running through his head, read them as clearly as if they were written on the tablecloth between them: if I say this, if I promise her that . . .

And yet, after all, he'd survived. Broken in body and – so she understands – almost certainly in mind; but still alive. Maybe she'll do something about that if he ever emerges from the coma. Or maybe she'll let him have his half-life, useless and miserable. She doesn't need to decide straight away. There are more important things to think about.

She opens the carrier bag and removes the small, round objects. Fifteen of them – more than enough if they're positioned properly, close enough together. She pushes them into place on the bedside table, arranging them in a pattern of concentric circles, the kind of thing she imagines Lucy might do.

She's worked so hard to get here. It's taken planning, self-discipline. God knows it was hard enough not to simply finish it all that night, when she had Lucy at her feet, sweating and reeking of vomit. But it wouldn't have been enough, she knew that. She'd summoned up the memory of that day, the figure turning in the lift, her arm reaching out for the button to close the doors. Lucy deserved to suffer for what she'd done.

So she'd put her to bed, let her sleep it off while she searched the house, found the front and back door keys and had them copied. She hadn't been sure then how she'd use them, but she knew it was important to be able to come and go as she pleased.

And now, all that care, the hours of observation, have paid off. Only someone as meticulous as she is would have found out about the fire; only someone who watched so carefully would have spotted the scars it had left. None of Lucy's so-called friends have noticed: the way she looks for the smoke detectors in whatever room she's in, the way she always sits facing the door; the fire blanket in her kitchen and the extinguisher tucked into the corner of the hallway. And then, that evening at Tom's house, all those pretty candles standing sentry down the centre of the dining table. She'd watched Lucy flinch every time someone reached for their glass, her eyes on the flames, waiting for them to lick upwards and catch a stray sleeve, the corner of a napkin.

She knows now what she has to do. She knows how to make the punishment fit the crime.

Chapter 33

I locked the door as soon as I was inside, and stood with my back against it as if at any moment Alice might charge over and try to batter it down. My teeth were chattering and the words ran in circles through my mind: *fire and blood and anguish, fire and blood and anguish.*

I remembered the calendar, that jaunty doodle of a flame next to today's date. Alice's little joke. I'd thought at the time she was simply telling me she knew what had happened in Leeds. Now I knew better, and I wondered why I'd never seen it for what it was: a threat.

She was going to set fire to my house.

I couldn't stay here. I'd go to Rebecca's, tell her everything – for once, I'd tell the truth – then wait there, safe with her and Sam, until the police arrived. The keys were still in the lock. I half turned and stretched out my fingers for them.

And then above my head, a floorboard creaked.

I froze, listening. I listened so hard I swear I heard the blood pulsing in my veins. And there it was again: a low, stealthy creak, directly above me. My bedroom.

I should go now, lock the door behind me. Alice would have to break out if she wasn't going to be caught trespassing, and there'd be evidence then, evidence that I wasn't just some paranoid woman who didn't like her neighbour.

I reached for the keys. And then I stopped.

Why didn't I open that door? Why the fuck didn't I just go? But when my fingers brushed the cold metal, something made me pause.

I tried to imagine what I'd tell the police. I tried to imagine them talking to Alice, asking her what was going on; and Alice, polite, bemused, making them tea and telling them she didn't understand what I was saying; how she'd thought we were friends, how just that evening I'd been at her home for the book club. And the book? *Oh yes, I dropped it off for her, Officer; we'd been reading it, you see, and I spotted it in a second-hand shop, thought she might like it. Writing? What writing? Oh no, I had no idea; I suppose it must have been a previous owner. Some people like making notes, don't they?* And the officers nodding, frowning, scribbling in their little notepads, knocking on my door and telling me that there was no evidence of a crime, to contact them again if there was any threat of violence; or worse, that it was a serious offence to waste police time.

I found myself turning from the door, looking up the stairs, one foot already on the bottom step. I thought: *This has to end.*

From above me I heard another sound, a rustle of plastic. A carrier bag, perhaps. Maybe it held the petrol can. I paused, sniffed the air; but there was nothing now except a faint, sick smell of fear and sweat. I knew it was coming from me.

I reached for the handrail, trying to put as little weight as possible on the wooden stairs. I knew the cottage, knew which steps creaked and groaned, and I ascended silent as an assassin, holding the knife before me, pointing the way.

The bedroom door was closed.

I stared at it, knowing I'd left it open as I did every day; knowing that Alice was on the other side. My courage failed me then and I stopped, unable to take another step.

I don't know how long I stood there. I know that every muscle trembled, and my mouth was dry, and each breath sounded as loud as a foghorn to my ears. I know that the knife grew heavy in my hand and needles of pain ran through the knuckles of my fist, but I couldn't have released it for anything. I know that I stared and stared and stared at that door until it no longer seemed like a real object in a real world, but a picture, a collection of lines, empty of meaning.

And then I heard it. A sigh. It was soft and yearning, and filled with such sadness that in that moment my fear drained away, replaced by pity. She was lonely, that was all; she needed help. She needed a friend.

My grip loosened on the knife and I walked to the door, no longer caring if Alice heard, my hand on the latch, white fingers against the black metal, the door opening, a warm, flickering light – and then pain, a hand across my throat, something sharp at my neck, darkness.

I woke with a weight on my body; everything so heavy that I couldn't move, not even my eyelids. I had to concentrate, to focus all my energy to open them, and then it was there: a sliver of light, golden grey, and a shape moving in front of me.

A voice said, 'Wake up now. It's time to wake up.'

And the fear should have made me cold all over, but I couldn't feel anything, and the colours were bleeding into each other, and—

I gasped, water on my face, dripping down my forehead into my eyes, running off my chin, soaking my chest. The shock brought back feeling and the colours snapped into place, and I could see her, Alice, standing above me, an empty glass in her hand.

'That's better.' She smiled, all teeth. 'Hi, Lucy.'

I tried to move my lips, tried to form words, but my tongue was thick and wouldn't work. My perspective was all wrong and I tried to lift my head, make sense of what I was seeing, but it was too heavy, everything was too heavy.

Alice moved away from me, a shadow in my peripheral vision. She said, 'Do you know where you are?'

A door. A white door. A hand lifting the latch. My bedroom. I'd come into my bedroom. I rolled my eyes, trying to take in my surroundings: more white, just white, but then there, a black line. I grasped the detail, focused on interpreting it. A beam. The ceiling. I was lying on my back. I was in bed.

Alice was talking again. I tried to concentrate on what she was saying, but the words were slipping and sliding through my brain and I couldn't catch them. I looked at the black line. *Beam. Ceiling. Beam. Ceiling.*

Hands under my arms, lifting me. Something hit the back of my head and I heard the thud, loud so that I knew it should have hurt. But my eyelids were drooping again and a voice was shouting a long way away, too far away to make out the words.

'. . . given you too much.'

I opened my eyes. There was a bin in front of me, a sour smell rising from it. The taste in my mouth told me I'd been sick, and the ends of my hair were wet with it.

A woman was coming closer. I could feel her and I tried to move away – I didn't want anyone seeing me like this – but my muscles belonged to someone else. I felt her hands on my shoulders, bony fingers digging into the skin, pulling me upright, twisting me in the bed. She propped me against the bedstead and I sat there like a rag doll, listing to one side, my head resting on my shoulder.

I could see the duvet, the end of the bed with its cast-iron frame, the door to the landing wide open. Everything was tipped sideways and bathed in the pale yellow light of the bedside lamp. The woman appeared in my line of sight, her back to me. She was moving away, passing through the doorway. Where was she going?

I heard her step on the carpeted landing, then a series of light thuds. She was going downstairs. I sat there watching the rectangle of the doorway. There was something I had to do. What was it? It was important, I knew that. Somewhere in my brain words were repeating themselves, over and over. I could feel the shape of them, but they wouldn't come.

I tried to remember. How had I got here? A picture flashed in front of my eyes: a dial, the needle on red. The car. I'd been trying to go somewhere. I had *needed* to go somewhere. I had smacked my hands against the steering wheel. Did I still need to get there? Was someone waiting for me?

But someone had been here, just a moment ago. A woman. I tested out the name: Alice. My lips moved as I tried to say it – *Alice* – and the words shimmered in my head. They were closer now. I could almost touch them. Alice. Something about Alice.

Why was she here? Why was I in bed? Was I sick? Yes, I'd been sick. I could still taste it. She must be looking after me. But no, that didn't feel right. A picture swam in front of me: silver ballet pumps on carpet. Another time. I'd been sick then too, helpless. She'd been there. She'd been to blame.

Alice. Alice.

I was afraid of her. And then I started to shake.

She'd done this to me. I was sure of it. She'd been waiting for me. There'd been a pain . . . I'd been there, by the door, and I'd felt it, a sharp bite at my neck. I tried to lift my hand to touch the spot, but my arm was too heavy. A needle. She must have injected me with something.

The words were closer now. I had to reach for them. They were important, the most important thing there would ever be. *Alice, Alice . . .*

Get away from Alice.

And now the pictures were flooding back to me: the pages of a book, pencil marks in the margin; the blade of a knife; my feet on the stairs. These stairs.

I had to move. *Movemovemovemovemove!*

I felt it: a flicker in my fingers. Oh Christ, no. I had to do better than that. The words were screaming now, filling my head. *Get away from Alice.* I looked down at my legs. *Get away from Alice.* They didn't move. I shifted my gaze to my feet, my toes. *Get away from Alice. Get away from Alice. Get away from Alice or you'll fucking die!*

My toes moved. I saw them. A twitch, no more, but they'd moved. I tried again. My left foot inched across the duvet. Again. Another inch. Again, again.

But it was too slow. There were footsteps climbing the stairs.

Get away from Alice.

Now my other foot was moving, sliding across the duvet. She was almost on the landing and there was no time.

The knife. I'd had a knife. My head turned. There was nothing on the table beside me except the lamp, an alarm clock and what looked like a wine bottle. How did that get there? Perhaps I could break it – if I could just reach out . . .

'You're looking more lively.'

Her tone was so normal that for a moment I thought I was losing my mind, that some kind of fever had been making me hallucinate. But then she came closer and I saw the look in her eyes.

Hatred. Nothing but hatred.

'That's good. You had me worried there.' She had something in her hands. I tried to make out what it was: a bowl. One of the glass mixing bowls Mum had got me. Oh God, Mum. What would she do when I'd gone? At least she'd still have Nat. And Dad. They'd have each other.

'Come on now, Lucy, don't cry. Behave like a grown-up.' She dipped a cloth into the bowl and brought her hand close to my face. I jerked backwards. 'Well then. You *are* feeling better. I think we'd better get on with it, don't you? But we do have to get you cleaned up.' She passed the cloth over my lips and chin, scrubbing at crusted vomit and saliva. The water was cool, refreshing. I couldn't help myself: I was grateful.

She pulled back and inspected me. 'There, that's better.' Her eyes narrowed and she smiled. I saw neat white teeth. 'Not that there'll be much left afterwards, but it never hurts to be careful. Though that's not something you'd understand. People like you aren't careful, are you, Lucy?'

There was a hardness to her voice now. I had to say something, find a way to make her stop. My lips were working, but the sounds that came out made no sense.

'What's that?' She leaned into me. 'What are you trying to say?'

I tried again. 'Surr . . . Surrrr . . .'

'Was that "Sorry"? Was that what you were going for?'

I moved my head in an approximation of a nod.

Her laugh split the air and my stomach churned at the sound. 'You're sorry! A little late for that. A day late and a dollar short!' She shook her head at me, a disappointed parent. 'You don't even know what you're sorry for, do you?'

I took a breath, concentrated on forming the word. 'R-Richard.'

She stared at me, the skin between her eyebrows pulled into a perplexed little V. And then her expression cleared and she smiled. 'Richard! You think I'm upset that you were having an affair with Richard!'

She put the bowl on the bedside table and perched on the edge of the bed. I could feel the weight of her next to my knees. 'Oh Lucy.' She sounded almost amused. 'You think you're going to be punished because you're an adulterer?'

An adulterer? Was she some kind of religious nut? I tried again to say I was sorry, but she put her finger to my lips.

'No. No more talking. It's time for you to listen.' She leaned towards me, and I could feel her breath on my face. 'It's not adultery you're being punished for. It's murder.'

Chapter 34

She told me that I'd killed her baby.

She said that Richard and I had taken the lift, and she'd seen me close the doors even though I'd heard her coming. She said she'd had to take the stairs. She said she'd fallen. She'd been pregnant and she'd fallen on the stairs and lost the baby.

Except those were my words, not hers. She'd told me what had happened and my tongue thick, stupid-sounding, I'd said, 'You lost the baby?'

And she screamed at me, no, no, she hadn't *lost* it. She hadn't put it down somewhere and forgotten where it was. We'd killed it, Richard and I. Murdered it. *I* had murdered it.

She said it was a little girl. She showed me this picture, a tapestry. She said she'd been making it for the nursery. She told me that her daughter would have loved it. Laura would have loved it. That was what she was going to call her.

I didn't know. How could I have known? How could I be blamed for Alice falling on the stairs? How could I even be sure she was telling the truth?

Except that I knew she was. I knew when it had happened.

I remembered pushing the button in the lift, the doors closing against the sound of heels on the corridor; Richard's smile as he'd pressed the alarm and pulled me into his arms.

That was why she hadn't waited, she said. We'd been fucking like animals in the lift, and the alarm had gone off and she'd had to take the stairs. And everyone knew what we were doing, everyone knew what a whore I was, and that Richard was a cheating bastard, but no one knew what we'd done to her. But we knew now, and we were going to pay.

I tried to tell her that she couldn't blame us for what had happened. I tried saying that it wasn't our fault any more than it was hers for choosing to leave the office then instead of five minutes earlier. But even as I spoke them, the words sounded hollow. Because she was right, wasn't she? It was our fault, mine just as much as Richard's. If we hadn't been in that lift, if we'd never been together in the first place . . . Nothing good had come of it. I'd always known it wouldn't. But I couldn't have known it would lead to something so horrible.

I wanted to know how far she'd been into her pregnancy. I wanted to ask her, but I was afraid that she'd say something terrible, that it hadn't just been a group of cells, that it had been a baby. And what did it matter anyway? It was a baby to Alice. It was her little girl. It was Laura.

I tried to say I was sorry. My mouth was working better by then, and my voice sounded more like my own. I said I knew nothing could make up for what she'd lost. I said I knew that we'd done a terrible thing, that I'd spend the rest of my life regretting it. I said I'd do whatever she wanted.

At first she didn't listen to me; she was shaking her head, twisting that long neck, flecks of spittle on her lips. I tried to ignore the way her neck moved, focused instead on her hands, her narrow fingers, her slender wrists. She held one hand in the other, linked her fingers as if praying, twisted them inside out. I remembered a rhyme from my childhood: *Here's the church and here's the steeple, open it up and here are all the people.*

I told her again that I'd do anything, anything to prove how sorry I was. She stopped then and her hands stilled. She looked at me, those cold grey eyes deep and empty, and she said, 'Anything?'

I nodded, gabbled, pleaded with her while she picked something up from the floor. A white carrier bag.

She said, 'I told myself that. I said I'd do anything to make you pay for what you did.' She was reaching into the bag, her hand closing around something. 'I was so patient. They kept telling me they were going to rent out that cottage.' She withdrew her hand from the bag. A bottle, golden liquid inside. She carried it to the other side of the bed. 'But there was always something: the boiler needed to be repaired, the roof timbers needed treating.' She was putting the bottle on the other bedside table. I strained my neck trying to see what it was.

'Do you remember how long you were here before I moved in, Lucy?' I began to answer, but she wasn't listening. 'Three months. It was three months. I drove up here a couple of times, just to see how you were getting on. But I knew I couldn't do it often, not in a place like this. Someone might have noticed me, wondered what I was doing.'

She was reaching into the bag again.

'I told myself it was for the best. I thought, give her some time to get herself settled, find a job, make some friends. I thought it might be enough to take them from you. I thought if you cared about them it might hurt you the way you'd hurt me.'

She was holding something in her fist. I could just see the end: purple plastic, translucent. It caught the light and I felt something turn over in my stomach.

'But you didn't bother with a job, did you, Lucy? I suppose you didn't need one, what with all that money from Waites. Richard must have been really sick of you to give you that much to leave. Or was it payment for services rendered?'

She sat back down on the bed. 'And you didn't give a shit about your so-called friends.'

I was only half listening to her, all my attention focused on the object in her hand.

'Do you have any idea the trouble I had to go to? Do you have any idea how hard it was? Trying to keep an eye on you and them at the same time? All those hours listening to Cynthia's gossip, following them around, having to break into houses like a common criminal? And for what?'

She was on her feet again, walking to the window then back to the bed, her fist still clenched around the thing from the bag.

'Did you even get it? *Did you even get the point?*'

I looked up at her. 'The book club.'

'Yes, Lucy.' She sank back onto the bed, exhausted by my stupidity. 'The book club. A story for each of you. A chance to expose all your lies. A chance for you to repent.'

'I do repent—'

'Shut up.' She sounded tired now. 'You didn't even see it. I put it right there in front of you, and you still didn't see it.'

'*An Inspector Calls.* That was for me. That was my story.'

She uncurled her fingers, looked down at the object in her hand. The breath caught in my throat.

'And why was it for you, Lucy? Let me know you understand.'

I could hardly speak, but I had to find my voice. I had to keep her talking until the strength came back to my limbs. She ran her fingertips over the plastic, and my stomach churned.

'Because . . .' I could barely hear myself. I swallowed and tried again. 'Because I didn't think about the con . . . the cons . . .' I couldn't get the word out.

'Take a deep breath, Lucy.'

'The consequences of my actions.'

'That's right. Because everything you do has consequences, doesn't it? For you and for other people.'

I nodded, my eyes still fixed on the piece of plastic. 'I know that now.'

'But it's too late, isn't it? The damage is done.'

I felt the tears well up in my eyes. 'No, no, I'm sorry, Alice.'

'Not Alice. I think we can dispense with that. My name is Emily.' She was watching me, waiting for the spark of recognition. 'Emily Archer.'

I said, 'Emily, yes, I remember now.' But I didn't. I didn't have a clue and she knew it.

'Please, Lucy. Please just don't.' She sighed. 'At least say you remember the lesson.'

My frazzled synapses struggled to spark. What was she talking about? What lesson? Another test, and I was going to fail this one too. *What fucking lesson?*

Everything stopped as she held the piece of plastic in front of my eyes. 'Shall I give you a clue?'

My mouth gaped as she ran her thumb over the metal wheel of the lighter. Once, twice. Then a third time, and she pressed down on the black plastic at the bottom and with a click there it was, a long yellow flame.

'I wouldn't have thought you'd have forgotten the lesson. Not after what happened on that hen weekend.'

The flame danced in front of my eyes. I could feel its heat on the tip of my nose.

'So what was it, Lucy?' She sounded patient, a schoolteacher with a particularly slow pupil. 'How does the inspector tell us you'll be taught your lesson?'

I wouldn't answer her. If I didn't answer her, she couldn't do it.

She brought the lighter closer to my face. I had to move. I had to grab her or this was it, I was going to die right here in this bed. I closed my eyes, shut out the dancing flame, summoned all my energy. *Move now.*

My hand lifted a few inches and fell back to the duvet. *Oh Jesus, God help me, please, someone help me.*

'I can see we're running out of time.' Alice snapped off the lighter and got to her feet. 'The answer is fire. Fire and blood and anguish.' She walked around the foot of the bed, back to the other bedside table. Back to where small, round white things were arranged in circles on the surface, one inside the other. I'd been so focused on trying to see what was in the bottle she was carrying that I hadn't noticed them before, but I knew what they were. Tea lights. No holders, no mats beneath them. Too close together.

I said, 'Please, Alice . . . Emily. I'm sorry . . .'

'I expect you are.' She was lighting them now, holding each one at an angle to the lighter so she wouldn't burn her fingers, one flame turning into many. I smelled citrus. 'Being sorry won't help, though, will it? Being sorry won't bring back my little girl.'

She was putting the lighter down, and it was too near the tea lights, that little parcel of fuel too close to the metal containers, the hot wax that would spill from one to another, a burning pool of oil. And now she was picking up the bottle and I could see what it was.

She read the label, as if giving a demonstration. 'Citronella oil, to go with the candles. We could be here all night otherwise, and we can't have that.' She unscrewed the cap.

I was talking to her, pleading with her, begging for my life; but she didn't listen. She didn't care. She picked up the carrier bag and took a last glance around the room, checking that she hadn't left behind anything incriminating. Then she looked at me one last time. She didn't smile. She didn't seem happy, or frightened, or angry, or relieved. She just looked blank. She tipped the bottle of oil, watching it flow onto the bed, and the carpet, up the side of the bedside table; and when there was only an inch or so left in the bottom, she looked at me and said, 'This is what you deserve. Goodbye, Lucy,' and emptied the last of it over the candles.

There was a *whumpff* and a sheet of flame shot up to the ceiling. I screamed, and before the sound had died on my lips, the flame had subsided, the first droplets of oil evaporated; but on the bedside table a pool of fire coiled and writhed, snaking down its legs to the sodden carpet.

I looked to the door in time to see Alice leave. She didn't look back.

I called out, screamed for help, but my voice was still weak and I knew no one would hear, no one but Alice. Black smoke was billowing from the oil, and at any moment a spark would catch the duvet. I had to get out.

My hands and feet were made of lead, but if I concentrated hard I could move them. My arms and legs were a different matter. I turned my head away from the flickering flames. I couldn't afford to panic. I'd done this before. I'd escaped a fire. I could do it again.

I slid my feet across the bed, one at a time. Acrid smoke was filling the room, smothering the scent of citronella. My eyes were tearing up and I tucked my chin to my chest, squinting through the moisture to watch my feet slip over the edge of the bed. The sensation was returning to my legs: I could feel the cotton of the duvet on my skin, the sweat damp and sticky.

The flames were crackling and spitting, the heat reddening the side of my face, and wreaths of smoke drifted in front of my eyes. Already it was hard to see, harder to breathe. If I didn't take my chance now, I would be disorientated, choked by the smoke, unable to find my way out of even this small room.

My heart was pounding, the adrenalin coursing through my body. I could do this. I *had* to do this.

I stared at my legs. They were part of me. They would do what I told them to do. I needed them to move. I needed them to move *now.*

They swung to the carpet and I shouted in triumph; but the shout came out as a croak as the smoke filled my mouth. I swung my body upwards, but my legs wouldn't hold my weight and I fell to the floor, my knees and elbows scratching against the carpet. I was coughing, horrible grating sounds, but the air was clearer here. I reached forward, swearing at my arms to respond, and now at last they did. My muscles screamed as I pulled myself along on my stomach, trying to turn in what I thought was the direction of the door; but it was too hard, every movement cost too much, and I was going to die there, die alone, just like Liz, and no one would ever know what Alice had done.

Fire and blood and anguish.

My hand hit something hard. I tried to push it away, but it was too big and it didn't move. And now my other hand was against it and I realised it was the wall. My spirits leapt: I could follow the wall; if I kept flat against it, I'd find the door. A voice whispered that there was no time, that even if I found it, it was too near where the fire had started to be passable now; but I ignored it. I had to try.

I crawled closer to the wall, my hands moving upwards as my body closed the gap. Something brushed my fingertips, something soft, and my mind raced, trying to interpret it. Fabric.

The curtain.

The window. Why hadn't I thought of the window?

I clutched at the curtain, handfuls of fabric in my fists, and pulled myself upwards, praying that those old cast-iron curtain poles were as sturdy as they looked. Space opened up in front of my body and I fell forward, onto the low, deep windowsill. I felt my throat constrict as I cried out, but the sound was drowned by the roar of the flames. The fire must have reached the bed.

I reached out, feeling the glass warm against my hands. I had to find the catch, but something seared the flesh of my fingers and I pulled back in shock – the metal was too hot to touch. I balled my fists instead and pummelled at the glass. And now I heard the sound that rose from my scorched throat, shrill against the fury of the flames: the sound of someone about to die.

No. I was stronger than this. I would not let her win.

I summoned every scrap of energy and raised my fists to the glass again. Pain streaked through my knuckles and something warm ran down my hand, and I felt air. I was punching and pulling at the glass, my hands red in the light of the flames, but the gap was too small, I'd never get through. I was close, so close. I could see the catch of the window and I gritted my teeth and held onto it as the pain streamed through me; but I didn't let go and there was nothing but emptiness, and I screamed as the flesh of my hand was torn away and I fell, down and down and down into the dark.

Now

There's the sound again: that shrill beeping sound. I can't make out what it is. It's persistent, though. Whenever I concentrate, I can hear it. But I forget. My mind wanders. It's just as well. If I had to listen to it all the time, I think I'd go mad.

I'd almost prefer the music. They were talking about having music in here, I remember. There was a woman, she was saying something about a song she liked. But no, that wasn't it. She was talking about me. How strange, I remember now. She was saying that I'd always liked it.

I try to look around, but it's too bright in here. The sun streams through the windows and bleaches the faces of the people.

That light. It's right in my eyes. I strain to move away, but my head feels too heavy on my neck, and there's something pressing on my eyelid. I want to reach up and brush it away, but my hands are heavy too, and there's a pain, a burning pain in one of them.

Where have they gone? All the people? I can't hear them any more. Just that sound, the beep; and something else. Something low and jagged-sounding. It rises and falls: *Hmm*-hmm, *hmm*-hmm.

It's getting clearer. It's a voice; *her* voice. The woman I know. The one who wanted to play the music. She's saying something. She wants me to listen to her.

And I'm not afraid any more.

* * *

The doctor bends over the bed, fingers on her forehead, his thumb lifting an eyelid and shining a light into her eye, testing for a reaction. The mother hovers next to him, hands clasped to her chest. A little way behind her is the father. His eyes are fixed on the floor.

This isn't the first time it's happened. His wife has seen it before, or so she's said. A flicker of the eyelids, a twitch of a finger. Who knows, maybe she did. They've spent so many hours at this bedside that he's lost the ability to see change: every day it's the same white sheets, the same grey plastic panels at the side of the bed, the blue tube snaking from the mask over her mouth and the dull beep of the machine that monitors her heart rate and blood pressure. There's another tube running from the back of her right hand. It was in her left hand until last week, but there was an infection and they've had to move it, despite the burns. He'd flinched and had to look away as the needle had gone into what was left of the ruined skin; but Lucy hadn't stirred.

If his wife sees the things she believes she does, these movements, they mean nothing. Their daughter still lies there, eyes closed, the machines feeding her and breathing for her. He will not tell his wife this, but he no longer hopes. He feels in his bones that she will not wake.

But something has shifted in the air.

The doctor is still bending over the bed and now he peers closer, his face almost against Lucy's. He says something, is calling someone, and as he steps back, Lucy's mother moves into the space he has left, grabbing her daughter's hand, sobbing her name.

He can't move, can't bear to look down at that bed again and see her still sleeping, the delicate veins on her eyelids, the pallor of her skin.

But his wife is calling, 'Lucy, Lucy, come back to us, sweetheart,' and now he can't bear *not* to look; and he steps forward and puts his hand on his daughter's knee because he can't reach her other hand and he must touch her, even though he can't speak.

And he sees it too: her eyelids are trembling, and his fingers bunch up the cotton sheet around her knee. And his wife says again, 'Lucy,' and their daughter opens her eyes.

* * *

Emily peers into the mirror and picks a stray hair from her lapel. She hadn't been sure about going short to begin with, but the hairdresser had been convincing and, after all, she'd wanted a change. She likes it now: it fits with the new flat and the new town. She'll get another job soon enough, something better than the post office, and the haircut will work well for interviews. Neat and professional.

The doctor at the hospital told the parents not to give up hope, that Lucy might yet wake up – but Emily isn't worried about that. Even standing along the corridor, she could tell he was just saying what they wanted to hear. And besides, she knows better than to trust doctors. That woman she'd seen after the fall had tried to tell her she'd never been pregnant: *The symptoms of phantom pregnancies can be very real.* As if Emily were stupid. As if she didn't know what was happening to her own body.

No, Lucy isn't coming back.

At first Emily had been sure she wanted to stay in Willowcombe, but she hadn't really thought it through. There'd been some damage to her own cottage – inevitable really – and options for alternative accommodation were thin on the ground. She'd stayed with Maggie for a few nights – with David gone, it wasn't as if she could have claimed not to have the room – but Maggie wasn't the company she'd hoped for, snapping and snivelling and staring into the middle distance, and in any case, Emily preferred her own space. Rebecca had taken her snotty-nosed children and gone running back to her parents, a grim-faced couple in cardigans who'd come to collect them in an estate car. And as for Tom: well, he'd been a concern, coming up to her in the post office a few days after the fire, fixing her with a glare and telling her he couldn't imagine Lucy doing anything so stupid as going to sleep with a table full of candles next to her head, drinking or not. It had been alarming, and for a while she'd contemplated doing something about him. In the end, she'd satisfied herself with tracking down his parents and sending them an anonymous letter explaining how their son lived so comfortably on the proceeds of his 'art'. He wasn't a real threat, but it didn't hurt to have his attention elsewhere for a time.

All in all, Willowcombe had lost its charm. It was Maggie who'd put the idea of Bath into her head. David was staying with friends on the outskirts, apparently. Emily had never been, but it was always popping up in Austen novels and she'd heard it was an attractive city.

She looks around the hallway in approval. It's a pretty flat, well located, bright and airy. The estate agent said she was lucky to get it, and while she knows they all say things like that, she can't help feeling he was telling the truth. There's a newsagent's just a few minutes' walk away too, handy for bread and milk. That's where she's going now.

Downstairs in the lobby there's a table, an elegant thing in polished mahogany. You wouldn't have got anything like that in the lobby of her flat in Pimlico; not anywhere in London for the money she's paying here. The post is put there, and people sort through it and take what's theirs. There are only three flats in the building, one on each floor, so it doesn't take long. You have to do it every day, though: it's not the kind of place where sheaves of takeaway menus and cards for cab firms are left to fester for weeks.

Today, someone has sorted the post into three neat piles. Hers is on the left, *Emily Archer* peering up at her from the window of an A5 envelope. Her council tax statement, she guesses. She likes being Emily again. Alice was necessary, but she was a lie all the same.

There are a few other items in her pile: something from the cable company, confirming the details of her phone and internet package, no doubt; a flyer from a local gym; and at the bottom an envelope with a Post-it note attached to the front. She holds it up, examines the message:

> Sorry, picked this up by accident!
> Jessica (Flat C)

The envelope is thick creamy paper, her name written on a large white label with something printed at the bottom. She looks closer: *Mailer and Todd Literary Agency, 53 Goldfinch Crescent, Bath.* Something lifts in her chest. It's one of the jobs she's applied for, the admin assistant at the literary agency. The one she really wants.

She puts down the rest of her post and scrabbles at the seal, her fingernails sliding against the paper. The letter is short and she scans it joyfully: they've invited her for an interview. She's smiling as she reads it again, taking in the details: 15 March at 3 p.m.

So that's . . .

No. No.

She reads it again, checks, but the numbers don't change.

Today is the 17th. The letter is dated over a week ago. She's missed the interview.

The paper is crumpling in her hands and she can hear the crunch of her teeth grinding against each other. She tries to breathe. Why? Why, when everything was going so well? She would have got that job, she knows it. She would have got it and they would have loved her, and they'd have seen how much she knew about books and after a while they'd have said that she was wasted as an admin assistant, that she should find her own writers to represent. It would have been a whole new career, a whole new life; and now it's gone. Gone because some bitch was too stupid to read the name on an envelope, too lazy to return the mail she had taken – *stolen* – from her in good time.

Emily looks at the Post-it again. Jessica. Flat C.

She slips the envelope into her handbag with the rest of her mail. She has things to do today and she'll do them quickly, because now other tasks are crowding onto her itinerary. She has plans to make.

Jessica has to be taught a lesson.

Acknowledgements

Once upon a time I thought writing was a solitary occupation. Now I know differently.

A huge thank you to all the friends, family and colleagues who've put up with me banging on about this story, read drafts and given their advice and encouragement. Special thanks to Lisa Oyler, Melanie Sturtevant, Kathryn Thomas, Barry Upshall, Sheena Leng and Trevor Diesch.

Thank you to Henry Tam, my writing partner in crime, who's borne with angsty emails with far too many exclamation marks, and dispensed patient, wise counsel in return. And thanks to Lisa Goll and the members of the London Writers' Café for all those wonderful evenings sharing stories and feedback.

Thank you to Nicola Barr, who first made me believe there was a chance people might be interested in my writing. Thank you to Julie Cohen, my unofficial (and unknowing) fairy godmother, whose sage advice at critical moments has meant more than she knows. And my unending gratitude to Sally Haslam, my anti-Alice, whose intervention on my behalf changed my life – in a good way.

Thanks to the brilliant Hannah Wann and Ellie Russell for

their careful and insightful suggestions, to Krystyna Green for taking a chance on me, and to everyone at Constable and Little, Brown who've had a hand in making this an actual, real book. I still can't really believe it's happening.

My deepest thanks to my mum and dad for telling me I could do anything I put my mind to; the greatest gift any child could ask for. And to my husband, Mark, for all the things I can't put into words. You know what they are.

Finally, thank you to you, for reading and breathing life into this story. I'm more grateful than I can say.

Reading Group Questions

1. What are the main themes explored in *The Book Club*?

2. What role does the setting play in the story? Why do think the author chose a Cotswolds village?

3. Do you have a favourite character in the book and, if so, why?

4. Alice tells Lucy 'Everything you do has consequences . . . for you and for other people'. To what extent do you agree with this? Is there any truth in Alice's belief that Lucy is responsible for her fall down the stairs?

5. Throughout the book, Alice has a strong desire for revenge against people she believes have wronged her. Where do you think this comes from? Did you feel any sympathy for her?

6. How does the author create a sense of claustrophobia in the novel?

7. Lucy believes that Alice set up a book club as 'a way to get inside their heads'. How much do you think a book club discussion reveals about the people talking about the book?

8. Tom argues that the characters in classic novels are 'products of their time'. Do you think classic literature is relevant to our lives today?

9. Why do you think neighbours are a popular topic in thrillers?

10. What did you think of the ending of the novel?

Read on for the opening chapters of C. J. Cooper's new thriller

The Verdict

When Natalie finds herself on the jury of an unsettling trial, she is shaken when the verdict of 'not guilty' is greeted by a scream from the public gallery.

As the weeks after the trial pass, she can't shake the feeling that they made a terrible mistake with their verdict; that a dangerous man is walking free.

When she crosses paths with the accused by chance, Natalie decides that she has no option but to get close to find out the truth.

But just how far will she go to set the verdict right?

Prologue

I could feel him there, on the periphery of my vision. He must have been looking at me. Everyone was looking at me. But I didn't look back.

I kept my eyes on the clerk, corvid and Dickensian in his cloak and wig. From my perch in the jury box I towered above him, above all of them. It was borrowed power, the authority of office – I understood that. For all the theatre, I knew it wasn't a performance. That was why it had to be me standing there. Why it was always going to be me.

He said, 'Answer yes or no to the first question only,' and I felt a ripple of annoyance. I didn't need to be reminded how it went. I knew not to rush my lines.

'Have you reached a verdict on which you are all agreed?'

They knew the answer already. That was why we were all here. Just four days together, and this would be our last. I said, for the sake of the occasion, 'Yes.'

'And do you find the defendant, Ian Craig Nash, guilty or not guilty?'

I knew it wasn't fair to prolong the moment. I didn't hesitate. I said, 'Not guilty.'

Around me I felt the tension leave the bodies of the other jurors. The woman next to me gave a quiet sob.

And then the scream rang out across the courtroom.

Chapter 1

It landed on my doorstep on Valentine's Day, one of two envelopes among the pizza flyers and minicab cards. It looked official, so I opened the other envelope first: a letter from an estate agent, promising that properties in my road were in high demand. I wasn't disappointed, truly I wasn't. I had no expectations of Aidan any more. No doubt *she'd* be getting something, propped on a breakfast tray with croissants and a rosebud. She looked like the type who'd expect it.

I tore at the brown envelope carefully, and there it was, bulky text in Valentine's pink: *Jury Summons*. I wasn't sure whether I was daunted or excited. It was my first summons, and at thirty-six I supposed I'd got off lightly. I'd have to take time off work. Get Alan to cover. I checked the dates – two months away. If Easter fell then, he wouldn't be happy. I felt a shiver of *Schadenfreude*. Tough.

I misted the leaves of the dragon tree with a mixture of water and plant food – low dose for the winter months, just enough to keep them green and shiny – picked up my bag and left for the office.

One thing I've always liked about civil servants: they don't do Valentine's Day. I worked briefly in a magazine office when I was younger, and there would have been at least one ostentatious flower delivery, a minimum of three cards left on keyboards and hushed giggling in the kitchen. At Her Majesty's Revenue and Customs, no one seemed to see any significance in the date. Or perhaps they were being sensitive. I suppose that's possible, even for people who work on VAT policy.

Alan was at his desk already. He always gets in before me, though not nearly as early as he claims. Once or twice I've arrived before my usual time and he's turned up ten minutes before I'd normally get in, looking shocked and muttering some nonsense about delayed trains. He thinks, you see, that if he arrives before me, he's justified in sloping off at five on the dot, regardless of whatever shit is hitting the fan. It annoys me but I don't say anything. It's not like I have a lot to get home for myself.

I logged into my computer and went straight to my diary, clicking through to April. There was bound to be some post-end-of-financial-year stuff to deal with, but nothing had been scheduled so far except the usual team meetings and staff one-to-ones. I ticked the box next to Alan's diary and viewed his schedule: nothing there that wasn't in mine. I blocked out the week then wondered if it would be enough. The letter had only given me a date to turn up at the court. How long did jury service take?

'Alan?'

He swivelled his chair in my direction. After the office reorganisation he'd somehow got the seat at the window, the one next to mine. I was flanked on either side by desks. So much for seniority.

'Morning, Natalie. Good weekend?'

'Fine, thanks. You?' He started to reply, but it wasn't like I was interested. 'Have you ever done jury service?'

He leaned back in his chair, pleased to be able to dispense his wisdom. Alan's older than me, in his pre-retirement phase, and he likes to instruct me when he gets the chance. It doesn't happen often.

He said, 'Twice actually. I got a murder the first time.'

I was impressed in spite of myself. 'How long did it take?'

'About a month.' He read the dismay on my face. 'The other one was arson, though. We were in and out in a week. They were going to give us another case, but it was coming up to Christmas and they didn't bother in the end.'

Beyond the partition behind my desk, Malcolm, another of my team, raised his head like a meerkat. 'Have you been summoned then, Natalie?'

I nodded. 'How are you supposed to plan how long you'll be away for?'

'They say to assume two weeks, but it depends. Look on gov.uk.' Alan again. He had that look he gets when he's thinking, like he's constipated. I could guess why: he wasn't sure whether to be pleased I wouldn't be around to keep tabs on him or dismayed that he might actually have to cover my work.

'Right, you'll be holding the fort for the second half of April then.' Might as well strike while the iron was hot. I'd better tell Fiona, my boss, too; let her know I wouldn't be contactable and to keep an eye on Alan. The idea was faintly thrilling. It had been a long time since I'd been able to forget about the BlackBerry while I was on leave.

Malcolm was talking again, saying something about fraud cases going on and on. Would I want that? I wondered. The complexity could be enjoyable. And it might be good to have some proper time away from the office, interesting to lose myself in something other than work. And better fraud than something horrific – child abuse, say, or rape.

‘I was the foreman both times I was on a jury.’ Alan’s lips had a self-satisfied curl. ‘You probably will be too, Natalie.’

I didn’t like him knowing things I didn’t. ‘Why?’

‘Oh, you see all of human life on a jury.’ He laughed. ‘You forget that not everyone . . . Well, this kind of job is good training in a way.’ I stared at him. VAT policy? ‘I mean, we’re used to looking at evidence, formulating conclusions. Even just chairing a discussion. Most people don’t have that kind of experience.’

God, he was full of it. But he had a point. After all, what was a trial but a process? I understood process. I trusted it. I’m a bureaucrat, that’s what we do.

And sitting there then, I thought: he’s right. I am well qualified for this. Whatever case I get, I’m going to do my best to do a good job.

That was what I thought. Exactly that. Pay attention, because this bit’s important. Back then, that was all I wanted: to do a good job; by which I suppose I meant that I’d play my part in making sure all the evidence was scrutinised, that I wouldn’t allow myself to be blinded by prejudice or carried away on flights of fancy. That I’d do what I could to make sure the jury reached a conclusion on the basis of whatever facts were presented to us.

What I didn’t aim for back then, before I’d set foot in that courtroom, before the witness statements and the diagrams and the photos and the video, was to find the truth.

That came later. After the scream. And I think now it might have been better if it had never come at all.

Chapter 2

I'd brought two books. Everyone said there was a lot of hanging around. Someone told me they'd waited three days even to be assigned to a case. It sounded like a monumental waste of time, though I'm not knocking my colleagues at Her Majesty's Courts and Tribunals Service. All those private-sector idiots who claim that if they ran their businesses the same way as the DVLA or the NHS or the courts or whatever bit of the public sector they're whinging about at the time, they'd go bust . . . Well, how many businesses have to serve everyone, whether they can pay or not? How many of them are led by people who have to get re-elected by their customers every five years? How many have a few hundred other people who see it as their job to take a pop at them every week at Prime Minister's Questions?

So I'm not going to complain about the waiting. I'm not.

I'd started out with some book on change management – *Reaching for the Stars*, or some such rubbish, which a colleague had pressed earnestly into my hands on learning I'd be out of the office for a couple of weeks. I'd just volunteered to run a staff group on the topic, hoping to tick off the required corporate contribution for that year's performance appraisal, doing your actual job no longer being sufficient for the top of the office. I'd stuck with it for a couple of chapters, but my eyes were glazing over and I'd switched to P. D. James in the interests of being awake if and when I was called. The woman opposite glared at me when she saw the cover – perhaps she considered reading something called *The Murder Room* poor taste in the circumstances – but I ignored her.

A slight woman with short grey hair and an east London accent had already talked us through the housekeeping arrangements: the passcode for the door into the jury corridor, the evidence needed for travel and expense claims, the location of the canteen and the loos. She'd taken a register, and we'd watched the video on how it all worked, shown on a TV that got wheeled into the room on a stand. It was like being back at school, and I found that oddly reassuring; for once, it was someone else's responsibility to make sure everything went according to plan.

There were two other TV screens in the room, mounted on the walls at either end. They showed a table with a list of cases – the name of the defendant and the judge, the number of the courtroom, a reference number and a column headed 'Status', which was mostly empty. The court served south-east London, and the defendants sounded as cosmopolitan a bunch as you could hope for: a David and a Mark, Jayden and Tyrone, a Sayid, and Aaliyah and Lisa for the girls.

All of human life.

I wondered who I'd get. Just before lunchtime, I found out.

The grey-haired woman reappeared and read out a list of names. *Isabelle Fernandez, Brian Clifton, Natalie Wright . . .* I got to my feet, and around the room others stood too, exchanging nervous smiles. We trooped out trailing scarves and bags and lined up against the wall of the waiting room as if about to face a firing squad. An usher, a motherly woman in spite of her voluminous black cape, introduced herself as Janet and led the way down a corridor and up a flight of stairs, turning to put her finger to her lips before opening the door to a second corridor, off which the courtrooms apparently lay.

Portraits lined the walls, stern-looking photographs of judges past. All of them white, all but a couple men. About halfway down, Janet stopped and pushed open another door, standing to one side and gesturing to us to pass. The court opened up before us, all dark wood panelling, the judge in scarlet robes and others – the barristers, I presumed – in black, just like I'd seen on TV. Janet guided us to the jury box, squeezing us onto the wooden benches, hips and elbows touching. But the crush was temporary: more names were read out and a handful of jurors were escorted from the room. I didn't understand why. Had it been random, or had those of us who remained passed some kind of test? But there was no time to ponder, because now we were twelve. The Twelve. And there was an oath to be taken.

We spoke in turn, Janet whispering to each of us to check which version we wanted – Christian, Muslim, the affirmation of the atheist. We were a mixed bunch, Spanish, Chinese and Scottish accents amongst the London and Estuary English, some stumbling over the words, one man confounded by the task of holding the bible in one hand and the laminated card with the words of the oath in the other. I gave my affirmation flawlessly, if I say so myself. *Foreperson material*, I imagined the others thinking.

When we were finished, the judge leaned forward and peered at us over her spectacles. The Honourable Victoria Something – her name sounded Nigerian, but I didn't catch it properly – was a kindly looking soul, though I imagined her atypical background meant there was steel there somewhere. She told the usher to hand a folder to each of us. She was still talking, her accent pure

RP, as I followed her instructions to open it and lift out the first sheet of paper; then for a moment her voice faded away as I read the words of the indictment.

Intentionally penetrated . . . did not consent ...

Oh God, no.

. . . did not reasonably believe . . . consented . . .

Rape. It was a rape case.

I swallowed, and my hands were cold as I replaced the folder on the ledge in front of me. I tried to stop the thoughts that were already running through my head: the statistics on conviction rates; the difficulty of proof . . . I breathed deep.

The clerk was speaking now, addressing someone on the right-hand side of the room. The defendant. 'Are you Ian Craig Nash of 236A Mountford Road, Lewisham?'

Lewisham. Like me. I raised my eyes and looked at him. Short brown hair, unremarkable face. He was wearing a dark-blue T-shirt, lightly muscled arms sticking out of the sleeves. Why didn't he have a jacket? The courtroom was so cold. I pulled my own coat more closely around me.

'Yes,' he replied, his voice quiet. The clerk read out the charge and asked for his plea, and then one of the lawyers was on her feet – they were all women, I saw now. Of course: only a rape case would have bucked the norm like that. She was calling a witness. It was all too quick – shouldn't there be some kind of interlude, a chance to catch our breath? The woman on my right coughed, then cleared her throat and coughed again. A police officer was stepping into the witness box. I picked up my pencil and held it poised over one of the scrappy sheets of notepaper I'd taken from my folder.

I can do this, I told myself. I just had to watch, and listen, and think. I would focus on the evidence, the stories they told. There had to be proof, evidence beyond a reasonable doubt. I'd watched enough courtroom dramas to know that was how it went. That was the bar: no more, no less. All I had to do was to test what I heard, assess whether the standard had been reached. I could keep a cool head – it was what I did every day. And I'd make sure the eleven other people on the jury did the same.

The police officer was holding up his hand, swearing his oath in the voice of someone who had done this before but still didn't like it. I wrote the date at the top of the paper, then *PC Alex Watson*.

It had begun.

We heard only two witnesses that day: the first, PC Watson, twenty-something, awkward but seemingly diligent; then a young detective, DS Emma Willis-Jones. I didn't like her, her pointy nose and her tanned face – a drop of winter sun somewhere – shiny hair tied back in a ponytail, just the way I bet it was when she played netball with the other popular girls at school. Unlike the constable, she wasn't wearing uniform, and her blue and white striped shirt was unbuttoned at the neck to show a silver pendant. She gave her evidence in a clear voice, not needing to check her notebook. She was capable, composed. I suppose in that way she was a bit like me.

They were easy to listen to – dry facts delivered without emotion. I scribbled away as they spoke, my pencil hardly pausing: the arrival at the neighbour's flat, a woman in tears, the allegation, knocking at another door in the small block where they both lived, the arrest. He had seemed calm, PC Watson said; there hadn't been any trouble getting him to the station. I noted it all down, my pencil growing blunt, a soft crackle as I finished one sheet of paper and started on the next.

I sat in the second row of the jury box and from time to time I looked at my fellow jurors, the four in front and the three beside me. They seemed alert enough, but they scarcely picked up a pencil between them.

At one point we were asked to leave the court; it wasn't clear why. Janet led us back up the stairs between the rows of benches and through a door in the panelling at the back. This was the jury room, and from then on, we would enter and exit the court that way. It was small and windowless, with grubby cream walls and a large table in the middle with just enough room on each side to squeeze into the seats around it. A door at the end opened into a tiny loo with a sink, and in one corner a smaller table held an aged television, a bottle of water and a stack of plastic cups.

We shuffled into seats, excusing ourselves as we went, unsure of each other. A tall woman with blonde hair took the seat opposite me. I'd seen her in the waiting room – she'd been knitting. I liked that, that she'd come prepared to wait, to fill her time doing something useful. She said, 'I saw you taking lots of notes.'

I shrugged self-deprecatingly, though I suppose it might not have been a compliment. 'It's the way I listen. I find I concentrate better if I write things down.' It was half true. The other half being that I thought it might be helpful to have a record of what people had said, given that we were supposed to be using that to decide whether or not a man was a rapist.

She said, 'I'm no good at taking notes. Can't read my own writing.' She laughed raucously and I wondered whether the sound would carry into the court. I wanted to tell her to shush, but it seemed a bit much given we'd only just met. Maybe when I was foreperson . . .

I wondered whether I should suggest some introductions, treat it like a meeting. Perhaps the others would be relieved if someone took charge. I sat up a little straighter in preparation, looked around the table. A few seats down, a stuffy-looking kid in a jumper adjusted his glasses on his nose and said, 'Shall we do introductions?'

Oh shut up, *foetus.*

But before anyone had the chance to respond, the door opened and Janet was ushering us back in. The judge watched us as we took our seats. We'd been able to leave our bags in the jury room, and there was less shuffling and arranging of arms and legs than there had been on our first arrival. I picked up my pencil, poised for action, but there was no need. Quarter to four and apparently we were done for the day. I looked up at the dock as we trooped back out. He was staring straight ahead, the skin on his arms a bluish pallor. I hoped he'd wear something with long sleeves the next day.

Out in the spring sunshine I found myself shaking off the air of the courtroom, grateful to be able to go home. I was already wondering about her – Chantelle, that was the name of the woman who said she'd been raped. Not 'the victim', I reminded myself; it wouldn't be right to think of her that way. We hadn't seen her yet, and I let my imagination wander to what she'd be doing this evening, whether there'd been people in the public gallery who'd tell her what had happened today. Whether she wanted to hear every detail or couldn't bear to talk about it. Whether she'd be able to eat, or later, to close her eyes and sleep. I imagined how I'd feel standing in that witness box: was there anything she could do to ready herself for that?

And I thought about him, the accused. Ian. Would they let him go home, or would he be spending the night in a cell? I had no idea how it worked. We'd been told the trial would last three to four days. It didn't seem long. Three to four days and he'd be either walking out under the same sky as the rest of us, or taken away to locked doors and iron gates, to a world without choices. I wondered if he suspected which way it would go. I wondered if he hoped for justice or feared it.

As I crossed the car park I heard footsteps quickening behind me.

'Natalie?'

I turned to see one of the other jurors, a woman with a tired smile and sensible eyes. 'It is Natalie, isn't it?'

'Hi, yes. Sorry, I don't think . . .'

'Helen, Helen Owens.' I saw her wondering whether the surname had been a good idea. Then, 'Don't worry, I know we're not supposed to talk about the case.'

I smiled as if the thought hadn't occurred to me. 'It's nice to be out so early. I hadn't realised court days were so short.'

She nodded. 'I know. Someone at work told me to make the most of it. I think we're all in the wrong jobs.'

'What do you do?'

'Social worker. I'm based in Hackney.' That explained the tired eyes, I thought; she must have seen it all. 'You?'

'Civil servant.' I added my standard dinner-party line in case she thought I was a spook. 'I work for the taxman.'

She was quiet for a moment. It usually has that effect. Then, 'Are you heading back to London Bridge?'

She chatted for the ten minutes or so it took to reach the station, not seeming to require much in the way of a response. She was a few years older than me, a couple of daughters in school, no mention of her husband but she wore a ring. As we parted, she said, 'I don't see how we're going to reach a verdict.'

I shrugged, knowing what she meant and trying not to worry about it. 'It's only the first day. They might have more.'

'Yes. I just hope . . . You know, one person's word . . .'

It was what I feared too. I said, 'It's innocent until proven guilty. If there's no real evidence, I suppose there can only be one verdict.'

And even as I said the words I thought: can it really be that simple? But Helen was nodding. It *was* that simple. There was no other way for it to be.

At home, I picked up my BlackBerry and tapped in the password. I hadn't taken it to court, unsure whether I'd be allowed to keep it with me, and as far as Alan was concerned I was out of commission for all but the direst emergency. He'd been given strict instructions to leave me a voicemail if there was anything that needed my attention; I was pleased to see there were no messages. I scrolled quickly through the day's emails – as quickly as it's possible to scroll through 186 items, anyway – but resisted the temptation to respond to any of them. If I gave Alan the opening, he'd assume I'd pick up anything difficult.

When I'd finished, I went to the sitting room and pressed a finger into the soil in the pot holding my dragon tree. *Dracaena marginata* is one of the easiest house plants to keep, but nevertheless it's important to water it at appropriate intervals. Too much is as bad as too little: it starves the roots of oxygen. The soil was on the edge of crispness, so I added a moderate amount and gave the leaves a spray of plant food.

Later I settled in front of the TV with my dinner on a tray. Maybe I'd watch a film, enjoy the luxury of the extra time; but flicking through the channels, a nature programme caught my attention. A squirrel was burying some nuts, watched from a distance by another one. I thought I recognised the voice providing the commentary – an actor, Scottish. Who was it?

'*The would-be thief is in for a surprise.*' Shot of the nut-burying squirrel peering suspiciously over his shoulder. '*He's been spotted, and this squirrel has a trick up his sleeve . . .*'

Was Chantelle watching television now? Or reading a book or a magazine, trying to take her mind off things? Or was she lying in bed, staring up at the ceiling, imagining how it would be to stand there in that courtroom, the things she would have to say? And what about Ian? Was he desperate for his chance to tell his side of the story? Or terrified that when the moment came, he'd be caught out, his lies exposed in the harsh glare of the fluorescent lights?

'*The squirrel has only pretended to bury the nuts, and now he's off to find another hiding place.*' Squirrel number two had come out of hiding and was pawing at the spot recently vacated by squirrel number one. After a while, he stopped, empty-handed, realising he'd been duped.

Such deceitfulness, even in the animal kingdom. Why expect people to be any different? We're hard-wired for it. We're the worst of the lot.

I thought of Aidan. He'd thought he was going to get away with it. He'd thought he was the cunning one, but he was squirrel number two. It had taken me a while, but I'd got wise to him in the end. I found myself smiling as I reached for my glass of wine. Yes, I'd seen through him eventually. And then Aidan found out he was dealing with squirrel number one.